BY NAOMI NOVIK

Uprooted

League of Dragons

League of Dragons

Naomi Novik

DEL REY • NEW YORK

Published in the United States by Del Rey, an imprint of Random House, a division of Penguin Random House LLC, New York.

DEL REY and the HOUSE colophon are registered trademarks of Penguin Random House LLC.

Library of Congress Cataloging-in-Publication Data
Names: Novik, Naomi, author.
Title: League of dragons / Naomi Novik.
Description: New York : Del Rey, [2016] | Series: Temeraire ; 9
Identifiers: LCCN 2016008015 (print) | LCCN 2016013985 (ebook) | ISBN 9780345522924 (hardcover : acid-free paper) | ISBN 9780345522948 (ebook)
Subjects: LCSH: Great Britain. Royal Navy—Officers—Fiction. | Napoleonic Wars, 1800–1815—Fiction. | Ship captains—Fiction. |Wizards—Fiction. | BISAC: FICTION / Fantasy / Historical. | FICTION / Fantasy / Epic. | FICTION / Science Fiction / Adventure. | GSAFD: Alternative histories (Fiction) | Fantasy fiction.
Classification: LCC PS3614.O93 L43 2016 (print) | LCC PS3614.O93 (ebook) | DDC 813/.6—dc23 LC record available at http://lccn.loc.gov/2016008015

Printed in the United States of America on acid-free paper

randomhousebooks.com

2 4 6 8 9 7 5 3 1

First Edition

To Charles
sine qua non

20°

10°

0°

● Edinburgh

N

50°

ATLANTIC

OCEAN

LONDON ●

Dover ●

40°

● PARIS

Fontainebleau □

**EMPIRE
OF
FRANCE**

30°

**KINGDOM
OF
PORTUGAL**

● Salamanca

MADRID ●

**KINGDOM
OF
SPAIN**

● LISBON

20°

□ Vitoria

Mediterrane

10°

0°

Part I

Chapter 1

THE CHEVALIER WAS NOT dead when they found her, but the scavengers had already begun to pick at her body. A cloud of raucous crows lifted when Temeraire's shadow fell over the clearing, and a stoat slunk away into the underbrush, coat white, muzzle red. As he dismounted, Laurence saw its small hard shining eyes peering patiently out from beneath the bramble. The French dragon's immense sides were sunken in between her ribs so deeply that each hollow looked like the span of a rope bridge. They swelled out and in with every shallow breath, the movement of her lungs made visible. She did not move her head, but her eye opened a very little. It rolled to look on them, and closed again without any sign of comprehension.

A dead man sat in the snow beside her, leaning against her chest and staring blindly forward, in the ragged remnants of what had once been the proud red uniform of the Old Guard. He wore epaulets and the front of his coat was pockmarked with many punctures where medals had once hung, likely sold to whichever Russian peasants would sell him a pig or a chicken for gold and silver. Flotsam from Napoleon's disintegrating Grande Armée: the dragon had most likely been driven by hunger to go too far afield, searching for food, and having spent her final strength could not then catch up the remaining body of her corps. She had come down a day ago: the churned ground beneath her was frozen into solid peaks, and her captain's boots were drifted over with the snow which had fallen yesterday morning.

Laurence looked for the sun, descending and only barely shy of the horizon. Every scant hour of daylight now was precious, even every minute. The last corps of Napoleon's army were racing west, trying to escape, and Napoleon himself with them. If they did not catch him before the Berezina River, they would not catch him; he had reinforcements and supply on the other side—dragon reinforcements, who would spirit him and his troops safely away. And all this devouring war would have no conclusion, no end. Napoleon would return only a little chastened to the welcoming cradle of France and raise up another army, and in two years there would be another campaign—another slaughter.

Another laboring breath pushed out the Chevalier's sides; breath steamed out of her nostrils, billowing like cannon-smoke in the frigid air. Temeraire said, "Can we do nothing for her?"

"Let us lay a small fire, Mr. Forthing, if you please," Laurence said.

But the Chevalier would not take even water, when they melted some snow for her to drink. She was too far gone; if indeed she wished any relief with her captain gone and a living death already upon her.

There was only one kindness left to provide. They could not spare powder, but they still had a few iron tent-poles with sharpened ends. Laurence rested one against the base of the dragon's skull, and Temeraire set his massive claw upon it and thrust it through with a single stroke. The Chevalier died without a sound. Her sides rose and fell twice more while the final stillness crept slowly along her enormous body, spasms of muscle and sinew visible beneath the skin. A few of the ground crew stamped their boots and blew on their hands. The snow heavy upon the pine-trees standing around them made a muffled silence.

"We had better get along," Grig said, before the final shudders had left the Chevalier's tail; a faint note of reproach in his high sparrow-voice. "It is another five miles to the meeting-place for to-night."

He alone of their company was little affected by the scene, but then the Russian dragons had cause enough to be inured to cruelty and hunger, having lived with both all their days. And there was no real justification for ignoring him; they had done what little good there was to be done. "See the men back aboard, Mr. Forthing," Laurence said, and walked to Temeraire's lowered head. The breath had frozen in a rim around Temeraire's nostrils while they flew. Laurence warmed the ice crust with his hands and broke it carefully away from the scales. He asked, "Are you ready to continue onwards?"

Temeraire did not immediately answer. He had lost more flesh than Laurence liked these last two weeks, from bitter cold, hard flying, and too little food. Together these could waste the frame of a heavy-weight dragon with terrifying speed, and the Chevalier made a grim object lesson to that end. Laurence could not but take it to heart.

He once more bitterly regretted Shen Shi, and the rest of their supply-train. Laurence had already known to value the Chinese legions highly, but never so much as when they were gone, and all the concerns of ensuring their supply had fallen into his own hands. The Russian aviators had only the most outdated notions of supply for their beasts, and Temeraire, with all the will in the world, had too much spirit to believe that he could not fly around the world on three chickens and a sack of groats if doing so would put him in striking distance of Napoleon again.

"I am so very sorry Shen Shi and the others had to go back to China," Temeraire said finally, in an echo of Laurence's thoughts. "If we were only traveling in company, perhaps . . ."

He trailed off. Even the most relentless optimism could not

have imagined a rescue for the poor Chevalier: three heavy-weights together would have had difficulty in carrying her. "At least we might have given her some hot porridge," Temeraire said.

"If it is any consolation to you," Laurence said, "remember she came into this country as a conqueror, and willingly."

"Oh! What would the dragons of France not do for Napoleon?" Temeraire said. "When you know how much he has given them, and how he has changed their lot: built them pavilions and roads through all Europe, and given them their rights? You cannot blame her, Laurence; you cannot blame any of them."

"Then at least you may blame *him*," Laurence said, "for trading so far on that loyalty to bring her and her fellows into this country in a vain and unjustified attempt at conquest. It was never in your power to prevent her coming, or to rescue her. Only her master might have done so."

"I do," Temeraire said. "I do blame him, and Laurence, it would be beyond everything, if he should escape us now." He heaved a deep breath, and raised his head again. "I am ready to go."

The men were already aboard; Temeraire lifted Laurence to his place at the base of his neck, and with a spring not as energetic as Laurence would have liked, they were aloft again. Beneath them, the stoat crept out of its hiding-place and went back to its feasting.

The ferocious wind managed to come as a surprise again, even after so short a break in their flying. The last warmth of autumn had lingered late into November, but the Russian winter had come with a true vengeance now, more than justifying all the dire warnings which Laurence had heard before its advent, and to-day the temperature had fallen further still. He was used to biting cold upon the deck of a racing frigate or aloft upon a dragon's back in winter, but no experience had prepared him to endure this chill. Leather and wool and fur could not keep it out. Frost gathered thickly on his eyelashes and brows before he could even put his flying-goggles back on; when at last he secured them, the ice melted and ran down the insides of the green glass, leaving trails across his sight like rain.

The ground crew traveling in the belly-netting, shielded better from the wind, might huddle together and make a shared warmth; he had given his scant handful of officers permission to sit together in twos and threes. He could permit himself no such comfort. Tharkay had left them two weeks before, on his way to answer an urgent call to Istanbul; there was no-one else whom Laurence might sit with, without awkwardness—Ferris could not be asked without reflection on Forthing, and equally the reverse; and he could not ask them both, when they might at any moment be attacked. They had to be spread wider than that across Temeraire's back.

He endured the cold as best he could beneath wrappings of oilcloth and a patchwork fur made of rabbit- and weasel-skins, keeping his fingers tucked beneath his arm-pits and his legs folded. Still the chill crept inexorably throughout his limbs, and when his fingers reached a dangerous numbness and ceased to give him pain, he forced himself to stand up in his straps. He carefully unlatched one carabiner, working slowly with thick gloves and numbed hands, and hooked it to a further ring; he then undid the second, and made his way along the harness hand-over-hand to the limits of the first strap before latching back on.

The natural hazards of such an operation, with half-frozen hands and feet and on a dragon's back made more slippery than usual with patches of ice, were outweighed by the certain evil of staying still for too long in such cold: he had to stir his blood. At least the instinctive fear of the plummeting ground below was in this case his ally, rather than an enemy; his heart jerked and pounded furiously when his feet slipped and he crashed full on his side, clinging to the harness with one hand and one strap, trees rushing by in a dark-green blur below.

Emily Roland detached herself from a nearby knot of huddled officers, and clambering with far more skill came to his side—she had been dragon-back upon her mother's beast nearly since her birth and was as much at home aloft as on the ground; she expertly caught his loose strap as the carabiner came banging against Temeraire's side, and latched it to another ring. Laurence nodded his thanks, and managed to regain his footing; but he was flushed and panting when he regained his place at last.

Temeraire himself kept low to the ground, his eyes slitted almost shut against the glare and the breath from his nostrils that came streaming back along his neck: it made clouds filled with needles of ice that stung Laurence's face. Grig flew behind, making as much use as he could of the air churned up by Temeraire's wings. Below them rolled the endless snow and the black bare trees frosted with ice, the fields empty and glittering and hard. If they passed so much as a hut, it remained invisible to them. The peasants had taken to covering their houses in snow up to the eaves, to conceal them from the sight of the marauding feral dragons: they ate their potatoes raw, rather than light a fire whose smoke might betray them.

Only the corpses remained unburied, the trail of dead that Napoleon's army left behind it. But even these did not linger in the open long: a host of feral dragons pursued them, savage as any murder of crows. If a man fell, they, too, did not wait for the body to grow cold.

Laurence might have called it the hand of justice, that Napoleon's army should now be hunted and devoured by the very ferals he had unleashed upon the Russian populace. But he could not take any solace in the dissolution of the once-proud Grande Armée. The pillage of Moscow trailed grotesquely behind them: silken cloth and gold chains and delicate inlaid furniture discarded along the sides of the road by starving men who now thought only of bare survival. Their misery was too enormous; they were fallen past being enemies and reduced to human animals.

Temeraire reached the rendezvous an hour later, on the edge of nightfall. He inhaled a grateful deep breath of the cooking-steam from the big porridge-pit as he landed, and immediately fell-to upon his portion. As he ate, Ferris approached Laurence: he was holding several short sticks which he had tied together at the top, making a skeleton for a miniature tent. "I have been thinking, sir, if we propped these over his nostrils, we might drape the oilcloth over them, and have his nose in with us after all. Then his breath shan't freeze in the night; and we can open a chimney-hole at the top to let it out again. Whatever warmth we might lose thereby, I think the heat of his breath will more than make up."

Laurence hesitated. The responsibility of their arrangements was the duty of the first lieutenant, and ought to be left in his hands; the interference of the captain on such a level could only undermine that officer's authority. Ferris would have done better to apply to Forthing rather than to Laurence, allowing the other man to take the credit of the idea, but that was a great deal to ask when Forthing stood in the place that should have been his; that *had* been his, before he had been dismissed from the service.

"Very good, Mr. Ferris," Laurence said, finally. "Be so good as to explain your suggestion to Mr. Forthing."

He could not bring himself to refuse anything which might improve Temeraire's situation, already so distressed. But guilt gnawed him when he saw Forthing's cheek color as Ferris spoke to him: the two men standing mirror, the one stocky and squared-off in shoulders and jaw, and the other tall and lean, his features not having yet lost all the delicacy of youth; both of them equally ramrod-straight. Forthing bowed a very little, when Ferris had finished, and turning gave stiff orders to the ground crew.

The oilcloth was rearranged, and Laurence lay down to sleep directly beside Temeraire's jaws, the regular susurration of his breath not unlike the murmur of ocean waves. The warmth was better than anything they had managed lately, but even so it was not enough to drive out the cold; at the edges of the oilcloth it waited knife-like, and slid inside on any slightest breath of wind. Laurence opened his eyes in the middle of the night to see a strange rippling motion in the cloth overhead. He put a hand out and touched Temeraire's side: the dragon was shivering violently.

There were faint groans outside, grumbling. Laurence lay a

moment longer, and then groggily forced himself up and went outside. The fur he had wrapped over his coat was useless as armor against the cold. The Russian aviators were up already, walking among their dragons and striking them with their iron goads, shouting until the beasts stirred and got up, sluggishly. Laurence went to Temeraire's head and spoke. "My dear, you must get up."

"I am up," Temeraire said, without opening an eye. "In a moment I will be up," but after a little more coaxing he climbed wearily to his feet and joined the line the Russian dragons had formed: they were all walking in a circuit through the camp, heads sagging.

After they had walked for half an hour, the Russians permitted their dragons to lie down again, this time in a general heap directly beside the porridge-pit. A thick crust of ice had formed over the top; the cooks at regular intervals threw in more hot coals, which broke through the crust and sank. Laurence urged Temeraire to huddle in as well; a great many of the small white dragons curled in around him. The oilcloth was slung again; they all returned to the attempt to sleep. But it seemed to him the cold grew still worse. The ground beneath them radiated chill as a stove might have given off heat, so intense that all the warmth which their bodies could produce was not adequate to push it back.

Temeraire sighed behind his closed teeth. Laurence drifted uneasily, rousing now and again to put his hand on Temeraire's side and be sure he was not again shivering so dangerously. The night crept on. He roused Temeraire with the other dragons for another circuit. "The banners of the Monarch of Hell draw nigh, Captain," O'Dea said, he and the other ground crewmen stamping along with Laurence alongside Temeraire's massive plodding feet. His hands were tucked beneath the arm-pits of his coat. "No wonder if we are o'ertaken, and the dawn find us locked in ice eternal; God save us sinners all!" Then the cold stopped even his limber tongue.

They returned to their place; they slept again, or tried to sleep. Laurence stirred some unmeasured time later and thought morning must be coming near, but when he looked outside the night remained impenetrable: the light was only from torches. A Cossack courier had landed, his small beast already crawling into the general heap. The other beasts made grumbling protests at the cold of her body. Her rider was chattering so badly he could not speak, but waved his hands in frantic haste in the faces of the handful of officers who had gathered around him, the movements throwing wild shadows through the torchlight. Laurence forced himself out into the cold and crossed to join them. "Berezina," the man was saying. "Berezina."

A young ensign came running with a cup of hot grog. The man gulped, and they closed in around him to give him some little share of their own warmth. His clothing was coated white, and the ends of his fingers where he gripped the cup were blackened here and there: frostbite.

"*Berezina zamerzayet,*" he managed; one of the officers muttered a curse even as the courier stammered out a little more around another swallow.

"What did he say?" Laurence asked low, of one of them who had French.

"The Berezina has frozen," the man answered. "Bonaparte is running for it."

They were aloft before sunrise, and reached the camp of the Russian advance guard as the dawn crept over the frozen hills. The Berezina was a clouded ghostly lane between high-piled snowbanks. To the north of the Russian camp, a handful of French regiments were streaming across the river in good order, men marching two abreast, with narrower lines to either side of camp-followers and soldiers who had fallen out of the ranks, struggling across alone as best they could: women and children with their heads down, hunched against the cold; wounded men leaving bloody marks upon the ice as they limped along. Bodies lay prostrated beside the lines, and here and there a figure huddled and unmoving. Even with escape open before them, some had reached the limits of their strength.

"That cannot be all of his army?" Temeraire said doubtfully: there were not two thousand men. Upon the hills of the eastern bank, a small party of French dragons huddled together around a pair of guns, established to provide cover for the retreat, but there were only four beasts.

"They are spread out along the river to the north," Laurence answered, reading the dispatch which Gerry had come running to bring him. The division was a clever stratagem: if the Russians came at any one crossing in strength, Napoleon might sacrifice that portion to save the rest; if the Russians divided themselves to attack more than one, Napoleon could use his advantage in dragons to concentrate several of his companies more quickly than the Russians could do the same. Each group remained large enough to fend off the Cossack harrying bands.

Laurence finished reading and turned to the crew. "Gentlemen," he said, "we have intelligence that Napoleon has declared to his soldiers that he will not go dragon-back while any man in his army remains this side of the Berezina; if he has not lied, he is somewhere along the river even now."

A low murmur of excitement went around the men. "If we can only get *him,* let the rest of them get away!" Dyhern said, pounding his fist into his palm. "Laurence, will we not go at once?"

"We must!" Temeraire said urgently, hunger and cold forgotten. "Oh! Why are the Russians only standing about, waiting?"

This criticism was unjust; the Russian sergeants were already bawling the men into their marching-lines, and even as Laurence ordered his officers to make ready for action, orders were sent running around the rest of the dragons: they were to go and survey the French crossings, and bring back word of any company of unusual strength. "Temeraire," Laurence said, as he loaded his pistols fresh, "pray have Grig pass the word to look for Incan dragons in particular: there were not many with the French, and those few will surely be devoted to Napoleon's protection. Ma'am, I hope you will be comfortable in camp," he added, to Mrs. Pemberton, Emily Roland's chaperone. "Mr. O'Dea will do his best for you, I trust."

"Aye, ma'am, whate'er can be done," O'Dea said, reaching to pull on the brim of a cap he no longer had; his head was swathed instead in a makeshift turban of furs and flayed horsehide, flaps dangling over the ears and the back of the neck. "We'll strike up a tent and do what we can about some porridge, Captain."

"Pray have not a thought for me," Mrs. Pemberton said; she herself was engaged in low conversation with Emily and handing her an extra pistol, one of her own, and a clean pocket-handkerchief.

The French dragons on their hill lifted wary heads when they saw the Russian dragons coming, but did not immediately take to the air themselves; the guns beside them were heaved up, waiting if they should descend into range. Laurence looked across at Vosyem, the Russian heavy-weight nearest him; there was little love lost between himself and Captain Rozhkov, but for the moment they were united in their single goal. Rozhkov looked back, his own flying-goggles blue, and they shook their heads at each other in wordless agreement: Bonaparte would not be with this company, the most exposed to Russian attack; in any case, there were no carriages nor wagons, and very few cavalry.

They flew northward along the line of the river: already a dozen marching ant-lines dotted across the frozen white surface. Behind them, the French company fired up signal-flares in varied colors, surely signaling to their fellows ahead. As the Russian dragons closed in on the next crossing, a volley of musketry fired to greet them, and they had to go higher aloft: painful in the cold weather, and there was not an Incan dragon to be seen; only a few French middle-weights gathered by their guns, who eyed the mass of Russian heavy-weights with some anxiety.

There were, however, a dozen wagons crossing the river under guard by the company, pulled by teams of horses, many of them having lost their hoods: they went frantic and heaving with the dragons overhead. And the wagons were laden not only with wounded but with pillaged treasure, and in alarm Laurence heard Vosyem rumble interest, cocking her head sideways to peer down, as one of the wagons toppled over, and a load of silver plate slid out across the snow, blazing with reflected light.

Laurence heard Rozhkov shout at her, and haul brutally upon the spiked bit she wore, to no avail. The other Russian heavy-weights had seen the treasure as well—they were snarling at one another, snapping, throwing their heads violently to shake their officers off the reins. "Whatever are they hissing for?" Temeraire said, craning his head about. "Anyone can see Napoleon is not there. Napoleon is not there!" he repeated to the Russian dragons, in their tongue.

Vosyem paid no attention. With one last heave of shoulders and neck, she flung Rozhkov and his two lieutenants off their feet, leaving them dangling by their carabiner straps, and her reins were loose. With a roar, she banked sharply, her wings folding, and stooped towards the baggage-train. The other Russian heavy-weights roared also and flung themselves after her, all of them, claws outstretched: worried more about which of them would reach the laden carts first than about the enemy.

"Oh! What are they doing!" Temeraire cried; Laurence looked away, sickened. In their savage eagerness, the Russian beasts were making no effort to avoid the hospital-carts or the camp-followers, and wounded men were spilling out across the ice with cries of agony. The Russian dragons skirmished among them, heedless; others were smashing the rest of the carts, dragging them up onto the bank, mantling at each other with hisses and displays of their claws and teeth.

Temeraire turned wide circles in distress aloft, but there was nothing to be done. He could not force a dozen maddened dragons to come to heel, even if the Russian beasts had not already dis-dained him. "Temeraire," Laurence called, "see if you can per-suade the smaller beasts to come along with us. If we can only find Napoleon, we can return and perhaps by then marshal the other heavy-weights; we can do nothing with them at present."

Temeraire called to Grig and the other grey light-weights, who were not unwilling to follow him; none of them could hope for a scrap of treasure with so many heavy-weights engaged. Even as they turned away, two of the Russian dragons went smashing into the frozen surface of the river, clawing at each other, rolling over and over, and the ice broke with a crack like gunfire: three wagons and dozens of screaming men and women sank at once into the dark rushing water beneath.

Temeraire's head was bowed as he flew northward, leaving the hideous scene behind them. They flew past another four crossing-points: Marshal Davout's regiments, much diminished yet still in fighting-order. He had few guns and almost no dragons left, most of them forced to flee ahead of the retreat outside Smolensk, but his soldiers had climbed up onto the edges of their hospital-wagons, holding their bayonets aloft to form a bristling forest of discouraging points. "A courier has told him, I suppose," Temeraire said, "how the Russian dragons were behaving: oh! Laurence, I hardly know how to look at them. That they should think *I* would do such a thing, go after a hospital-cart, and only for a little silver!"

"Well, it was quite a *lot* of silver," Grig said, in a faintly envious tone, then hastily added, "which does not of course mean they were right to do it: Captain Rozhkov will be so very angry! All the officers will, and," he finished glumly, "I expect they will take away our dinners."

Temeraire flattened his ruff, not liking this speech very much. He beat away quickly, urgently. The river swung back eastward beneath them, snow blowing in little drifts across the ice. Over the next stand of hills, they found one smaller crossing already completed: tracks through the snow on both sides of the bank, and the ground atop the highest point on the eastern bank trampled and bared of snow, where dragons had lifted away the guns and followed the company. But the soldiers had already vanished into the trees on the western bank.

Laurence swept the countryside and the river ahead with his spyglass, anxiously. As little as he wished Napoleon to escape, he feared crossing the enemy's lines. The Russian light-weights were not accustomed to any combat beyond their own internal skirmishing; they did not make a strong company, and now there were French dragons on every side, backed with guns and companies in good order. "We must begin to think of turning back," he said.

"Not yet, surely!" Temeraire cried. "Look, is that not a Cossack party, over there? Perhaps they will know where Napoleon has gone."

He flung himself ahead, eagerly. It was indeed a Cossack raiding party: seven small beasts, courier-weights perhaps half Grig's size, each of them carrying a dozen men hanging off their bright hand-woven harnesses. The Cossack men were armed with sabers and pistols; their clothing was stained dark in places with dried blood. Parties such as theirs had been harrying the French rear all the way from Kaluga; they had been largely responsible for the speed of Napoleon's collapse, but they had neither the arms nor the dragon-weight to meet regular troops. The chief man waved them a greeting, and Dyhern shouted back and forth with him in Russian, through Laurence's borrowed speaking-trumpet; they landed, and Temeraire came to earth beside them. Dyhern leapt down and went to the Cossacks, carrying Laurence's best map; after a quick conversation, he came back to say, "The Prince de Beauharnais is crossing over the next two miles with nine thousand men and twelve dragons: none of them are Inca." Laurence nodded silently, grim with disappointment; but then Dyhern moved his finger further north on the map and said, "But there are two Incan beasts with the Guard company crossing here, where the river forks, with a carriage and seven covered wagons."

"Only two dragons?" Laurence said sharply.

The Cossack captain nodded and held up two fingers, to confirm, and then moved his hand in a circle and flung it in a gesture westward, conveying flight. "He says all the other Inca dragons flew away west four days ago in a great hurry: they took nothing with them," Dyhern said.

"They must have run out of food," Temeraire suggested, but

Laurence doubted. For the Incan dragons, all the potent instincts of personal loyalty were bound up in their Empress, now Napoleon's consort. He was the father of her child, which had secured their devotion to him. That in extremis he should have chosen to send away those beasts who could have been relied upon to protect him, first and foremost, seemed unlikely.

"But we have not seen any other French heavy-weights, either," Temeraire said. "None, except that poor Chevalier—so perhaps he had to send them all away, and kept only those two." He was hovering, looking yearningly north, his ruff quivering. "Laurence, surely we must *try*. Only imagine if we should learn that he escaped us, so near—"

Laurence looked again over the map. Only the merest chance, and between them and the fork lay a force of twelve French dragons, and a strong company of men and guns. If the French should see a danger to Napoleon, and turn back in force—"Very well," Laurence said. He could not bear it, either. "Dyhern, will you ask them to show you a way to come at the fork from the east? We must go around de Beauharnais, far enough to be out of sight, to have any hope of coming at his chief."

Temeraire flew low, just brushing the snow from the tree-tops, and flat-out; setting such a pace that the small Russian dragons fell behind, just barely keeping in sight. Laurence did not slow him. Speed was the only chance, if there were any. If the Cossacks' intelligence were good, then Temeraire alone could halt Napoleon's party, if he arrived in time to catch them out in the open; then the Russian light-weights might catch them up, and provide a decisive blow. But if the Cossacks had been mistaken, if there were more heavy-weight dragons or more guns, a company too great for Temeraire alone to stop, then the Russian light-weights could not make victory possible. There was no chance, either, of going back to get the Russian heavy-weights—and just when their power might have told significantly, if the French truly had sent away all of their own larger beasts.

Laurence was well aware that if they found a force too large for them, he would have a difficult struggle against Temeraire's inclination to keep him from an attempt which could only end in disaster. When Temeraire turned at last sharply westward again, going back towards the river, Laurence stood in his straps, despite the still-ferocious wind and cold, and trained his glass ahead of their flight. The trees broke; he could see the two branches of the river flowing, the marshy ground around them, and then his heart leapt. A very large covered wagon was trundling up the far bank onto a narrow road, being pulled not by horses but by one of the Incan dragons; and behind it rolled a carriage, large and ornamented in gold, with a capital N blazoned upon the door. Another Incan dragon waited anxiously beside the guns on the eastern bank, its yellow-and-orange plumage so ruffled up the beast looked three times its size—but even so, not up to Temeraire's weight. There was not another dragon in sight.

"Laurence!" Temeraire said.

"Yes," Laurence said, his own much-restrained spirits rising; two dragons and guns, and on the order of three hundred men, to guard only a carriage and a wagon-train? He reached for his sword, and loosened it in its sheath. "At them, my dear, as quickly as you can. Mr. Forthing! Pass the word below, ready incendiaries!"

Temeraire was already drawing in air, his sides swelling; beneath his hide trembled the gathering force of the divine wind. Faint cries of alarm carried to Laurence's ears as the French sighted them; the Incan dragon in the lead abandoned the wagon and leapt aloft, beating quickly, and the second came up to join it, both going into a wide, darting, back-and-forth flying pattern, making themselves difficult to hit. The men on the ground sent up a volley of flares even as Temeraire swept in.

"Ware the guns," Laurence shouted to Temeraire; a flick of the ruff told him he had been heard. Twelve-pound field guns, two of them, spoke together, coughing canister-shot and filling their approach with shrapnel; but Temeraire had already beaten up out of their range, skimming the top edge of the powder-smoke cloud, and as he swept over the emplacement, the bellmen let go a dozen incendiaries.

"Ha! Well landed!" Dyhern shouted: fully half of the incendiaries were exploding among the French gun-crews. Others rolled away; one burst on the river and sank into the hole it had blown itself in the crust. And then Temeraire was past; he doubled back on the guns and unleashed the divine wind against their rear—the endless impossible noise, ice-coated trees on the bank shattering like glass bottles, the housing of the guns cracking and coming apart. One still-smoking barrel rolled down the hill and carried away two massive snowbanks; it struck the back wheel of the carriage, shattering it, and the cascade half-buried the entire vehicle in snow.

The Incan dragons dived, ready to make raking passes along Temeraire's vulnerable sides. But Temeraire twisted sinuously away to one side and traded slashing blows with the heavier beast: blue-and-green plumage with a ring of scarlet around its eyes, which gave it a fierce look. There were nearly two dozen Imperial Guardsmen on its back; rifle-fire cracked from their guns, the whine of a bullet passing not distant from Laurence's ear, and six of them leapt for Temeraire's back as the dragons closed.

The sky wheeled around them, a tumult of colors and cold wind; then Temeraire pulled away, leaving the Incan beast bleeding. "Make ready for boarders!" Forthing was shouting. The Guardsmen had leapt across to Temeraire's back latched one to the other; only two of them had made hand-holds, but that had been enough to hold the rest on.

The Guards made intimidating figures: they were all tall, heavily built men, bulky in leather coats and fur caps drawn tightly around the head, with broad sabers and four pistols each slung into their harness-straps. They steadied one another until they had all latched on; then in a tense, disciplined knot they came forward swiftly along the back, covering one another's advance with pistols held ready.

Laurence now had cause to regret his threadbare crew. He had but few officers; his choices had been scant, in New South Wales, and of that motley selection only a handful had survived the wreck of the *Allegiance:* small Gerry, who could not yet hold a full sword, brandishing a long knife instead; for midwingmen, besides Emily Roland, he had only Baggy, still gangly in the midst of getting his growth and only lately advanced from the ground crew; and thin, stoop-shouldered Cavendish: brave enough, but likelier by the look of him to be blown overboard by a strong gust of wind than to cross swords with one of Napoleon's Grognards.

Laurence had not wanted to take men from his fellow-captains; Harcourt had offered, handsomely, when they had parted ways in China. But Laurence knew he and Temeraire were deep in the black books of the Admiralty; he might have been reinstated, as a matter of form and necessity, but no-one could imagine that those gentlemen would turn a kindly eye on any officer coming from his crew. That consideration might now doom the men he did have, or even Temeraire.

By unconscious agreement, Roland and the boys were thrust back to make a final defense between the oncoming boarders and Laurence—a prospect which he could only find grotesque; and yet the fault was his own, for not taking more pains to fill out his crew. Forthing had no second or third lieutenant behind him, no older midwingmen who might have bolstered their resistance; there were no riflemen aboard.

Ferris and Dyhern drew their swords; they joined Forthing, clambering along the line of Temeraire's back to meet the Frenchmen. Laurence drew his own sword and his pistol—the metal painfully cold to the touch; he could only hope it would fire.

The world turned over again, a dizzying spiral, and then suddenly they were in a steep climb: the Incan dragons were pursuing Temeraire hotly, trying to prevent him getting his breath back again; they were wary of the divine wind. Laurence had learned the trick of leaning hard into his straps, his boots planted firmly against hide, to keep from falling over during hard flying, but even so he could not avoid a disorientation that blurred all the world into meaningless shapes and colors.

He shook his head and blinked streaming eyes. The Guards had all kept their feet. Forthing climbed into range—he stood up in his straps—he fired his pistol; one of the Guards fired his at the same instant. A cloud of smoke, and the Guardsman fell; Forthing jerked, twisting around in his straps. A spray of blood burst from his cheek and was slapped back onto his skin by the wind, bright red around a torn bleeding hole: the bullet had gone into his mouth and through the side of his face. Another pistol fired off, the grey smoke anonymous; Laurence could not tell whether the shot was on their side or the French.

Dyhern was grappling with one of the Guardsmen; he was a big man himself, but the other, a younger man, was bearing him down. Ferris looked down Temeraire's back, and then, greatly daring, reached down and unlatched his second strap, and let go the harness: he fell ten feet straight down onto the man overpowering Dyhern, and managed to catch onto one of his straps. Before the Frenchman could recover, Ferris had pistoled him in the face. He thrust the spent pistol into his belt, and bent to latch himself on in the dead man's place; the corpse went falling away.

All sensation of weight abruptly vanished. Temeraire had opened just enough distance from his pursuers to turn; now he arced over, mid-air. He hung suspended a fraction of a moment, and then he was plummeting, down onto the two Incan dragons so close on his heels. The dragons shrieked, bending their heads away to protect their eyes from Temeraire's claws and teeth, entangled with one another. The world fractured: Temeraire roared in the dragons' faces as they all fell, the divine wind drumming beneath his skin again; he roared again, and a third time, his wings beating the air wildly. They were falling, all falling together; Laurence clung to the straps, straining, and saw the other men doing the same. Like being in the tops mid-gale, struggling to reef a sail. And then Temeraire smashed the two dragons together down into the riverbank beneath him, tree-limbs snapping, snow and ice erupting all around like gunpowder smoke.

Laurence shielded his eyes with his sleeve, but the flying snow

thickly coated the top of his head, covered over his mouth and
ears. They had stopped moving. If Temeraire had been wounded in
the fall—

He dropped his arm only to see one of the Guardsmen slash his
own straps and come leaping in four quick strides directly towards
him. Emily Roland lunged at the man from one side, Baggy from
the other; but he had more than a foot in height on either of them,
and bulled his way past them. He had a saber ready in his hand;
Laurence pulled up his own pistol and fired—with no result; the
powder was too wet. He flung the pistol into the Frenchman's face
instead, and met the descending sword on his own: a brutal impact. The Frenchman pounded down on Laurence's sword with
main strength, trying to beat it out of his grip, and seized his arm.

The surface shuddered beneath them, Temeraire shaking himself free of the coating of snow. The Frenchman let go his hold on
Laurence's arm and seized his harness instead, to keep his footing.
They were close enough to have embraced; Laurence managed to
lean back far enough to club the man across the jaw with the guard
of his sword-hilt. The man shook his head, dazed, but struck down
again with his saber; the Chinese sword shrieked as the two blades
scraped against each other, but held.

They were matched and straining; then the bright crack of a
pistol, and hot blood and brains spurted into Laurence's eyes. He
jerked aside. Emily Roland had shot the man in the back of the
head. Laurence wiped blood and ice from his face as Temeraire
reared up onto his feet and shook himself steady. The two Incan
dragons lay still and broken beneath him, shattered by the divine
wind more than by the fall; the green-blue-plumed head had fallen
back limply across the ice, a blaze of incongruous color.

Laurence looked back. The last two Guardsmen on Temeraire's back had surrendered: Forthing was taking their guns and
swords, and Ferris was binding their arms. All their fellows upon
the dragons had been slain: the bodies of men lay scattered around
the wreckage of the beasts.

Further up the river, the soldiers around the carriage stood frozen and staring back at them, clutching their rifles, pale. Laurence felt Temeraire draw breath, and then he roared out once more over all their heads, shattering, terrible. The men broke. In a panicked mass they fled, some scrambling and slipping up the river in blind terror; some flying back eastward, undoubtedly into the waiting arms of the Cossacks; most however ran for the western bank, vanishing into the trees.

Temeraire stood panting, and then he threw off the battle-fever; he looked around. "Laurence, are you well? Oh! Have you been hurt? What were those men about, there?" he demanded, narrowly, catching sight of the prisoners.

"No, I am perfectly well," Laurence said; his shoulders would feel that struggle for a week, but his skin had scarcely been broken. "It is not my blood; do not fear." He laid his hand upon Temeraire's neck to soothe him; he well knew what the fate of the prisoners would be, if Temeraire imagined them responsible for having harmed him.

For once, however, Temeraire was willing to be diverted. "Then—" Temeraire's head swung back towards the gilded carriage, standing now alone upon the bank and still buried deeply beneath the snow. He leapt, and was on the riverbank. He pushed the large wagon away, with a grunt of effort, and scraped the bulk of the drift away from the carriage with his foreleg. Laurence sprang down, with Dyhern following; they went to the door, which had been thrust half an inch open against the snow before it stuck, and dragged it open against the remnants of the drift.

Two women inside were huddled in terror half-fainting against the cushions: a beautiful young lady in a gown cut too low for respectability, and her maid; they clung to each other and screamed when the door was opened. "Good God," Dyhern said.

"The Emperor," Laurence asked them sharply in French. "Where is he?"

The women stared at him; the lady said, in a trembling voice, "He is with Oudinot—with Oudinot!" and hid her face against the maid's shoulder. Laurence stepped back, dismayed, and looked back at the wagon: Temeraire reached for the cover with his talons, seized, tore.

The sun blazed on gold: gold plate and paintings in gilt frames; silver ornaments, brass-banded chests and traveling boxes. They threw back the covers: more gold and silver and copper, sheaves of paper money. They had taken only Napoleon's baggage: the Emperor was safely away.

Chapter 2

"IT DOES NOT SEEM reasonable," Temeraire said disconsolately, "that when I should have liked nothing more than to have a great fortune, none was to be had; and now here it is, just when I should have preferred to catch Napoleon. Not," he added, hurriedly, so as not to tempt fate, "that I mean to complain, precisely; I do not at all *mind* the treasure. But Laurence, it is beyond everything that he should have slipped past us: he has quite certainly got away?"

"Yes," Hammond answered for Laurence, who was yet bent over the letters which Placet had brought them all from Riga. "Our latest intelligence allows no other possibility. He was seen in Paris three days ago, with the Empress: he must have gone by courier-beast the instant his men had finished crossing. They say he has already ordered another conscription."

Temeraire sighed and put his head down.

The treasure remained largely in its wagon, which was convenient for carrying. Laurence had insisted on returning those pieces which could be easily identified, such as several particularly fine paintings stolen from the Tsar's palace, but there were not so many of those; nearly all of it had been chests full of misshapen lumps of gold, which had likely been melted in the burning of Moscow, and which no-one could have recognized.

Temeraire did not deny it was a handsome consolation; but it did not make amends for Napoleon's escape, and while he was not at all sorry that the Russian heavy-weights now looked on him with considerably more respect and had one and all avowed that in future they would listen to him when he told them not to stop, they would not believe that he had not done it for the gold. "I was doing my duty," he had said, stiffly, "and trying to capture Napoleon, which is what all of you ought to have done, too."

"Oh, yes," they all answered, nodding wisely, "your duty: now tell us again, how much gold is in that middling chest with the four bands around it?" It was not what he called satisfying.

"And now Napoleon is perfectly comfortable at home again," Temeraire said, "having tea with Lien, no doubt; I am sure *she* has not spent the winter half-frozen: I dare say she has been sleeping in a dozen different pavilions, and eating feasts. And *we* are still here."

"*Still* here?" Hammond cried. "Good Heavens, we took Vilna not three days ago; you cannot consider our residence here of long duration."

But Temeraire personally did not make much difference between Vilna and Kaluga; yes, he could see perfectly well that upon the map there were five hundred miles between them, and it was just as well to have crossed them, and anyone might *say* that they were in Lithuania instead of Russia; but he found little altered, and nothing to be very glad of, in their present surroundings. The coverts, on the very fringes of the city, were unimproved; the ground frozen ever as hard as in Russia proper, and though there was more food to be had, it remained unappetizing: dead horses, only ever dead horses. Laurence had arranged for a bed to be made up for him of straw and rags, which daily the ground crew built up a little more, but this was a very meager sort of comfort when Temeraire might look down the hill at the palace in the city's heart lit up with celebrations from which dragons were entirely excluded, although the victory could not possibly have been won without them.

"Indeed I am almost glad," Temeraire said, "that the *jalan* had to return to China; I should not know what to say to them if they had met with such incivility; not to speak of ill-use. It is one thing to endure any number of discomforts in the field, on campaign; one must expect these things, and I am sure no-one would say we were unwilling to share in the general privation. It is quite another to be left sitting in mud, in *frozen* mud, and offered half-thawed dead horsemeat, while the Tsar is feasting everyone else who has done anything of note, and yet he never thinks of asking any of *us*."

"But he has," Hammond said earnestly. "Indeed, Captain," he added, turning towards Laurence, "I am here to request your attendance: it is the Tsar's birthday to-day, and it is of course of all things desirable that you should attend as a representative not only of His Majesty's Government—" Temeraire flattened his ruff at the mention of that body of so-called gentlemen, but Hammond threw an anxious look at him and hurried on. "—but of our friendship, indeed our intimate ties, with China; I wondered if perhaps you might be prevailed upon to wear the Imperial robes of state, which the Emperor has been so kind as to bestow upon you—"

Despite a strong sense of indignation at being himself neglected in the invitation, Temeraire could not help but approve this idea, wishing to see Laurence, at least, recognized as he deserved. But Laurence had a horror, a very peculiar horror, of putting himself forward. He would at once refuse, Temeraire was sure; he always required the most inordinate persuasion to display himself even in honors which he had properly earned—

"As you wish," Laurence said, without lifting his head from his letters; his voice sounded distant and a little strange.

Hammond blinked, as though he himself had not expected to meet with so quick a success, and then he hastily rose to his feet.

"Splendid!" he said. "I must do something about my own clothes as well; I will call for you in an hour, then, if that will do. I hope you will pardon me until then."

"Yes," Laurence said, still remote, and Hammond bowed deeply and took himself out of the clearing nearly at a trot. Temeraire peered down at Laurence in some surprise, and then in dismay said, "Laurence—Laurence, are you quite well? Are you ill?"

"No," Laurence said. "No, I am well. I beg your pardon. I am afraid I have received some unhappy news from England." He paused a long moment still bent over the letter, while Temeraire held himself anxious and stiff, waiting: what had happened? Then Laurence said, "My father is dead."

Lord Allendale had been a stern and distant parent, not an affectionate one, but Laurence was conscious that he had always had the satisfaction of being able to respect his father. While not always agreeing with his judgment, Laurence had never blushed for his father's honor, both in private and in public life unstained by any reproach; and in this moment, Laurence was bitterly conscious that his father could not have said the same of his youngest son. His treason had broken his father's health, had certainly hastened this final event.

Laurence did not know if his father could ever have been brought to understand or to approve the choice which he had made. He had reconciled himself to his own crime only with difficulty, and he had before him every day all the proofs which any man could require, of the sentience and soul of dragons. He had seen those dragons dying hideously, worn away by the slow coughing degrees of the plague; he had with his own eyes witnessed their agony and seen the carrion-mounds of a hundred beasts raised outside Dover. He had known what the Ministry did, in deliberately infecting the dragons of Europe with that disease: a wholesale murder of allies and innocents as much as of their enemies.

All this had been required to turn his hand to the act, to make him bring the cure to France and give it into Napoleon's hand. And even so, he had recoiled from the act at first. He had dreamt of the moment of crisis again only three nights ago; of Temeraire saying, "I will go alone," and afterwards in the dream Laurence found himself in an empty covert, going from clearing to clearing, calling Temeraire's name, with no answer.

With an effort, Laurence recalled himself to his circumstances: Temeraire's head was lowered to peer at him, full of anxiety. "I am well," he said again, and put his head on the dragon's muzzle as reassurance. "I am not overset."

"Will you not take anything? Gerry," Temeraire called, raising his head, "pray go and fetch a cup of hot grog for Laurence, if you please; as we have nothing better it must do," he added, turning back down. "Oh, Laurence; I am so very sorry to hear it: I hope your mother is not hurt? Have the French invaded them again? Ought we go at once?"

"No," Laurence said. "The letter is a month old, my dear; we are too late for the funeral rites." He did not say that he should scarcely have been welcome, with or without a twenty-ton dragon. "He died in his bed. My mother is not ill, only much grieved." His voice, low, faded out without his entirely willing it to do so. The letter was in his mother's hand, brief, sharp-edged with sorrow. His father had been hale and vigorous five years ago, still in his prime; she might justly have hoped not to be made a widow so soon. When Gerry came running with the hot cup, Laurence drank.

"In his bed?" Temeraire was muttering to himself, as if he did not understand; but he did not press any further for explanation; he only curled himself around Laurence, and offered the comfort of his companionship. Laurence seated himself heavily upon the dragon's foreleg, grateful, and read the letter over again so he might at least have the pleasure of being unhappy with those whose unhappiness he had caused.

"I am sorry, Laurence; I do not suppose he could have heard that your fortune was restored," Temeraire said, looking over at the wagon-cart, still piled high.

"He would have known me restored to the list," Laurence said, but this was only a sop to Temeraire's feelings. He knew that neither his fortune, nor his pardon and the reinstatement of his rank, which might restore him in the good graces of the world, would have weighed at all with Lord Allendale. That gentlemen could more easily have brooked his son's public execution, on a charge he knew to be false, than to see his son laureled with gold and praised in every corner, and known to him as a traitor.

He might have told his father that worldly concerns at least had not weighed with him; he had acted only as his conscience had brutally required. But he had not seen his father since his conviction; he had not presumed to write, even after his sentence had been commuted to transportation, nor since his pardon. And they would now never speak again. There would be no opportunity for defense or explanation.

And Laurence could not but regard Temeraire's extravagant hoard with dismay, although the Russians had been more astonished by his being willing to return any part of the treasure than by his keeping it entirely for himself. Laurence had asked how and where they should surrender the pillaged goods; the other aviators had only stared uncomprehending, and asked how he had managed to persuade Temeraire to surrender even the Tsar's paintings, which could not have had a plainer provenance. He knew perfectly well what his father would have thought of a fortune obtained with so little character of law to the process.

But there was something too much like bitterness in that thought. Laurence made himself fold up the letter, and put it away in his pocket. He would not dwell upon what he could not repair. They were still at war; the French Emperor might have escaped, but the French army was yet strung out between Vilna and Berlin, what was left of it, and there would surely be more work to do soon enough.

There were other letters; letters from Spain: one from Jane Roland and one from Granby, with an enclosure addressed to Temeraire directly. Laurence meant to open them, but Temeraire said tentatively, "Laurence, I suppose you must begin to dress: Hammond will be calling for you in a quarter of an hour. Roland," he called, "will you pray bring out Laurence's robes? Be sure you do not track them in the dirt."

Too late, Laurence recalled the conversation he had not attended; too late, protest sprang to his lips. Emily Roland was already with great ceremony and satisfaction unfolding the immense and heavily embroidered robes of silk which belonged to the son of the Emperor of China, and not to that of Lord Allendale.

When Laurence had gone, Temeraire brooded, watching the celebrations get under way. Even the magnificent display of fireworks which opened the evening did not please him: a stand of trees blocked a great deal of the covert's view, which he felt might have been taken into account, and the faint drifting smoke only reminded him that he and every other dragon had eaten nothing but porridge and burnt horse for months.

"And it is not as though they did not know any better, anymore," Temeraire said resentfully. He had refrained from making any remarks, while Laurence might be distressed by them any further, but after he had left for the celebration, Temeraire could no longer restrain himself. "It is not as though they had not seen, for themselves, that dragons should like to eat well, or live in a more orderly fashion; they have seen the arrangements of the Chinese legions."

Churki, Hammond's dragon—or rather, the Incan dragon who had decided, quite unaccountably in Temeraire's opinion, to lay claim to him; Hammond by no means wished to be an aviator, nor even liked to fly—lifted her head out of her ruffled-up feathers; she had huddled down to await his return. "Why do you keep complaining we have not been invited to that ceremony? Plainly it is a gathering of men: how could any dragon come into that building where they are holding it?"

"They might make buildings large enough for us to come into, as they do in China," Temeraire said, but she only huffed in a dismissive way.

"It is inconvenient for people to always be in buildings built to our size; it means they have too far to go to get from one thing to another," Churki said, which had not occurred to Temeraire before. "Naturally they like to have places of their own; there is nothing wrong in that, nor that they should hold their own celebrations. And as far as I can tell, *you* are the senior dragon here; who else should be offering thanks for victory, and arranging the comforts of your troops, but you?"

"Oh," Temeraire said, abashed. "But how am I to arrange any comforts, when we are only thrown upon a miserable covert, and have nowhere else to go?"

Churki shrugged. "This does seem a poor city," she said, "and there are no large plazas of stone where dragons would ordinarily sleep or gather; but something may always be contrived! There is good enough timber in those woods there, and it would not be more than a few days to put down a floor of split logs, if you sent all those Russians to fetch a few dozen. Then you must pay men and women, if you have not enough in your own *ayllu* to carry out the work, to prepare ornaments and a feast. I do not see that there is any great puzzle about it," she added, rather severely.

"Well," Temeraire said, and would have protested that the woods were certainly property belonging to someone or another, but he could not help feeling it would be really complaining, then; the sort of complaining that shirkers did, when they did not want to work. Laurence had a great disgust of shirkers. "Ferris," he called instead. "Will you be so good as to go into town for me, and make some inquiries? And pray can you see where Grig has got to?"

The crush of the ballroom would have been sufficient to stifle a man wearing something other than heavy silk robes. Laurence endured grimly both the heat and the attentions of the company. The robes were meant for a man presumed by their makers to be the natural center of any gathering he attended, and in this setting they had the happy power of ensuring him that position; he certainly outshone every man present, and most of the women. Hammond was aglow with delight, presenting him without hesitation to men of the highest rank as their social equal, and presuming upon the association to address himself to them. Laurence could not even check him, in public as they were, when Hammond was the King's representative.

And the solitary one here, even though he was not even properly an envoy to Russia at all, but to China—but no other British diplomat had managed to keep up with the Tsar during the tumult of both retreat and pursuit. Lord Cathcart had been forced to flee St. Petersburg early on when Napoleon's army had seized it; the ambassador in Moscow had decamped that city shortly before its fall, and Laurence had no idea what had become of the man. Only Hammond, with the benefit of a dragon as traveling-companion, had been able to stay with headquarters all the long dusty way.

"I am entirely reconciled to Churki's company—entirely; I cannot overstate the benefits of having made myself so familiar, to the Tsar and his staff," Hammond said, in low voice but with a naked delight that Laurence could not help but regard askance. "And, quite frankly, they think all the better of me, for being as they suppose her master; they value nothing so much as courage, and I assure you, Captain, that whenever we have caught them up, and I have been seen dismounting her back, and instructing her to go to her rest, without benefit of bit or harness, I have been received with a most gratifying amazement. I have arranged to have it happen in sight of the Tsar three times."

Laurence could not openly say what he felt about such machinations, or about Hammond saying, "My dear Countess Lieven, pray permit me to make you known to His Imperial Highness." He could only do his best to escape. A storm of cheering offered him an opportunity at last: the Tsar making his entrance to the pomp of a military band, and soldiers strewing the path that cleared for him with prizes: French standards, many torn and bloodstained, symbols of victory. Laurence managed to slip Hammond's traces and take himself out onto a balcony. The night air, still bitterly cold, was for once welcome. He would have been glad to leave entirely.

"Ha, what a get-up," General Kutuzov said, coming onto the balcony with him, surveying Laurence's robes.

"Sir," Laurence said, with a bow, sorry he could not defend himself against any such remark.

"Well, I hear you can afford them," Kutuzov said, only heaping up the coals. "I have not heard so much gnashing of teeth in my life as when you brought that wagon-load of gold into camp, and all the rest of those big beasts nursing along scraps of silver, over which they nearly quarreled themselves to pieces. Tell me, do you think we could buy off these ferals with trinkets?"

"Not while they are starving," Laurence said.

Kutuzov nodded with a small sigh, as if this was no more than he expected. There was a bench set upon the balcony. The old man sat down and brought his pipe out; he tamped down tobacco and lit it, puffing away clouds into the cold. They remained in silence. The revelry behind them was only increasing in volume. Outside on the street, on the other side of the back wall around the governor's palace, a single shambling figure limped alone through a small pool of yellow lamp-light, leaving a trail dragged through the snow behind him: a French soldier draped in rags, occasionally stopping to emit a dry, hacking cough; dying of typhus. He continued his slow progress and disappeared back into the dark.

"So Napoleon has got away," Kutuzov said.

"For the moment," Laurence said. "I believe, sir, that the Tsar is determined on pursuit?"

Kutuzov sighed deeply from his belly, around the stem of the pipe. "Well, we'll see," he said. "It's good to have your own house in order before you start arranging someone else's. There are a thousand wild dragons on the loose between St. Petersburg and Minsk, and they aren't going to pen themselves up."

"I had hoped, sir, that you had thought better of that practice," Laurence said.

"Half my officers are of the opinion we should bait them with poison and hunt them all down. Well, what do you expect, when they are flying around eating everything in sight, and sometimes people? But cooler heads know we can't afford it! If it weren't for you and those Chinese beasts, Napoleon would have had us outside Moscow last summer, and we wouldn't be here to chat about it." Kutuzov shook his head. "But one way or another, something must be done about them. We can't rebuild the army when our supply-lines are being raided every day. You'll forgive me for being a blunt old man, Captain," he added, "but while I can see why you British would like us to finish beating Napoleon to pieces, I don't see much good in it for Mother Russia at present."

Laurence had already heard this sentiment murmured among some of the Russian soldiers; he was all the more sorry to hear it espoused by Kutuzov himself, the garlanded general of the hour. "You cannot suppose, sir, that Napoleon will be quieted for long, even by this disaster."

"He may have enough else to occupy him," Kutuzov said. "There was a coup attempt in Paris, you know."

"I had not heard it," Laurence said, taken aback.

"Oh, yes," Kutuzov said. "Two weeks ago. That is why his Incan beasts went racing off home—back to that Empress of theirs. She seems to have managed everything neatly enough: all the men involved were rounded up and shot before the week was out. But Bonaparte is going to be busy enough at home for some time, I expect. Anyway, as long as he doesn't come back to Russia, I don't see that it's our business to worry about him. If the Prussians and Austrians don't like their neighbor, let them do something about him."

At this juncture, Hammond appeared to retrieve Laurence and draw him back into the ballroom; he was worried and yet unsurprised when Laurence related the substance of the conversation to him. "I am afraid far too many of the Russian generals are of like mind," Hammond said. "But thank Heaven! The Tsar, at least, is not so shortsighted; you may imagine, Captain, how profoundly he has been affected by the misery and suffering which Bonaparte has inflicted upon his nation. Indeed he would like a word with you, Captain, if you will come this way—"

Laurence submitted to his doom, and permitted Hammond to usher him up to the dais where the Tsar now sat in state; but when they had approached the Tsar rose and came down the steps, much to Laurence's dismay, and kissed him on both cheeks. "Your Highness," the Tsar said, "I am delighted to see you look so well. Come, let us step outside a moment."

This was too much; Laurence opened his mouth to protest that he was by no means to be treated as royalty; but Hammond cleared his throat with great vigor to prevent him, and the Tsar was already leading the way into an antechamber, advisors trailing him like satellites after their Jovian master. "Clear the hallway outside, Piotr," the Tsar said to a tall young equerry, as they came into the smaller room. "Your Highness—"

"Your Majesty," Laurence broke in, unable to bear it, despite Hammond's looks, "I beg your pardon. I am foremost a British serving-officer, and a captain of the Aerial Corps; I am far from meriting that address."

But Alexander did not bend. "You may not desire the burden which it represents, but you must endure it. The Tsar of Russia cannot be so uncouth as to insult the emperor who chose to bestow that honor upon you." Nor, Laurence unwillingly recognized, be so unwise as to insult an emperor who could send three hundred dragons to Moscow; he bowed in acknowledgment and was silent.

"We will take a little air together," Alexander said. "You know Count Nesselrode, I think, Mr. Hammond?"

Hammond stammered agreement, even as he cast an anxious sideways glance at that gentleman, who certainly meant to begin issuing demands as soon as his Imperial master was out of ear-shot of haggling: demands for money, which Hammond was far from being authorized to meet on Britain's behalf. But Laurence could do nothing to relieve his discomfiture. He followed the Tsar out upon the balcony.

A greater contrast with the scene which he had overlooked, from the other side of the palace, could scarcely be envisioned: the streets before the palace gates were thronged with celebrating Russian soldiers, shouting, screams of laughter, a blaze of lanterns, and even the occasional squib of makeshift fireworks contrived from gunpowder. Alexander looked with pardonable satisfaction upon his troops, who had pursued Napoleon across five hundred barren miles in winter, and yet remained in fighting order.

"I trust you were not put to excessive trouble to return the portraits, Your Highness," the Tsar said. "I was given to understand it quite impossible to extract prizes from the beasts, once taken."

"By no means, Your Majesty," Laurence said. "I must assure you that dragons, while having no more *natural* understanding of property rights than would a wholly uneducated man, may be brought to an equal comprehension; Temeraire was entirely willing," this a slight exaggeration, "to restore all the stolen property to its rightful owners, if only provenance might be established." Laurence paused; he disliked very much making use of an advantage he had not earned, but the opportunity of putting a word into so important an ear could not be given up. "It is a question of education and of management, if you will pardon my saying so. If a dragon is taught to value nothing but gold, and to think of its own worth as equal to that of its hoard, it will naturally disdain both discipline and law in the pursuit of treasure."

But Alexander only nodded abstractly, without paying him much attention. "I believe you were speaking with good Prince Kutuzov, earlier this evening," he said, surprising Laurence; he wondered how the Tsar should already have intelligence of an idle conversation, held not an hour since, in the midst of his ball. "I am sorry to have dragged him so far from his warm hearth. His old age deserved a better rest than his country—and Bonaparte!—have given him."

Laurence spoke cautiously, feeling himself on the treacherous grounds of politics; did Alexander mean to criticize the old general's views? "He has always seemed to me a great deal of a pragmatist, Your Majesty."

"He is a wise old warrior," Alexander said. "I have not many such men. And yet sometimes the wiser course requires such pains as may make even a wise man shrink from them. *You*, I am sure, understand that Bonaparte's appetite is insatiable. He may lick his wounds awhile; but who that has seen the wreck of Moscow could imagine that the man who went on from that disaster to continue a futile pursuit will long be dismayed?"

The pursuit had not seemed nearly so futile at the time, to one among the prey. If Napoleon had been able to feed the Russian ferals for another week, if the Chinese legions had reached the end of their own supply a week earlier; on so narrow a thread had the outcome turned. But Laurence did not need to be persuaded of Napoleon's recklessness. "No," he said. "He will not stop." Then slowly, he added, "He cannot stop. If his ambition was of a kind which could be checked by any form of caution, he would never have achieved his high seat. He does not know fear, I think; even when he should."

Alexander turned to him, his face suddenly alight and intent. "Exactly so!" he cried. "You have described him exactly. A man who does not know fear—even of God. Once even I permitted myself to be lost in admiration of his genius; I will not deny it, though I have learned to be ashamed of it. And yet at that time, it seemed to me such courage, such daring, demanded respect. But now we have seen him for what he is; in the ruin of his army he has been revealed: a fiend who gorges on human blood and misery! If only we had captured him!"

"I am very sorry he should have escaped," Laurence said, low.

He had tried to comfort himself, after the first bitter disappointment, with common sense: Bonaparte would surely not have left himself exposed in any way that might have rendered him vulnerable to capture. He had undoubtedly crossed with a strong company, in good order, and remained always in the very heart of his Old Guard. There had not been any real chance. But common sense was insufficient relief; Laurence feared Alexander was too right, when he said that Napoleon would not be checked for long. He would raise a fresh army, the drum-beat would begin again. The Russian Army and the Russian winter had won them not a year's reprieve.

"I am determined it will not be so," Alexander said. "He may have slipped away; but we will not allow him to escape justice forever. God has granted us victory, and more than that, has left our enemy weakened. We must seize this opportunity of destroying his power. It is our duty to liberate not only Russia but all Europe from this scourge of mankind. I *will* pursue him; I *will* see him brought down! When my soldiers stand in Paris, as his trampled into Petersburg and Moscow, then I will be satisfied to go home again; not before!"

Alexander's face was flushed with vehemence. Laurence regarded the Tsar soberly. It was impossible to doubt the sincerity of his inspired wrath. But the Tsar spoke not of forcing Napoleon to sue for peace, or make concessions of territory; he spoke of driving Napoleon from his throne. To take Paris—the very idea was fantastical. All of Prussia yet lay under the yoke of France; Austria was docile and shrinking before him; and Napoleon would surely defend the heartland of France desperately, with every resource in his power—which, Laurence well knew, included a vast and devoted army of dragons. And behind them, the greatest cities of Russia lay in rubble and in ruin; feral dragons roamed the countryside pillaging at will. Kutuzov's might be the loudest voice, but it would not be the only one advising Alexander to go home and put his own house in order.

———

"Well," Hammond said, as they left the palace together, a little while after, "I suppose I will either be knighted, or sent to prison; I have left the Government very few alternatives."

Laurence regarded him with concern. "What have you promised the Russians?"

"A million pounds," Hammond said.

"Good God!" Laurence said, appalled. "Hammond, what authority have you to offer a tenth such a sum?"

"Oh—" Hammond gestured impatiently. "I am overstepping my orders, but the plain truth is, it cannot be done with less; likely it must be twice as much. Their finances are in the most monstrous wreck imaginable."

"That, I can well believe," Laurence said. "Can it be done at all?"

"I am not going to tempt fate by making any such prediction," Hammond said. "Bonaparte has overturned too many thrones and armies. But I will say—if it is ever to be done, it must be done now. He has been pushed over the Niemen already; Wellington is ready to strike in Spain. We will not get a better chance. But if we are to get anywhere at all, we must bring the Prussians over; and to do *that,* we must empower the Russians to make a real showing. I will call it cheap at the price, if a million pounds should have that effect."

Hammond concluded almost defiantly, as if he were making an argument before the king's ministers, rather than in a half-deserted street in Vilna, before a man nowhere in their good graces. Laurence shook his head.

"Sir," he said, "I think you have forgotten one critical point. Can you conceive that the King of Prussia should ever agree to join us in opposing Bonaparte while his son and heir remains hostage in Paris?"

Hammond said, "His officers will force him to it. All of East Prussia longs to throw off Bonaparte's yoke. A few Russian victories, and his own generals will be ready to mutiny to our side if he does not embrace the effort—"

"And then what do you imagine will happen to the prince?" Laurence snapped; Hammond paused, as if so minor a consideration had not occurred to him.

"Bonaparte cannot mean to offer any harm to the boy," Hammond said, uneasily.

"His father may be less willing to rely upon such a conviction," Laurence said.

Chapter 3

TEMERAIRE COULD NOT HELP but enjoy Laurence and Hammond's surprise, when they came back into the covert and found the work quite advanced: a central plaza already laid out, full of squares framed with logs. The Russian light-weights were filling these with stones and sand, which they were gathering from the riverbed and the hills near-by, using the water-troughs for shovel-scoops.

"Yes," Temeraire said, with what he felt was a deserved complacency, "we are further along than I should have expected. I did not imagine that the heavy-weights would make themselves any help at all, but once they understood that I meant to feast them, many of them became quite interested."

"But what have you done!" cried Hammond. "You must have torn up an entire stand of timber—"

"We have," Temeraire said, "but that is all right: I paid for it, and the owner told Ferris he did not mind at all, as long as we would not eat his cattle; and then I bought those, too, so he was perfectly satisfied."

The cows were already roasting upon spits over a roaring fire, under the interested supervision of Baggy. "Only, I thought it would be a shame to see such good beef go to waste, sir," he said, looking at Laurence sidelong. "And Temeraire said he thought there wouldn't be any harm this once—"

"Yes, very well," Laurence said, not entirely with approbation.

Temeraire privately did not understand why Laurence considered cooking strictly the province of the ground crew, as it seemed to him quite one of the most important functions of his crew as a whole, but he knew that Laurence was strict with Baggy: the boy had been promoted from the ground crew, to try and fill the dearth of officers, and there seemed to be some need to keep him only at an officer's tasks. "I hope you do not mind, Laurence," Temeraire said apologetically, "as it is for the party, and not just ordinary eating: so it needs a close eye upon it. Yardley *will* let the meat overcook, and say that it is healthy, when it is only quite inedible."

"I am sorry that he has not learned better; I will contrive to hire a proper cook, if I can," Laurence said.

"That," Temeraire said, "would be splendid. Oh! How lovely it is, Laurence, to be in funds again—although of course," he added hastily, "ten thousand pounds' worth of the treasure is properly *yours*, not mine: I have not forgotten my debt, in the least."

"I know of no debt whatsoever you owe me," Laurence said, very nobly, although Temeraire knew that Laurence had lost all his money in a law-suit, which had been settled against him because everyone had thought him a traitor at the time. That hideous memory had long preyed on Temeraire's spirits, and he could not help but rejoice that he had the power to restore Laurence's fortunes at last; he did not at all mean to let Laurence refuse, out of generosity. But Temeraire was puzzled, a moment, to think how he might induce Laurence to take the gold; Laurence certainly could not have carried it himself, if Temeraire pressed it upon him.

Inspiration struck. "Perhaps you would prefer if I should arrange repayment in some nicer form," Temeraire said. "—I suppose there are jewelers, somewhere near?"

"I do not suppose it," Laurence said, very quickly. "Let us by all means put it into the Funds; I will see if I can find a banker, instead."

"That will suit me perfectly, if you prefer," Temeraire said triumphantly, and then belatedly wondered if there had been something unpleasantly smacking of artifice, in this maneuver; if it were the sort of thing that Lien might have done. He almost asked Laurence, but realized that he could not do so without undermining the good effects, so instead he excused himself privately that no-one could really complain of being given ten thousand pounds.

"And," he added thoughtfully, "I do not suppose, Laurence, that you might put us in the way of some fireworks of our own? I should like to have them set off from that mountain-ridge, up there, so we can see them very clearly from this plaza; and also, if it might be arranged, some musicians."

Laurence by no means begrudged Temeraire or the dragons a share in the feasting; and indeed he could scarcely wish Temeraire to spend the pillaged treasure of Russia better, than to feed her army's dragons. He only chafed to be arranging entertainments rather than engagements; but the latter could not be had merely for the asking. There was no supply for heavy-weights ahead of them, nor likely to be, unless Hammond's outrageous promise were fulfilled.

In the meantime, they should have to sit in Vilna and watch Napoleon's army fleeing westward, knowing that the disordered companies and solitary officers who this day escaped would be marching back to meet them in springtime: their ranks fleshed out, their equipment restored, once again the instruments of their master's limitless ambition. Laurence thought again of the Grand Chevalier, panting out her life in slow gasps on the frozen ground; the corpses in their dotted lines running all the way from Moscow. Pale faces stared from the corners of his mind, and he could not help seeing among them his own father's face, equally pale and still, lying blind in the chapel at Wollaton Hall. A sense of futility dragged upon his spirits as he walked from the covert the next morning, to be thrown off only with an effort; Laurence thought perhaps he ought be glad for any employment.

He presented himself to the colonel of the foot artillery regiment stationed nearest the covert: the soldiers had been among those who had been borne dragon-back during the escape from Moscow, and had lost some of their fear of dragons. "Your Highness," the colonel said, bowing deeply, when Laurence had been shown in; Laurence sighed inwardly, and accepted the greeting as well as the far more welcome offer of a cup of tea—strong and flavorful, although the Russians did not know anything of introducing the beverage to milk.

"I should be grateful for the loan of your regimental band," Laurence said, after the niceties were observed, "if they should not object to coming into the covert this evening. The men should not need to remain the night," he added, "—only until we have drunk the Tsar's health: in vodka, of course." He was well aware of the power of this inducement to obtain the cooperation of many a reluctant soldier.

The colonel looked rather relieved than otherwise, and far from objecting, expressed his gratitude at their having been singled out for such an honor. He could not have meant this with any sincerity; likely the man had been expecting some far more egregious demand, presented on the grounds of his supposed rank.

Whatever the cause, however, Laurence could only be pleased by the extraordinarily stirring marches that evening, which accompanied the fireworks from the heights. Any remaining hesitation he might have felt at what seemed frivolity was overcome by the fixed and rapt expressions upon the faces of all the Russian dragons, while they stared skywards and their tails beat upon the ground in an unconscious accompaniment to the martial music.

This was succeeded by dinner: roast cattle, each stuffed and laid upon a bed of boiled potatoes and turnips, sufficient to sate even the hungriest beast. It had proven impossible to find even one dragon-sized vessel of brass, much less anything like an elegant service, but Temeraire's ingenuity had contrived a solution: the bed of a wagon had been taken off its frame, painted gaily and festooned with tinsel, and this was loaded up and ceremonially presented to each dragon in turn, while Grig, at Temeraire's side, described the military achievements of that beast in glowing terms. The dragons swelled visibly with both dinner and pride, and those still anticipating their turn were loudest in applause.

Not all the dragons had come, at first; some were restrained by their own disdain, and some by their officers. But the noise and the aroma drew the laggards in by degrees, and not only them; some of the Cossack dragons looked in, and after this even some wholly unharnessed dragons whom Laurence supposed must be the local ferals. These were not the half-starved Russian beasts escaped from their breeding grounds, but small wild dragons, green and sparrow-brown, with narrow heads and large bony crests atop them in stripes of oranges and yellows.

They were wary, but full of yearning, and Temeraire was quick to welcome them: he nudged the other beasts to make room and called them in; they were invited to gnaw upon the roasted carcasses. By way of making thanks for this hospitality, the ferals made a great deal of approving noise after every speech Temeraire made describing the work of the fighting-dragons; so there were no objections to their presence.

When at last every beast of three dozen had been fed, and they lay sprawled out and nearly somnolent upon the floor, Temeraire straightened up and cleared his throat, and made them all a long speech in the Russian dialect of the dragon-language. Laurence could not follow this very well, but it was certainly well-received; the dragons snorting approval, and sometimes even rousing up enough to roar. And then, at its conclusion, Emily Roland and Baggy came solemnly forward and presented each military beast with a chain of polished brass, upon which hung a placard carved—a little crudely, but legibly—with the dragon's name.

A more thunderstruck company, Laurence had never seen. The Russian heavy-weights had been used to spend their many hours of leisure squabbling ferociously, and even skirmishing with one another; the light-weight beasts had to devote their energies to stealing scraps for their dinners. They had never been taught anything of generosity or of fellowship, and before now they had been too resentful of being pushed aside to learn anything from the practices of the Chinese legions, except to envy them their more regular supplies of food. But even the most disdainful beast was overcome by this display; they presented their heads low in orderly turn to receive their decorations, and as they departed to their several clearings, each almost humbly thanked Temeraire for his hospitality, while their officers stared in amazement. The success of the evening was complete.

"I do think it came off well, Laurence, do you not agree?" Temeraire said, in a victorious mood. He was settling at last to sleep upon the floor, with the pleasant company of four or five small ferals huddled around him, their bodies warming him. The remnants of the feast were being cleared away: the bones, picked clean, had been heaped up onto the wagon and driven away to be put into the porridge-pot for tomorrow. "Even if it cannot compare to the dinners which we have enjoyed in China," he added.

"Your company was entirely satisfied, which must be the aim of any host," Laurence said. "I cannot think they found anything wanting."

"That is true," Temeraire said, "even if it is because they do not know any better; but I am too pleased to be unhappy tonight, Laurence, and that dinner has set me up entirely. Do you suppose we will be sent forward to rejoin the pursuit tomorrow? Surely Napoleon is getting even further away while we are waiting here."

But Laurence said, "My dear, I am afraid there can be no question of that."

Temeraire had been drifting to sleep even as he spoke, but this unwelcome news woke him quite. He listened in dismay as Laurence explained: more supply was needed, and more money, and the Prussians should have to throw in with them, and it seemed the Austrians were wanted, too, and any number of conditions.

"But Napoleon and his army are running away *now*," Temeraire said in protest. "You and Hammond were saying only yesterday that we cannot afford to let them escape, if we are to defeat him in the spring."

"It will certainly make the task more difficult," Laurence said. "But we cannot defeat him in the spring in any case, unless we have the Prussians; if they will not join us, the Russians cannot risk pressing on."

"I do not see why the Prussians should be so necessary to us," Temeraire said. "Napoleon beat them quite handily at Jena, after all; he rolled up all the country in a month's time. If they would like another chance to show what they can do, of course they might have it, but as for waiting for them—!"

However, there was nothing to be done without supply. That much, Temeraire understood reluctantly. He had not liked to say so to Laurence, but he had really not felt like himself, those last few weeks of the campaign, when it had been so cold, and with not nearly enough food. There had been no use complaining—one could only keep flying, and hope that sooner or later one came to something to eat. But the gnawing in his belly had been extremely distracting, and he had often felt a strange distance from himself; once to his horror he had even found himself looking at a dead soldier down in the snow thinking that the fellow might go into the porridge, with no harm done anyone.

Temeraire shuddered from the memory. "If the Russians will not send forward the supply, we can do nothing," he said, "I do see that much: so how are they to be worked upon? When will the Prussians come in?"

But this was evidently to be left to diplomats. As Temeraire had very little confidence in those gentlemen accomplishing this or any task in any reasonable time, he was by no means satisfied, and when Laurence had gone to sleep, he yet lay wakeful and brooding into the night, despite his comfortably full belly and warm sides.

"Pray will you stop shifting?" one of the little ferals said drowsily: they spoke a dialect not far at all from Durzagh, the dragon-tongue, although flavored with a variety of words borrowed from Russian and German and French. "No disrespect," she added, "only it is hard to get warm if you are always moving."

Temeraire hastily stilled his claws: he often could not help furrowing the earth when he was distracted, even though he was ashamed to have so fidgety a habit, and this time he was still more annoyed to see he had accidentally torn up some of the handsome new flooring. "I beg your pardon," he said, and then he asked, "Tell me, do any of you fly over Prussia, now and then? It starts two rivers over from here, I think. Have you seen any Prussian fighting-dragons, in the breeding grounds there? Or perhaps further west? I suppose Napoleon would not have kept them close to their officers."

The ferals conferred among one another: they had not, as their own territory stopped at the Niemen. "But I am sure we can pass the word, if there is someone you would like to send a message to," one of them said.

"That," Temeraire said, "would be very kind of you; I should be very grateful for any news of a dragon named Eroica, in particular."

"One of the dragons who live near Danzig might know something," the first feral said. "They take a lot of fish there, so a few of them like to change places now and then with one of their neighbors, and they get the news there. We will have a wander over to their territory in the morning, if," she added, a bit craftily, "we don't have to spend too much time looking for breakfast."

"Not as much as would fill a cup of tea!" the quartermaster said belligerently, when Temeraire would have let the ferals take a share of the porridge, the next morning.

Temeraire flattened down his ruff. That Russian officer had spent all the day before scowling at the preparations for the feast, as though he did not like them doing anything to feed themselves. Temeraire had very little use for him anyway; in his opinion, the man might at least have improved on horsemeat by now if he had only made a push to be useful. The quartermaster added something in Russian, which Temeraire recognized as impolite, and put his boot on top of the large lid.

"I do not see myself why we ought to be sharing with those dragons," Grig said, peering over Temeraire's shoulder.

"That is because you are very shortsighted," Temeraire said, but he knew perfectly well that he could not start a quarrel with the quartermaster over the food: that was a sure road to having all the Russian dragons join in, all of them trying to get more of it for themselves, and then all the food would be spoilt, or nearly; he had seen it happen more than once. "Laurence," he called instead, and when Laurence came from his tent, he explained the circumstances.

"That the attempt ought to be made is certain, and cheap at the cost of some porridge: I will speak to the quartermaster," Laurence said soberly. "But pray do not speak of this project before Dyhern: it can only be cruelty to raise hopes whose fulfillment is so uncertain. I very much hope that your efforts will be answered, but you must not expect a positive reply. We are a thousand miles from France, and I would be astonished if Bonaparte had not taken the cream of the Prussian aerial forces straight to his own breeding grounds."

He went to draw the quartermaster aside. While they conferred, Temeraire considered Laurence's warning; he could not help but see that it would be very difficult to get word from so far away. The ferals should certainly grow bored, or decide that they did not want the trouble of crossing through someone else's territory.

When the porridge was finally served out, and the ferals had eaten, Temeraire announced, "And if someone should really bring me word of Eroica, I will even give them—" he drew a deep breath and went on, heroically, "—I will give them this box full of gold plate. Roland, will you unlatch it, if you please?"

Not without a pang, he watched her lift the lid to display the contents: the heaped plates of Napoleon's own service, stamped with eagles around the letter *N*, lustrous and beautifully polished. The ferals all sighed out as one, as well they might: Temeraire could almost not bear to really mean it, although he had steeled himself to make the offer.

He drew his eyes away with an effort. "But," he added sternly, to the wide upturned eyes of the ferals as they looked at him, "I do not mean to be taken in; I must be able to tell that the message really is from Eroica, otherwise I will certainly not give the reward."

The ferals flew away, fortified and inspired, already making plans with one another gleefully about how they should share the treasure, or a few loudly announcing that *they* should find Eroica all alone, and not have to share it at all. Temeraire looked dismally at the box. "Pray close it up and put it away, Roland," he said, feeling it was already lost; he sighed and felt that after this, at least no-one should say *he* was unwilling to make sacrifices for the war.

Chapter 4

What is happening with the egg? You have been very slow in sending me reports these last few weeks, and I cannot see any good reason for it, when the French have just been running away and you have not even had any fighting.

We have been very busy here ourselves. I am sorry to say that Wellesley, or Wellington, or whatever his name is at present, insisted on our retreating back on Ciudad Rodrigo for the winter, only because Soult and Jourdan came up with half a dozen dragons and some few thousand men; and to make matters worse, the food was all sent by the wrong road, so we none of us had anything to eat, not even porridge, for four days. Fortunately, we discovered there were a great many handsome pigs running wild in the forests, which made good eating; and it was not in the least my fault if some of them ran away across the army's march, nor can I call it unreasonable that the soldiers should have shot a few of them to eat. I cannot see why Wellington should have made such a fuss over it.

*But I took it very meekly when he shouted, and I did not
even snort a little fire in his direction: I have decided I will
not quarrel with him at all. I had a word with him when I
came, about making Granby an admiral, and Wellington
said he is quite certain Granby deserves all the honors which
a grateful nation might possibly bestow, and he has
promised will see they are given, if only we should get the
French out of Spain.*

*We will certainly manage it in the spring, even if
everyone is lazing in winter quarters at present. I do not
suppose you will have got them out of Germany by then,
however. It is a great pity you have let Napoleon get away.*

ISKIERKA

PS: The Spanish fire-breathers are much smaller than I am.

Temeraire received this piece of provocation with strong indignation. "And this, when I wrote to her only three days ago," he
said, his tail lashing in expression of his sentiments, and threatening to demolish a stand of young ash-trees, "as soon as we had
come to Vilna, and after we have had so much trouble: nothing to
eat for four days, she says, with pigs running wild everywhere just
for the taking! I should have given a great deal for a pig, anytime
these last four months."

"You must make some allowances," Laurence said absently,
reading between the lines, where Granby's hand had noted the
rather more alarming numbers which had actually provoked the
retreat: *90,000 men & cavalry.* "The courier-route to Portugal is
sadly beset by French aerial patrols, and nearly all the post must
go by sea. Iskierka will not have received your letter yet."

This did not much incline Temeraire to forgiveness, however,
and worse yet, Iskierka's complaint only increased his brooding
concern over their egg. As this wonder of nature was presently
resting within the precincts of the Imperial City in Peking, tended

and watched over by a dozen anxious dragon nursemaids and a
battalion of servants, he might reasonably have remained free
from alarm. But while they had traveled in company with the Chinese legions, Temeraire had enjoyed near-weekly reports about the
egg, relayed by Jade Dragon couriers to and from the Imperial
City, and had indulged himself in any number of inquiries, suggestions, hints—every form of eager interference by which he might
assure himself of the safety and welfare of his future offspring.
Now that those lines of communication had been severed, their
keenly felt absence made Temeraire more anxious than he might
have been if they had never been opened at all.

"You do not think, Laurence," Temeraire said, fretful, "that
one of the Cossacks might go, perhaps? They seem very handy at
traveling light; and I am sure it is not above three weeks' journey,
through friendly territory."

This was a very fanciful way of describing a route across four
thousand miles of frozen, half-deserted countryside, lately ravaged
by two enormous armies and full of savagely angry feral dragons
and equally angry peasants, either of which might offer violence to
one of the feather-weight Cossack beasts. These, in any case, were
neither especially speedy nor inclined to travel alone: as raiders
and scouts they were matchless, but they were not reliable couriers.

"I am afraid not," Laurence said, and Temeraire sighed.

Hammond had been on the other side of the clearing, giving a
final reading to his own dispatches, which would go by the return.
As Temeraire's voice could not be called confidential, and Hammond had no notion of respecting privacy, he now intruded upon
their conversation. "You are quite certain it is impossible, Captain?" he asked, which could only encourage Temeraire. "I had
thought perhaps Captain Terrance might go—"

"What's that?" Placet said, cracking open an eye: the afore-
mentioned Terrance was fast asleep upon the slope of his back, hat
tipped over his head and snoring, having dosed himself liberally
with brandy against the chill of the flight from the Baltic. "Fly to

China? I should like to see us do any such mad thing. No, indeed: we have enough to do, flying back and forth to Riga, and going all over the sea trying to find wherever the ships have got to, to-day."

"Only it is naturally of the greatest importance to re-establish our communications with the Imperial court," Hammond said to Laurence, as they walked together to the next of the dinner-parties: Laurence's attendance had become *de rigueur,* by virtue of the Tsar's having recognized his rank.

That doing so was of the greatest importance to Hammond's position, Laurence had no doubt. Hammond could hardly be considered to be fulfilling his duty as Britain's ambassador to China when he was halfway around the world from any representative of that nation. But what value such a connection should have to the war effort, Laurence doubted extremely.

"We cannot expect that the Emperor will once more consent to loan us any considerable force, when we have been unable to maintain the previous one," he said.

"I am by no means of your mind, Captain," Hammond said quickly. "By no means—I think you give insufficient weight to the spirit of amity which has been established between our nations, and the sense of alarm which the extent of Napoleon's ambitions have raised, in the better-informed members of the Imperial court—"

"An alarm which his defeat in Russia must now greatly allay," Laurence said.

For this Hammond had no answer. After a brief pause, he resumed by saying, "Perhaps if we were to establish a way-station, as it were? I have consulted some of the Russian maps of the northern coastline, and I thought perhaps I might propose to the Admiralty that a frigate be stationed in the Laptev Sea—"

Laurence stared. Hammond trailed off, uncertainly. "Sir," Laurence said, "if you are willing to delay until next August, when I believe some portions of that body of water may have melted, I suppose a ship could be navigated along the Siberian coast; she should have to get out of the Arctic before October, however."

"Oh," Hammond said, and lapsed into a gloomy silence. He had given Terrance the fatal packet, with its extravagant promise of a million pounds. In three days' time it would arrive in London; within a week, he would have an answer, and might well be recalled to England in disgrace. And if Hammond were recalled, Laurence knew he would likely be ordered back as well. Once back in Britain, he and Temeraire would undoubtedly be sent to the most unpleasant and useless posting which malice might contrive: some isolated sea-washed rock off the western shores of Scotland, with no chance of any action at all, nor communication with other dragons who might be influenced by Temeraire's heretical notions of justice.

He might refuse that order, of course, if it came. The Admiralty would court-martial him again, Laurence supposed, with a kind of black humor; he knew he should feel a greater distress at the prospect than he did. But indeed, the event could not cause him much pain. Even under his present circumstances, he could scarcely envision any future where he might resume a place in British society. So be it: he would let them try him in absentia, this time, and ignore the outcome. He would only need to grieve another conviction insofar as it retained the power to distress his mother.

They had reached the steps of the house; the footman was holding the door. Laurence could not but find the contrast absurd, to step from such thoughts onto the threshold of a glittering ball and find generals and archdukes bowing to him; it lent the scene a kind of unreality, as though he sojourned briefly in a fairy-world which would vanish away as soon as he had left it.

"They must see the necessity," Hammond murmured worried, to himself. "They must, they must. If you please, Captain, I should like to present you to Prince Gorchakov—"

Laurence moved through the room still suffused with that feeling of falsehood, all the world a theater-stage; the men and women he spoke to flat as playing cards, all surface and no substance. Everyone spoke of the same things, repeated the same remarks: Napoleon had been seen in Paris, Napoleon was raising another army. Ferals had destroyed the estate of Count Z—and the summer house of Princess B——. The two threads were often wound together, and Napoleon almost blamed more for having unleashed the starved and chained dragons than for his invasion, it seemed.

"Murat should be hanged like a spy, in my opinion," one gentleman declared, whom Laurence did not recognize: he wore a uniform free from decorations. "And his master after him, if he had not been permitted to escape! And the beasts slaughtered, one and all. A few porridge-vats full of poison—"

"And when Napoleon returns, with a hundred of his own beasts in the air?" Laurence said, distant and dismissive; he would have turned away.

"Then poison them, too!" the man said, glaring and belligerent. "At least I hope some hero might be found, who would go into a French camp and make the attempt, instead of this rank folly where tenderly we nurse monsters who would devour us all. Now I hear we are to take porridge out of the mouths of our own serfs, over whom God has set us as fathers and mothers, and set it out to feed the beasts—Oriental corruption! Because *they* are slaves to their own dragons, they would see the rest of us brought low and groveling in the dirt beside them—"

He was drunk, Laurence realized, cheeks suffused with a stain that owed more to wine than heat. It did not matter. "Sir, you are offensive," Laurence said. The company around them were drawing away, slightly; faces turning aside, hiding behind fans. "You must withdraw the remark."

"Withdraw!" the man cried. He shook off the hand of another gentleman, who was trying to whisper in his ear. "Withdraw, when murdered children cry out for justice, from the serpents' bellies? By all the holy saints, when I think that God above sent a plague, which would have cleansed them one and all from the earth—!" Here he was forcibly interrupted, by his friend and another officer, who were both speaking to him in urgent low Russian. But he paused only a moment, and shook their hands off. "No! I will not knock my head to a man who chooses to parade himself around under the supposed dignities bestowed by a barbaric king—"

Hammond's hand was on his own arm, but Laurence took it

away, and struck the man sharply across the face, breaking him off mid-sentence; the man fell stumbling back into the hands of his friends. Laurence turned away before he could get up again and walked for the door, quickly. People made way murmuring, glancing towards his face and looking away again. Laurence did not know what they saw written there. He felt only weary, and disgusted, and angry with himself: if he had been less distant from his company, he must have seen that he was speaking with a man too drunk to be answered. But now there was nothing to be done.

Hammond caught him by the door and trotted down the steps beside him, his face stricken. "I hope you will act for me, Mr. Hammond," Laurence said.

"Captain," Hammond said, "I must ask whether—if the gentleman should seek satisfaction, then—as I understand, there is a prohibition against dueling for aviators, strictly enforced—"

Laurence halted in the road and turned to stare at him. "Mr. Hammond, if you can explain to me how, having agreed to call myself the son of the Emperor of China, I am to make amends to a man who has so egregiously insulted him to my face, and call myself a gentleman, much less a prince, in future, I am ready to listen."

Hammond gnawed on his lip. "No, no," he said. "No, I quite see; it would entirely undermine the claim," as though he merely considered the matter in a pragmatic light. "Ah! But wait; I am certain—I am almost certain, the gentleman is neither a prince nor an officer. As an Imperial prince, your rank, your elevated rank, must preclude your meeting anyone of such markedly inferior rank—you cannot distinguish someone so far beneath you. I must find out his name; I must speak to Kolyakin, in the Imperial household—I will call on him in the morning—"

Laurence turned away from Hammond's mutterings and back to the drudgery of the ice-crusted snow, his head lowered. He could not quarrel with Hammond's point, and it aligned too well with what he knew to be his duty; and yet all feeling revolted at making such a use of the distinction which the Emperor had bestowed upon him—to deny satisfaction to a gentleman whom he had so deeply and deliberately offended. And yet the severity of the insult had merited the reproof. Laurence had struck the man precisely because he had felt he could not accept anything but an apology so complete as to be abasement. But he had done so with the intention of giving satisfaction if asked for it, as the man surely would.

"You will speak with the gentleman's friends, first, I hope," Laurence said heavily, "and make it known to them that I will consider an apology. I should be glad to excuse his behavior on the grounds of drink." He did not like soliciting an apology for an offense so great, and he did not see how the other man could offer one remotely satisfactory without appearing a coward, after receiving a public blow. But he could not stomach giving the man no recourse at all.

"Oh, yes, naturally," Hammond said, already looking more relieved with every moment. "I will certainly arrange the matter."

"And if you cannot," Laurence said, "I must ask you to inform the gentleman's friends that they must be ready to get him away instantly, should any mischance befall me."

Temeraire roused when Laurence came back to the covert, and peered up at the stars. "I did not expect you another two hours, Laurence. Are you taken ill?" he asked, anxiously. He had overhead some of the Russian officers say that more than a thousand men had died yesterday, of some sort of fever, and Temeraire could not but recall that Laurence's father had died in his *bed,* where nothing ought to have menaced him.

"No, I am well. I did not care to stay," Laurence said. "Shall we read something?"

The temporary relief brought by this answer vanished by the next day: Temeraire was quite certain Laurence was not well after all. He was very silent, and spent nearly all the morning in his tent, writing letters and arranging his papers as though before a battle.

"Would there be any chance of some of the French army coming this way, after all?" Temeraire asked, when Laurence came out at last; perhaps Laurence had not said anything, because he did not wish to raise hopes.

But Laurence answered too easily. "I am afraid not," he said. "I believe they have all crossed the Niemen, by last report." So it was not that, either. Temeraire did not like to pry; he knew Laurence felt it a great rudeness to ask questions, and solicit information which had not been volunteered. But Laurence remained too-silent and grave all that day, and did not eat much of his dinner, which he took at the covert that evening for the first time since they had come to Vilna.

Temeraire had nothing to occupy him sufficient to distract him from these anxious observations. The Russians had no notion of aerial drill under ordinary circumstances, and on the amount of supply they possessed, all the dragons were inclined to sleep more than fly, anyway. Temeraire had made arrangements, through Grig, for some of the smaller beasts to spend the afternoon in his clearing, where Temeraire recited some poetry to them, and afterwards tried to spur them to discussion. But they mostly yawned, and then he yawned, too, and it was so very easy to drowse, even though Temeraire took very much to heart the instruction, from the Analects, that a dragon ought not spend more than fourteen hours of the day in sleep.

He tried to read alone, or have Roland read to him from the newspapers, when one might be found in a language which she read sufficiently well—Temeraire again felt the injustice that Sipho should have gone away with his brother and Kulingile; Kulingile had gone to the Peninsular Army, where would be no shortage of English newspapers, and perhaps even books, which anybody at all could read to him; and meanwhile Roland could only read in three languages, and not very well in any of them—or he might amuse himself by doing some mathematical problems in his head, only these made him drowsy as well.

So he was very much at leisure to worry, and think up new

sideways questions which might approach the question of Laurence's health. None of these produced a satisfactory answer. Laurence was not tired; Laurence was not too hot, nor too cold; Laurence did not have the head-ache. Laurence did indeed recall vomiting over the side during that typhoon in the year six, but he did not feel the least inclination to be similarly ill at present.

"Laurence," Temeraire said finally in desperation, "perhaps you have heard of typhus?"

"I have," Laurence said. "It is going through the hospitals, I am afraid; poor devils."

"Oh! The hospitals only?" Temeraire said, much relieved. "*You* would have no thought of typhus, would you?"

"What, of being ill? None whatsoever. Whence has this sudden concern for my health arisen?" Laurence said, raising his head from his pistols, which he was cleaning.

"Only, I do not quite understand," Temeraire said, "how your father seems to have died in his bed, and you have been so very quiet—"

Laurence said, "My father was seventy-two, and had been ill a long time, my dear; I may hope for another two score years myself, if nothing should—" He stopped very abruptly.

Temeraire was immediately alarmed, and only more so, when Laurence said, "Temeraire, I beg your pardon. I am not ill; but it is true that my thoughts are occupied. I am sorry that I should have let you see it, when I cannot confide their subject to you; honor demands my silence at present. Having said so much, I trust you will not press me further."

"And I did not, but I very much *wished* to," Temeraire said to Churki, unhappily, that afternoon, when Laurence had left with Hammond on yet another social occasion. Laurence's speech had done nothing to make Temeraire feel less uneasy: entirely the reverse. Laurence's idea of honor was very peculiar, and nearly all-encompassing; it had led him into dangerous situations before now.

"I should think so," Churki said. "Why did you not insist on being informed further at once? What if he has got himself into some difficulty, which you ought to manage for him? Men do not always like interference, and by and large," she added, "I do not hold with *unnecessary* interference; they ought to be allowed to manage their own affairs. But there are some matters which a respectable dragon ought not allow to go forward among her people; why, I have known men to be lured out of their *ayllu* to visit a woman in another, and then they are snatched up by some other dragon and never seen again, all because their own dragon did not intervene soon enough."

"Well, I am sure Laurence has not been visiting some woman," Temeraire said uneasily; it did occur to him that Laurence had been attending all these parties, at which he understood there were a great many ladies all in very dazzling gowns; and Laurence did have odd notions about what might be due the reputation of a gentlewoman. "Perhaps you are right; perhaps I ought to inform myself. Roland," he said, turning to break in on her sword-drill with Baggy, "Roland, you would not happen to know which party Laurence has gone to, this afternoon? You might go after him, and just keep an eye upon him."

Baggy dropped his sword at once and sat down looking grateful for the respite: he was finally filling out his well-stretched frame little by little, but remained still very lanky.

"I mightn't at all," Roland said, with feeling, wiping sweat and strands off her brow; she wore her sandy hair braided in a queue, but a great deal of it had escaped during the practice: her enthusiasm for the exercise was considerably greater than Baggy's. "I should have to put on a dress. You had better ask Forthing to go after him, or Ferris: he can do the pretty when he has to."

"Ferris, certainly," Temeraire said, mindful of the wretched condition of Mr. Forthing's coat, which he could hardly bear to have seen even within the confines of the covert, much less out in the world, as associated with any officer of his; neither was his appearance at all improved by the large wadding of bandages bound up over the wound in his cheek. "—pray ask him to go at once, if you please."

"I'll go!" Baggy volunteered, and scrambled up and away with a flailing of thin limbs and an expression of relief.

Ferris went out in a condition of which any dragon might be proud: in a neat grey coat, freshly sponged down and with a golden stick-pin in the lapel, trousers faultlessly white and boots well-polished. "I will find him, never fret, Temeraire," Ferris said. "I have enough Russian to ask about, and there aren't so many aviators about that people won't remember a flying-coat."

"And perhaps you might find Grig for me," Temeraire said to Roland, after Ferris had gone, just in case: if any other dragon *had* been nosing about Laurence, Grig was sure to know of it.

But Grig did not need to be summoned: he was at that very moment darting into the clearing in a rush. "Temeraire, some of those ferals have returned, that you asked to go west for you; but they have come in over Symerka's clearing, and he thinks they are trying to get at his treasure."

"Oh! What treasure has he got to speak of, but three silver plates, dented!" Temeraire said, in some exasperation.

But this paucity in no wise deterred Symerka, who was indeed beating aloft furiously, launching himself at the two cowering ferals, who together could have fit under one of his wings. Temeraire had to roar very loudly to get his attention; so that the entire infantry battalion at the foot of the hill burst out of their tents and began milling around, and a few of them fired guns in panic.

"These are my guests, who have come to bring us intelligence, not to take anything," Temeraire said to Symerka severely, putting himself in front of the ferals. "You cannot be supposing everyone a thief, and jumping on them without so much as a word."

"Well, as *you* are vouching for them," Symerka said, "I suppose they are all right; but I am sure that one looked towards my plates," he added, stretching his neck as he flew back and forth before them a few more times, before at last subsiding and returning to his clearing.

"I am sorry you should have had so unfriendly a welcome," Temeraire said to the ferals: it was their chief come back again, and one other with her, a thin pale-grey creature almost as white as Lien, except with grey eyes instead of red. Temeraire was sorrier yet when the feral chief declared herself quite overset, and in need of restoration after their fright: she could not speak a word until they were fed. The quartermaster refused to be of any use, and in any case the dinner porridge would not be ready for another four hours yet. Roland had to be sent down to the city with a gold coin, and Temeraire then had to see this go down the gullets of his visitors in the form of two handsome round-bellied pigs.

"*Now* then," Temeraire said pointedly, when at last they had licked the last specks of blood from their muzzles.

"First," the feral chief said, uncowed, "I should like us to be very clear on terms. I suppose you would agree I have had a share in bringing you the message, even if I don't bring it myself, so long as I introduce you to someone who does?"

"Certainly," Temeraire said, "and that is quite enough of terms to discuss, until there *is* such a message, as I suppose you mean that you don't have it."

"Well, no," she said, "not yet: Bistorta here was not ready to believe me, that there was gold in it, and she says it is getting dangerous to go into France."

"They are all gone mad for this Napoleon down there," the pale-grey dragon said, in French, when Temeraire inquired of her. "All of them, whether they are harnessed or no. It has come to be so that they will herd you down for questioning as a spy if they do not know you. But your Prussian friends are there, yes, in the breeding grounds outside Moirans-en-Montaigne: I have seen them. It used to be I would take a sheep off their herders now and then, before the patrols grew so unfriendly. But these days, I would not risk going in *except* for gold, and as I told Molic here, I will believe in gold when I see it in front of my face; although you have certainly given us a handsome meal," she added, "and so behold, I am ready to be persuaded." She folded her wings neatly and tucked her head back in an expectant curve.

Temeraire sighed deeply and resigned himself to salting the wound: Roland and Baggy were told off to display the golden plate service once more, and the appreciative sighs of his guests only made him feel, all the more, what he would be losing. But he cheered himself that Bistorta could not say for certain whether Eroica himself were there, nor recall the names of any particular Prussian dragons; she might be entirely mistaken.

"But I will certainly attempt it," she said, after one last acquisitive squint at the engraving upon the largest platter. "Oh! Will I not! But tell me now what I must say to this fellow Eroica, when I find him."

"*If* you should find him," Temeraire said, with emphasis, "you shall tell him that Dyhern is quite at liberty, and here with us, and we should like him to rejoin; and also all his comrades. Roland," he turned his head, "I do not suppose you can learn from Dyhern which other Prussian aviators have been set free? Without telling them why, of course: Laurence is quite right that Dyhern ought not be distressed, when very likely we will not find Eroica after all."

This list took some time to obtain; the ferals did not object to the delay, nor to eating a substantial share of Temeraire's dinner when the porridge did at length finally come. "Eating fat, morning and night," Molic said, with a replete sigh; her belly was noticeably rounded. "It makes you think twice about harness, doesn't it?"

"No, it does not," Bistorta said positively. "I mean no offense," she added, "but it is not for me: following orders from one, who takes orders from another, for the sake of a third. Some of those dragons in France, they have never met this Napoleon at all, yet now they are ready to fight if you so much as hint he is not made of diamonds, all because he has given them a few pavilions and firework-shows. For me, I will stay in the mountains and be free; I would rather sleep in a meadow than beneath a painted roof."

"Firework-shows," Temeraire muttered, in fresh irritation: he was quite sure that the French dragons did not have to arrange their own entertainments; Napoleon would certainly see them invited to any general triumph.

At last Roland came with the list, written out in large letters, and Temeraire read it out to Bistorta; she listened carefully and permitted Roland to strap the list onto her foreleg, wrapped in several layers of oilskin and tucked into a map-case. "That will do," she said, shaking it to be sure it wouldn't fall off. "As long as I can take it off with my teeth, if I need to."

"Perhaps we had better stay until morning?" Molic said hopefully, meaning breakfast, but Bistorta had been too much inspired by the display of gold to wait; she nodded a farewell and was aloft, Molic trailing after her with a little more reluctance. Temeraire saw them go, and then noticed the aviators were going to their beds; it had grown late.

"Why, Laurence has been gone a long while," Temeraire said, "and Ferris is not back, either—I suppose he has found them, and has stayed in their company," he added, striving not to be anxious, unnecessarily anxious. "I wonder where they are."

Chapter 5

A CARRIAGE HAD BEEN WAITING for them, as close to the covert as the driver and his horses were willing to come. Hammond led Laurence to it with a miserable and anxious look, but in silence. Laurence had nothing he wished to say, and Hammond did not breach the wall of reserve which had risen around him.

The streets were busy with mid-day traffic, and their progress was slow. Laurence sat in the close stuffy box and watched the city move past through the window. "I am sorry for the inconvenient timing," Hammond at last ventured. "The gentleman's friends would not agree to meet earlier; they expressed doubts of his being entirely sober, by then."

Laurence only inclined his head. He could not find any emotion within but a concern for Temeraire's unhappiness, and this he could only permit himself to feel distantly. Hammond blamed himself that matters had come to such a pass, but wrongly; he had made every effort—he had made too much of an effort. His discreet inquiries to the Russian Imperial household had brought an instant answer: Baron Dobrozhnov was certainly beneath a prince of China, and the Tsar would as certainly order his immediate execution, for having offended an ally of such importance.

"But of course, you need make no official complaint," Hammond had tried, desperately, after he had very reluctantly conveyed the message to Laurence.

"Have you heard from the gentleman's friends?" Laurence had said, ignoring him, and to do Hammond credit, he did not pursue the attempt; it was absurd to suppose that the world would not know of it, if Laurence refused to meet Dobrozhnov by standing on the grounds of his Imperial rank.

He was not afraid; some deadening of the natural instinct of self-preservation had grown habitual, from long use, and he did not think he had anything to fear but his own harm or injury. The usual arguments for the prohibition of dueling, by an aviator, did not hold in his own case. Most dragons little felt the significance of their fighting work; they received no encouragement to be attached, themselves, to the causes for which they fought, and when their captains died would not remain in the field. But Temeraire would not abandon the struggle against Napoleon only because he was bereaved, thinking of nothing but his own grief and caring nothing for the larger cause; Temeraire would carry on their work.

Perhaps half an hour past the city walls, the carriage slowed as the wheels turned into a dirt lane and halted. Laurence opened the door: they had halted near a small stand of trees, on a narrow street barely dug out of the snow, ice mingled with pebbles and dust underfoot. A small solitary farmhouse stood atop a nearby hill, dark, with a peculiar weathercock in the shape of a rabbit; a few shaggy dark cows with snow dusted across the tops of their backs were browsing at a pile of hay in a nearby meadow. They were alone as yet: the cattle watched incuriously as Laurence and Hammond walked through the packed snow towards the trees. Beneath the laden branches, the ground was nearly clear, browsed down to the grass beneath.

"Perhaps he will not come," Hammond said. "Maybe his friends have persuaded him . . ."

Laurence did not listen; he marked out the clearing and its length with his eye, noted that the wind was high enough to alter a bullet's course. He was sorry that Dobrozhnov was not a military man; he disliked having so much advantage, where he could not be conciliatory. The wind was cold, and he walked back and forth, swinging his arms, to keep his blood moving. Hammond shivered beneath his heavy fur coat and hat. The time dragged. Laurence was conscious of the slow shift of the shadows of the tree-branches upon the snow.

"You are certain you have not mistaken the place?" he said finally.

"Quite certain," Hammond said. "Baron Von Karlow mentioned the rabbit; and that is his groom up there with our driver, who gave us the direction. But Captain, if the other gentleman is late, perhaps has chosen not to come—"

"We will wait another quarter of an hour," Laurence said.

At the very end of this period, they saw in the distance a carriage approaching slowly; in another ten minutes it had drawn up, the horses only lightly exercised. "You have certainly made very poor time," Hammond said, sharply, when the gentlemen descended; a doctor followed them out of the carriage.

"I am *very* sorry," Baron Von Karlow said, heavily, with a strange emphasis. Laurence knew him a little: another Prussian officer who had thrown in with the Russians rather than accept the French yoke, like Dyhern; he had distinguished himself in the battle of Maloyaroslavets. The friendship had likely a pecuniary ground: Dobrozhnov was wealthy, and given to sponsoring Prussian officers who required some support.

Von Karlow bowed to Laurence very stiffly; his look was unhappy and constrained. Laurence belatedly understood: they had not come so late by accident. Dobrozhnov had kept him waiting, in the cold, deliberately.

That gentleman looked better than the last time Laurence had seen him; clear-eyed and his skin no longer flushed with drink, although the bruise across his cheek had purpled. He avoided Laurence's eyes, and said, "Well, let us get on with it," and walked away to the other side of the clearing.

"Captain," Hammond said, low and angry; he, too, had understood. "I will require a delay, and see if we cannot arrange for something hot to drink; the goodwife of the farmhouse, perhaps, would provide—"

"No," Laurence said. He felt a heavy weariness and dismay, as if Dobrozhnov had gone to his knees and begged for his life. "There is no need. I have killed men in colder weather than this."

Hammond took the dueling-pistols to the center of the clearing, and met Von Karlow there; they inspected the weapons together. Hammond took some time over the examination, and carried the pistols back with the case tucked under his arm and his ungloved hands wrapped around the guns, warming them. Laurence was grateful, for the sentiment more than the act; the fire of Hammond's indignation lifted some of the oppression from his own spirits. He took one of the pistols, checked it, and nodded to Hammond; Von Karlow turned from his side and nodded as well. He walked back to the middle of the clearing and held up his handkerchief.

"On a count of three," he said, "when I have dropped the handkerchief, you may fire."

Laurence turned his side, to present a narrow target, and took aim; Dobrozhnov also turned, and Laurence was sorry to see the man's hand trembling, a little. He did not look at the gun, or the man's face; he looked at his chest, chose his point, and adjusted his pistol for the wind. "One," Von Karlow said. "Two—"

Dobrozhnov fired. Laurence all in one moment heard the explosion, saw the smoke, and felt the impact in his whole body; a sharp, shocking blow, knocking the air from his lungs. Then he was on the ground, without any consciousness of the fall. "My God!" Von Karlow cried aloud. He sounded far away.

Hammond was kneeling by his side in the snow, bending over him, ashen. "Captain—Captain, can you speak? Here, Doctor, at once!"

Laurence drew a shallow breath, and another. The pain was

startling, but general; he could not tell where he had been hit. Hammond's hands were on him, and the doctor's, opening his coat and his shirt, and then the doctor was sliding his hand down over Laurence's back. The doctor was speaking in Russian. "Thank Heaven! He says it has gone cleanly through," Hammond said. "Captain, do not move."

That was not, at present, a necessary instruction; Laurence's arms and legs felt weighted down as though by iron bands. The doctor was already working on him with needle and thread, humming to himself, a strangely cheerful noise. Laurence scarcely felt anything beyond a little pressure; a deep chill was traveling through his body. Hammond spoke to the doctor and then he bent down and took the pistol from Laurence's hand and stood. Laurence heard him saying, with icy formality, "Sir, I hope you will agree with me that a return of fire is required, under the circumstances of this unhappy accident. I am ready to oblige your party at any time."

"I agree, unquestionably," Von Karlow answered, his voice harsh.

"It was an accident," Dobrozhnov was saying, his voice trembling, "—a perfect accident. *Bozhe!* My finger slipped—"

He stopped talking; neither of the other two men spoke. After a moment he said, "Of course—of course. But we should see if the gentleman will recover to take his own shot—a hour can do no harm—"

"Such agitation of his wound can in no wise be recommended," Hammond said. "Nor that he go on lying here, in cold, any longer than he has already been kept in it. I add, sir, that I will be delighted to stand for another exchange of fire, should the completion of the first not achieve a decisive result. We may alternate, and so go on as you have begun."

"I agree to your proposal on behalf of my party," Von Karlow said.

Their united coldness was not less palpable than the frozen ground; Dobrozhnov said, "—yes. Yes, of course."

His footsteps crunched away a small distance, and then halted.

Laurence opened his eyes. He had not been conscious of closing them. The doctor was still humming, and putting a thick compress upon the wound. The sky above had that peculiar blue brightness of a very cold day. The sun had already passed its zenith. Laurence heard, a moment later, the explosion of a second pistol, and Dobrozhnov's exclamation.

"Well, sir?" Hammond said. "Can your party continue?"

"My arm is hit," Dobrozhnov said.

"A graze to the off-arm," Von Karlow said. "The wound is not grave."

"I do not know any reason why I must wish the other gentleman harm," Dobrozhnov said. "I am very willing to consider the matter closed."

Von Karlow said, after a moment, heavily, "Do you consider honor satisfied, sir?"

"Under the circumstances, I think I must request a second exchange," Hammond said. "Your party may fire whenever ready."

There was a brief pause. Laurence was already a little more aware of himself. He would have tried to sit up; the doctor pressed his shoulders back to the ground with the firmness of a nursemaid to a small child. Laurence shut his eyes again, and heard the pistol-shot, a thick hollow wooden thump; the bullet had hit a tree.

"You may fire when ready," Von Karlow said, after a moment.

A second shot. Dobrozhnov gasped. The doctor made an impatient grunt, and pushed himself up and left Laurence's side. Hammond was there in his place, a moment later. "Pray hold still, Captain," he said. "I will get the driver; we will remove you to the farmhouse in a moment."

He stood up again. "Sir, is honor satisfied, on your side?"

"My party cannot answer, but I consider the matter closed," Von Karlow said. "I hope you will permit me to express my regret for any irregularity; I would be glad to shake your hand, sir, if you would take my own."

"I am very glad to do so, sir; I find no fault in your arrangements," Hammond said.

A fence stile was brought, and the driver helped Hammond put him on it. Laurence was by then conscious only of cold; the movement caused him some discomfort, but this was brief, and he knew very little of the next passage of time. Bare tree-branches like lacework crossing over his field of vision; the warm stink of cows and pasture; the cry of several anxious chickens; the thump of a fist on a door, and then finally warmth again: they lay him near the fireplace, a roast on the spit turning and a sizzle of fat on the logs. Footsteps came and went around him; voices spoke, but they largely spoke in Lithuanian—a peculiar music not at all like Russian or German to his ear. He drifted, or slept, or dozed; then he opened his eyes and looked at the window. It was dark outside. "Temeraire will have missed me," he said aloud, and reaching groped for something to help him sit up.

He could not manage it. He fell back gasping to the floor. A woman came to his side—he stared up at her: a girl not twenty years of age, extraordinarily beautiful with clear green eyes and dark-brown hair; she returned the stare with immense interest. A sharp word drew her away; Laurence turned his head and found her mother glaring at him, with the same green eyes. Laurence inclined his head a little, trying to convey his lack of ill-intentions, if that were necessary under the circumstances.

His chest ached. A dressing was wrapped around his body, pressing upon the ribs. Blood had not quite soaked through the topmost level on the front. "Captain," Hammond said, kneeling beside him. "Are you—do you feel improved?"

"Temeraire," Laurence said, saving his breath.

"Von Karlow has gone back to town," Hammond said. "He has promised to send a message to the covert that we have been asked to stay the night at a hunting-lodge, outside the town. Pray try and rest. Are you in a great deal of pain?"

"No." There was no use in saying anything else. Laurence closed his eyes.

———

Forthing read out Laurence's note loudly: it was brief, but quite clear; Laurence would not come back to-day. "Oh," Temeraire said, disappointed; he had anticipated with pleasure revealing the initial success of his scheme. Laurence would surely approve all his arrangements, and in particular the generosity of his offering so remarkable a reward, and the result which it had already achieved. Indeed, Temeraire had quite counted upon that approval to salve the regrets which could not help but assail him, when he thought too long about the burnished luster of the golden plates, and imagined himself handing them over.

At least he had hoped to enjoy the satisfaction of showing Laurence that he, too, was not a slave to fortune; that he was quite willing to make the most extraordinary sacrifices in a worthy cause. There did not seem to Temeraire to be any need to defer that enjoyment until the final outcome was determined; after all, he had already made the gesture, and even now suffered the pains of anticipation. Even if Bistorta should *not* find Eroica in the end, Temeraire had still committed himself, and might as well have the credit of so doing.

So he sighed; but he only meant to resign himself to waiting, and thought nothing more of the note, until Churki said, "There is something I don't care for going on here. Lay that out where I can put an eye on it."

There was a great deal of sharp authority in her tone; Forthing had automatically spread the letter open on the rock before he recalled she was not properly entitled to give him orders. But by then Churki had already bent her head, and was peering closely at the small note; she said, "I thought so; it did not sound like something Hammond would have written, and that is not his hand. Is it your Laurence's?"

Temeraire peered at the letter very closely. It was difficult to make out the very small letters, but finally he decided that it was not.

"And the contents are too scanty for my taste. Where is this hunting-lodge, and who is their host?" Churki said. "Hammond is not given to sailing off without good reason, and he dislikes hunting extremely; whyever has he gone to such a place? None of this looks reliable. Whatever peculiar business your Laurence is engaged upon, it looks to me as though he has drawn Hammond into it, too."

"When Laurence has only been going about town because Hammond has made him go into society!" Temeraire said, but this protest was distracted; if anything had happened, it was surely not Laurence's fault, at all, but in every other respect he found Churki's remarks uncomfortably plausible.

"*And* we will have a bad time of searching," Churki added. "There isn't a moon to-night."

"Searching!" Forthing said. "What do you mean, searching: flying about and roaring and scaring good people in-doors? No talk of that, if you please. You are both working yourself up over nothing. Here's a note that Captain Laurence and Mr. Hammond very kindly asked someone to send for them, so you shouldn't worry when they came home a little late even though they are two sensible gentlemen perfectly able to take care of themselves, and instead here you are brewing it up into a proper conspiracy for no reason."

"I do not think it is *no reason,* at all," Temeraire said, with dislike. He did not think Forthing was as devoted to Laurence as he should have been, considering how Laurence had condescended to have him as first officer. Churki might be a little over-fretful on account of how Incan dragons were giving to stealing one another's people, but certainly there was no harm in being cautious. "Only it would do no good anyway for us to begin flying around without knowing anything of where Laurence and Hammond are: we will never find them without some direction. Who brought the letter, Roland, and where did they get it?"

"Just one of the street boys, the ones who aren't afraid to come near the covert," Roland said. "We'll see if we can catch him; like as not he'll have gone for one of the bun-sellers down the road." She tapped Baggy and Gerry, and went running with them for the gate of the covert.

Baggy returned the first, some twenty minutes later and out of breath. "Tisn't *my* fault," he said, when Churki demanded what was taking them all so long. "When we found him, he could only say he brought it from a message-boy who brought it this far but didn't want to come in the covert; so we had to go after *him,* and it is only luck I even got that one at all. And then *he* said it came from an officer, a Prussian officer named Von Karlow, at a public house near the German Gate, and *that* is all the way on the other side of the town."

"Ah!" Dyhern said. "Von Karlow: I know the man. I have fought with him: a good man—an honorable man. He would not send you a lie, Temeraire, I am sure."

"There, you see," Forthing said.

"I do *not* see," Churki said. "I have never heard this man's name. How does he know Hammond or Laurence at all, and how does he know that they are at this lodge? Why should it be his business to send a letter on their behalf? I am by no means satisfied."

Forthing was inclined to argue with her, but Temeraire interrupted. "Dyhern," he said, "if this gentleman is your acquaintance, perhaps you will oblige me by going to call upon him, and asking him the direction of this lodge. After all, it must be outside the city somewhere; there could be no real harm in our going to look in upon them, and if they have only stayed the night because of their horses being tired, we might bring them home."

He finished decidedly, with a flip of his tail, and felt he had struck a sensible, a reasonable course of compromise, without permitting himself to grow overly alarmed as Churki had. But Forthing, of course, could only bleat objections. "There is no call for your chasing off after Captain Laurence," he said. "What if he should have left by the time you got there? He would come straight here, and want to know what had become of you; meanwhile you would be flying about half-distracted, supposing the worst, and what if we should get orders to fight?"

"We will *not* get orders to fight," Temeraire said. "We have wanted orders to fight for three weeks, and we have not had any; we are not going to get some now."

He turned his head even as he spoke: at last here was Ferris coming back into the clearing. Forthing said, "Mr. Ferris, I hope you have word from the captain; I am sure you will tell us everything is well, and there is no reason for any sort of alarm."

"Oh, will I," Ferris said, and Temeraire, looking closely, saw that his face was set and furious. "He is gone to a meeting; some caper-merchant Russian lag-wit insulted the Emperor of China to his face at a party last night, and he struck the man. I cannot find anyone to tell me where it is, but I have learned for a certainty that one of the man's friends called on Hammond this morning, some fellow named Karloff or Karlow."

"Good God!" Forthing cried, and there was a general noise of excitement and babble among the crew, which made it quite impossible at first for Temeraire to understand what exactly had happened, and why they should be so distressed that Laurence had—quite justifiably—chastised a rudesby, and what any of this had to do with meetings or hunting-lodges. "Captain Dyhern, pray will you go at once," Forthing was saying, and Dyhern was already coming out of his tent, in his coat and his hat, and Baggy said, "I will run ahead and get you a carriage, sir," and pelted away towards the street again.

"What is the to-do?" Roland said, looking as Baggy flew past her; she was coming back the other way. "Did Baggy have any luck finding the message-boy?"

"Roland," Temeraire said, putting a forefoot before her, so she could not be swallowed up in the general chaos, "pray tell me at once what it means, that Laurence has gone to a meeting."

"He wouldn't," she said, but at once said, "Oh, but he *would*, wouldn't he; has he?"

"Yes," Temeraire said, gripped with horror. "Roland, what *is* a meeting?"

"The worst nonsense anyone ever heard of, and he knows perfectly well better; if Mother were here, she would throw him in stocks for it, if he has not got himself shot," Roland said, stormily.

"Shot?" Temeraire said blankly. "Shot?"

"He has gone to fight a duel," Roland said.

Nearly the most dreadful hour of Temeraire's life followed on this intelligence: an hour in which he could do nothing, knowing all the time that somewhere not an hour's flight away, Laurence might at this very moment be stepping upon a field of honor. This was aptly named, it seemed to Temeraire, as *honor* was a word which seemed associated with every worst disaster in his life: a hollowness for which Laurence had before now been willing to die in the most unnecessary fashion, and this one more unnecessary than ever. "For no-one *could* suppose Laurence was a coward," Temeraire said. "Not even anyone who disliked him extremely: I have heard the Admiralty tell him he had not *enough* fear."

"It isn't the captain that anyone would call a coward, sure," O'Dea said, "but the other fellow that he struck; and the captain's too much a gentleman to hit another and not let him have satisfaction, if he ask for it. Ah, the sword and the pistol have made much food for worms ere now out of men of honor, and watered the soil with blood and the tears of their relics. I have known eight men shot dead in duels, on the greens of Clonmel." He patted Temeraire's foreleg, in what perhaps was meant to be a comforting gesture; but Temeraire was too stricken to feel any sense of gratitude.

His crew had scattered out into the city, all of them trying to learn where the duel was to be held, and when; Dyhern was engaged in canvassing his acquaintance among the Prussian officers to find some intelligence of Von Karlow. Temeraire had thought of flying passes over the town, but Ferris had dissuaded him. "As likely as not, they are fighting somewhere outside the city, or beneath some trees, and if you terrify everyone into hiding behind closed doors and shutters, we will never find out where in time."

He spoke of *in time,* but Laurence had been gone so long already; and every minute dragged onwards. Some of the crew came straggling back, without anything to report, until a pale and sweating Cavendish came back; he said, "Is Mr. Forthing anywhere?"

"He has not come back yet," Temeraire said. "What have you heard?"

"What about Mr. Ferris?" Cavendish said, and then he wished to wait for Captain Dyhern to return, and then desperately, "Well, perhaps Roland will be back, in a little while," and Temeraire realized he was trying to put off bad news.

"Tell me at once," Temeraire said.

"I don't know anything," Cavendish said, but a low awful growling was building in Temeraire's throat, thrumming against the ground, and Cavendish swallowed and said, "I don't, nothing certain! Only I went along of Captain Dyhern to the public house, where that Karlow fellow is supposed to have rooms; he wasn't there, so Captain Dyhern went on, but I overheard a couple of fellows in the taproom, from an infantry regiment, talking over a duel—but they didn't know anything, not really; they didn't know it was our captain—"

"What did they say?" Temeraire said.

"They said," Cavendish said, "they said someone had fought a fatal duel, somewhere outside the city," Temeraire felt the world drag to a halt, suspended, "and they said—they said it was Von Karlow's own fault, seconding a coward, because—because his man fired ahead of the signal."

"He is dead, then," Churki said. "And without even a single child! I am so very sorry, Temeraire."

"No," Temeraire said, "no; he is not dead," blindly, and Dyhern came panting up the hill, shouting, "He is *not* dead! He is not dead, thank the good God."

"He is *not?*" Temeraire said, thrusting his head down low to the ground, the world lurching back into motion.

Dyhern caught Cavendish by the ear and shook him. "What do you mean by repeating nonsense like that, you young sow's head? Keep your mouth shut, next time. He is not dead," he re-

peated, and had to let go the wincing Cavendish to bend himself
double, hands braced on his knees, to get back his air: Dyhern was
a big man, and though he had lost a great deal of flesh to grief and
to winter, his wind was not so remarkable that he could cheerfully
run up the steep hillside to the entry gates.

"Then what has happened?" Temeraire cried.

"The other man," Dyhern said, "is dead."

"Oh! That is just as well," Temeraire said, immensely relieved.
"If he were not, I should certainly have killed him; but I am glad
Laurence has already done so. Why has he not come back?"

"He did not kill his man," Dyhern said. "Hammond did."

"What?" Churki said, sitting up sharply. "What has Hammond to do with killing anyone? He is not a soldier!"

Dyhern did not say anything more, waving away the questions as he heaved for breath; then he went to his tent and came
out with his harness. "I will tell you all, once we are in the air,"
he said. "We are flying west. Von Karlow has given me their direction. Here, be useful now," he added, to Cavendish, "and get
aboard. We may need hands. You there, O'Dea, you will tell the
officers where we have gone. Give me your paper, I will write the
direction."

Temeraire did not argue, because he agreed with Dyhern: Laurence was alive, and all further intelligence might be deferred in
the interest of going to him at once. He waited impatiently for
Dyhern to finish scribbling his note, and then held out his claw for
him and for Cavendish, to put them up more quickly on his back.
"Well?" he said. "Have you latched on?" and hearing the carabiner-
clicks did not wait for an answer, but launched himself into the air.

Laurence woke in the night coughing, a sharp pain in his side, and
found Dyhern bending over him and the household in weeping
terror. "Take him, take him!" the goodwife was saying in rough
German, making pushing gestures at Laurence with her hands.
"Give the dragon!"

Dyhern calmed her with a stern speech in that language, too quick for Laurence to follow, and turning back said, "Rest, Captain, I will tell Temeraire you cannot be moved," and then was gone again. Laurence fell back into fitful and uneasy sleep and woke again with the household in fresh dismay, shrieks rousing him: it was daylight outside, and Temeraire had put his enormous eye up to the window to peer in at him.

"Temeraire," Laurence tried to say, and then he was dreaming again, of beef: fresh hot roast beef, the juices running red and rare, until these became rivulets of blood dripping from Dobrozhnov, a dead groaning corpse who came close and closer and put out clammy hands to grasp Laurence's arms; he woke with a jerk in an unpleasant but welcome sweat, too warm: his fever had broken. There was a pot of beef broth cooking over the fire.

He drank nearly all of it, and then realized that the groaning soul in the cot across the room from him *was* Dobrozhnov: still alive, despite a bullet gone through his chest. "Good God, why is he here?" Laurence said to Hammond.

"I am very sorry for the circumstances, Captain; he could not be moved, and indeed, we hardly foresaw any reason to do so," Hammond said uneasily, looking towards the cot. "The doctor was quite sure of his being dead before now. But I am very glad to see *you* so improved: will you eat a little more?"

"With pleasure," Laurence said, "when I have spoken to Temeraire."

This required the support of Dyhern's strong shoulders, and the use of the household's only bed and its meager supply of pillows; limping across the chamber was even so a remarkably painful process of transfer, and when Laurence at last was lying upon the bed, he was forced to accept another swallow of laudanum from Hammond, and catch his breath for some twenty minutes before he could again speak to let them know they might open the door.

Temeraire put his head up to it, anxious, deeply distressed. "Anyone might have *guessed*," he said with immense reproach, "that the sort of person who would insult the Emperor *would* cheat, and here you are wounded!"

"I assure you I feel very much better," Laurence said, although he was indeed in severe pain, which the laudanum only served to cloud and not remove. He heard and understood only distantly: his attention was fixed on his own words, struggling to keep in mind that he must say nothing of Dobrozhnov, still lying helpless in the room behind him. Temeraire could not know him still alive.

"I have been speaking with Dyhern a great deal on the subject of dueling," Temeraire said, "and it seems plain to me that something must be done. You must give me your word, Laurence, that if anyone ever *should* insult you again, they must be told at once that I will insist on being your second myself. I am very much indebted to Mr. Hammond for having killed that wretched fellow, but in future, if anyone likes to prove they are not a coward by insulting you, they may fight me, and then they cannot complain of not having had satisfaction: I am sure everyone will agree they *were* brave, once they are dead. Pray promise me, and then you must go have some more beef broth," he insisted.

Laurence said vaguely, "As you wish," having become unable to follow the conversation, and was grateful to be carried back to the fire, still in the bed, and to eat a little more broth. This the daughter of the house brought him, and sat by him for a while frowning, and then in a little awkward German spoke to him, asking quite seriously if the dragon obeyed him because he was a devil. This notion she proposed with an air of interest more than horror, and seemed reluctant to accept Laurence's denial. When he awoke from a long drowse, he did so finding her carefully putting his hand onto the family crucifix, and in some exasperation he took hold of it, showed her he had not the least hesitation in doing so, and kissed it: a Popish gesture, but convincing. She seemed however disappointed, and demanded to know how he *did* control the dragon.

"Ask Hammond," Laurence said, too weary to struggle on in

German, of which he had very little even under better circumstances. "He has a dragon also."

Hammond was meeting with very little success in controlling his dragon in any manner, however: Churki was in a mood of great severity, which had been not at all improved by learning the details of Hammond's behavior in the duel, which she loudly characterized as ridiculous and inappropriately dangerous. The next day Laurence felt improved enough to be carried out of doors for a brief airing; he was glad to escape the cottage briefly despite the cold, as Dobrozhnov persisted in not dying and had begun to moan almost incessantly from pain. By then he found a serious quarrel brewing between the beasts: Churki was inclined to blame him for having dragged Hammond into the affair, and Temeraire was inclined to blame Hammond for the reverse, and an atmosphere of resentment had settled between them.

"A pretty thing to be accusing you of," Temeraire said, snorting with sufficient force to blow the snow before him into a cloud, "when you are so badly wounded you groan day and night," and then he paused with a sudden puzzled expression and looked over at the cottage, from which had just issued one of these groaning noises.

"I do not cry out, I assure you," Laurence said hastily, hoping to divert Temeraire's attention: Temeraire would certainly kill Dobrozhnov at once if he learned of the man's survival, and very likely have the house in ruins on all its occupants besides. "—I am not uncomfortable."

"Still, *you* are the one who has been shot," Temeraire said, not mollified, and it was of no use to point out that Hammond had stood the same hazard; indeed Laurence found it best not to discuss the particulars of the duel at all.

The remainder of his crew had arrived the previous day, driving the wagon-load of gold and treasure—much to Temeraire's relief—and Laurence could not help but be aware that his officers were very shocked; their disapproval was a palpable thing. Of Jane Roland's reaction he was left in no doubt, from Emily's furious looks, and he was uncomfortably certain that the absent Granby, too, would have upbraided him in the strongest terms. The ground crew, who did not themselves suffer from the prohibition against dueling, were more tolerant, and indeed rather more pleased than not to have a captain who would fight a duel in the teeth of prohibition; they considered his ferocity as reflecting well upon them. But Laurence did not care to have an act of unpleasant necessity be approved as barbarism, so this was not much consolation.

The officers of course could not express their feelings through any open reproach, but they were worsening the quarrel by ranging with Churki in blaming him. Temeraire was now torn between his own anger with Laurence and his unwillingness to cede ground to Churki, and Laurence was very dismayed to find the quarrel migrate onto the person of Miss Merkelyte. Hammond had introduced this young lady to Churki, by way of answering her questions and, he hoped, reconciling the family to the continuing presence of two large dragons in their acreage. Churki found much to approve in the girl's youth and beauty—too much to approve; she informed Temeraire, in haughty tones, that she would accept the young lady, on Hammond's behalf, as a kind of apology.

"Well, I am *not* going to make her an apology," Temeraire said, indignant on very wrong grounds. "I do not see why Hammond should have her at all. She is very beautiful, at least all the crew tell me so. She may marry Ferris."

Laurence would have upbraided both beasts for their scheming, as an insult to the already-unwilling hospitality of their hosts, but when he had marshaled Dyhern and Mrs. Pemberton to make apologies to Mrs. Merkelyte and ask her to keep her daughter indoors, that lady held a conference with her daughter, and then demanded instead to know the situations of both gentlemen, and the particulars of bride-price and settlements. They were serfs, despite their relative prosperity, and had much to be wary of in seeing their nation absorbed by Russia, where their caste was notoriously oppressed. It was perhaps not surprising that Mrs. Merkelyte was ready to seize an opportunity of lofting her child to the security of a far higher sphere of society, even at the cost of losing her.

The proposed grooms were more hesitant. Ferris, while by no means indifferent to Miss Merkelyte's charms, had sufficiently disappointed his family, through no fault of his own, to wish to further provoke them by presenting them with a wife of whose birth and education they would have strongly disapproved; meanwhile Hammond had vague but firmly held plans to ally himself with a woman of wealth and influential family, when he should have achieved sufficient success to recommend himself to such a lady. Laurence could not blame them, but the natural consequence of their failing to come up to the mark was to permit every other man of their company, of remotely marriageable age, to imagine himself as the lady's partner instead.

Forthing, whom Laurence was sorry to learn a widower, hinted himself willing to pay his addresses, while Ferris reddened with indignation; Cavendish quarreled with Baggy though they had not half a beard between them. Even O'Dea made it his business to sit by Laurence's bedside and recite poetry, casting soulful looks across the room while struggling to contrive rhymes for *Gabija.*

No young lady who had been so thoroughly sheltered could be blamed for enjoying such attentions; meanwhile her mother kept a hawk's eye on the proceedings, but did not demur so long as her sense of propriety was not crossed. Temeraire hurled fuel upon the fire by regularly ordering some item of his treasure brought out from under the tarpaulins, to be polished and displayed in the thin wintry sunlight. Churki grew incensed with the competition offered to her own ambitions and began to hold long insistent conversations with Hammond, from which he escaped with an expression so mortified that Laurence could not imagine what had been said.

"What has *not* been said?" Hammond paced the room, pale with red spots. "I will not forbear to say, Captain, that the morals of dragons are *very sadly flexible,*" and Laurence realized appalled that Churki was proposing that Hammond take the girl into his keeping, if he did not wish to marry her.

"Well, of course there is no reason for her to go into Hammond's keeping," Temeraire said, "but she might go into *yours*. Indeed, that seems to me an excellent solution: we can pay bride-price now, and she may choose which of my crew she likes when she is ready. Or perhaps she might marry someone *else,*" he added, struck as though by a remarkable inspiration, "and then they should join my crew also: I have thought, Laurence, that we might do well to have a few more officers."

After this conversation, Laurence said to Hammond, "For God's sake, send for that doctor and ask if I am not well enough to be moved before we have more to reproach ourselves with than we already do; I am sure neither of these wretched beasts would scruple to make themselves procurers, only to win their point."

The doctor came and pronounced Laurence on the mend, but not well enough to be allowed a flight in cold air; after this disappointment he inspected Dobrozhnov, and further complicated the situation by announcing that the gentleman evidently meant to live after all.

Dobrozhnov still moaned incessantly that night, but by the following morning, he began to be well enough to sit up and make an even worse nuisance of himself. Most unfortunately, he spoke Lithuanian. Nor felt, so far as Laurence could tell, any compunction about abusing the hospitality he had received: indeed he was no sooner well enough to speak, than he began to make clear by his behavior that he considered Miss Merkelyte fair game, and himself entitled to enjoy her favors, if only he should conquer her resistance ahead of his competitors. Laurence did not understand the words with which he addressed her, but the tone was so familiar it might have been better suited to a bawdy-house, and covered her with confusion.

Laurence had been determined to say nothing to the man; indeed, to ignore his presence insofar as possible: the situation was impossible otherwise. But he could hardly sit by and watch the progress of the seduction of an innocent girl, whose character was so alarmingly threatened, and not least through the actions of his own crew. "Hammond," Laurence said, "he must be induced to leave that girl alone. Can you get rid of him?"

"I hardly know how," Hammond said dubiously. "We can scarcely get him out of the house without the dragons seeing him: they are watching the door every minute to see who is coming in or out to speak with Miss Merkelyte."

Just when he would have preferred to be ill for longer, Laurence found his own recovery speeding; he was well enough to stand up by himself the next day, and when he went slowly and haltingly outside, on Ferris's arm, the cold did not bite with more than its usual ferocity. But he could not avoid knowing that their own departure would now leave the girl unprotected. Dobrozhnov had spent an hour in close conversation with the mother that very morning, and Laurence had seen gold change hands—ostensibly in thanks for the house's hospitality. The coins were a trifle to a man as wealthy as Dobrozhnov, but to the household they meant ten years' work and good fortune, and Mrs. Merkelyte plainly did not conceive that such a sum had been pressed upon her by a man with anything other than serious intentions; nor did Dobrozhnov have any hesitation letting her imagine he meant to offer her daughter a respectable marriage, rather than an arrangement as dishonorable as it was likely to be of short duration.

"Forthing," Laurence said at last, grimly settling on the least of the many evils from which he had to make his choice, "*will* you marry her?"

"If—if she likes," Forthing said, a little uncertainly; he had not received much encouragement. He was not rich and had never been handsome, even before the fresh scar which marred his face, nor were his manners of a sort that could impress a young woman, and he was besides this a little too practical to be entirely in love himself. "Only, I don't know what I'm to do with her. I could send her to my sister. I suppose she'd learn English quick enough?"

"Whatever use is *that*?" Temeraire said, objecting immediately. "Why should she go away? I wish her to remain with us."

"We cannot be taking her to war," Laurence said.

"Why not?" Temeraire asked. "Roland comes to war, and so does Mrs. Pemberton. And Laurence," he lowered his head, if not much his voice, "must it really be Forthing? I am sure she is too beautiful for him: only look at his coat!"

"Pray come and speak with her mother," Laurence said to Forthing, deferring this argument; he felt not a little guilty at Forthing's doubtful expression, but under the circumstances he could see no better solution.

However, Mrs. Merkelyte was grown particular: not entirely remarkable, when she had a wealthy Russian baron sleeping on her floor making a pretense of courtship, and two dragons busily trying to offer her the choice of a British diplomat and a younger son of the nobility, however unwilling these latter two might be. Dyhern awkwardly demurred from serving as go-between, for which Laurence could hardly blame the man, so Hammond had to be recruited to the task. He tried to persuade her through the barrier of German, but he was nervous lest he make a remark too easily misconstrued to commit *him* as the bridegroom, rather than Forthing. The discussion continued for only a little while; mother and daughter exchanged a glance; the girl looked away—the mother shook her head. Meanwhile Dobrozhnov watched all the proceedings sidelong from his own cot, with an amused and half-incredulous expression, as though he thought the offer absurd; Laurence was conscious of a strong desire to knock him down again.

Gabija did not admire Dobrozhnov; her own preference was quite certainly for Ferris, on whom her eyes often lingered: with his sword and pistols and flying-coat, and the military carriage which had never deserted him, he presented the qualities of an officer even though he no longer possessed the rank. He had a smooth high forehead beneath auburn locks, and over the course of the preceding year he had filled out in muscle to match his height; if not a match for her in beauty, he could reasonably have been called handsome even by a judge with more basis for comparison. She was too shy to even attempt to speak to him, but she made excuses to be in his way, and even dared to linger near Temeraire, who might be relied upon to call Ferris over whenever she was by.

But despite these evident signs of calf-love, Laurence feared her susceptible to Dobrozhnov's persuasion: she plainly did not wish to settle, any longer, for the quiet country life which would have been her natural lot. If no better offer were made her, she might well be persuaded to accept Dobrozhnov's suit, without under-standing what fate she embraced.

And yet Laurence had reached the end of what solutions he might offer: he could not press Ferris to marry under the circum-stances. Temeraire however felt no such hesitation, and when the failure of Forthing's suit had been reported—to Churki's visible and ruffled-up satisfaction—he urged at once, "Ferris, are you *sure* you would not like to marry her," while Laurence, catching his breath upon the camp-chair which had been arranged for him, could not yet object.

"I must beg to be excused," Ferris said, and dragged his eyes away from Miss Merkelyte's appealing glance with an effort: she was feeding the chickens in the yard, and made a remarkably charming portrait with her dress hiked up to her knees, and curls of her dark hair escaping from under a kerchief. He swallowed, and added with some bitterness, "It would be too much to pros-trate my mother a second time," and took himself away.

"Temeraire," Laurence said, "you cannot be tormenting him so: leave off."

"But if *we* do not object, I do not see why he ought to imagine his mother will; after all, she has never seen Gabija," Temeraire began, but he stopped and raised his head, his ruff pricking up.

A small dragon came dropping out of the clouds in the dis-tance: one of the local ferals, green, with a remarkable bony crest atop her head in orange and brown stripes. She sighted them and came on, circled once and descended. "So here you are!" she said, in accusatory tones. "What do you mean by hiding yourself away like this?"

"I beg your pardon?" Temeraire said, glacially. "I have come here to look after Laurence, who was injured in a duel; and I do *not* propose to let anyone object to it, either."

"Hm," the feral said, "well, as long as you aren't trying to get out of it, at least: I hope you wouldn't be that sort of dragon."

"I am *not* that sort of dragon, at all!" Temeraire said. "And it is quite outrageous that you should come flitting back again to accuse me of any such thing. It is not as though I were going to wait about forever on the very thin chance that you should return. After you have found Eroica, then it will be very well for you to start talking about my *trying to get out of it:* as though I were a scrub."

"What?" Dyhern said, standing up; he had been sitting upon a log near-by, occupying himself with whittling while Laurence spoke with Temeraire and Ferris, and to Laurence's regret, he had heard his dragon's name mentioned.

"All right," the feral said, "so go on and bring out the plate, then: we are here, aren't we?"

"I believe," Temeraire said in awful tones, "that there was a small matter of *proof,* and as for *we*—" Here he stopped, and Laurence heard Dyhern make a short, sharp inhalation, audible even across the farmyard, and then he was running, his arms open wide as a boy as he pelted downhill, shouting: there were half a dozen heavy-weight dragons breaking through the cloud cover, wisps of fog boiling away over their grey and brown bodies, and Eroica was in the lead.

Chapter 6

$\mathcal{L}$AURENCE HAD RARELY SEEN a man so overcome: Dyhern could not manage any language but German, and his speech was so choked with tears that it could not have been comprehensible if he had been speaking the most fluent English, but he wrung Laurence's hand with fervor enough to make words superfluous. Eroica, too, was beyond words, attempting as well as any dragon of twenty-three tons and armored in bone plates might to make himself a lap-dog, nearly knocking Dyhern over with attempts at caressing, while his fellows crowded around with enormous anxiety and peppered Dyhern with questions, asking after their own captains, their own officers. The noise was extraordinary.

"Temeraire," Laurence said, almost too baffled to share in the delights of so unlikely a reunion, "I suppose you must have engineered this, but I cannot conceive how."

"Oh," Temeraire said, in despairing tones; he was regarding the touching scene with his ruff flattened so thoroughly against his neck as to make it nearly impossible to see at all.

"Well?" The little feral popped up to prod Temeraire, nudging him with her nose. "I suppose *now* you cannot argue we haven't done our part." Another small feral dragon landed, a grey-white beast with suspicious eyes for the crowd of Prussian beasts, and joined the first. "We are here. We have brought them. Where is the gold?" she demanded. "I want to be on my way: I mean to get it somewhere safe, before there are a lot of rumors about it."

Temeraire heaved an enormous gasp, his entire chest bellowing out, and said chokingly, "Ferris, will you pray have the gold plate brought out—Napoleon's service? I do not suppose, Laurence," he added, in a sudden burst of desperation, "that you object to my having offered it as a reward? If *you* think it an excessive gesture—"

"My God," Laurence said, with feeling, "if you have bought us half a dozen Prussian dragons, you might have spent every last ounce of coin in your wagon, without my raising the least objection," and Temeraire gave a shudder and put his head under his wing, as the plate was brought out and handed over to the two exultant ferals.

They fell almost at once to squabbling over the equal division of their spoils, which the presence of various serving-vessels of varied size made difficult. Temeraire flinched from the dispute. Laurence could not pretend to share his feelings, but nevertheless laid a hand upon his muzzle to try to comfort him. "My dear," he said, "I am very sensible of the pain which this sacrifice must have given you; will you permit me to say that I rejoice in the character which you have displayed in enduring it? And to urge you to console yourself by observing the pleasure you have given our friends, entirely aside from the manifest benefits to our war effort."

"I am very happy to have been of service, of course," Temeraire said, monotonously, but Hammond emerged from the cacophony quite nearly incandescent with his own joy, and seized his hand and cried, "Laurence, Laurence, the beasts say there are another forty of them, spread across Prussia, the entire Prussian aerial corps: they have *all* run for it. I cannot conceive how they were persuaded."

"Well, it's plain enough, isn't it?" the grey feral demanded, lifting her head. "If this Napoleon isn't knocked down, they will never see their captains again, who might all as well be dead. There wasn't any sense in their sitting about in the breeding grounds anyway, and they weren't even being bred, for that matter."

"What?" Temeraire said, lifting his head, at least briefly distracted from his unhappiness.

She shrugged. "I gather this Lien dragon doesn't think much of the Prussian lines: she even had them kept apart on purpose, the males and females, so they shouldn't have *any* eggs."

"Why," Temeraire said, "how insulting, and when they were so brave—even if they did insist on formation-flying, that was not *their* fault, really, and they did not know any better; Eroica, I am very sorry you should have endured such rudeness," he added, but Eroica reared his head up away from Dyhern, his yellow eyes widening suddenly, and cried out, "Mein Gott!"

He lunged back onto his feet, with such force that tremors ran through the ground; Laurence had to put a hand on Temeraire's leg to steady himself. "Eggs! Temeraire—forgive me! That I should not tell you at once! She is a fiend, a fiend—"

"Of course she is, but whatever are you talking about?" Temeraire said, pulling his head back on his neck, wary.

"The white dragon came to the breeding grounds not two weeks ago," Eroica said. "Her insulting remarks—I will not repeat them all! But this we overheard her say," and he turned his head one way and another, to the other Prussian dragons, who all nodded energetically, "that she considered it her duty to protect the lines of France no less than the lines of China: that she meant to prevent our breeding even as she meant also to see to *a mongrel egg,* which a *traitor to her kind* had produced, to seal a corrupt alliance between China and the most evil nation of the West—"

Temeraire oversaw the hasty packing with blank calm. "I see now, Laurence," he said, "that you are quite right, that one must not be a slave to fortune: if I had kept all the gold plate, and never offered the reward, I should never have known that the egg was in danger, and Lien might have—" Here he faltered, with a shudder which wracked his entire frame; he did not wish to imagine what Lien might have done to the helpless, too-fragile egg. "But will you be well enough to travel?" he added instead, with dull anxiety.

"I will do," Laurence said. "But Temeraire, you and I must go alone; we cannot take the crew with us on such a journey."

"As you think best," Temeraire said. The ground crewmen took the lid off the porridge-pit, and he put his head within to eat as much as he could, though he felt no sense of appetite.

Hammond and Forthing and Ferris had already been arguing with Laurence in low voices, telling him that it was madness to try to cross all Russia in the worst cold of winter, without escort; they redoubled their arguments now. Temeraire overheard, but made no answer. It would be very difficult, of course, but there was no alternative: to take the southern road would be a loss of three months' time.

"Gentlemen," Laurence said, without looking up from his writing-table, where he leaned heavily upon his elbow as he slowly scratched out a letter, "Temeraire will go: do you imagine there is any question of that? Therefore I am going. Mr. Forthing, I will give you a letter for Whitehall, but until you receive further orders, I hope you will be guided by Mr. Hammond's advice. I imagine that there will be a great want of men to crew the Prussian dragons, and you cannot, I think, do better than to return the favor which Dyhern has done for us heretofore. Mr. Hammond, I would be very much obliged to you if you will ask safe-passage for us from the Tsar."

"Good God!" Hammond cried, "as if he can give you any such thing, with five thousand mad and starving ferals scattered across his countryside. Captain, I beg you to try all your influence, all your energies—"

"Those," Laurence said, cutting him off, "I must conserve for efforts more likely to succeed."

Hammond gave over arguing, but a little while later, when

Laurence had gone into the house to eat a little supper, he came to Temeraire and made a final attempt. "Temeraire," he said, "I must say to you what Captain Laurence will not: this journey will be his death. He has scarcely risen from his sickbed; he is weak and ill. To attempt to cross a frozen wasteland in his condition, with insufficient food and shelter, will be a death sentence even in the absence of any other hazards which you might encounter. Will you insist upon taking him to so cruel a fate?"

"Oh!" Temeraire cried. "That *you* should speak to me so: why is he weak and ill, but that you put him in the way of this wretched duel, and did not let me know anything of what was happening? You may be sure *I* would not have permitted him to be shot by a worthless coward."

So he sent Hammond packing, but could not help but feel all the force of the argument: Laurence lost his breath so easily now, and looked very weary and grey. It was not two days since he had been first able to stand. Temeraire furrowed the ground uneasily, and then he leaned over and roused Eroica, who was sleeping after his long and arduous flight. "Will you come and have a word, if you please?" he asked, low, and when they had padded a little distance away—carefully, so as not to knock down any of the sheepfold or the trees—he summoned his resolve and said, "Eroica, Laurence cannot come with me—he must not come with me—he is not well. But I must go to the egg, of course. Will—will you look after him for me, until I return?"

"Temeraire, best of friends!" Eroica said. "I swear to you I will guard him like my own captain: how could I do any less, when you have restored Dyhern to me?"

"I hoped you would feel so," Temeraire said, although a deep hollow sensation of unhappiness made itself present in his breast, as though having spoken, he had already parted from Laurence. His head bowed with misery.

Eroica leaning over nudged his shoulder beneath Temeraire's and offered its massive breadth for support. "Courage! That you will save your egg and come back again, I have no doubts. And

while you are away, Dyhern and I will make it our business to keep
your captain safe. So, too, will all my companions: there is many a
dragon of Prussia who owes you a happy reunion."

Temeraire tried to accept this consolation, but it was hard; he
told himself he left Laurence with an immense treasure, and many
friends to watch over him, but he could not pretend he was not
also leaving Laurence exposed in the midst of war. But the egg—
Lien would send assassins, or pay them—Temeraire trembled all
over again, envisioning the egg—*smashed,* that delicate opalescent
shell in pieces across the marble floors of the Imperial City, all its
guards murdered—

"I must go," he gasped. If Laurence were not coming with him,
there was no need for packing; no need for preparation or supply.
He would go on the wing, and hunt as he flew. "Eroica, pray tell
him—pray tell Laurence—" But here Temeraire's invention failed
him; he could not suppose what there was to tell Laurence that
Laurence did not already know.

"I will tell him you are sorry to leave him behind," Eroica said,
"and that I will stand in your stead as his protector, until you have
returned."

Temeraire only bobbed his head blindly in agreement, then
flung himself aloft; he beat his wings in great scoops of air and
lifted away, turning his head to the east, and flew.

Laurence heard the shouting outside, and saw the great shadow
crossing the fields, and knew at once: Temeraire had gone without
him. He was sitting at the rough-hewn table which stood in the
house's kitchen. He did not immediately make a push to gather his
strength to stand: it was already too late. Temeraire would not be
caught by any dragon here, not when he went unarmored, unbur-
dened, and stretching himself to the limits of his speed.

Hammond appeared in the doorway, stricken, and Laurence
looked him in the face; Hammond hesitated, saw that he already
understood. His face fell; he did not speak.

"You will pray send to the Tsar for a safe-passage regardless," Laurence said quietly. "It is not likely to be of much use, but the Russian couriers may at least pass the word ahead, so he will not meet any official obstacles."

"Yes," Hammond said. "Captain, I must beg your pardon—"

Laurence forestalled him with a hand, and shook his head. There was nothing to be gained by upbraiding Hammond now. He pushed himself up from the table and went back to the cot: there was nothing more he could do at the moment.

He slept, and woke in the late hour of the night to the sound of a soft scuffling across the room. The embers of the fire lit Dobrozhnov in orange: he was sitting sideways upon his cot, smiling, and holding Gabija by the wrists; she was pulling against his grip and whispering urgently. He said something in cajoling tones, pulling her down towards him, and Laurence pushed himself up and said, "You damned blackguard, let that girl go, or I will have my men horse-whip you in the yard."

Dobrozhnov let her go, his face purpling with indignation, and she ran from the house in long fleet strides, gasping like a deer set loose from a snare. The mother's head popped out of the bedroom door, frowning, and a moment later Ferris wrenched wide the front door and stormed in, tall and furious with his sword drawn, and said, "Now you will give *me* satisfaction, you wretch—"

He was only restrained with difficulty from dragging the man from his sickbed at once; a difficulty only increased by Dobrozhnov saying contemptuously, "What a to-do! I am not going to fight you over a warm peasant armful, you young ass; make a fool of yourself if you wish."

"You cannot kill a wounded man," Laurence said tiredly, "nor force a coward to face you, Ferris; leave off. Tomorrow he will go back to the city in a wagon-cart, and we will return to the covert, and there will be an end of the matter. Hammond, tell that woman to keep her daughter in the bedroom until we have all of us left."

Most of the Prussian dragons had already been sent back to the covert, where they could be supplied. Eroica alone had remained. When Laurence emerged that morning, the great dragon came to the door and earnestly assured him of his protection, a promise which Temeraire had evidently extracted from him before departing. "He is sure to return very soon," Eroica said, with draconic optimism. "So pray have no fear for yourself, or this magnificent treasure which he has left you: be assured not so much as a single coin will I permit anyone to take from it!"

Dyhern was in equal earnest, though more conscious of the grave danger which Temeraire now faced. "But while there is life there is hope, as my own example may show," he said, "and you must permit us to make what small returns we may for the gift you and he have given us. Come. We will go back to Vilna. You will rest, you will recover. And Laurence, though your dragon is gone, duty remains: you must be our instructor. The old ways are of no use against Bonaparte; Jena taught us that. It will not be enough that we renew our discipline and our daily practice. We must have new tactics, from the East, and you are best fitted to aid us in contriving them."

Dyhern's voice, and the example of his conduct, could not fail to carry enormous weight: while imprisoned, he had struggled for his liberty; while grounded, he had pursued service afoot; while his nation had been pinned beneath treaties, he had gone even to Russia to make himself of use in the struggle against the tyrant. Laurence nodded silently. Duty remained.

The wagon-cart was unnecessary: Dobrozhnov tried to protest he was not yet well enough to travel, but when it had been borne in upon him forcibly that his alternative was to be flung out of doors, he sent for his well-sprung coach and was borne into it by his tall footmen, still groaning and muttering protests. They drove away, not before he pressed a little more gold into the mother's hand, and gave Gabija a broad wink which brought fresh color to Ferris's cheek. Dobrozhnov might well intend to send for her, or return when he was well; but for the moment he was gone from the house, at least. Laurence could see little more that they might do, and he could only trust to society to distract the man with more satisfying entertainments than he might have found while prostrated in a solitary farmhouse.

The treasure had been well-packed into its carrying-wagon, and Churki and Eroica fed; she was urging Hammond in a low voice, making one final push to persuade him to bring the girl along. Ferris had gone away to Eroica's other side, and busied himself with unnecessary harness-work, to avoid looking upon Miss Merkelyte. He at least had no further cajolery to face, although he looked as though he might have wanted some; his obligations to a family both distant and already disappointed perhaps seemed less compelling than the attractions of the lady before him.

But when Laurence had been helped carefully aloft, and secured beneath blankets and oilcloth, he looked down Eroica's shoulder and overheard Dyhern asking, "My young friend: you are determined not to pursue her? I wish to be certain you have made your choice."

Ferris kept his head bowed and swallowed, then said in stifled tones, "Thank you, Captain; I cannot."

Dyhern nodded. "Well, you are a young man, and there will be many young ladies yet! I have some heart to put into you, also: will I not write to my King's ministers, and request your commission in his service? We have more dragons now than men to fly them, and I need not even ask Laurence if he would release you to us: his answer is a certainty."

Ferris flushed scarlet in his fair skin; he averted his eyes. "I— I am very much obliged to you, sir," he said, unsteadily, and bowed; Dyhern clapped him on the shoulder and left him, and Ferris came aloft. Even distracted by the mingling of anticipation and unhappiness, he clambered up with all the nimble speed that youth and practice could offer; he hooked on his carabiners with a habitual motion, and sat staring down at his hands. The ground crew were loading their gear and adjusting the makeshift harness, which had been cobbled together for Eroica out of the one Temeraire had left behind, and only imperfectly fitted him, as his breadth and bony plates gave him an entirely different configuration.

The officers were coming aboard; Hammond had persuaded a disgruntled Churki to give up her matchmaking and put him upon her back at last. Dyhern was speaking with Mrs. Merkelyte and her daughter, making their last farewells. Laurence shut his eyes; he had drunk laudanum against the pain, so he might not be unmanned by the flight, and he felt dizzy and ill. He opened them again: Ferris had made a small startled noise behind him. Dyhern had taken Gabija's hand, and was speaking to her earnestly, gesturing to Eroica; she was looking up at him with surprise, a little shy. She glanced once at Ferris, who was staring down at her. But then she bit her lip and raised her chin, and nodded to Dyhern.

Dyhern spoke to Mrs. Merkelyte again, who held a low muttered conversation with her daughter, and then laid her hand in Dyhern's, and nodded her blessing over them.

Dyhern flew back to the farmhouse the next morning with a special license, and returned to the covert with his bride. Eroica had by then gathered enough from Churki's openly expressed indignation to be very satisfied with his own captain's victory, as he could not help but see it. He was however gracious in his temperament, and assured Churki heartily that Hammond was sure of finding a splendid partner very soon, if not one quite so lovely and charming as *his* captain's wife.

"I hope you do not blame me, Laurence," Dyhern said candidly, stopping by Laurence's small hut the following morning to see his progress. "But I am sure the boy will get over it soon enough: at that age, I did not think much of women when there was battle to be had. Six years grounded is long enough to cool a man's head, however: I have had much time to be sorry that I had nothing to occupy my mind and my days, when my dragon was gone."

Laurence could understand his sentiments; he would himself have been grateful for distraction, any distraction, from his own fear and anxiety. When Dyhern had left, he spread out the maps and reports again, which he had politely put aside during the visit, and returned to his self-appointed torment: marking out the likely routes which Temeraire might pursue, and referring to the dispatches to learn all the worst of the circumstances which he might encounter. These were unhappy indeed. Ferals had devoured and ruined so many stores in the western part of the country that famine was spreading widely; the nobles were paying peasant bands by the head to slaughter dragons while they slept.

When pain and fatigue overcame Laurence's strength, and he closed his eyes to sleep a little, he walked through thick crusted-over snow, between black trees and a leaden sky above, and found Temeraire's corpse lying still and alone in a field with a red-mouthed stoat feasting on his sides.

Chapter 7

WHEN TEMERAIRE SCRAPED AWAY the snow around the protruding hoof, he discovered why the horse had not yet been devoured: the rest of the corpse was barely visible beneath several feet of blued ice. He contemplated it wearily, but he had not seen anything else left to eat, anywhere, so he gathered himself and roared at the block of ice: the divine wind thrumming through his chest and cracking the surface. He roared again and dug into the block with his talons; at last the ice broke apart. The corpse broke, too, but that was just as well; he picked up each piece with his jaws, held it in his mouth until it thawed a little, and then he could swallow it.

He was shivering when he had finished, but at least he did not feel quite so ravenously hungry. The light was beginning to fail, though, and he could not go much further. He went aloft to try to find something like shelter: after half an hour's flight, he caught sight, to his grateful surprise, of a large barn—not quite a barn; it only had one rough wall of heaped stone, and a roof of half-rotten planks held up on columns, so the other sides were open to the elements. It seemed to have been left half-finished: a heap of tall logs stood to one side, as though waiting to complete the building and forgotten.

Even so, it was better by far than the stone wall he had sheltered against last night; the ground beneath was heaped with leaves and even some hay, and nearly clear of snow. He landed, and crawled with some difficulty beneath the roof. Once within, the close quarters were all to the better; he was out of the worst wind, and by lapping his wings to either side and tucking his head beneath them, he warmed a little.

He slept almost at once and deeply, exhausted with worry and effort. He was aware of nothing until he stirred some hours later, still in the dark, coughing and puzzled by his own warmth: he was *uncomfortably* warm. That seemed unimaginable, but when he tried to move his head out to see what was burning, he could not: something was keeping his wing in place. He managed to wiggle the wing-tip down a little, and discovered in alarm that while he slept, the heavy logs had been put up to complete the walls, and beyond them a great fire was crackling up from heaped tinder which had been buried beneath the snowbanks. He uttered a cry as a burning ember fell upon his back, between his shoulder blades, and looking up discovered the whole roof was heaped with tinder also. The hay beneath him was catching.

Voices were shouting to one another over the crackle of the fire, in Russian. Temeraire peered out between the logs with one eye and saw shadows moving, men with pitchforks, and he called out, "Help! Help!" in that language, and saw them turning to stare and cross themselves. But none of them came near, and he realized, despite a peculiar groggy dullness, that they had set the fire deliberately: they meant to burn him alive.

He tried to draw breath to roar, but the smoke rasped his throat and set him coughing instead. He tried to wriggle, but the logs had been driven deep, and there were so very many of them. His wings were cringing against his body as more cinders began to rain upon him. He had no other choice; he set his legs beneath him and pushed: sharp searing pain along his wing-blades where the heat scorched the delicate membranes, and the roof pressed as heavily upon him as though they had loaded it with boulders. He pushed once, twice; he had to stop, coughing dreadfully—a third push, and the roof creaked and groaned.

The men began shouting; they ran in closer, and thrust pitchfork-jabs at his head and his forelegs; he squeezed his eyes shut with a cry as one sharp point sliced the flesh and skin tight along the muzzle-bone, only just barely catching upon the heavy ridge of bone beneath his eye. The man drew back for another attempt, and Temeraire with real desperation gathered all his strength and heaved up, straining.

The roof cracked abruptly above him. Heaped stones like hot coals came raining down upon his body, and the flames roared suddenly roasting-hot everywhere all around him. He tried to leap aloft, but his legs and wings were unwilling to answer; he floundered up and forward, smashing through the collapsing structure, gasping for the clear, cold air. Clouds of steam and smoke boiled furiously out of the furnace of the fire. Temeraire blundered away through them, his whole body scorched and stinging, until he could fling himself into the snow and roll over onto his back, writhing vigorously to try to cool the burns.

But the men came again, shouting, and Temeraire had to roll back to his feet. They were running towards him, carrying scythes, pitchforks, axes all raised; the metal glowed orange-red in the fire-light. Temeraire pushed himself with an effort up on his haunches, and opened his wings wide; he spread his ruff and roared out his pain, furious, and as a breaking wave they crumpled to the earth before him, and lay still.

Those men further behind slowed, halted, their heads tilting back as they stared upwards at his full breadth. They dropped their weapons and torches and they ran. Temeraire dropped to four legs and stood trembling and panting. His wings stung dreadfully; he gingerly brought them forward and could see the orange-dyed snow through the burns, his membranes pierced in many places by ragged holes like worn-through sailcloth.

He dug himself into a snowbank for a little more relief, but soon he was cold again despite the burns. He shivered in the frigid air, and he could not keep himself pressed into the snow for long. He even crept back a little towards the raging fire afterwards to warm himself, and curled into a heap near it: exhaustion trembled through him, and yet he could not sleep. The men might come back; they might return with guns. He flinched as the last corner of the false barn crashed down into the rising bonfire, orange sparks erupting in a blaze of fireworks-glory.

He thought of trying to fly away some distance, but he did not want to try his wings. They stung so, and ached along all the ribs, and his throat was rubbed-raw and painful. And the night was so very cold.

But he had evidently closed his eyes; he was sleeping. He opened them again at an unpleasant clanging noise, very close by, and reared his head up and away from a sharpened iron pike planted point-downwards in the snow, scarce inches from his eye. The man holding the shaft stared up at him, a face ringed in fur like a lion, and then in the next moment was already running away, his heels kicking up clods of snow behind him. Another man was still standing by the head of the pike, a drawn sword in his hand, which he had used to deflect it.

Temeraire gazed down at him dully: it was Tharkay, although that it did not make any sense, of course. However, there was a more pressing matter: there was a horse running away, too, in the distance. "Is that your horse?" Temeraire asked. "Would you mind a great deal if I eat it?"

He could only hope that the answer was not *yes*, because he could not bring himself to wait to hear it: in a few moments more the horse would be out of sight in the trees ahead, and perhaps lost. His wings stung and ached dreadfully when he unfurled them, and he had to overfill his breath to keep aloft—he felt ungainly, a lumbering hulk in the air, but none of that really mattered; the world had narrowed to a line of small hoofprint indentations in the snow, shadowed deeper blue, and the dark body of the running horse ahead.

He devoured her hooves and tail one and all; he only remembered to spit out the saddle because the stirrups caught on one of his teeth. The hot blood ran comfortingly down his sore throat. When he had swallowed the last bite, he could be a little ashamed, and looked around guiltily as Tharkay trudged towards him, breaking a path through the snow. "I am very sorry," he said apologetically. "And I will certainly get you another horse, as soon as ever I can; at least, once there are other things to eat. But what are you doing here?"

"Looking for you," Tharkay said. "Or rather, for the army you are with: I supposed that a message should reach you quicker, if I found the lines of communication, than I could bring it to Vilna myself. I was able to hire a dragon to bring me to Kiev, but no beast would go further north than that, nor any closer to the Russian Army."

"Well, they are quite sensible to refuse," Temeraire said, "for I have never met any people so unfriendly as this, anywhere, at least not when I had not given them *cause* to be unfriendly. But Tharkay," he said, misery seizing him fresh, as he recalled his circumstances, "I cannot take you to Laurence—I must go on. I must get to China—"

"I beg your pardon for interrupting you," Tharkay said. "But I think you will find you are mistaken: you must get to France. They stopped in Istanbul with your egg, two days ago. There may yet be a chance to intercept them, I believe, in the Alps."

Part II

Chapter 8

"WELL, LAURENCE, YOU HAVE a gift for establishing yourself in the more benighted places of the world," Tharkay said, his voice rasping with the cold even after they had warmed their hands and throats with a cup of tea. Laurence could hardly quarrel with the remark: they were huddling upon a ledge inside an icy crevasse which plunged away beneath them in rings of blue shading to midnight-dark, even though above their heads the clouds wheeled across a wide and sunny sky.

They were at least not in present danger of a fall to their deaths: Temeraire, crouching, filled the pit beneath them very much like a cork sitting in the neck of a bottle, looking entirely as uncomfortable as this description might suggest despite a thick matting of dried leaves and straw which protected his hide from the walls. But he was very nearly invisible against the dark; two French patrols had flown directly overhead in broad daylight to-day, quite clearly visible from their hiding-hole, but Temeraire had not been spotted even by the sharp eyes of the Pou-de-Ciel dragons.

"I will admit this is an unsurpassed bolt-hole," Tharkay added.

"I imagine I could walk past the opening a dozen times without the least suspicion, even if I had the certain knowledge you were within a hundred yards of me."

"I cannot think it so splendid as all that," Temeraire put in, a little plaintively. "It is very strange to feel that there is nothing beneath me: I feel as though I am flying, but I am not; and these walls are quite cold. But pray let us look at the maps again, and see if you can tell a little better, which way they are likely to come?"

These Laurence had just finished tacking to the walls of the crevasse with small nails, and they were more the work of his hands than their original surveyors' by now, with a great many alterations drawn atop the long line of the Alps, and dozens of passes marked for being shut by snow and ice. The ferals had made a great many snickering comments about the quality of the maps when he had first displayed them for their consideration; dragons made considerably better surveyors than men.

The French company might fly over a closed pass, but he thought it unlikely. Great inconvenience would attend such a choice: the dragons required places to rest the night, safe from avalanche and rockfall, and their passengers would have little comfort trying to make camp. Even French couriers going with all speed back and forth to Italy avoided the closed passes, and the company from Istanbul would have no reason to suspect they needed to brave so inhospitable a route: these were the walls around the very heart of France, and Napoleon did not yet suppose his citadel likely to be stormed.

"You do not suppose they will try that crossing Bistorta told us of, where her friend was nearly buried?" Temeraire shuddered. "Oh! If they should let the egg be smashed, or frozen—"

"You may rely they will do no such thing, having brought it so far, so carefully," Laurence said. Even if Lien would have preferred to see Temeraire and Iskierka's egg destroyed, Napoleon plainly did not mean to discard so priceless a cross-breed, nor hesitate to use it to his best advantage: whether to bring Celestial and Kazilik blood into his own lines, or perhaps even to compel Temeraire and

Iskierka to surrender to him, removing them from the field of battle. The egg might remain unhatched and vulnerable for another year, perhaps even as much as two.

"They have alternatives enough, without risking any of the worse passes," Laurence finished. "Our best chance must be to ask our friends to disperse themselves widely through the passes, and bring us news of any unusual party of dragons seen coming into the mountains. Was there a heavy-weight among them?" he asked Tharkay, who nodded.

"A Fleur-de-Nuit, I am sorry to say." It was indeed unwelcome news: the party might well travel by night with such a guide, and if caught at such a time would have all the advantage of the night-flying breed's better vision.

"Only find them for me," Temeraire said, with unwonted savagery, "and I will answer for any number of dragons, if they even have the gall to try and defend *egg-stealing* to my face: I wonder they should not be heartily ashamed of themselves."

That evening, the Alpine dragons promptly scattered on this mission—they were none loath to accommodate the request, Temeraire having brought two substantial chests packed brim-full of gold plate and handsome jewels—and after devouring the goat which they had brought him, Temeraire fell into a fitful drowse, his head curled awkwardly atop his body, which rose and settled uneasy in the bottle-neck of the chasm with every breath.

The ferals had also brought another load of hay, likely pilfered from some highly perplexed farmer more used to dragons stealing his sheep than their feed. With this, Laurence and Tharkay repaired the gaps which had opened in Temeraire's protective waist-coat; an operation which, requiring them to clamber precariously around the ice-walls secured only with a pickax while they thrust handfuls of straw down Temeraire's sides, left Laurence shaking and weary when it was done. He climbed only slowly back up to the ledge that was their shelter; Tharkay was adding the rest of the straw into the matting that was their own protection from the ice.

"This is a peculiar sort of place for convalescence, Laurence,"

Tharkay observed as they huddled back beneath their makeshift heap of oilskins and furs, gnawing the dried meat which was all the supper they could have: fire could not be risked in the night, where the glow would illuminate all the crevasse for any Fleur-de-Nuit within fifty miles to see. "I cannot recall when I have seen either of you look more ragged."

"There is nothing to be done for it," Laurence said shortly. He was almost too cold to speak. The bullet-wound pained him deeply—an ache which drew all the chill of the ice into his body, and barred sleep. He dug out his brandy-flask, and swallowing handed it on to Tharkay. "I am sorry if your work in Istanbul was interrupted."

"No," Tharkay said, permitting the change of subject. "My work was finished, some days before the French dragons came through. It was just as well to have an excuse to leave. It is a very damnable thing, Laurence, to be forever reminded that one is too much betwixt and between to belong to any settled place." He drank deeply, and handed the flask on. In the dark, his face could not be seen, and his voice had kept light, but Laurence was sorry. He thought he knew what had sparked that rare flash of bitterness: Tharkay had gone to Istanbul to see Avraam Maden, whose daughter had married another man.

"How did you manage to hire a dragon, for your passage?" Laurence asked quietly.

"An hour's ride east from the city, I found an isolated place and staked out a handsome cow, and waited; a couple of ferals landed at twilight. They were inclined to be suspicious, but they understood Durzagh well enough for me to make myself understood, and bribery did the rest. They flew me over the Black Sea, nearabouts to the outskirts of Odessa, and made my desire to be carried onward known to the dragons there with whom they could speak, and handed me over to them like a piece of peculiar baggage. In this fashion I arranged to have myself bundled along. I cannot call it a comfortable way to travel, but for speed it was re-markable."

They exchanged the flask a few more times, choked down the rest of the meat, and eventually slept, curled almost as awkward as Temeraire over their own knees, pulled in tight to make small warm knots of their bodies. Laurence jerked awake at uncertain intervals from discomfort and shrieks of wind, in pitch darkness, only Tharkay's presence at his side and the steady low hissing of Temeraire's breath to orient him. The sky above turned, stars in their paces, and the night crept onward; he woke again with the first brightness creeping into the sky, and dozed fitfully until the dawn was fully advanced. No word had come.

They built their small fire, and Tharkay made the climb to the top of the crevasse to pack a pailful of snow to be melted. They brewed tea, and soaked their hard bread and dried meat until it became a little more edible. Temeraire stirred, and looked longingly up at the open sky, but did not propose risking even a short flight. The day crept even more slowly than the night, and when Bistorta dropped into the crevasse at dusk, Laurence was not more startled than he was glad. She had brought Temeraire a small sheep, but no news: no party of dragons had been seen coming into the mountain, nor even a single heavy-weight.

"But Tharkay did say they were visiting at the Sultan's palace," Temeraire argued with his own disappointment, "and I dare say meant to stay in Istanbul a little while, so we ought not have expected them yesterday: to-night, perhaps, or tomorrow."

"Or the day after, if I misjudged their haste," Tharkay said.

Laurence did not say, that it had taken Tharkay three days to find Temeraire, and more than a week to reach their present camp, where the search had consumed another; that the egg might already be gone into France, and beyond their reach.

"Well, perhaps it will be to-night," Temeraire said, low, half to himself.

But there was no sighting that night or the following, and by the third Temeraire was in a fever of anxiety: the possibility that the egg was near acted upon him as a goad. Only the strongest persuasion kept him from struggling out of their bolt-hole and attempting his own search, and Laurence had no confidence that even this would restrain him when the next dawn came.

But in the late dark hours, the moon having set, he jerked awake as Temeraire moved, scrabbling against the ice walls: he looked up and saw the outline of a small dragon against the stars, peering in: Bistorta. "Laurence," Temeraire was saying, urgently, "Laurence, quickly, at once."

Temeraire put them up out of the crevasse, small showers of snow and ice drifting down as the ice walls shivered and groaned around him. He had barely put them down before he came scrabbling out himself, emerging like some unexpected monstrous beast from the depths of the earth. Great chunks of ice crashed away beneath him with a shattering noise as he heaved himself onto the slope, back legs clawing for purchase at the mouth of the crevasse. Then he shook himself, put out a taloned forehand, and caught Laurence and Tharkay up and put them on his back: barely a moment for them to clip their carabiners onto his abbreviated harness and he was launching aloft, his still-ragged wings churning furiously, and circling up into the air.

He could fly no quicker than his guide, for which Laurence was grateful, as otherwise he feared Temeraire would have pressed past his strength. Even keeping Bistorta's pace, his whole body was laboring, his breath coming with some difficulty; they were neither of them, as Tharkay had said, having a healthy convalescence. Thin blades of mountain air drove through the gaps in Laurence's own huddled-on wraps, the corners of his oilskins escaping often to flap noisily in the wind until he could catch them back around himself.

The mountains were shadows, black shapes jagged against the sky. Bistorta and Temeraire did not talk; they flew and flew southward, and after perhaps an hour's travel Bistorta landed and made a small sharp whistling noise, piercing, and then stood with her head cocked, listening. No reply came; she came back aloft and said, "Further!"

After perhaps another ten minutes, she tried again; this time in the distance a similar whistle answered her, and she altered their course slightly. Another brief span, and the whistle was very close: then another of the small dragons was leaping up to meet them, chirping to Bistorta and to Temeraire: Laurence could not follow much of the conversation, but they wheeled after this newcomer and plunged into a valley between two of the tall sharp peaks. The new guide led them to a narrow ledge—narrow by Temeraire's standards, at least; he had to stand on his hind legs almost embracing the cliff face to keep himself upon it. "They are coming," he said to Laurence, his voice trembling with urgency. "A heavy-weight dragon, but not a Fleur-de-Nuit; they do not know what she is, he says."

"Alone?" Laurence said, and looked at Tharkay, who shook his head doubtfully.

"What I heard in Istanbul was three dragons, traveling in company," he said, "but rumor on the streets is often amplified; I would not rely upon it."

"I must stop them," Temeraire said, "but I must be sure not to hurt the egg—oh! If I should use the divine wind upon them, and the shell were to—" He could not finish, his voice breaking off into misery.

"We must try and pen them in," Laurence said, looking at the narrow pass, "and ask the ferals to make something of a screen above them. If it is not a Fleur-de-Nuit, we may well take them by surprise, and they will not be sure the size of our party; caution may persuade them to surrender the egg. You are sure the other dragon will not think of harming the egg?"

"Unless it is Lien, herself," Temeraire said venomously. "*She* would do anything, I am sure, even to a helpless egg: you see what she has done already!" He twisted his neck about to look as another feral landed, to chirp a new report: their quarry was perhaps ten miles distant, coming quickly.

They could not use the divine wind against the mountain-side for fear of warning the oncoming dragon; but Temeraire's weight and fury served well enough to tear down a great heap of stone and ice and snow to block the far mouth of the valley: still a terrible noise, but not an unfamiliar one in those mountains. On the ledge, Laurence cleaned and loaded his pistols, and the rifle he had brought with him from Vilna, and put fresh wicks on his pair of incendiaries. They would not do much to bring down a heavy-weight, but they might do to make a convincing show of arms; he lined the guns up in a row, ready to be fired off as quickly as possible. Tharkay also added his own pistol and rifle to the collection.

And then Temeraire returned to his perch, and they all held stiff and cold and silent, listening for the rhythmic flap of wings. The ferals—another five or so had joined them—gathered on either side, but in a much more celebratory spirit; they were quiet but chirping softly to one another, and Laurence caught more than once the exultant word for treasure passing among them.

But their voices fell silent, soon, and then they were listening, too: their prey was close. The Alpine ferals all sat up alertly, their narrow heads giving them a look of eager greyhounds trembling for the sign to spring. Laurence heard the dragon coming: if Granby had been here, he might have been able to say what the breed was, by the wing-gait. Laurence could not guess, but the beast that passed below their ledge was certainly a heavy-weight and a large one, throwing a long sinuous shadow blue on the blue snow, with drifting scraps of cloud clinging to its sides.

Temeraire managed to restrain himself until the dragon had gone through the pass; then he flung himself off the cliff in a leap, twisting as he did mid-air to come about, and then he roared—not in the dragon's direction, which might have threatened the egg, if the other beast was carrying it, but at the rock face.

The shattering force of the divine wind blasted the snow-laden peak on the other side of the pass, and an avalanche came roaring down: rock, snow, ice all together, a great cloud. Laurence squinted through his flying-goggles as snow spattered his face; the Alpine ferals had all jumped aloft and were keening their high-pitched hunting song as they went in circles over the valley, forming a ceiling for their trap. The cloud of snow and ice hid the other beast.

Temeraire roared again, not the divine wind this time, only a challenge; he was hovering mid-air, darting a little to one side and then another, waiting for an opening to dive in.

Laurence glimpsed the shadow of the other dragon as it twisted around upon itself wildly, taken by surprise, turning towards them, and then a long painfully brilliant gout of flame came erupting through the cloud, dissolving the blizzard into boiling steam. A tongue of fire licked at the mountainside, and Laurence and Tharkay dived into the snowbank as the flames came spilling up the rock and past their ledge, heat and cold both intolerable at once. The dragon came roaring out behind its flames and struck Temeraire mid-sky, and the two beasts rolled, twisting around each other, hissing and furious. Alarmed, Laurence dug out of the snow, squinting uselessly: Flammes-de-Gloire did not travel alone; they were too rare for that; were there more beasts coming? He could see almost nothing of the struggle: his eyes were streaked with dazzle from the flames, and a handful of trees and scrub in the valley below had caught like dry tinder, blazing small suns that made the night around them into pitch.

But he did not need to see: he heard the snarling of the fire-breather's voice saying, in clear wrathful English, "Oh! How dare you leap on me out of the dark, like a coward! I will tear you into pieces, see if I don't!"

"Whatever are you doing here?" Temeraire said, struggling with a crushing sensation of disappointment. But if the egg had not come *this* way, surely it had gone another; he turned without waiting for an answer to Bistorta, who had at last crept cautiously back: the other ferals had scattered in high alarm at the torrents of flame. "What do you mean, setting me on Iskierka?" he demanded. "She is not a French dragon, at all; and where is the *egg?*"

Bistorta defended herself smartly. "How were we to know she was not a French dragon?" she said. "They have so many peculiar kinds; and anyway, you did not say you wanted a *French* dragon, you said you were looking for a heavy-weight and a fighting-dragon, and you cannot say she is not *that*."

"What am I doing here?" Iskierka said, paying no attention to their conversation. "I am here for *my egg,* which you promised me and promised me would be perfectly safe in China, and should have an emperor as companion, and now only look what has happened! Why are *you* jumping out upon me out of nowhere like this? Granby, did you put him up to it? I did not think you would *betray* me so," she added reproachfully, her head swinging around.

"I didn't, but you may be sure I would have done it in a heartbeat, if I had any notion of his being anywhere near," Granby said without even a little hesitation as he clambered down her side. "Hell-bent on going straight into France, and bearding Lien in her den," he told Laurence and Tharkay, as he shook their hands. "Nothing would hold her, when she knew. It was all I could do to persuade her we had to swing out over the Med, and not fly straight across over every Frenchman and French gun in Spain."

He sat heavily down upon a boulder and rubbed his arm across his forehead. The golden hook which had taken the place of his left hand gleamed with reflected flame: half a dozen bushes and scrubby trees were still alight, where they clung to the walls of the mountains. His brown hair was unbraided and in a wind-tangled mess, his clothing disordered and his face unshaven, as though he had been flung dragon-back without any warning and dragged across Europe for days, very likely the case. He gratefully accepted the offer of Laurence's canteen.

"Well, that is quite absurd," Temeraire said, "for if ever Lien gets the egg, she will have it well-hidden, and any number of soldiers and dragons guarding it."

"It is *not* absurd," Iskierka returned. "Of course we must go to her, if she has the egg. What use is there going anywhere else?" Which had an uncomfortable ring of truth to it, Temeraire had to admit; only that was plainly hopeless, so he could not allow Lien to have the egg, yet.

"When I have scorched her a few times, I dare say she will turn it over," Iskierka continued. "What good did you suppose it would do for you to leap upon *me*?"

"I did not mean to!" Temeraire said. "We have been laying a trap for the dragons who are bringing the egg back from China."

Iskierka snorted. "I see how well *that* plan has worked. If you cannot tell the difference between me and an egg-stealing French dragon, I do not see how you ever expected to get the egg back this way."

"It is dark!" Temeraire said. "And I could not go and look closely at you, or else the *element of surprise*," on which he laid especial emphasis, as a point of strategy that surely even Iskierka might understand, "should have been lost."

She remained unimpressed. "It was certainly a surprise, because it was a ridiculous thing to do. What if the egg-stealer should be one of those night-flying dragons? I dare say she should have flown straight around you. I saw one of them yesterday evening at a distance, while I was trying to work my way around these wretched mountains, and I thought I should make her show me the way; but as soon as it was dark she managed to lose me, even though I should have had her in an hour in daylight—"

"What?" cried Temeraire, seizing upon this intelligence. "Where did you see her?"

"You are not paying attention; what difference does that make?" Iskierka said crossly, but when Temeraire had made her understand that a Fleur-de-Nuit had stolen the egg, and very likely it was the same one she had seen, she ceased to be quarrelsome at once.

There was no sense in retracing her steps, but Laurence, dear Laurence, had brought his maps; Temeraire remembered with a moment of shame how he had privately resented Laurence's taking those few moments, when they had been leaving the crevasse, to take them down and pack them up: how useless they had seemed in the moment! And how priceless now, as Laurence drew them out and laid them before Granby, who squinting by the light of a torch found the place where Iskierka had sighted the Fleur-de-

Nuit. From there, they found the nearest pass she would have taken through the mountains, perhaps twenty miles distant. Their best chance—Temeraire refused to name it their *only* chance—was to catch her on the western side. Inside the borders of France.

"The ferals cannot match your pace," Laurence said, as he rolled the maps up again. "But ask them to follow us, so long as they are able and willing: we may well be grateful of their aid at the end; or they may sight her coming out of another pass, if we have mistaken her course."

He did not say, *This Fleur-de-Nuit may only have been a patrol-dragon; you must not raise your hopes,* or *It has been a day and a night; the egg may already have been carried deep into France,* or *Iskierka was sighted, they are looking for us; we are sure to run into a French patrol.*

Laurence said none of these things, and nevertheless Temeraire was unwillingly conscious that Laurence *might* have said them. He did not wish to think these things; he struggled not to think of anything so much like despair and surrender, but the long dragging weeks of fears and searching had worn away at his own blind determination. It seemed his mind *would* fix upon them, no matter how he tried to evade the thoughts.

"If you would prefer to leave us," Laurence was saying to Tharkay, low, "we might bribe the ferals thoroughly enough, I think, to buy your passage back to some company of the Russian army: the Cossacks were already nearing the Oder."

"That is a sufficient distance to make it likely I should meet a company of Frenchmen, first," Tharkay said.

They were in headlong flight by then, Iskierka outpacing him badly; a circumstance which on any other occasion would have been deeply mortifying. At present, Temeraire did not care. Iskierka might outfly him by a hundred leagues, so long as she reached the egg before the Fleur-de-Nuit reached the ominous mark upon Laurence's map: the great network of caverns just beyond the Alps labeled simply, L'ARMÉE DE L'AIR: the training grounds where the French aerial corps hatched most of their beasts, and trained their recruits.

Temeraire's wings ached, but he fixed determinedly on the thin pale cloud of steam that trailed Iskierka's flight and pressed onwards. To the east, the edge of the mountains, ragged like an unsharpened knife, steadily grew more visible. The sun was coming.

The sky was deep rose-grey when they finally climbed over one last gasping ridge of mountains and plunged gratefully into the pass, an hour later: Iskierka still in the lead, but Temeraire had caught up a little, navigating the higher elevations; he had grown more used to the thinness of the air. Still he was dull and laboring, and he only distantly heard Tharkay say, "Laurence," and then a moment later, after the click of the spyglass, Laurence replying, "I see it."

He said nothing more, and Temeraire only flew on; slowly his mind turned it over and over and finally he said, "Laurence, what is it?"

Laurence did not immediately answer, and then gently said, "There is a small camp in the valley directly behind us, with the remains of a dragon's meal, I think."

"But that is splendid!" Temeraire cried, and meant to call to Iskierka with the news; but the tone of Laurence's voice held him. "Surely we are on their trail?" he added uncertainly.

"The fire is cold, my dear," Laurence said. "The Fleur-de-Nuit would have spent her day there; she will have been on the wing since nightfall."

They were a full night's flying behind her, then. Temeraire's heart sank, but then Iskierka gave a sudden roar, and even jetted a gout of flame: he jerked his head forward and saw in the distance a small dark figure against the sky, sunlight breaking over the crest of the mountains and catching its wings, and the dragon ducked its head away from the light, as if it disliked the brilliance, and dived back into shadow.

"Oh!" Temeraire cried aloud, and flung himself after Iskierka, all worry, all fear forgot; he beat desperately on even as she stretched herself out her full length, coils unraveling into a single red-and-green banner and steam hissing furiously from every spike. "How far, Laurence? How far?"

Laurence was standing in his carabiners and peering through his glass. "Not five miles distant. Surely they must have gone further in a full night's flying."

"It might not have been their camp," Tharkay said.

"It ought to have been, unless they made remarkably bad time the night before last," Laurence said, "and they had good reason to make haste." And then sharply he said, "Temeraire, wait—Temeraire! Listen to me," but waiting, listening, no; Temeraire could not bear to listen to anything which should make him wait. He roared out instead, a challenge that split the air, and saw the Fleur-de-Nuit—it *was* a Fleur-de-Nuit, it was!—pop up again from the valley, looking their way. And wrapped against her breast—impossible to be certain, for it was thickly swaddled in netting, in layers of white padding stark against the dragon's grey-black hide—oh! Impossible to *doubt*; it was the egg, the egg—

Laurence was shouting through his speaking-trumpet now, but Temeraire did not hear what he said; fury dimmed all his senses, and drove him in a surging rush forward. He and Iskierka were ranged alongside each other, their minds for once as one; he felt the churning steam of her fires jetting against his side and welcomed it even as the bitter air froze it to his scales. He was breathing in vast expanding gulps, the divine wind thrumming beneath his breast, rattling in his throat. The Fleur-de-Nuit had dived into the valley again, and as they came blazing into it they saw her cowering back against the cliff wall—too ashamed of herself to fly or fight—as well she should have been, Temeraire thought hotly, and he flung himself to the ground and roared well above her head.

She cringed down before him. "How dare you take my egg!" Iskierka hissed, landing beside him and pouncing forward; the Fleur-de-Nuit cried out as she raked her back, and the harness came loose—

"Be careful!" Temeraire leapt forward and caught at the forward edge of the netting as the whole mass of it came loose and the egg—

The egg fell out, unraveling into nothing more than a mass of cotton wadding and rags, empty. The netting hung on Temeraire's claws. His breath caught: the egg, where was the egg? He could not think, could not understand.

"Temeraire, it is a trap!" Laurence was shouting, hoarse as though he had been shouting it a long time. "Temeraire!"

"A trap," Temeraire repeated, numbly, as four heavy-weight dragons came down around them: all of them under full harness, loaded with men and guns, and a cloud of middle-weight beasts circled in the air aloft.

Chapter 9

LAURENCE SURFACED IN THE pleasant manner where sleep by imperceptible degrees became wakefulness, and the world only slowly intruded upon his consciousness. In the final stages of the process he at last opened his eyes, sunlight illuminating the woolen bedcurtains of deep blue, snugly drawn against draughts. A vast and cheerful noise was rising outside, roughly what might have been expected of a herd of elephants engaged in a melee. He rose and went to the window of his chamber—a window barred with iron, but set in a spacious and comfortable room elevated by the presence of a truly handsome wooden desk he would not have disdained to own himself, and a chamberpot of porcelain painted in flowers.

A species of chaos was under way in the large courtyard: dragons in harness descending, their crews spilling off their backs, and one and all making their way to tables. Even the dragons ate out of large clay bowls they carried for themselves, taken from heaped stacks at one side of the grounds to be filled in the cooking-pits at the other: Laurence could see the clouds of steam rising. The men were doing likewise, on a smaller scale, and the companies then gathered together again to devour their meal. The operation was not a novel one to Laurence, but it was the first time he had seen it executed in so expert a fashion by any Western army; he might again have been with the Chinese legions, save that there was a greater and motley variety to the dragons.

Laurence did not think he saw a single breed to recognize, but the characteristics of many scattered and shared out among many beasts. To his surprise, the light-weight Pou-de-Ciel was perhaps the best represented, mixed it seemed with larger and more notable sorts; one beast, with the conformation and size of the smaller breed almost exactly, had the brilliant yellow-striped black coloration of the Flamme-de-Gloire, a cross he would never have expected. Many others bore in varied patterns the long feathery scales of the Incan breeds.

He had been standing by the window for perhaps a quarter of an hour, watching, when the bell rang half-past noon and all quitted the field, the dragons and the men alike carrying their bowls to an enormous washing-trough, with large bundles of stiff straw tied above to serve as scrubbing-brushes, so they could scrape clean their dishes before depositing them back onto the stacks.

Then they lifted away, and exposed the large and sun-drenched field beyond them. Now Laurence could see the cooking-pits in their neat rows, still emitting a steady cloud of warm steam— which wafted tenderly, moistly, over the just-exposed shells of what seemed a thousand dragon eggs and more.

Laurence stood staring in appalled horror for some half an hour, trying to make an accurate count. It was not an easy task: the eggs were all half-buried in heaps of sand and surrounded by small fires, which a busy crowd of workmen tended out of wheelbarrows laden with wood, moving constantly up and down the rows. He was interrupted finally by a chambermaid knocking tentatively with his coat, cleaned and pressed, along with fresh linen; she asked him timidly if he would come to dinner. He washed and dressed; he would have liked to shave, but they had not left him his razor. The maid led him downstairs—trailed by two guards—into a small room, also barred and well-guarded, where Laurence found a disheartened Granby before him, attempting to make pantomime conversation with a handful of glum, grey Prussian officers.

"Well, Laurence, we are in the soup properly," Granby said, when they had sat down to table. "He is going to drown us in dragons if we give him another year. How he means to feed them all is a large question, but I dare say he has worked out some cleverness for *that,* too."

Their own dinner was brought out then, and Tharkay still had not come. Laurence turned and spoke to one of the guards: "Our companion, is he ill? *Il est malade?*"

The young man—very young, his mustache still a weak and struggling thing—stared at him so blankly that Laurence wondered too late if Tharkay might have contrived to pass himself off as a servant, or a ground crewman, and if he were in danger of undermining the ruse. Then the youth said suddenly, "Oh, you mean the spy? They are sending him to Paris to be shot."

"I hope they do not mean to try to put *me* in a cave, for I will not have it," Iskierka said loudly, with a snort of flame for the benefit of the two large dragons presently guarding them, who eyed her nervously. The training grounds stood at the foot of a steep cliff wall pockmarked with wide cave-mouths, and many dragons were peering out of them interestedly at the prisoners. Temeraire for his part had lived in a cave before, and in any case had no heart to defend his prerogatives against any kind of insult at the moment. He felt his spirits would have been ideally matched to a tenancy in a dismal swamp, or perhaps upon some comfortless lichen-covered rock.

But they were not taken to a cave. A small dragon, something between a Pou-de-Ciel and a Pascal's Blue, landed before them and announced in an incongruously deep voice, "Follow me, if you please," in French; he brought them over the wide martial fields to a spacious building, constructed of stone, with a small but elegant fountain in front. Plainly it had drawn upon the dragon pavilions of China for inspiration, but in style Temeraire had not seen anything like it: the roof was raised up on tall smooth round pillars, and there was something very pleasingly mathematical about the proportions of the rectangular floor, made of white marble and marvelously warmed through from beneath. Iskierka immediately sprawled herself to her full length upon it with a sigh. "Well, I call that something like," but Temeraire sat on his haunches and curled his tail about himself, resentful of this reminder of the perversity of the world.

"I wonder that you can make yourself comfortable under these circumstances," he said bitterly. It seemed to him almost heartless.

"I do not see that the circumstances are so very bad," Iskierka said maddeningly. "I was quite tired and hungry, and *you* could not even keep up with me, flying. Now we will have a rest, and eat something, and then we will find out where the egg and Granby are, and we will go and take them back."

"You are being unutterably stupid," Temeraire said. "They will not keep them in the same place. If we should try and get Granby and Laurence, the French will order us to put them back or else they will hurt the egg; if we should try and get the egg, they will order us to leave it or else they will hurt our captains. We are prisoners twice over, and there is nothing we can do about it. I dare say Lien is congratulating herself all this time," and he added, low, "on how well her plans have come about."

"I think *you* are the one being stupid," Iskierka said, mantling in some heat. "It is quite the other way round. If they should hurt Granby, even a little, or the egg, even a little, I will certainly burn up all of them, and they must know it. They will not dare harm them, I am sure: you see how respectful they are being."

"Oh! There is no use arguing with you," Temeraire said, but secretly felt a little comforted: perhaps there was something in what Iskierka said. The French did know enough to be wary of them both.

"Anyway," Iskierka said, "it is just as I told Granby, and as I told you: if they have the egg, there is no use our being anywhere *else*. I am just as pleased to be nearer the egg, and having a good dinner: here it comes! Now pray don't be absurd and sit there without eating: as though *that* would do any good."

The dinner was not elaborate, but a good hot porridge flavorful with meat, and it was brought to them in large bowls. "There was no time to make anything more," the deep-voiced dragon, whose name was Astucieux, explained apologetically, which implied there should be something better in the morning, and seemed to bear out Iskierka's way of thinking. Temeraire found his appetite quite restored by the thought, and made a hearty meal, but when the dishes had been removed, they were left alone again with their guards, a ring of large dragons, who became silent, looming shadows as the light failed.

Far off he still heard companionable chatter, voices calling to one another from the caves; the warming orange glow of firelight shone all over the large nearby field, and faintly in the distance he could glimpse yellow squares of windows looking out of a large building, if he stretched up on his rear legs. He sank down again. The distant noise only made him feel their isolation more, and his worries returned afresh. After all, how would they *know* if anything had happened to Laurence or to Granby or to Tharkay; or to the egg; the French would certainly lie to conceal it, if any of them came to harm.

"I beg your pardon," he called out to the guards, and one of them came close, warily: she was a Grand Chevalier, very near Maximus's size—and Temeraire realized in surprise she was not under harness, and indeed looked rather ill-kept, as French dragons went; her scales between her shoulders, where she could not have reached with her snout, were even dirty.

"What do you want?" she demanded.

"I am Temeraire," he said, meaning to be polite. "Will you pray tell me your name?"

"I am Efficatrice, but I don't see why you should care," she said. "Unless you mean to make up to me, and you can stop that right away, if you do. I am not stupid, and I mean to win my harness: so don't suppose you can practice any tricks upon me."

"Win your harness?" Temeraire said, baffled, but the Chevalier evidently thought she was being insulted, for she drew herself up and regarded him very coldly out of narrowed eyes.

"I *shall*," she said, "see if I don't, even if I *am* too large," which was not a complaint Temeraire had ever heard leveled against any dragon before, in the West.

"Well, it would be silly to say you are not large, but I do not see that you are any larger than you ought to be; I have seen Chevaliers nearly your size before," he said, "and I am sure I wish you every success, although perhaps I shouldn't," he amended, "since you are on the French side, but Laurence is quite friendly with De Guignes, after all, so I suppose it does not matter in that way: but whyever cannot you have a harness, if you want one?"

"We eat too much," she muttered, after a moment, "and we quarrel with other big dragons, and so cannot work well together. But *I* will not quarrel," she finished.

"You are certainly being quarrelsome with *me*," Temeraire said, "even though I am being perfectly civil, when anyone would agree I have been badly wronged: when all of you are *egg-stealers*. And all I want is for you to take a message, to whomever has charge of this place, that I can repose no confidence whatsoever in the safety of my egg, and require assurances at once."

"Of course no-one has hurt your egg!" Efficatrice said. "No-one of us would hurt an egg, at all; there is no call to be rude."

"There is *every* call," Temeraire said, "when I think how you have snatched my poor egg from a safe place and carried it off halfway around the world, through the greatest dangers imaginable—barren deserts, winter cold, icy mountains—past armies and through battles—and not so much as a word to let me know that it was safe."

Efficatrice flinched and looked conscious, which was at least a small grain of satisfaction. Feeling all the moral force of his position, Temeraire drew himself up. "So I do *not* trust any of you, and I hope you may go to your commanding officer and tell him so, and that if I am not given *certain proofs* of the good condition of the egg, I will assume that these cannot be given because my egg is *not* safe, and you have been lying about it."

"And if you *have* been lying about it," Iskierka put in, having roused enough from her napping to follow the conversation, with slitted eyes, "you may be quite sure you will all be sorry: if anything has happened to my egg I will burn everything between here and whatever house Napoleon is hiding in, and then I will set *that* on fire, too."

The senior officer overseeing the camp was Admiral Thibaut: at only a few years Laurence's senior, he was a young man for his rank and post. Napoleon would soon need a host of trained officers, when he had so many new beasts to man. But at present Laurence had other, more immediate concerns, and could only be grateful that Thibaut had been so willing to receive him: a single request passed through the guards on their mess had almost at once brought him to the admiral's office.

"No, sir, I thank you," Laurence said, refusing the amiable offer of a glass of brandy, "I have come to urgently beg you to permit me to acquaint you with the peculiar facts of Mr. Tharkay's position, and then I hope I can rely upon your sense of justice not to prosecute so deadly a charge against a man who is in every way entitled to be treated as a honorable prisoner of war." Admiral Thibaut indicating with a courteous bow that he might continue, Laurence marshaled his arguments and plunged forward.

"—I grant that Mr. Tharkay's circumstances might have justly raised questions. He is a British officer: but he accepted his commission from His Majesty's Aerial Corps under the demands of exigency, when your master launched his invasion of Britain: I trust you agree no gentleman could do otherwise, in those conditions, than make himself of use to his country in whatever manner was asked of him. His active service then was but brief and irregular. I do not deny that in this last campaign, he was for all intents a member of my crew, and served in Russia in that capacity; but he had lately taken his leave of us, and rejoined only a few scant weeks before to-day, under such circumstances as made it impossible to provide him with anything in the way of uniform or insignia, or indeed anything but the bare necessities of survival. For this, I can offer as proofs the appearance which I myself make before you, which I trust you will do me the courtesy to believe not the manner in which an officer of His Majesty would present himself under conditions allowing otherwise.

"Besides this, I must also express to you the evident—" Here Laurence caught himself back, not wishing to offend where he must court, "—rather, what seemed to me the evident truth that no man in my service could expect himself to be taken for anything other than a member of Temeraire's crew, when captured in his company, regardless of his appearance."

The admiral's frown deepened as Laurence spoke, but it was an expression less angry than concerned; somehow disquieting. With a sense of urgency, Laurence added, despite a sense of delicacy which would otherwise have forbidden him to mention the point, "And if it should weigh with you, sir, I should mention that we took many of your own country-men prisoner in this last campaign, behind our lines, whose clothing at that time could not by any stretch of imagination have been made to resemble a uniform, and without calling them spies for it."

Here he finished; after a moment the admiral said, "Captain Laurence, I beg you to believe that I have permitted you to speak at such length in the hopes, the greatest hopes, of finding myself persuaded of there having been a mistake of some kind. No Frenchman—no French aviator—who knows what you have done for our dragons, and the sacrifices which you have endured in consequence, could wish anything but to oblige you in any manner where it fell in his power and his duty. But I fear greatly that to pardon M. Tharkay does not fall within my own. I thought

perhaps you might say we had mistaken the gentleman, that he
was not M. Tharkay at all, or perhaps a different M. Tharkay—
a relation?—but all you have said must indeed confirm the reverse."

Laurence said slowly, "Sir, he is the only man of that name of
my acquaintance." It was the truth, and therefore the only thing
he could say, despite a certain faint wheedling hint in the admiral's words, to suggest that the man might almost have welcomed
a lie.

The admiral nodded. "I am desolate, Captain, but your friend
has not been taken up on the grounds of a mere lack of uniform,
or even a suspicion of disguise: there is indeed a considerable price
lately laid his head, for spying, and I am informed M. Fouché desires conversation with him at the earliest moment."

Laurence could not answer; taken aback, and yet not enough
so, to say with conviction that the accusation was mistaken. He
had known that Tharkay often served as an agent of the East India
Company; his movements had always been secretive, and he had
rarely volunteered his motives. That he should have been acting on
behalf of Whitehall instead was not so unusual; certainly there
were few men better suited for ranging across the world, if he
could have been persuaded to undertake the work.

The admiral was regarding him with regret—sincere regret—
but without any hesitation, and indeed Laurence could not ask the
man to betray his duty, which certainly would have been to execute a spy so notorious to his nation. Only one course remained:
almost intolerable, and Laurence could only be surprised that his
voice remained steady. "Sir, I wish I could tell you there had been
a mistake: I cannot, with certainty, nor can I dispute your understanding of your duty. I can only ask you to postpone the sentence,
if you will be so kind as to permit me the time to seek his pardon
from—from one who has the right to give it."

The admiral was quite willing; and gave him pen and ink,
though Laurence could as cheerfully have drawn his own blood
for the task. But the letter had to be willing.

Sir, Laurence began,

> *You at one time expressed a sense of obligation to me, for*
> *having brought you the cure for the dragon plague, an act*
> *which as you know I performed only from an understanding*
> *of my duty as a man and a Christian. I therefore cannot*
> *claim that obligation as my right, but if you should*
> *nevertheless be glad of a chance to discharge it, I would*
> *solicit—*

There he had to pause a while before he could continue, slowly, and finish the note: a clumsy, graceless thing unfit to send to any gentleman, much less the emperor of half Europe: Laurence feared every word betrayed his resentment. He would gladly have cut his own throat before accepting any reward or personal recompense; he did not want thirty pieces of silver for betraying his country's interest, and he knew better than to seek anything which might have altered the course of the war—Temeraire's freedom, the return of the precious egg: Napoleon was a sovereign before he was a gentleman.

But a pardon, Napoleon might grant, as he would not any larger request. Would almost surely grant, his own vanity gratified by a gesture which would cost him little: he might as well keep Tharkay in a prison as cut off his head. That knowledge did not make the request easier to make; only more imperative. Laurence could not let Tharkay die when the sacrifice of his pride might save him.

"I will be glad to send the letter," the admiral said, "and glad to delay. I will hope with you, Captain, for a favorable answer."

Laurence passed his evening in his comfortable cell with its uncomfortable view. By now he had counted several times over: although he had reached a different tally each time, there were certainly more than a thousand eggs laid out so widely across the field, perhaps even twice as many. Four rows of large eggs in the middle were easily distinguishable by their blue-and-yellow shells: Granby had mentioned them in particular. "Fleur-de-Nuits," he had said gloomily. "A whole company of them, and nearly ready to hatch, by the dullness of those shells." Such a company could threaten an entire army encamped at night, and strike to devastating effect while others were halted by darkness.

And the rest of that enormous host was not so far from hatching, either. The first ranks had already begun to hatch, Laurence suspected, for he could pick out the signs of unfledged youth among many of the dragons in the camp, the hint of ungainliness where some limbs were disproportionate, or as yet unfamiliar to their possessors.

Watching the dragons jostle one another at the feeding troughs for their evening meal, a memory broke into his thoughts, in the slightly peculiar way they now from time to time resurfaced, vivid as though newly experienced: the morning after Temeraire's hatching, that neat, self-possessed creature all absurdly tangled up in the hanging cot in his cabin, no larger than a dog and furious at the loss of dignity. But Temeraire had never been graceless; he had always seemed to be just his proper size throughout, so that Laurence could recall no single day when he had been struck by the vast transformation under way, when he had looked at Temeraire and thought, *Look how large he has become!* or seen him clumsy with new growth.

The same was not true here: many among the crowd of young beasts were inclined to snarl their wings upon a talon, or overfly and dump themselves into a squalling heap upon the ground. But soon enough they would outgrow their awkwardness.

The young dragons lifted their heads from their meal all at once: their attention had been arrested by a sudden flaring light somewhere near the base of the mountains, bonfire-high flames leaping. Iskierka? Laurence wondered, but could not tell; at this distance there was only a golden-red bloom of light, which vanished away nearly at once. He was not so very surprised, however, to hear footsteps come along the corridor not a quarter of an hour later: a young officer knocking on the door, asking him if he pleased to step along.

Admiral Thibaut received him and Granby in his dressing-gown, and after polite apologies for disturbing their rest said, "We have had a little difficulty, which I would not wish to conceal from you: Temeraire and Iskierka have formed the notion that if we do not immediately demonstrate the good condition of their egg, and their captains, the worst must have happened; they are some way along to convincing themselves of the case, with all the evil consequences this must entail."

Laurence's first thought was fear for Temeraire: they were not at present in circumstances where rebellion could have anything but a fatal result. The dragons here would be neither sympathetic nor persuadable, as the beasts of the British breeding grounds had been, and there were too many of them: even a simple headlong flight could have been stopped. But Granby said, in heat, "And who has set them going, I would like to know, putting word about that their egg is *unfit,* and talking of smashing: a handsome way of going about your business, I will not scruple to say."

Laurence looked at him in surprise: Granby had a temper, but not an ungovernable one, to be provoked to such an outburst; and then his meaning became clear.

It had not before occurred to him that Lien had deliberately spoken in so inflammatory a manner about the precious egg. But as soon as the idea had been proposed, it was hard to imagine anything else. Laurence recalled that had never seen any dragon face with complacency the idea of outright, deliberate harm to any egg; it was a crime universally reviled among them. He had supposed Lien's hatred of Temeraire to have overcome this instinctive reluctance, but her hatred had never been of a fiery, violent nature. How much more likely that calculation had spoken instead, and made so hideous a threat exactly to lure Temeraire into a cold, malicious trap.

At once Laurence understood, and at once shared Granby's

feelings. It was an underhanded piece of scheming, as vicious as threatening the life of an infant to induce its mother to come running headlong into danger for its sake. Even the admiral was silent before the accusation in Granby's voice, as though he could say nothing in defense of the act, and therefore in duty could say nothing at all. "We wish to do our best to reassure their feelings," he said only, with a small bow.

They were put on a smallish dragon called Souci: somewhere between a heavy courier and a light-weight combat-beast, with a certain lean greyhound look reminiscent of the Jade Dragons: a fast flyer, certainly, and big enough to hold an armed guard of six men along with them. "All goes well back there?" the dragon asked, snaking his head around on a long and flexible neck, without any sign he thought it unusual to speak to his passengers without the intermediary of a captain. "Good! Up we go," and launched himself with a grunt and a spring, and after a startling amount of flapping he leveled and was off like a shot towards the mountains, tearing so rapidly along that Laurence's eyes streamed.

Souci landed panting not a quarter of an hour later. They had come down near a large building incongruously like an ancient temple: as though a Roman troop had marched out of the dim reaches of the past to erect it, then marched away again leaving it planted here in the French countryside. It was all of a piece with Napoleon's affecting the trappings of Caesar, and yet not impractical, Laurence realized, as Temeraire and Iskierka came pouring out between the enormous columns, eager for a glimpse of them.

He was asked to stand up, and Granby also: the guards held lanterns near their faces to make them visible. Laurence raised a hand hoping to reassure: they were too far distant to speak. Even so, the dragon nervously took a nimble hop back when Temeraire and Iskierka would have approached a little. "That's enough, then," the little beast said, too hastily: Laurence would have liked some more reassurance himself of Temeraire's health. There were a few lanterns hung on the pavilion, but these showed very little of a black dragon in the dark, and Temeraire did not spread his wings.

But Souci would not linger; he thrust himself into the air again, with that same storm of flapping, and as quickly as they had come dashed back across the camp. When they had dismounted, he indulged himself in a shudder of his whole body. "That is more than I undertake to do again!"—this to the admiral, in reproachful tones. "Those two monstrously large beasts! Going right up to them like that and dangling their captains in front of them just as if to say, *Look what I have got, ha ha!* I am all astonishment they did not leap upon me at once. I hope they did not get a clear look at me. If ever they saw me again I am sure they would not let it pass."

"I beg you not to repine upon it," Laurence said. "Temeraire understands well that orders must be obeyed, and will not hold it against you; he knows it was not in your power to deliver us to him."

"Well, but it *was*," Souci said, not conciliated, and Granby said nothing reassuring at all. Iskierka did not allow of assurances of her behavior, good, evil, or otherwise.

They were returned by their polite but firm escort to their rooms, and Laurence did not try to speak with Granby, both silent with their own shared and private unhappiness, and shared anger as well. Laurence had in some sense felt they *deserved* to be captured: that it had been the only reasonable outcome of skulking about on the very borders of France. That feeling had spared him real regret, like a gambler at the table who had staked all upon one unlikely throw, knowing all the while it would not come, and even in despair had accepted the natural course of the event. But now the trick dice had been uncovered: indignation burned in his chest, the resentment of having been taken by what felt a low cheat.

He slept well, despite it all. He could have slept for a month. In the morning, he was asked to the admiral's rooms for breakfast, and met with a bow. "Captain Laurence," Thibaut said, "I hope to gratify you," and handed to him a letter; Laurence steeled himself to meet with a reply which, however generous, could only stoke his still-hot indignation.

But surprise banked the fire. The letter was addressed to Thibaut and written in the neat hand of a secretary, but the words, abrupt and decisive, were all Napoleon: *Tell me you have shown him every courtesy! Nothing is too good for such a man,* adding the phrase, *il a bien plus de valeur que les perles,* a phrase which Laurence, half-amused despite every will to be otherwise, recognized as the description of the virtuous woman.

Napoleon continued,

> *We have sent an escort to bring him and his companions to Fontainebleau, and the dragons as well: let them depart at once. Here they will see the egg in its safe repose, and arrangements will be made for their comfort.*
>
> NAPOLEON

"I have sent to ask M. Tharkay and Captain Granby to join us for breakfast," the admiral said, "while the dragons of your escort make their own. You will leave immediately."

Chapter 10

"You will forgive the Emperor's absence," Empress Anahuar-que said, in quite fluent English, improved still further beyond what she had acquired at great effort in her own country; she had evidently kept up her studies.

Laurence had last met her in her own court at Cusco, dressed in the Incan style in bright-woven wool and adorned in gold; yet she seemed not a whit out of place here in the sitting room where they had been received, nor the least uncomfortable in a morning gown of white made elaborate by gold embroidery, striking against her dark-brown skin, and her black hair bound up behind a tiara of diamonds: overdressed perhaps for a private visit, yet not inap-propriate to an empress. Laurence was surprised to find the crown prince of Prussia in her company: a gangly young man of seven-teen, who bowed and spoke to them in very fluent French. Her own child, a handsome and sturdy-looking boy with a cap of dark hair and large dark eyes, was playing upon a blanket in the corner of the room. He was overseen by a trio of nursemaids and a fourth just outside the house: the massive feathered head of an Incan dragon, one of the sleek and venomous Copacati, peered in through the barn-wide glass doors at the end of the chamber.

Laurence offered his congratulations on the child, as a little more awkwardly did Granby: difficult to know how to behave to a woman to whom he had so nearly been forced to pay his addresses—and who had ordered an attack upon them, while they had been guests in her court. She seemed not the least conscious of any awkwardness herself, however, and merely inclined her head accepting those congratulations as her due; then she said, "There will be another in the fall," with a calm complacency.

Laurence bowed again; there was nothing else to say, although any enemy of Napoleon might feel some regret at his finding so much success in securing his dynasty, and his alliance with the Inca.

"My husband wished to be here to greet you, but matters in Paris demand his attention for a few days more," Anahuarque continued. "But I greet you in his stead, and I assure you that you will be made comfortable. Although the unhappy state of war between our nations makes you our prisoners, feeling must make you our guests," a pretty sentiment, though of course meaningless.

She sat with them a quarter of an hour—unusually gracious, particularly as a heap of letters upon the writing-table and a silent and hovering pair of secretaries made plain there were many demands upon her time. It fell to Laurence to carry the conversation on their side; Granby was stifled by embarrassment and by the surroundings, and Tharkay only sat observing with a sardonic expression in his eye. But the Empress was well able to supply her own share, and when Laurence had asked her how she liked her new home, she recounted with charming frankness several amusing stories of the misunderstandings that had plagued her on arrival, and laughed at her ongoing travails in learning to read and write: the Inca had been used to rely instead upon a system of knotted cords to communicate.

The handsome clock against the wall chimed the hour softly, and a footman came in to speak to her in a quiet voice; the Empress rose to her feet, and they rose with her. "Gentlemen, I am afraid I must bid you farewell," she said, giving them her hand to kiss in dismissal, and they were escorted out past another visitor waiting to be taken in. The gentleman was standing at the other side of the antechamber, studying the large landscape upon the wall; Laurence saw him only briefly and from the back, but some vague sense of familiarity tugged at him, and when they had gone on into the hallway, he almost stumbled a moment in surprise: it had been Talleyrand.

"A remarkable performance," Tharkay said, when they were at last shown to their own quarters—a magnificent suite more suitable for a visiting dignitary than prisoners of war—and private once more, the guards having withdrawn politely past their doors. The garden outside the windows gave a handsome illusion of liberty, if one did not go close enough to see the additional soldiers standing to attention across the paths, just out of view. "She makes quite the picture of domesticity. You would never think to look at her that she is the absolute ruler of several million people and some five thousand dragons, and a nation larger than Europe.

"Talleyrand is an interesting visitor for her to host. He quarreled with her husband several years ago, after the failure of the invasion of Britain. I wonder where he is getting his money from these days: Austria, perhaps."

Laurence had of course said nothing of the means by which he had engineered Tharkay's release, nor asked anything about the charge laid against him. He only knew as much as he did by unhappy accident; he could invite no further confidences on a subject where he had intruded without invitation in the first place. But nevertheless he could not help but perceive in Tharkay's remarks a professional assessment, and Laurence could not but recoil at the idea of a man taking funds in exchange for his own country's secrets.

"Spying is not the cleanest business," Tharkay said, perhaps reading his face.

Laurence shook his head sharply: he felt certain whatever

might be distasteful in the work Tharkay did could have nothing to do with this kind of selfish treachery. "There can be no comparison," he said, and then realized he had betrayed himself unintentionally.

Tharkay nodded a little, but did not speak directly to the subject. "The two are not unrelated, I am afraid," he said only. "A man rarely will compromise himself without assistance."

"That does not justify the act upon *his* side," Laurence said. "No man may be made a traitor without his consent."

He could speak from experience; he had given his own consent, once. He could not understand the coarseness of spirit which could permit a man to do such a thing for money and not the bleakest imperative of honor.

He paced the room round twice, troubled, and abruptly asked, "Are we not obligated by ordinary humanity to warn her she ought not be in his company? A man who would do treason for money—what would he not do?" Even if Talleyrand was in some sense on their side, Laurence could not help but feel uneasy to have knowledge of his treachery, and yet say nothing as the man was admitted to the private company of the expectant Empress and her small child—the worst fears of Napoleon's enemies realized.

But Tharkay said dryly, "You seem to be under the impression she does not know exactly the sort of man he is. At the very least she cannot suppose him fond of her husband; a man who has been publicly called a shit in front of half the Marshals of France by his emperor is not likely to be easily conciliated. In any case, certainly Fouché knows as well as I do that Talleyrand's expenses outrun his public income."

"Why would she entertain such a visitor, if he had not persuaded her of his having been reconciled with her husband?"

"He might be safer company, if he were the Emperor's loyal servant," Tharkay said, "but he would not be half so useful, if she cares to maintain any sort of communication with the other courts of Europe when they have declared war upon France."

To reconcile this kind of cold scheming with the charming

young woman they had only just left was an incongruous task, but Granby said, "Well, I am not forgetting any time soon that she set a hundred beasts on our tail hunting us across the Andes, however meek and mild she chooses to look at present," which was a useful reminder. "I am sure I wish Napoleon every joy of his wife: better him than me."

"But not, perhaps, for us," Tharkay said. "Our present circumstances leave a great deal to be desired. Not that I mean to make you regret your happy escape," he added, with a faintly amused glint.

"No fear of that," Granby said. "I don't mean to say I wouldn't rather be back in the Peninsula, where I can do some good, but I would as lief kick my heels in France the rest of the war as be married in Cusco. I don't suppose one dragon can make all that much difference, even Iskierka, when he has a whole horde of them breeding up." He sighed.

Tharkay was silent; then he said, "And yet Napoleon *does* suppose it."

"What do you mean?" Laurence said.

"We are not here by accident, after all," Tharkay said. "Temeraire and Iskierka were deliberately tempted here, as you have divined, by those threats against the egg; but if you will pardon me, we have not considered *how* they were tempted: where you heard these threats."

"The Prussian dragons had overheard them," Laurence said, and then slowly, "—you mean that they were deliberately permitted to escape?"

Tharkay inclined his head. "You would have been a good deal more skeptical of threats sent directly to you, and having received those threats, you would not have supposed you could intercept the egg. Not to mention that it does pass credulity that some thirty dragons were able to flee the breeding grounds of France without challenge."

"But surely credulity is passed much more thoroughly to suppose that Napoleon let half the Prussian aerial corps loose, just to get Temeraire and Iskierka here," Granby said. "Not that they don't make a good deal of noise, but they are only two beasts: they aren't worth the exchange."

"With as many dragons as Napoleon has in prospect, the relative value of keeping the Prussian beasts captive must have been diminished," Tharkay said. "But nevertheless, you are right—if the dragons were judged solely for their fighting-qualities. Which must mean there are other considerations which have prompted the act."

Lien's unblinking expression, fixed on Temeraire, managed somehow to convey without a word that she was astonished that he should have got himself into such a state, and even disappointed: that her satisfaction in his defeat was somewhat reduced by his looking so ragged, as though it were not much, after all, to have brought him low. Temeraire had not given a thought all this month to his torn-up wings, to his fresh scars; the scales where the fire had burned him worst had grown back hard and dull instead of glossy. None of these had mattered.

But now he could think of them again, for beyond Lien stood a small but elegant little pavilion, and beneath the roof, an enormous basket lined with silk and much padding held the beautiful shining egg, its delicately speckled shell unharmed, even to the small mark which looked so much like an eight. Half a dozen braziers stood around, warming it, and there were screens to shelter it from the wind, which the servants had drawn aside only to let them see.

With the worst anxiety eased, others crowded forward to take its place. Temeraire could not help but realize that he made a very disreputable figure at present; as slovenly as Forthing, with no power of repairing his appearance.

Iskierka felt no consciousness; she was sniffing around the pavilion with immense suspicion. "Are you sure that the egg is warm enough?" she demanded. "Look at all this snow everywhere around; what if it should take a chill? And how has it been brought here, anyway; did you shake it? Did it get wet at all?"

"All proper measures have been taken for its care, of course," Lien said, with cool disdain.

"I don't see what is *of course* about it when you have been going on and on about *smashing,* and hauling it all over the world," Iskierka said, rounding on her. "What do you mean by it? How dare you go anywhere near my egg?"

Lien did not—quite—edge away from Iskierka's flaring anger, but she stiffened her back visibly, which Temeraire found a little gratifying. "Surely one must ask why *you* left your egg behind in the care of those who were not capable of its protection," she answered.

"Oh!" Temeraire said: that was too much. "When you certainly had your friends in China bribe some of the guards, and murder the rest; I hope Crown Prince Mianning puts them all to death just as soon as he is emperor."

"I will have cause for sorrow enough if China should be brought so low," Lien said venomously, "as to have an emperor who has lost all the favor of Heaven: his own Celestial companion lost, and willing to pledge his empire to a nation of low opium-merchants to acquire another. But I will not call it the fault of the *egg,* nor have I permitted any harm to come to it, poor mongrel creature though it is sure to be; but that is more cause to pity it than harm it."

"So this has all been more of your scheming against the crown prince, after all," Temeraire said, nearly choked with indignation at this speech, so wholly different from the report which Eroica had brought him. "And you never meant to hurt the egg at all? I suppose we are to believe *that*—"

"I care nothing for what you believe," Lien said cuttingly. "And need not care. Through an excess of headstrong anger, you have compromised yourselves and your *masters,*" this with a sneering emphasis, "and now you only see your egg by the grace of my lord the Emperor, who chooses to be kinder to you than you deserve: a reflection of his nobility and not your merits." And here she gave Temeraire a look, up and down, to make plain these were few indeed, before she went aloft and left them.

He returned in some irritation of spirit to their own pavilion—also charming and comfortable, with heated stones and everything nice, standing amidst a garden of stone and pine trees and a pond delicately iced over and traced in frost with patterns like leafy vines. Temeraire could not but feel put-upon even by these luxuries, as though he heard Lien's voice coming from every smooth pebble, saying, *Look how well I am situated, and what a poor creature you are,* and feeling the truth of the remark all too strongly.

A troop of servants and three small dragons appeared shortly, bearing great steaming water-buckets in yokes on their sides, and offered to bathe them. Temeraire felt so very dirty and wretched that he could not even bring himself to make a grand refusal, and had to be grateful instead to be standing under the hot sluicing water, with delightful scrubbing-brushes going busily at every talon and dirt-crusted scale, and then to lie down on the hot stones to dry, feeling unavoidably refreshed.

"*Now* what is the matter?" Iskierka demanded. "Everything is going splendidly, and still you keep sulking."

"Splendidly!" Temeraire said.

"Yes, of course," Iskierka said. "A month ago, we had no notion of where the egg was, or even if it had been smashed; a week ago, we were a thousand miles away. Now here we are, just round the corner, and Granby and Laurence are somewhereabouts, too; now we only need to work out how to get us all away."

"Only that!" Temeraire said, a little annoyed to find he could make no better rejoinder.

"We are still better off than *before,*" Iskierka said. "I think you are being very poor-spirited to keep moaning."

Temeraire bristled, but did not argue: they were in the very heart of France, surrounded by Napoleon's best guards and legions of dragons—but it did feel rather poor-spirited to mutter about such details when the egg was not only safe but so very near-by, and Laurence as well. However, he was not willing to fully share in Iskierka's satisfaction.

"And why *is* Napoleon being so nice to us, I should like to know," he said, "for I am sure there is a reason for it: Lien would not mind at all the chance to keep looking down her nose at us."

"I dare say they are afraid of us," Iskierka said, "as they should be," but Temeraire lay his head down and brooded over alternatives, each less pleasant than the next. Perhaps they were only being lulled into complacency, that the pain when at last inflicted should be all the deeper.

"And what *does* Lien mean to do with the egg," he added suddenly, as a fresh unpleasant thought struck him, "now that she has it? Very well to say she only wanted to deny it to Crown Prince Mianning, but now what? It is sure to be a large dragon, as we are both large, and France does not want large dragons anymore. What if it is left all alone and companionless—told it must *win* its harness! How insupportable!"

"Now, *that* is an excellent question," Iskierka said, jetting steam from her spines in full agreement. But the guard dragons could not give them an answer, and were anyway not inclined to talk, but only stared pointedly until Temeraire curled back into the pavilion in frustration.

The gardens sprawled out of sight in either direction; the beautiful house only glimpsed in the distance. "If only I could be sure Granby were not in there," Iskierka said broodingly, "I would go and set it on fire, see if I wouldn't, and then I am sure they would tell us," but Granby *was* in there, very likely, so that was no help.

And escape did look rather hopeless, however sanguine Iskierka liked to be. The estate was nearly swarming with dragons of every size and description, darting here and there over the course of the day—some very large and laden with goods; then a steady stream of lighter beasts, then a large party of French combat-dragons, in war harness: middle-weights and light-weights, and then a stream of small motley companies, very different in character from one another.

Temeraire idly counted some nine or ten different groups, so peculiar and distinct from one another in appearance that he could not work out what sort of dragons they were; none of them even looked like the French dragons he had known. Not even the newer cross-breeds, which at least had some distinguishing feature to remark upon, or at least a consistent shape of the second wing-joint, quite characteristic to most French breeds.

He could not make any real sense of it, but he was only observing dully, without giving the question much thought: what did any of it matter when half so many dragons would have done to keep them penned up? But late in the evening, a company of heavy-weights in remarkable colors and familiar conformation landed at a pavilion not distant, and his attention finally sharpened.

"What is it?" Iskierka said, as Temeraire raised his head to peer at them through the dimming twilight.

"Those are Tswana dragons," Temeraire said slowly. "What are *they* doing here?"

"Your Imperial Highness," Napoleon said, and when he had heartily embraced Laurence in the Gallic manner, with a kiss upon either cheek, he had completed Laurence's discomfiture: a welcome more suited to a fellow head of state and an ally than his prisoner. Not content to finish there, Napoleon with cheerful familiarity greeted Granby, and rallied him a little with a sly apology for having stolen his bride out from under his nose, a bit of pleasantry to which poor Granby was hard-pressed to make answer; then the Emperor noticed Tharkay, saying, "Ah! So this is the infamous gentleman? Laurence, you do not know how much you are in my debt: Fouché outright gnashed his teeth at me when I told him he must give up his prey"—a none-too-subtle reminder of the favor Laurence had asked; and Tharkay's narrow glance told him the remark had not passed unnoticed there, either.

The Emperor was not alone, although the force of his presence at first commanded all attention in the room, but when he had turned to unnecessarily badger the servants to add to their comforts, one of his companions stepped forward to make Laurence a bow, and Laurence was surprised to belatedly recognize Junichiro, his hair pulled back and wearing an aide-de-camp's uniform.

"I am glad to see you well," Laurence said, a little constrained.

"I would be glad if it were so, Captain," Junichiro said forth-rightly, "but I do not presume to expect such consideration from you."

Laurence's feelings were indeed divided, and so opposed to one another as to be difficult to reconcile. Junichiro had placed him under such profound personal obligation, in aiding him to escape execution in Japan, that Laurence had given himself no real hope of discharging the debt. That Junichiro had provided that aid not for Laurence's sake, but to save his own beloved master, in no wise diminished that lingering obligation. The boy had made himself a criminal in his own country, had forfeited all hope of rank and place and home.

And yet—Laurence had done his best to discharge the debt: he had given Junichiro a place among his crew, and sought to establish him as an officer—not impossible in the motley ranks of the Aerial Corps. He had done everything in his power to secure the young man a respectable future, and to make him comfortable if not happy. But Junichiro had spurned all these good offices, in the end, and gone—gone to the French, hoping to promote among them an alliance with Japan, as counterbalance to the threat he saw to his nation from the deepening connection between China and Britain.

It was impossible to see him now and not realize that here was the architect of Temeraire's distress and his own. Junichiro had been among their party in China; he had known everything of the negotiations which pledged Temeraire and Iskierka's egg to Crown Prince Mianning, in exchange for the alliance that had sent the Chinese legions to the war in Russia. He had seen with his own eyes the pavilion where the egg had been established in state, and the guard placed upon it. His intelligence had undoubtedly been responsible both for Napoleon's forming the design of capturing the egg, and for its success.

—And yet Junichiro had not behaved dishonorably. He had

openly avowed his intentions before resigning Laurence's service, despite the personal risk he ran thereby. And it was by no means clear to Laurence that Junichiro understood his duty to his nation wrongly. While desiring nothing but peace with Japan, Hammond had made no secret of valuing higher an alliance with China: Britain would certainly look the other way should that power decide to turn their attention to their smaller neighbor, an event not so unlikely when Prince Mianning ascended his throne: the crown prince had already demonstrated his intentions to broaden China's reach, and bring his nation more into the world.

Laurence could hardly feel *pleasure* at finding Junichiro here under these circumstances, and established deep in Napoleon's councils—but if he meant to be civil to Napoleon, who had waged a relentless war upon Europe for near twenty years now, and invaded his own country—and who, for his part, showed no disposition to be less than gracious to Laurence, who had been instrumental in thwarting his destruction of the Russian Army—he could yet greet Junichiro with courtesy, and he returned the bow the young man made him.

"Captain Laurence," Napoleon said, turning back again, having commanded an array of refreshments, the addition of several comfortable chairs, a change of drapery, an increase in their firewood, and the assignment of a footman to carry out their errands, "I am remiss. You must permit me to offer you my condolences upon the loss of your father."

"I thank Your Majesty," Laurence said quietly.

Napoleon remained with them nearly an hour, talking freely and walking the room as though among intimate friends. Laurence could not but be sensible of the compliment the Emperor paid him with such a degree of attention and time, and perplexed by it; if he had not succumbed to Napoleon's blandishments five years before, when by so doing he might have saved his own life and Temeraire's liberty, the Emperor could hardly expect to seduce him now. Or so Laurence hoped, unhappily conscious that he might have given encouragement to such thoughts, in asking a favor, and contemplating with no pleasure the prospect of having to refuse any en-treaty which the Emperor might now make him.

But Napoleon asked him nothing, except his opinion on this or that new provision for the dragons of France, which he had under consideration. There were many of these: Napoleon passed freely from schools for hatchlings, to a scheme of using dragons in laying new trails over the Alps—inquiring for Laurence's opinion on the Alpine ferals as he did so. "They have resisted all our offers most stubbornly," Napoleon said, shaking his head.

"They have a remarkable bent for independence, I should have said, Your Majesty," Laurence said.

"Which you admire!" Napoleon said, with a keen glance. "But nothing can be accomplished by one alone and friendless, without support. If I should ride into the field alone, what use would I be? And yet with an army beside me, what can I not accomplish?— They would do much better for themselves to accept the protec-tion of France."

Laurence refrained from making a remark about the value this protection had been to the Russian ferals Napoleon had loosed and then abandoned. "I think you may find them hard to per-suade," he said only, and Napoleon moved onwards.

His designs ranged almost absurdly wide. He talked of estab-lishing great trade routes by dragon-back even to India and to China; he talked of building pavilions all across the breadth of Europe and Asia. His plans grew ever more ambitious as he spoke, and Laurence wondered. Napoleon spoke not at all of the disas-trous reversal he had lately suffered—betrayed no consciousness either by word or look, or even by moderation, of the wreck of a million men, of ruin and defeat. Indeed he spoke of the war only briefly, to complain of his stepson, Eugene de Beauharnais. "He is too openhearted. He has given you quite a generous gift—the Oder!" Napoleon said. "All because a few Cossacks have given him a little trouble, and a handful of Prussian dragons." Laurence could not but rejoice at the news: so the Tsar had sent his troops forward after all. But the censure in Napoleon's voice made not the slightest acknowledgment that he had left that army wrecked, in an untenable position.

There was something dreadful in this determined avoidance, as though Napoleon could not bear to recognize his own defeat and had instead to delude himself, even knowing as he must that his audience in this case knew the truth. Laurence was sorry to see it. He had thought in Russia that the Emperor was not himself— sallow, thickened: he had gained another stone in weight and did not carry it well, his face settling into heavy lines. The grey eyes were dulled; he stared into the fire often as he spoke, and did not meet his listeners' eyes often.

But he remained Napoleon, for all that. Laurence said, wanting only to escape the painful sense of omission, "We were impressed by your training grounds outside Grenoble, Your Majesty."

"Ha!" Napoleon cried, turning round. "—you mean, by the number of eggs." Laurence could not deny it; he bowed. "Yes," Napoleon said, "for seven years now we have attended the wisdom of the Princess of Avignon—Madame Lien as you knew her— and you have seen the fruits of our labors. There are four thousand eggs laid upon the sands of France, and soon they will come to their maturity.

"The old ways of war are done, Captain. You have seen their death-knell," Napoleon added. "The army which can bring more power to bear upon the battlefield, more quickly, will always be the victor: the weight of metal and of men will carry the day—if their generals are wise. You were at Tsarevo Zaimische?"

"I was," Laurence said, surprised to hear the Emperor now at last mention anything of the campaign: although in some wise the battle had been his triumph.

"What a morning that was!" Napoleon said. "A little of my own sauce, as they say: to be woken in the first hours of the day to hear of five hundred dragons coming for me. You ought to have had me! But you could not bring your full weight to bear." His face was illuminated again with vivid satisfaction; he seized upon a scrap of writing paper and a pen, and with a quick hand sketched out the defensive emplacements, his own forces behind their wall of defensive guns and the narrow corridor left; the Russian Army and the Chinese legions spread wide before it. "—You did not do as you ought. If you had committed your forces decisively, you must have overwhelmed us, and secured a complete victory, the destruction of my army. But you permitted caution to rule you," he finished, flipping the pen from his fingers with a shrug; and Laurence knew well that no one would ever say the same of this man.

Napoleon stood studying his own diagram a moment longer, then abruptly said, "Come, let us go and take the air—you are no delicate courtier; you are a soldier," and Laurence had no objection to make; indeed agreed heartily, privately hoping for a glimpse of Temeraire somewhere upon the grounds.

The gardens of Fontainebleau had been expanded and transformed into a covert, but not resembling any Western notion of that word. Large and imposing pavilions were made private by stands of young trees and elaborate trellises of vines, fountains playing among them: something from an imagined pastoral landscape, only with dragons instead of sheep. Dragons of every description: smaller feral-looking beasts, heavy-weights in every color and conformation, until Laurence, at first bewildered by the variety, spied down a narrow walk the heavy sinuous curve of a Kazilik dragon, unmistakably marked by the steam-hissing spines.

But the dragon was not Iskierka: the hide considerably more black-green, and Laurence realized only then that these were not all French beasts. These were dragons from every corner of the world: besides the Turkish beast, he caught sight of several not unlike Arkady and his fellow Pamir-dwellers; over there to the north a huddled group of Russian ferals, lean and savage-looking; in a green-marbled pavilion along their way a pair of dragons conversing in broad colonial English. And as they turned back for the house, Laurence saw a dragon he was sure he recognized: Dikeledi, one of the beasts of the Tswana, whom he had last seen sailing for Africa with a transport full of slaves liberated from the Brazilian plantations.

The dragon took notice of him also, peering back curiously, then turned to speak to a man—to Moshueshue, Laurence realized in deepening astonishment; the crown prince of the Tswana, here? Nothing could account for it, but to suppose that Napoleon had somehow gathered all these dragons here, in secret. Questions trembled on Laurence's lips, although constrained: he was an enemy of France. And yet Napoleon had brought them here of his own volition; he had not needed to promenade Laurence about the grounds, inevitably to notice the presence of so many foreign beasts. Laurence asked, therefore, only a little diffidently.

"What secrecy has been necessary?" Napoleon said. "*You*, Captain Laurence, know well the willful ignorance cultivated by my enemies of the lives of dragons. I have made no efforts at concealment: what use, when my couriers have gone throughout the world, and spoken with dragons in every part of it? We could not have expected them all to keep it secret, if we wished to. If you have had no intelligence of our convocation, it is no doing of mine: you see there we have even Russian beasts among us." He gave a disparaging snort. "Your old men and generals will not have it that dragons are thinking creatures, and throw a few coins at them to keep them contented. What do they know of it, when my couriers land even in their own breeding grounds, and speak to the creatures they have penned up and expect to remain quiescent even in the face of their outright destruction? You may be sure that the pitiable condition of the Russian ferals has not been forgotten *here*—those monstrous wing-chains! I wonder that you can with complacency range yourself with the architects of such cruelty."

Laurence could not easily answer this charge. He might have said that Napoleon had been little kinder in leaving them to starve and be hunted down, all so that they might wreak havoc among the Russian supply-lines. He might have said that the Russians had been on the point of freeing the ferals. But he could not bring himself to make these arguments. He would have chosen starvation over slavery, himself, and the Russians had been no less calculating in their decision than Napoleon: they had planned to make their ferals into troop-carriers, and that decision had been made only under the duress of Napoleon's own lightning-quick advances. In truth, he had nearly resigned his post and gone when he had learned of the brutalities by which the Russian ferals were kept confined to their breeding grounds: only Kutuzov's assurances that the ferals would be freed, under his and Temeraire's own supervision, had kept them at their post.

"Not with complacency," Laurence said finally. "But war makes strange bedfellows, sir."

"By your decision," Napoleon said sternly, as though chiding a low subordinate. "You know the masters you serve: you cannot expect otherwise under their rule." Laurence closed his mouth on a reply: he could make none that would be civil, nor politic, to an emperor and a gaoler. Napoleon presently seemed to think better of his tone; he added, "But I will not wound you with reproaches! I know *your* conscience is not of that soft metal, which bends before a wind."

True to his word, the Emperor instead returned to enlarging upon those plans he had earlier described—which seemed now less grandiose, if he meant to accomplish them by an alliance with all the dragons of the world, direct: an unlikely but not impossible endeavor, Laurence thought. The evils of the condition of dragons in nearly every nation of the West, and the wholly unimproved situation of most ferals, would offer a fertile ground for Napoleon's proposals: if he could afford them, which seemed the greatest bar.

"But now you must pardon me," Napoleon said, when they had circled back into sight of the palace. "The guards will see you back to the house. You have my word, Captain, that I will see you are given the chance to speak with your dragons soon, and as often, henceforth, as safety can allow—I know well how bitter that separation must be!"

He left them, walking swiftly away down one of the garden paths towards an exceptionally beautiful pavilion of black marble here and there adorned with gold, and set upon the bank of a lake;

and as he went a great white dragon head lifted to greet him—Lien's voice musical as she called a greeting in French.

He had *that* weapon, too—and an immensely dangerous one. Laurence had seen too many times for his present satisfaction how the power and grace and swift intelligence of a Celestial united to command the respect of other dragons, particularly if supported by self-interest: how many times and how easily Temeraire had persuaded other dragons to act in concert, and tolerate without resentment his leadership.

"Well, we had better hope they eat him out of all the cattle in France for a month or two, and then go home again," Granby said, with an equal pessimism. "I don't suppose he *can* talk them all round, but Lord! If he did, it would be a nasty business. Those purple ones near the oak-trees were Nilgiri Cutters out of Madras, or I am a donkey-herder: I dare say *they* would be glad to serve us out—if he would only give them harness, and guns and powder, and a few dozen cannon to back them! But he would have to stretch a long way to find anything that could make a dragon in the Pamirs care a fig for anything that he says in France, without sending them a chest of gold with every command; or in Japan, I suppose," he added in challenge, to Junichiro, who had accompanied them to their stoop: every outer room in the palace had been altered, to have large wide doors that opened onto the grounds, evidently to permit dragons to share in the life of the house.

Junichiro paused by the door; then he said quietly, "You are mistaken, Captain Granby: he has already made all those beasts a gift which commands both their interest and respect—the cure of the dragon plague."

Chapter 11

"IT IS INTOLERABLY UNFAIR," Temeraire said, feeling all the indignation of having done a good deed at great cost, nobly expecting no reward, only to see another get both the credit of it and the unexpected fortune of the result. "What has Lien done for any of them, or Napoleon; *they* did not find the cure. Oh! When I think of all those hideous messes that Keynes inflicted upon me; even now I cannot but shudder if I get a smell of bananas, sometimes."

"Napoleon however had the power of passing it on," Tharkay said. "I imagine there are few threats which dragons can feel so immediately as disease; the gift must have commanded gratitude."

Temeraire wished to ask—longed to ask—if Laurence was distressed. His only hesitation was fear of the answer. "Still, I do not see why any of them should give Napoleon the credit of the cure. He would not have had it to give, if Laurence and I had not given it to him."

"Just so," Tharkay said, in his dry way. "And now you and Captain Laurence are here at the convocation, to be seen in his company; I am sure Napoleon is delighted to be able to present such a portrait of amity to his assembled visitors. The arrangement must have recommended itself to him highly: enough to make it worth letting the Prussian dragons go, and lure you here."

"So it is all due to you that we are here," Iskierka said severely, as Temeraire sinkingly let his head drop to the ground. "—I might have known."

"Surely no-one would suppose we are here of our own volition," he tried.

"I do not expect Napoleon means to give you any opportunity of explaining the situation to his other guests," Tharkay said, very loweringly.

Temeraire had anyway to be glad of the visit, because Tharkay could tell him that Laurence and Granby were housed sumptuously in the palace, treated with enormous respect and every attention to their comfort: a little gratifying, at least. Temeraire brought himself finally to ask, "And—is he well?"

Tharkay paused and said, "His health improves daily. His spirits are as well-supported as might be expected," which was to say, Laurence was very distressed, and Temeraire did not need to trouble himself to find the cause: to be paraded about by Napoleon, so everyone should think he supported the Emperor's designs— knowing that whatever these should be, they would certainly mean nothing good for England.

It *was* intolerable, Temeraire realized, with a kind of terrible blankness—the situation could not be tolerated. He did not need to ask whether Laurence should have preferred to be put in prison, or even hanged, sooner than be used in such a fashion; he knew the answer perfectly well. Indeed, Temeraire was quite certain that if left to himself long enough, Laurence would find a way to arrange something of the sort; it only fell to him to act, before that should become necessary.

"Will they let you come again?" he asked Tharkay, slowly, wondering how to speak: a party of some ten guards had come with him, and stood rudely all the while in ear-shot; Tharkay had said, "I believe these gentlemen would prefer greatly that we should converse in French," when he had come: they were certainly going to report every word.

"I believe I will be permitted to come again next week," Tharkay said.

"Very well," Temeraire said. "Tharkay, will you pray tell Laurence that I beg his pardon, and tell him that I hope he knows how—how highly I value him, and that I should never wish to act in any fashion that would give him cause to doubt my respect and esteem."

Tharkay paused, looking at him for some long moments, after this speech. "I will certainly assure him, if assurances are required," he said. "I hope to see you next week, then; although I suppose we must not depend upon it, until the event."

"Yes, of course," Temeraire said, so he was tolerably certain Tharkay had understood, as far as it was possible for him to understand.

Then he had gone, escorted away back to the house; their own guards were eating their suppers, far enough away to be inattentive. Temeraire turned to Iskierka. "We cannot wait any longer," he said. "We must rescue the egg."

"*I* do not disagree; *I* have been saying so from the beginning," Iskierka said, swallowing down a haunch of nicely roasted kid with an easy gulp. "I am glad that you are coming round at last. I would have gone and taken it already, but there are too many of those guards. And I could not see how I would go and get Granby, afterwards. Have you thought of something clever? You ought to, since this business is all your doing, anyway."

"No," Temeraire said, "I have thought of nothing clever, it is not clever at all; it is only dreadful. We cannot do it: we cannot take the egg without some noise, and they will lay hands on Laurence and Granby at once. There will be no getting at them."

"What use is there in bleating 'we cannot wait,' then?" Iskierka demanded, with an irritated jetting of steam.

"That is what I mean," Temeraire said. "We must take the egg, anyway."

Iskierka hissed at him, bristling up. "And let them *keep* Granby?"

"Yes," Temeraire said, almost choking: scarcely able to think of it. Laurence alone in Lien's power, and surely the object of her malice. "Napoleon cannot execute them. Not when he is busily pretending Laurence is his good friend, and quite in amity with him; he cannot harm him at all. It would certainly look very strange to all the dragons here, if he did. So this is our only chance. We must go and take the egg, and—and we must leave Laurence and Granby behind."

"Temeraire is certainly planning something," Tharkay said, "but as to the details, I cannot speculate, except that he evidently supposed you might feel slighted."

"That tells me nothing, unless he means to lose me another ten thousand pounds," Laurence said grimly.

"Had we better try and stop them?" Granby said. "You know there is no use hoping that cooler minds will prevail, on their end. The madder the notion, the more sure it is to please Iskierka: I would not depend on her to restrain Temeraire from launching a headlong charge on Paris and trying to bring down the Tuileries."

"I cannot see how you mean to do so," Tharkay said, "unless by betraying their intentions to our gaolers, which will certainly preclude any future chance of escape. You can either trust them, or halt them forever."

Placed upon these terms, Laurence found his own decision easy, if no more comfortable. "That trust I can hardly deny him. The egg is no longer in mortal peril, nor are we. I do not think Temeraire suffers in his present situation the same desperation that drove him to those earlier extremes, which brought us to this pass; he may certainly wish to escape, but I do not believe he would enter into some real folly, in pursuit of that aim, which would endanger the egg or our lives. I do not deny he might overestimate his chances, as judged rationally by a more skeptical eye. But I cannot remove his power of taking action, only because I have no means of approving his course."

"Well, it would be an unhandsome turn to serve him, I don't deny," Granby said, "but what good can he possibly do while we sit here in the midst of Bonaparte's armies? If I could think of anything at all worth the doing, I should be less concerned about his getting up to something. I will be the first to say it is a wrench, going from Spain to a French prison—however pleasant," he added, with a reluctant justice almost demanded by their surroundings.

It had not been enough for Napoleon to see them established in a palatial suite of his own home, attended by servants, made comfortable in every particular. The fire now roared so enthusiastically that they had been obliged to open the doors to the garden to avoid stifling; an urn of silver magnificence dazzled from the sideboard, of a capacity sufficient to three men if those three men had nursed the ambition to drown themselves in tea like Clarence in malmsey; and they had but risen from a handsome turbot filleted in wine and a beef roast of melting tenderness, with six removes and a dish of magnificent oysters with which even Laurence's most exacting standards could have found not the least fault. And Chicken Marengo, it had to be admitted, was excellent, even if there was something vaguely unpatriotic in the enjoyment thereof, and of all their present comforts.

Laurence would have refused every such gesture if offered in exchange for the least form of cooperation; he would have welcomed, indeed, a chance of making such a refusal. But he had not been asked for so much as his parole. He could not easily put aside the dinner laid before him and demand to be fed on gruel and water, or housed in a damp cell, without rudeness and absurdity united; and even if he had, an acquiescence to his wishes would have been a worse, as being a greater, favor: the power to direct his own arrangements. There would have been too much of the quixotic guest about it, instead of the resisting prisoner. He could only share in Granby's feelings, when he lamented the battlefield.

"We have been doing some proper work, too," Granby said, dispiritedly, "and I was beginning to feel I did not have to blush every time I caught Admiral Roland's eye: do you know, after Salamanca, even Wellington sent us a bullock from his own pocket, and a note I dare say I treasure better than a knighthood: *I congratulate you on the disciplined performance of your beast and crew,* and it was even more than half-deserved. Iskierka snorted over it, and wanted me to write back that *she* congratulated *him,* that not so many of his men had run away from the battle as usual, but I assure you she has been listening better than I had ever hoped to see. She has even, from time to time, condescended to give a little thought to her actions beforehand—and now *this,*" and Granby sighed.

Laurence sighed also. As little pleasure as he had found amidst the grim brutality of the Russian campaign, he, too, would have exchanged his place without hesitation for the coldest and most cheerless camp of all the winter. "But I will not accept that nothing remains to us but to sit quiet in prison," he said, "if only because Napoleon himself evidently sees more for us to do, if only to be displayed as a jewel upon a cushion."

He looked at the open doors—guarded discreetly but thoroughly by six young, hearty, and exceptionally tall soldiers in the uniforms of the Imperial Guard who stood stoically outside upon the stoop. The senior of these, a fellow named Aurigny, had presented himself earlier: he was not much above twenty-and-five, and there was something cheerful in the lines of his ruddy, wind-weathered face, but he had been serious while in conversation: "I hope, m'sieur, there will be no occasion for our disagreeing with anything you should wish," a phrase that captured to a nicety his peculiar orders: to guard prisoners, but without giving any offense, save of course the deepest one of removing their liberty. A little absurd, but suggestive that so long as Laurence cut his desires to the cloth of his imprisonment, he should not meet with contradiction. He would not be permitted to go near Temeraire, surely, but—

"If I asked to walk about the grounds, to take the air," Laurence said after a moment, "the guards would not like to refuse me, I think."

"Where the dragons can see you?" Tharkay said. "No, I imagine not, when displaying you is indeed the Emperor's aim."

"Very well," Laurence said. "I will accept that cost, and exchange it for the opportunity, which I hope that my walking the grounds will allow, to try and have a word with Moshueshue. I hope he will remember me; and though we spoke only a little, and once, he impressed himself upon me in that meeting as a reasonable man, nor have the Tswana shown the least inclination to fall in with France for any other than the most practical reasons. At least he may tell me the purpose of this conclave; he has no reason to conceal it, and afterwards he will have the power of telling the other guests, where I myself cannot, that my presence here is unwilling, and that I do not in the least endorse Napoleon's designs."

"But if you do?" Tharkay said later that evening, after Granby had retired. "It is a hazard as well to consider before as after meeting it," he added, when Laurence did not immediately answer. "Napoleon cannot have commanded the attendance of so many dragons—so many ferals, and beasts of other nations—only with respect."

"You think he means to lay some proposal before them, which will make a marked improvement to their condition," Laurence said.

"I can see no other motive that would compel them to listen," Tharkay said.

Laurence had too many bitter proofs of the disdain and fear which prevailed among his own country-men—his own Government—towards dragons, and the determined persistence of their hostility. He knew which alternative Whitehall would have preferred, between the hideous Russian practice of wing-hobbling and starving any beast that would not go into harness, and Napoleon's eager efforts to win the love and loyalty of his beasts, and bring them into the full life of their nation. Necessity might force the admirals to grant, with immense and grudging reluctance, a few piecemeal rights and liberties: there were too many natural advantages to Napoleon's course to be wholly ignored. But necessity only would move them. England would do nothing for dragons from any sense of justice or charity, while Napoleon worked tirelessly to fling wide the barred gates of breeding ground and covert.

"But I have this to armor me against Napoleon's most pleasant aims," Laurence said, "that all he does has ever been for his own selfish vainglory. He wishes to be loved by the dragons of France not for their sake but for his. He has had no hesitation in spilling their blood, and the blood of his soldiers, to make himself a perfect tyrant, bestriding the world unopposed. He cannot suffer an equal—and so he cannot be suffered. His means, his immediate acts, may be noble; his ends are less so, and he has shown himself insensible to the wreck and horror of war."

He was silent however awhile after speaking. He knew Tharkay regarded him with concern, which he could acknowledge was not unmerited. He could not be easy to find himself the instrument, in however small and unwilling a part, of Bonaparte's success, and his spirits indeed required all the support which he could give them. His father's death returned to his thoughts easily—too easily; he could not help but indulge privately in a bitter kind of relief that Lord Allendale had not suffered the pain of hearing it put about that his son was, not the prisoner of the French Emperor, but his honored guest, in the midst of war.

Laurence put the thought aside. The evil deed which had occasioned his present circumstances had been finished long ago, and he had since then—not without severe difficulty—reconciled himself to the necessity of its commission. He would not now learn to regret that he had been the instrument of saving so many lives from a hideous and tormented end—that so many of the dragons here present should only have survived, even to become the enemies of his nation, because of his actions. Victory by such a method must have been hateful to any man of honor, and if some claiming that title justified themselves by willfully refusing to acknowledge the sentience of dragons, Laurence was not of their number; *he* could not so deceive himself.

"I am satisfied," Tharkay said, with a narrow, steady look, "except on one point. I know how greatly you have enjoyed Napoleon's generous attentions," this dryly, "but you must know I would never have desired, or still less urged you to invite them, for my sake."

"I hope," Laurence said, "that I would not require *urging*, to undertake any service on your behalf. In any case, we have had too much evidence of Napoleon's desire to make a parade of me to suppose that his attentions would have been long delayed, and he can have wanted neither excuse nor consent to set about them, since I have given him neither."

Tharkay shook his head a little, dissatisfied. "I would prefer you not to permit any such consideration to weigh with you again. I undertook the hazards of my, shall we say, *occupation,* freely and with full knowledge of the consequences were I ever identified to the enemy."

"That cannot make me less inclined to avert those consequences," Laurence said. "But you may be easy. If I have given Napoleon the power of making me appear his friend, I now mean to make him as well as his guests the best proofs to the contrary that I can, and I know you will not speak to stop me."

"Indeed not," Tharkay said. "I am only sorry to have been unveiled so inconveniently."

There was a hard look in his eyes, which made Laurence dare to ask, "Do you know how it may have come about?"

"A reward for success, I imagine," Tharkay said. "My latest report on the political situation in the Porte may have been excessively useful: the Sultan remains Napoleon's ally, and is unlikely to shift his position so long as we are aligned with Russia, but I discovered that a significant vezir was susceptible to persuasion. The Chinese legions we hope for will not encounter any direct opposition, if they come overland."

"That is an excellent piece of news indeed," Laurence said, low, "but how should it have exposed you?"

"I imagine the report has circulated a little too widely for my health," Tharkay said. "It so happens that one of my beloved cousins has a minor sinecure, somewhere or other under the Navy Board."

"Good God," Laurence said. "And you suppose him to have turned traitor?"

"Oh, I am sure he would call it no such thing," Tharkay said. "I doubt that the report was sold along with my name—which explains M. Fouché's eagerness to discuss the operation with me. No, I am sure dear Ambrose merely found it an irresistible opportunity to be rid of me and my inconvenient attempts to assert my right to my patrimony, and at a profit no less."

He spoke lightly, but Laurence knew to measure the depth of Tharkay's feelings less by what he said, than by what he did not say, and Tharkay had not mentioned his paternal family over a dozen times in all the years of their acquaintance. It was to a mere offhand mention that Laurence owed the knowledge of their existence; and to the accident of a shipboard communication that those relations, who had taken pains to furnish Tharkay with every apparent proof of family affection until his father's death, had since that event done everything in their power to steal his inheritance and deny his legitimacy.

They had succeeded so far to render him friendless and penniless in Britain, dependent on the kindness of an old acquaintance of his father's in the East India Company for even the little and dangerous foreign employment he had been able to obtain, as a go-between and a guide. Only the prize-money paid him, for having recruited some twenty feral beasts out of the Pamirs to Britain's service, had finally enabled him to press a law-suit to recover his rights; but this had dragged ever since.

"I am sorry to lose the power of disappointing your cousin's designs," Laurence said quietly. "I hope, Tenzing, you know that I wish I hazarded my safety equally with yours."

"Oh, permit me to comfort you on that score," Tharkay said. "Napoleon does not seem to me to care much for being balked. When you have gone romping around his carefully assembled guests, and done your best to overturn his remarkable conclave, I have every hope of your provoking him to all the outward displays of wrath that you might wish. You are as likely to be executed as I am."

The request had been made of Aurigny, and permission came the next morning swiftly and enthusiastically: they were to have the full run of the grounds, although the Emperor regretted they must not go near the northern edge of the gardens where Temeraire and Iskierka were housed. But their escort would gently guide them away if they should accidentally stray too far in that direction, and they would dine with the Emperor and the Empress tomorrow night, an honor Laurence received unwillingly, and Granby with outright dismay.

"There is not a moment to lose: let us do our best to put him in a towering rage at once," he said. "It won't be too late for him to withdraw the invitation, and for my part, I had rather be in the stocks than at another such dinner table."

Tharkay's memory of the plan of the grounds was good enough to bring them near the Tswana, not without a little circumnavigation that Laurence could not regret, as serving to deceive their escort of six excellent and determined Grognards. He spoke with Aurigny and his companions a little as they walked the paths; they spoke of their emperor with an extreme familiarity, and cheerfully cursed the vagaries of his will that had put them on "sheepdog-duty," as one fellow put it, and away from the front lines. "Ah, but he must let us have a little fighting sometime," one of them named Brouilly said, a little indiscreetly, "now that the Prussians are lining up for another drubbing—I was at Austerlitz," he added, with pardonable pride, and touching the medal in his lapel with a caressing finger.

Tharkay glanced round, when he had made another turn, and Laurence saw he had put them upon a narrow walk, between two pavilions. Beyond them was visible the carved pediment of the particularly large one where they had seen the Tswana, the day before. There remained only to find some excuse to go near enough to speak to them: Laurence regretted Temeraire's absence all the more, for having very little command of the Tswana-language, himself, but they might contrive somehow, if there were will on both sides. Laurence had no aim of concealing from the guards what he said and did: so long as they did not drag him bodily away before he had said as much as he could, he would be satisfied.

"I must compliment the design of your pavilions," Laurence said to Aurigny, not without an inward shading of distaste for this species of deceit. "The floors are heated, I believe? I hope there is no objection to our making an examination of some few of the buildings."

Aurigny did not demur, and in a half-counterfeit of interest Laurence went to the nearest pavilion and made a little show of discovering the heating-stove—an invention not of French but of Chinese origin, with which he had long been familiar, although this one had certain clever modifications, which brought the deception nearer truth. Laurence would gladly have acquired plans of the system, although the thought reminded him unpleasantly that he had few prospects of making any use of such a design—heating was not much required in New South Wales, and even if he and Temeraire were ever suffered to make their home again in England, they were not likely to have the power of setting up any pavilions.

"John, will you have a look?" he said, calling Granby's attention to the location of the heating-pipes, which carried the hot water from the low gurgling kettle and circulated it into the base of the pavilion, and thought nothing of it when the dragons sleeping within raised their heads to look over at them: two middle-weight beasts, bright sky-blue in color and of a sleek configuration not so far from Temeraire's lines, with large but tightly furled wings and banding across the ridge of a rounded nose not unlike a snake; they had long fangs hanging over their jaws. The guards showed no concern, although perhaps for the youngest of their number, *affected* no concern: his hand rested upon his pistol, and his eyes remained on the dragons instead of his prisoners.

And then one of the beasts hissed inward, a long and threatening whistle of breath, and said, *"British."*

Granby, anxious over playing his part, had been bent with excessive attention to examine the pipes; he jerked his head up, took one look at the dragons, and said, "Oh, Lord, they are Bengal," and turned reaching for Laurence even as one of the beasts brought a slashing, many-taloned claw down.

Instinct moved quicker, and the shadow of the falling blow: Laurence dived aside and took himself rolling into the brush, while Granby fell back in the opposite direction towards the path. The claws passed with tearing force between them, carrying away two of the hot-water pipes. Clouds of hot steam erupted whistling into the air, and the dragon jerked back its talons with a hiss of pain.

The guards were shouting protests and drawing their swords and pistols, but a party adequate to guard three men was not sufficient to give pause to an angry dragon. The two beasts came slithering to their full length out of the pavilion, clawing over the ground with startling speed even with their wings still folded to avoid the trees, their heads swinging to either side back and forth searchingly. The meager cover of the steam-clouds was quickly failing as the burst pipes ran dry. Laurence, getting his feet beneath him, made a crouching dash for a stand of trees—and threw himself behind it only just as the trunk groaned, spitting bark to either side of him, with a blow from the dragon's head.

Pistol-fire was cracking loud behind him, on the path. One of the dragons had turned that way; another had come after him. She had drawn her head back, shaking off the impact against the tree, and in the brief respite, Laurence dashed for a hollow between a pair of massive boulders, artfully arranged for decorative effect to conceal one pavilion from another; fistfuls of moss tore away beneath his hands as he hauled himself into the small space. The dragon came on after him, putting her gleaming yellow eye to the crack. *"British,"* she hissed again, full of hatred. She wore a neck-collar of gold, very dirty, which looked also as though pieces had been broken off at different times—perhaps to sell, for her keep. She was a lean and older beast, with scales showing the broadening of age.

He ducked back deeper into his hiding-hole as the dragon tried scraping a couple of talons through the opening, nearly catching him. She clawed against the rocks in frustration, a hideous scraping noise. He might have called out to her, but he had no argument to make which he thought would have any weight with an enraged and vengeful dragon. Laurence reflected grimly that he ought to have considered that not *every* dragon here would have cause to esteem him; Napoleon would surely have been as happy to recruit more dragons who shared his devoted enmity for Britain.

The boulders jarred violently: the dragon was hurling herself bodily against them. Dirt shook loose, stinging in his eyes, and both the great stones rocked back and forth, one wobbling out of its place. Another blow would shake them apart. Laurence twisted in the hollow, and squeezed himself out on the other side—and ran, with the hunted speed of any creature with death at its back, hearing the splintering branches behind him, the brute cracking of green wood, as its herald. He did not look back. The hissing breath drew close, but in the distance came the sound of more guns, and roaring: the French had summoned their own dragons to be peace-makers. He could not evade forever, but he could buy time. He twisted sharply to one side, and threw himself behind one of the larger trees; the dragon whipped to follow him, and as she clawed for the trunk he ran directly at her, instead, and passed under the arch of her forelegs. Her head doubled on herself, trying to keep sight of him, and she was forced awkwardly to twist herself around to come after him again.

He was panting, nearly out of breath. His chest ached. The dragon had made a wall of herself behind him now, and was slowing a little—which might have seemed hopeful, for a moment, and then he saw she was herding him towards the open path ahead: when he was out of the trees, he would be easy prey to spot and seize. A moment's calculation, and then he ran, as quickly as he could, and threw himself across the path and behind the wall of a hedge on the other side.

But she had anticipated the tactic; she too leapt, a monstrous jump over the path, her wings half-opening, and landed on his far side—herding him once again, from the other direction, and she had closed in on him. Laurence had rarely felt more sympathy for a fox being run to ground: there was something terrible in feeling the quick intelligence of the hunter on his heels, a sentience without mercy. She would have him in another moment; there was only one final hope to hazard. He gulped a breath, then broke onto the path and ran once more, straight and without evading twists, for the Tswana pavilion, not far, and shouted, "Help! Help!" in their tongue.

And then the world overturned with stunning force. Laurence had a brief peculiar impression of light shining directly through his skull, accompanied by a clamor of bells. *Eight bells,* he thought distantly, his whole body overcome by a heavy numbing languor. The dragon's head was lowering towards him, teeth bared; she had knocked him down with a claw, and two talons pinned him like a butterfly to either side of his chest. She peered at him. He was conscious of no pain, but he could not move. Evidently satisfied he was stunned beyond escape, she lifted away her head, and raised her claw for the final blow.

Still in that paralyzing stupor, Laurence saw very clearly as she was bowled over and away from him: a much larger dragon in mottled orange and grey knocked her away and put a protective cage of talons over him. She coiled back up to her feet, and drawing up her shoulders unfurled a large frilled flap which extended above and below her head, patterned peacock-bright in blue and green and violets, and hissing bared her long and vicious fangs. One of these was a little broken at the tip, and a touch of greenish ichor dripped from it.

The Tswana beast, not unimpressed, made a low rumbling comment—Laurence did not entirely follow the meaning, but felt it something vaguely profane and uneasy. But dust was rising from the path, and in a moment two more of the Tswana dragons had landed next to their companion: their massed weight made the blue dragon draw back, and after a moment the frill smoothed itself back down. She hissed at them all again, and slowly backed away down the path, retreating without ever taking her eyes away, until she rounded her own pavilion and was gone from view, the last curve of her tail vanishing.

Laurence found he was trembling in all his parts, in some belated reaction, and a moment later sensation returned: his heart was pounding with violent speed, and he put a hand over his chest involuntarily, imagining he would feel the beat palpable against his fingers. A few deep breaths restored him to something more like equilibrium, and then the sheltering talons came away. He pushed himself up sitting, and turning found himself under contemplation by five dragons, and some ten men wearing the gold jewellery and fur cloaks common to the highest ranks of the Tswana warriors— although their spears had been exchanged for rifles slung over their backs, adorned with exceptionally long bayonets.

"We have a little while to sit and talk, I think," Moshueshue said, in quite excellent French, pouring him a cup of red-brown tea. "The excitement is not quite over, it seems, and they will be some time determining that you have not been scattered over the grounds in pieces. I was most interested to find you a guest here, Captain Laurence. I had not expected you."

Laurence lowered the cup, for which he was grateful: a hot and pleasant brew, with nothing bitter about it, even if it were not very strong. He had as yet said nothing to explain his situation, but Moshueshue evidently already suspected certain aspects. "Sir, you are right to be surprised; I am not a guest, but a prisoner." He outlined in a few more words the circumstances which had brought him and Temeraire, while Moshueshue listened without comment, and then added, "I would be grateful to know more of the purpose of this convocation, and to what end my name has been used."

Moshueshue did not answer immediately, but sat with a thoughtful and inward-turned expression, which showed nothing of hot emotion. One of the dragons, growing impatient more quickly, spoke to demand an explanation. The prince glanced up, and after a considering moment answered briefly: Laurence understood *egg* and *thief,* and was a little startled to see the dragons all draw back their heads with a united hiss of distaste.

"Egg-stealing is a serious matter with us, Captain," Moshueshue said, seeing his surprise, and Laurence realized that it would of course be regarded as nearly the theft of a soul: since the Tswana believed their dragons their own great reborn, and made the belief true by regularly inculcating each egg with the history of the dead while the dragonet formed within, they would object violently to anyone taking an egg from the family and friends who were responsible for conveying that history.

"Then you can well understand the motive which brought us here, despite all other interest," Laurence said, "and I hope would not see the practice rewarded."

Moshueshue smiled very briefly, as if acknowledging a point neatly scored, but he did not pass his words on to the dragons. He was not a man easily read, or easily led; and few, Laurence supposed, better understood how to manage dragons, as he must to have any influence over beasts who considered themselves not only his protectors but his elders.

"I understand the French have suffered a reversal lately, in the east," Moshueshue said, an invitation Laurence was glad to accept, by furnishing him with the details of Napoleon's disastrous Russian campaign.

"There will be an army at his gates by the spring, I confidently expect," Laurence finished, silently grateful to the cheerful young Imperial Guardsman who had informed him that the Prussians had joined the alliance, "and perhaps you know something already of the situation he faces in the south, in Spain."

He knew well that he was making an argument. Moshueshue regarded him all the while with a thoughtful expression, and then abruptly nodding said, "Napoleon has proposed an alliance," answering the question Laurence had not yet asked, but wished to. "Not, as you might suppose, a military one. He desires rather that we should draw up borders among ourselves, among dragons, and he has proposed as well a code of laws, which should govern among us and resolve those disputes which arise over territory. It is a sensible code: its principles are good, and there is much to like in it," which Laurence, a little dismally, could well imagine.

"But it recommends itself to my people mostly," Moshueshue added dryly, "by seeking our opinions on how the world is to be divided. We find you Ropeans are inclined to consult no one but yourselves on these little matters, and decide from the other side of the world how best to divide up a country in which you do not live."

He beckoned to one of his servants, a young boy who ran and brought them the proposal. Looking over the maps therein, Laurence was astonished—although he knew he ought not have been, by any Napoleonic effrontery—to find all Europe and even Russia made into a French province, and from the air divided neatly into territories belonging to various feral dragons who should all owe allegiance to Napoleon direct. Even in England the French flag stood over a quilt of small patched territories. Laurence wondered at it, seeing one marked YELLOW REAPERS, as though Napoleon hoped to acquire the allegiance of the entire breed, and across Scotland a collection of wholly unfamiliar and peculiar names— RICARLEE, VINLOP, SHAL—whose meaning he could not divine. He wished not for the first time that Temeraire were at hand, to be consulted; he could only guess that these were each the name of some particular dragon, like Arkady, who had established himself as chief of a company of feral beasts.

All Africa below the Sahara had been made over to the Tswana, and Brazil marked out for them as well, abutting the Incan Empire's holdings in the west. Indeed Laurence could see nothing for Moshueshue to complain of in the arrangements, if they had been at all enforceable, with no other European power in a position to quarrel with them.

"Sir, I can tell you that he has no power to assign any of these lands, though he may claim to," Laurence said to Moshueshue, who shrugged a little.

"Had you the power to assign Cape Town to yourselves, or the Portuguese to claim Louanda? You claimed those places, and acted upon your claims; you took slaves and established your fortifications and your farms, and you would be there yet, if we had not driven you away by force. All maps are fiction when the world is seen from the sky. But if ten thousand dragons choose to believe in this one, I think you will find it nearer truth than otherwise."

Laurence looked at those neat lines, which divided the fields of Scotland among a dozen feral bands—who should, he found, reading into the *Code Napoléon Draconique*, be entitled to take a certain amount of cattle in their territory, and to call upon one another for aid if their claims met resistance—and he began to understand. He knew well the jealousy of dragons, over anything they considered their own possessions and their own territory in particular, even if very lately acquired, or by dubious means or even outright stolen. Napoleon meant to put all that possessive spirit to his own service: by telling the dragons they were entitled to these rights, he would make them willing to defend them, and by providing them with a network of alliances would enable them to do so—if not forever, then certainly for long enough to be a powerful distraction to the human nations whose borders they occupied.

It was his stratagem in Russia refined and writ large: he would make all the ferals of Europe into enemies of the very governments who presently fed them in the breeding grounds or ignored their small depredations. That most of those ferals would be slaughtered in reprisal, or starve in the ensuing chaos, he would ignore, save when convenient for him to come to the aid of one or another band, as an excuse for making still more war upon his neighbors.

Laurence looked up from the sheaf of papers. "And would you lend *your* aid, to a feral band in Britain, seeking to seize lands not their own?"

"Where would you prefer to see war made, Captain Laurence?" Moshueshue asked softly. "In your country, or on the other side of the sea?"

"War has a habit of spreading, sir," Laurence said. "I would prefer to see peace."

Temeraire settled back down uneasily. "Well, it all seems to have gone quiet again," he said to Iskierka, "only I cannot see what any of them were about, except some sort of quarreling—it does not seem to have gone near the house, or near the egg, so I suppose it can have done no real harm."

He felt unconvinced by his own words: he did not at all like the sound of gunshots so near-by, and such a squabbling of dragons. He had seen five all together go skirmishing aloft; a bright blue dragon fighting three and finally four of the French middleweights, until they had harried him back to the ground. Temeraire had not recognized the breed at all, and so knew nothing of his allegiance, but what should any dragon be doing here, if not a friend of France, and if a friend, why starting up such an enormous fuss?—and why putting on so disheartening a display? The French dragons had brought him down so very skillfully, even though he had been quite large and old and impressively scarred. Temeraire had not liked observing it at all. As dreadful as it must be to think of leaving Laurence behind in captivity, to save the egg, it was far worse to think of being captured in the attempt to do so—the egg taken away *again,* and locked up this time somewhere in secret, so there would be no second chance.

"You will insist on making trouble as though we hadn't enough," Iskierka said, eating her cow with unconcern bordering, in Temeraire's opinion, on a complete lack of sensibility. "So what if they are quarreling among themselves? If you ask me, this is as good a chance for us as anything. We had much better stop worrying and just go at once, while they are busy with the nonsense over there."

"Why," Temeraire said, beginning to explain why this was a singularly bad idea, as Iskierka's always were, and then discovered he could not find a satisfactory argument against it. He struggled a moment longer, then said, "Oh, very well, then," and gulped the last hindquarter of beef out of his own bowl—they had complained falsely of hunger, and asked for beef in the British tradition. Temeraire had felt a bit guilty at putting their guards to such trouble, but they could not be sure of getting anything much to eat between here and Dover. He and Iskierka had settled it between them they should make for the covert there.

The bowls were clean; they had drunk deeply from the fountain. The evening was fast approaching: the lights of the house shone golden against the blue night. Laurence was there now, perhaps, Temeraire thought miserably—safe and well, his health improved and all consideration taken for his comfort—and by this evening, when their flight was known, he would surely be taken from there, hurled into a cold dank prison cell, made wretched and ill—

"Let us go at once," Temeraire said, before courage and resolution failed him.

"Very well, but if anything should happen to Granby, I will never forgive you," Iskierka said, adding not a little to his unhappiness.

"Be quiet, and start that fire going," Temeraire said resentfully. He rose up on his haunches and spread out his wings, making as large a screen of himself as he could manage. They had surreptitiously scraped together a heap of old branches and leaves into the back corner of their pavilion over the course of the day; Iskierka put her head low to them and blew a narrow line of flame upon the pile until it had fairly caught, and the fire began to lick up the columns of the pavilion. In a moment, the roof was blooming with small flames, surprising Temeraire by a wholly unaccustomed feeling of deep terror, which sent him jerking out of the pavilion with a gasp of dismay.

Iskierka followed him out, snorting. "Whatever is it? What if they look over and see us too soon?"

"The fire is far enough along," Temeraire said, striving to sound calm and sensible, and to be so as well; when really he wanted only to be gone, aloft and away from the flames. He shook out his wings and looked them over, covertly—surely some embers had caught upon them? There was no sign of so much as a spark, but as soon as he turned away he felt the small stinging sensation of prickling heat upon the membranes. He looked again: there was still nothing there.

"Come on, then," Iskierka said, and there was no help for it: he reared up with her and together they fanned the flames energetically with their wings, until it climbed rapidly into a towering pillar, crackling and roaring as the roof went up. Temeraire managed to remain in place, but he was grateful when the cries of alarm rose behind them and he and Iskierka went aloft at last, circling away, the blazing flames making them invisible against the night to their guards.

The pavilion of the egg was not far, and Iskierka had been right, after all: half the guardians were absent, and evidently had gone to help with the squabbling on the other side of the grounds. Five remained, alert and peering into the night, but Temeraire roared furiously as he and Iskierka descended, at the stand of elegant trees bordering the clearing. As the divine wind shattered their branches into splinters, Iskierka blew a sheet of flame over the fragments, so they caught and rained down upon the guards like a hail of fire, piercing and scorching all at once.

Cries of pain reproached Temeraire; many of the dragons covered their eyes and folded in their own wings; he shuddered with sympathetic agony. But the attack served its purpose. Together, he and Iskierka seized the edges of the roof and tore it away, and he snatched up the egg and all its nest together into his talons—carefully, so carefully—

Immense relief washed over him the instant he had it safe. "I have it!" he cried, "I have it!" and Iskierka flung her head back and swathed the air over their heads with flame, snaking her head back and forth all the while she breathed out her fire, leaving a streak of violet-green dazzle upon the night sky. Temeraire was beating up as quickly as he could—up and through a wall of hot air, but as soon as he got his wings cupped over it, he began to rise swiftly, and Iskierka was on his heels.

The guards were clamoring below, bells ringing wildly out. "Quick, there!" Iskierka called.

"No!" Temeraire said. "They have already lit the lamps on that side of the grounds, we must try to the north—" But there were lanterns coming alight in that direction as well, hemming them in.

"Over the house, then!" Iskierka said, "and we may as well have a go at picking Granby up, after all."

"Don't be foolish," Temeraire said. "Our only hope is that they will assume just that, and all go to the house, and we must choose a way to get past whoever is left elsewhere. We must go over the lake, and then we must try for a woods somewhere to hide, or a very large barn."

"I cannot hide in a barn!" Iskierka said. "And neither can you, so don't *you* be foolish! The lake is a dreadful idea: if they should catch us there, and I breathe fire on them, they have only to duck into the water, or knock me into it, and it will be of no use, or at least much less. Be careful with that!" she added.

"I *am* being careful!" Temeraire said. "Only it is shifting all on its own," and as soon as he had said it, he realized, with a shock of breathless outrage, that the ungrateful thing was hatching, *now*, after all their trouble.

But there was no help for it: the egg was rocking so that it was sure to fall out of his grasp. He was forced to drop hastily into a small clearing just to the east of the great house. He had the small satisfaction of being proven right: in the lights of the house he could see nearly twenty French dragons milling about in the air, and there was a great noise going forth inside; they were certainly securing Laurence and Granby even now, he thought despairingly, as he put the egg down on the ground—very carefully, despite his resentment. But when the egg split wide down the middle in a single loud crack, and the dragonet inside popped up, Temeraire was entirely of a mind with Iskierka, who snorted a small tongue of flame and said, "Well, I like *that*! Why didn't you hatch yesterday, and save us all this trouble?"

The dragonet sneezed twice and shook the slime from her wings—quite mature, and certainly able to have come out anytime this last fortnight, Temeraire noted with some indignation—and answered without a qualm, "I hadn't made up my mind to hatch just yet. The situation did not seem entirely auspicious. But neither of you seems to know where you are going."

"It is no joke to find a way out when we are in the middle of the French Army, I will have you know," Temeraire said. "And what of Laurence and Granby? They will certainly be put into prison: we will never get them out of the palace now."

The dragonet turned her head to look at the building. "So that is a palace!" she said. "It is very handsome. But if you want someone out of it, I suppose you must go and take them."

"There are twenty dragons over it!" Temeraire said. "Iskierka, perhaps if we only go back to our pavilion now, quickly, and pretend that it caught fire by accident, and we had only taken the egg and gone to the lake to be safe—perhaps they will not punish Laurence and Granby, after all."

"Yes, but then you will be prisoners again," the dragonet put in, "and they will require an answer from me."

"What answer?" Iskierka said suspiciously, and Temeraire felt quite baffled himself.

"The French Emperor wants me to take his son to be my companion," the dragonet said. "I did not want to come out and at once have to say *yes* or *no,* when I did not know what was best.

There is so much that is unclear from inside the shell! I have been trying to think how I might arrange to avoid committing myself. It would certainly be best if we should get away quietly, before anyone knows I have hatched."

"Well, now you are out of the shell, you will have to manage things for yourself," Iskierka said. "I am certainly not going anywhere without Granby *now*."

"Or Laurence," Temeraire added, with a feeling of strong indignation: so all his fears had been for nothing, and the egg had never been in any danger of indignity at all. So much for Lien talking of *poor mongrels*—at least Napoleon could recognize true quality, in a dragon. "We are not going to abandon them, only because you cannot make up your mind."

"That," the dragonet said, "is quite rude. I hope I am not to be called *indecisive,* only because I mean to make a careful choice. But I will pardon you, as of course you are anxious for your companions. I do not expect you to abandon them! Besides, we will never get away with everyone looking for us like this. Plainly we must have a diversion, and at once." She looked over at the palace, and tipped her head consideringly. "It is a pity, of course, but I cannot see any alternative."

Temeraire was just about to inquire what additional sort of diversion she imagined they might be able to produce, which would not merely draw everyone's attention to them straightaway, when she shook out her wings and leapt into the air. "No!" Temeraire hissed out in alarm. "Wait, come back; you will be seen at once!"

She was flying directly towards the house. The heads of several of the dragons were already turning towards her wingbeats.

"That is all that we needed," Temeraire said, despairingly. "We had better go back to our pavilion at once, before she has got herself caught. Perhaps she will take the blame for it all: and serve her right."

"I don't want to go back to our pavilion!" Iskierka said. "We will only go back to being prisoners, and I am sure they will lock

Granby away much better, no matter what excuse we give. Anyway, what do you suppose she is planning?"

"I do not know, and I don't suppose she has *planned* anything," Temeraire began, only to jerk his head around as a thin
shrill whine pierced all the clamor, very like a pot boiling under-
neath a badly fitted lid. His ruff flattened against his skull involuntarily: a truly dreadful noise, and it kept rising so. The rest of the
dragons began to make complaining sounds—not merely the
guards but everywhere through the grounds, heads rising up on all
sides.

"Why must she make that dreadful noise?" Iskierka said, jetting out a ring of steam in expression of her own displeasure. It
was indeed the dragonet, Temeraire realized—she was hovering
directly over the house now, escaping notice because all the other
dragons were twisting their heads away from the noise, and then
abruptly she pointed her head down and blasted out a stream of
white flame directly along the ridge cap of the immensely long grey
roof. It was quite thin, but it ran away from her with tremendous
speed, rippling strangely, and a moment later a shockingly loud
thunderclap noise followed it, as nearly every window in the building burst.

Temeraire found he had hunched into himself, head ducked
under a wing for shelter, entirely without meaning to. He shook
himself out. Glass was raining down with a tinkling noise, like the
box of magnificent porcelain he had seen shattered on delivery, in
New South Wales, ruined beyond repair—he still remembered the
carnage with regret—and the roof was in flames, all over. "Laurence!" he cried out in staring horror, and flung himself into the
air.

"Is it Temeraire?" Granby shouted over the dreadful shrieking
noise, and Laurence could only shake his head without answering.
It was like nothing he had ever heard in eight years of his experience of the divine wind, but Temeraire before now had managed

to make some new and unexpected use of his abilities, and Laurence could not be sure. Their guards at least had no doubts, he saw from their faces, nor any lack of horror. Brouilly's grip on Laurence's arm, above the elbow, was bidding fair to squeeze all the blood from that limb as Aurigny led the way, the guards dragging them urgently down the staircase, surely towards some holding-place below.

Laurence was in an odd state to be flung into a dungeon: he had been dressing for dinner, and he was yet in the evening clothes which had earlier been sent him by the same emperor who had now commanded his imprisonment: knee-breeches with polished buckles, silk stockings and slippers, and his cravat just properly creased; a new coat in deep aviator's green, lined with golden-yellow silk. The guards had burst in upon them unannounced just as Laurence had shrugged his way into the coat, and without ceremony or explanation had bundled them all off at once down the hallway. Laurence understood well enough; he had not even been unprepared, thanks to Tharkay's earlier news. Temeraire and Iskierka had acted; they had been seen in some act of rebellion or escape, and the French now meant to secure their hostages. He would have liked to know what had happened, but there was no chance to ask in the confusion, and the guards in no mood to answer.

They had been bundled, pell-mell-tumble fashion, all the way along the hall and down one turn of the stairs, towards the ground floor and the kitchens. Then the thunder had come. Laurence looked round with his ears still ringing, and all down the full length of the hall the massive windows burst: a noise like a broadside full-on through the stern cabin of a first-rate, glass and splinters flying. A sheeting wave of white flame came washing down the outer wall, and reached in roaring through the shattered frames.

"Good God!" Granby said, shouting and yet muffled in Laurence's half-deadened ears. The carpets were already aflame, and smoke was pouring into the hallway through every crack and open door, grey waves accompanied with screaming.

Brouilly, single-minded in the face of disaster, tried to continue onwards onto the cellar stairs, but Laurence caught the corner of the wall and planted himself. "No," he said, shouting to be heard. "No: I would rather be shot here, than driven below to roast alive. I have no idea what has happened, but there will be no escaping this house in ten minutes. We must get outside at once: where is the nearest door?"

Brouilly looked down at his senior; Aurigny halted two steps down the stairs and turned, staring up at them a moment out of the dark, irresolute; abruptly he came back up and demanded, "Monsieur, will you swear you had no part of this?"

"I can give you my word as a gentleman," Laurence said, "and although I cannot answer with certainty for my dragon, I will say Temeraire is not a fool, and I do not suppose, even if he could accomplish the act, that he would willfully set fire to a house where he knew perfectly well I was prisoner. I do not know what has happened, but he is hardly the only one who might wish your master any ill: where is *he*?"

This decided the matter; Brouilly said to Aurigny, "My God! What matter if they do go free, if the Emperor is lost?" and deserting their prisoners, the Guardsmen turned and rushed up the stairs they had just descended, going in leaps and bounds over the smoke that came rolling down the stairs to meet them in eddying waves.

"We seem to be abandoned to our own devices," Tharkay said. "May I suggest the nearest window, however, in preference to a door? I will take being singed over choking."

Laurence halted in the landing, halfway to following him, when a dreadful thought struck: "The child," he said abruptly, as Granby and Tharkay turned to look back at him. "The Emperor and Empress meant to dine with us; the boy would have been in the nursery by now."

The smoke was growing ever thicker as they forced their way up, past the torrent, back to their own landing. Men and women were running down the stairs in a frenzy to escape, coughing and half-blind. Laurence stepped into the hall to seize one of the enormous vases along the wall, full of flowers; he flung the flowers down and wetted himself and his cravat, wrapping it over his face, and handed it on to Granby and Tharkay.

"I suppose this is a judgment on me, for saying I should be grateful for any excuse not to go to dinner," Granby said, grimly, dousing himself thoroughly. "Let's hurry: I am damned if I am going to die trying to rescue the crown prince of France."

They went up another flight. In their rooms they had now and again heard a noise of childish wails and nursemaids singing, coming from above; now they ran down the halls, opening every door, until they found a room strewn with toys: the curtains ablaze and the silken carpet beginning to catch, and the loud determined cries of a distressed child coming from behind another door.

While Tharkay and Granby took the bottom edge of the carpet and dragged it away from the flames, folding it double and stamping upon it, Laurence ran to the inner door and threw it wide to find the bedchamber thick with smoke: one of the nursemaids lying on the floor by the window screaming, on the sooty wreck of a blanket that been used to smother her, her hair blackened and her blistered hands covering her face, while another huddled against the back wall with the crying child in her arms. The third was standing before them, beating at the flames catching around them with a wetted rag.

Laurence hurdled a line of flames and caught her by the arm. "Get out of the room!" he said, and the young woman cried out and pointed: he turned to find a single monstrous smoke-reddened eye peering in anxiously through the shattered glass and flames, calling.

Laurence dredged up a few words of Quechua: "This way!" he shouted out to the dragon, motioning to the next room. He turning caught the second nursemaid, with the child in her arms, and wrapping the wet sheet around her dragged her through the flames, the child between their bodies. Granby had pulled down the curtains with his hook-hand, arm wrapped in his sodden cloak, and now the dragon was tearing out the burning window-frame, emitting howls of pain as it did.

All at once wood and brick gave way, crumbling open a wide

gap in the wall. The Incan dragon put its foreleg through the hole, and they got the nursemaids and the child carefully into its talons. Laurence and Tharkay dashed back into the burning bedroom— the other woman had fallen silent, and she lay heavy and limp in their arms as they carried her out, her skin red and scorched. As they heaved her into the dragon's claw, a roaring from outside, and the sound of beating wings: through smoke Laurence glimpsed Lien, her white belly lit brilliant orange by the flames, hovering before the house. She was calling something out; the Incan dragon called back, "Wait, wait!" urgently, and snatching its precious burden drew its talons out of the opening.

"Maintenant!" Laurence heard Lien call, and from above a sudden deluge of dirt and water came pouring down the sides of the house, splattering enormous gouts through the gap in the wall. Laurence put his head out, afterwards, for a quick look up: fires still burned inside the house, licking out of the windows, but at least the outside had been smothered.

He turned as the door behind him flung open: Napoleon, with a party of Guardsmen crowding behind him, Aurigny among them—the Emperor also resplendent in a magnificent coat of red wool, now badly marred with soot. He stared at Laurence wildly, with the momentary bafflement of one trying to make sense of an unexpected meeting, and then leaping forward seized Laurence by the arms. "My son?" he demanded.

"Safely away," Laurence said, pointing out at Lien, and the Incan dragon that had gone to join her.

One of the guards sprang to the opening—unwary, as Lien called out, *"Encore!"* and a second torrent came down the walls and carried him out of the window-hole and away, his feet slipping in the mud already present. The wave subsided; out of the hesitating body of guards Aurigny leapt forward, and cupping hands around his mouth bellowed, *"L'Empereur est ici!"*

Two others followed him, all calling together, and Lien's head swung around as though pulled on a string; she had heard. She dived through the smoke, and the Guardsmen pushed him forward in a knot as Lien reached in for him. "The Empress!" Napoleon said, resisting.

"Safely out by now, Sire!" Aurigny was shouting as the men thrust him into the urgent talons.

Laurence started: Tharkay had his arm and Granby's, and was drawing them back. "There is a room with no smoke coming out, three windows down the hall," he said, low. They covered their mouths and ran through the haze of the hallway to the third door, and kicking their way in found a bare room halfway through cleaning, the curtains stripped and in a heap on the floor. One of the window-frames was burning, but the other, though blackened, had not caught. They unhooked the window and pushed it wide. Down the side of the building, Lien was lifting away with Napoleon, and two middle-weight dragons were crowding in to the window to rescue the Guards.

There were many ledges running along the outside walls, some as wide as a man's foot, and the building was not pitching back and forth, which made the climb down light work for a sailor, much less an aviator. In ten minutes, they dropped down onto the lawns, not too wretchedly singed and bruised, and as he rolled to his feet Laurence heard a voice over the pandemonium, calling, "Laurence! Laurence!"

There was nothing to do but hope the confusion would save them: Laurence shouted, "Here! Temeraire, over here!" and Temeraire came down beside him with a gasp of relief.

"Oh Laurence!" he said, snatching him up at once. "I flew round and round and I could not see you in the least. I will wring her neck, see if I do not!"

"Don't tell me Iskierka has done all this!" Granby said, already tumbling into Temeraire's other claw with Tharkay.

"No!" Temeraire said. "It is not Iskierka's fault, except it is, for she *would* have an egg with the divine wind and fire both, and just look where that has landed us!"

"Free, and with your captains," the dragonet said, which silenced
Temeraire and Iskierka, in the midst of their heartily upbraiding
her. She lifted a claw and licked her talons neatly—bloodstained,
as though having fired the palace, she had taken a moment to go
get herself something to eat. Recalling the voracious appetite of
new-hatched dragons, Laurence supposed this was indeed the case,
as she would otherwise have been complaining extremely. He
stared down at the deceptively small creature in some dismay. She
seemed entirely untroubled by the enormous chaos she had
wreaked: in the distance behind them, clouds of smoke still blotted
out half the night sky, and the palace was still limned in the reddish
glow of embers.

"But that is only by good luck!" Temeraire said.

"I do not deny there was a risk," the dragonet said judiciously,
"but one must take risks occasionally to achieve one's ends, when
there is no better way of going about it. There is no sense lamenting a necessary evil."

"It was *not* necessary for you to nearly burn up Granby," Iskierka said stormily, "and the next time you mean to *take risks,* you
may take them with *your* companion, and not mine. Why you
couldn't have made up your mind to take Napoleon's son, I am
sure I don't know. He will be an emperor, too: it is all muchwhat-
like."

"That," the dragonet said severely, "is an extremely shortsighted remark. As though one emperor were just the same as another, to all purposes!"

"It would certainly *not* be as good, as to be companion to the
Emperor of China," Temeraire said, "but for my part I do not see
why you should have ever needed to consider becoming a *traitor,*
and joining the enemy."

"That term I reject, for I should have betrayed no-one in making such a choice: my loyalty has *not* been given either to China,
or Britain, *or* France," the dragonet said with a martial light in her
eye, drawing herself up and thrusting her head forward in challenge towards Temeraire, although his muzzle loomed larger than
her entire body. "I recall you telling me quite clearly that the choice

of companion should be my own: did you only mean, so long as I should choose a companion agreeable to *you*?"

"Oh, well," Temeraire said, and drew his own head back to rub against his flank in a gesture of embarrassment; Laurence indeed recalled overhearing him make such muttered lectures to the egg in its shell, when it had first sat in state upon the *Potentate*. "But I do not see why you should at all *want* to join the French, after they stole our egg, and after Napoleon has caused so much trouble for everyone."

Satisfied to have defended her honor, the dragonet settled back down onto her haunches. "I cannot say that I have perceived any distinction among the nations of the world," she answered, "which should entitle any of them to either my full approval *or* condemnation. I have heard more than enough, being carted here and there and exchanged from one side to another, to persuade me that none are without blame for this unhappy state of quarreling and perpetual warfare. *That,* I can heartily condemn. It seems perfectly plain to me that it is war itself which must be halted, without wanting one side or another defeated in particular."

She spoke severely. Laurence supposed her time in the shell had certainly been an alarming period enough to give her a distaste for its cause, if she had been aware through much of it to remember; but she did not seem to have grown shy—perhaps not surprising, when she had already produced a disaster of such magnitude while not yet the size of a pony. It augured ominously for her future capabilities, and he could not help but be concerned to find her so willing to entertain all suitors.

"Certainly the war must be halted," Temeraire said. "That is precisely why we mean to defeat Napoleon."

"That would stop *this* war," the dragonet said. "But I am quite certain that it would not end *all* war. I dare say you and your allies would all quarrel among yourselves straightaway, and start a new one."

"Well, if there were *no* war, anywhere, how could one ever take a prize?" Iskierka put in. "That would not be agreeable at all."

"I would be very happy to see war come to an end, myself; although a neat little skirmish now and then, with a prize after, no-one could really object to, I think," Temeraire said. "But I should like to know a great deal how you suppose anyone should accomplish *that*."

"Well, I don't know, yet," the dragonet said, "but I mean to find a way: just because the business will be *difficult* is no excuse for not making the attempt. But of course my choice of companion is of great importance. I am not sure that the Emperor of France would not be best situated, after all, to help me."

"You may be sure Napoleon will not want anything to do with you after *this*," Temeraire said.

"Nonsense," the dragonet said. "Most likely he does not even know I have hatched yet. Since you have escaped, I dare say he will blame the two of you, instead, and if anyone *did* see me do it, why, I am newly hatched, and no-one could expect me to know exactly what I was doing. Perhaps it was only an accident, or perhaps you even set me on it."

"We did not, at all!" Temeraire said, with a gasp of indignation.

The dragonet flicked her tail-tip back and forth to wave this away. "I am only saying there are any number of reasonable explanations he might settle on, should he wish to excuse me. And I am sure he would wish to, if I chose to join his side; I imagine he will be quite impressed with what I can do," which was inarguable. "I did hope it would answer," she added, with a note of satisfaction, "after all this talk I have heard in the shell of the conjunction of the divine wind and fire-breathing, but I could not be quite sure until I had tried it. I am glad to have made proofs of it!

"But I cannot yet tell whether the Emperor of China or the Emperor of France will be better suited to assist my task. Or," she added, earnestly, "perhaps the King of Britain: I hope you do not think I am unwilling to consider *him*. So hadn't we better be getting under way? Which way is this Dover of yours, that you want to get to?"

"Laurence," Granby said, when at last they bedded down just before dawn, "what a perfect terror: what are we going to do with her?"

They were some ten miles from Dieppe as best Laurence could guess—they had found an isolated farm in disrepair, the house and barn abandoned, the latter with a collapsing roof: Temeraire and Iskierka were now hunkered down behind it, with a stand of trees and undergrowth to screen them from at least a first glance, if not a second. The dragonet, having slept nearly all the day on Temeraire's back, had roused only long enough to go and fetch a heap of straw out of the gaping hayloft; she made herself a nest in the warmest hollow between her progenitors, and satisfied with her arrangements went directly back to sleep.

Laurence was arranging handfuls of dry straw himself, with splinters, to make tinder for the armful of wood Granby set down. The fire would be a fresh risk, but in the half-light of morning the smoke might pass unnoticed: they were a good distance from any road but a half-overgrown track. The night had been cold, and they had none of them been dressed for flying: even huddled with Granby and Tharkay in one of Iskierka's talons, and held against the churning warmth of her belly, a heavy chill had settled deep into Laurence's limbs; he thought they must have a little warmth before they dared sleep.

"What Napoleon would make of her, if she should throw in with him, I don't like to think," Granby went on. "Of all the dragons to come into the world unharnessed!"

"We will deliver her to Dover," Laurence said firmly. "I am sure Whitehall will be delighted to restore her to Prince Mianning, and repair the alliance with China thereby. I trust we can rely upon their skill in the handling of dragons, from there, to make her happy to be the future Emperor's companion. You will recall that they do not harness beasts, until later in their lives, at all."

"I suppose we can't do better," Granby said. "The Chinese

may say what they like, and I am sure it answers for *them;* but I should be a great deal easier if this one had a captain to call her to order from the moment she came out of the shell."

"You will permit me a little skepticism as to the hypothetical man's likely success," Tharkay said, coming back into the barn and putting down an armful of potatoes and carrots, which he might as well have conjured out of the air. "There is a vegetable garden against the side of the house; it seemed likely," he answered their surprised looks. "We are fortunate in our choice of hiding-place, I think: there were some letters inside from a son gone to be a soldier, written to a widowed mother—the latest half a year old, from Smolensk, and unopened. I dare say there are many young men who will not be coming home."

The sunrise was giving a mellowing warmth to the weathered grey boards of the barn, and gilding the edges of the bare branches. There was a comfortable familiarity to all the arrangements of the farm that made the absence of life all the more disquieting. There ought to have been lowing cows and a gabble of chickens, and a farmer hurrying with half-closed eyes to tend his stock. Instead, empty stalls and silence, and untended fields just beyond the doors: the cost of Napoleon's wars.

They roused Iskierka just enough to start the fire with a gout of flame spat onto their carefully scraped ground; her eyes lidded down again at once. The half-frozen bounty of the garden roasted in the coals as they warmed their hands and numbed feet, and melted snow to drink hot out of a tin pail left hanging on a hook. Laurence scratched in the dirt his best memory of the coastline, and they considered the distance.

"We had better go by sea, if we think they can manage it," Granby said.

"I will be so bold as to be certain that we are scarcely a hundred miles from Eastbourne, flown north-north-west," Laurence said, "and once we are fairly into the Channel, most ships of the blockade can throw us out some pontoons if we should get into trouble with a cross-wind. We may have some difficulty signaling, if they do not recognize us."

"*That* don't worry me," Granby said. "It would be wonderful indeed if any captain who has been in the Channel since the year seven didn't remember Iskierka, and curse to see her coming to snatch a prize out from under his teeth. They would be heartily delighted to see her drown, but I suppose they shan't turn us away if we appear on their doorstep, as it were. We'll have to go on from there to Dover straightaway, though—there's a covert at East-bourne, but it is not much more than a courier-stop; they won't like us dropping by with a couple of heavy-weights and a fresh-hatched beast."

"Do you insist upon making for a covert?" Tharkay said, un-expectedly. "I trust you will forgive my raising a point of con-cern," he added, when they looked in puzzlement, "but do you suppose your hatchling likely to be impressed by the conditions she will find at Dover, compared with those she has lately left behind—before she set them on fire, that is."

"Well," Granby said, and halted there. Of course he could not without pain admit any evil of Britain's coverts, when held against those of France, and Laurence shared his sentiments of loyalty to the service; but there was no denying that the disparity would be a marked one, unless such changes had been made in their five years' absence as they could hardly hope for. Temeraire had kept up an irregular correspondence with Perscitia, a comrade of his breeding-ground days who had energetically pursued in his absence the liberties—and prosperity—of dragons. Her letters when they came were universally a litany of complaint, cataloguing obstruction in every direction.

"Let us get out of France, first," Laurence said, after a mo-ment. "We must content ourselves with escaping Bonaparte's bor-ders before we can entertain other concerns."

Laurence stirred in the late afternoon, conscious of some near presence, and opened his eyes to find the dragonet staring very intently directly into his face, the long arrow-shaped head ex-tended to the full length of her serpentine neck. He could see her colors now, and also the difficulty of making them out: the underlying color of her hide was certainly black, but heavily overlaid with an opalescence of red and green and blue which became dominant at the extremities of limbs and wings, almost casting off a reflection.

"Good," she said, drawing back to let him sit up. "You have woken up. I am very sorry to be the cause of difficulty, but I am afraid I must have some more food at once."

She was not wrong about the difficulty. The sun was still well up, despite winter, and neither Temeraire nor Iskierka could possibly go aloft in settled countryside like this and not be noticed at once against the sky. The farmers would certainly raise an alarm, and even if there were no pursuit close enough to pounce upon them immediately, the entire coast in flying distance would be roused against them.

"Over the Channel, Temeraire will certainly be able to get you a decently sized tunny to eat," Laurence said. "Can you only wait until sunset?"

She looked up at the sky, and then turned back and said firmly, "I cannot."

"I don't see that we must wait. I would not mind a cow myself, now I think of it," Iskierka muttered, having been half-roused by the discussion.

"*That* is all we need," Granby said, rubbing a hand over his own face as he sat up.

"Perhaps we might make some broth, if anything more can be found," Laurence said.

They all dug in the garden for a few more leavings of vegetables, and Tharkay managed to take a squirrel with a stone, although this was not much to put into their stolen pot. A few handfuls of old barley were the only other addition, found in a cupboard. As they stirred the fire urgently, Granby said to Laurence, under his breath, "Are you sure you don't want to try and put some harness on her? I suppose Temeraire wouldn't like it in the least, but a dragonet's hunger is no joke. Her patience will go hang before we can make this fit to eat, I expect."

"*I* would not like it in the least, either," the dragonet said, poking her head up over the rim of the soup-cauldron unexpectedly, having overheard. "Besides, I am perfectly capable of seeing for myself that concealment is of the essence, at present. So that is quite enough of that sort of talk."

"Oh, Lord," Granby said, with a start.

"You might hurry up that soup, instead," she added, in reproachful tones.

"We are hurrying it as fast as ever we can," Granby said. "And in the meantime, you may as well decide, what are we going to call you? I suppose you can't wait for a captain to hand you a name, if you don't mean to settle for anything short of an emperor."

"You may call me Lung Tien Ning," the dragonet said. "That will satisfy the Emperor of China, as he does not expect to name his companion, but requires me to be considered a Celestial; and the Emperor of France may always give me a French name later, if I like."

"As though she has any right to be called *tranquility*," Temeraire muttered to Laurence, who could not disagree.

But Granby's pessimistic shake over the soup was at least mistaken: Ning did pounce upon the pot immediately the barley was toothsome enough to chew, but she waited patiently until they had pronounced it ready, and even then drank the soup down slowly in measured delicate swallows, pausing halfway through to demand that they add some more snow to the pot and heat it up again: evidently trying to trick her own belly into a temporary complacency.

"There," she said at last, having licked the pot not merely clean but dry, "I think I can manage until dark, now. I hope it will be soon!"

She slept again afterwards, and so managed to last until sunset: but then she had reached her limits. She roused Laurence again with a sharp nudge of her head, the sun lowering and golden beneath the tree-tops and a grey chill descending. "How long until I can have that fish?" she demanded.

There were lights clustered ahead of them to the west, gathering more closely as they neared the coast where five years before Napoleon had mustered and launched his invasion. Only a quarter-moon rising, fortunately. Ning hunched on Temeraire's back, restless and scraping the sides of her claws against his scales—a dusty noise that crept forward into Laurence's ears and along his spine.

He had preferred to stay aboard Temeraire for this flight, despite the cold, when they might too easily be separated from Iskierka during the crossing. There was too much uncertain in their position, under British law, for him to be glad to send Temeraire flying alone, without anyone who might more easily be heard by a naval captain who knew more of their disgrace and transportation than of their more recent pardon. Those men might remember Iskierka's pillaging their prizes, but they would remember also the final disaster of the invasion, the sinking of Nelson's fleet, and all accomplished by a single Celestial. The silhouette of the sinuous body, the horns and frilled ruff, had been the subject of many an artist's mourning, and whether dark or light would be unwelcome overhead to any ship or shore battery.

"There is a Fleur-de-Nuit flying out there, I think," Temeraire said low, turning his head back a little. "I saw someone cross against the stars, there to the south: she may have seen us."

Laurence nodded. The word would be out for them by now, all up and down the coast. He leaned forward to look down past Temeraire's shoulder, a cupped hand shielding his eyes against the wind: the bobbing of fishing-boats tied up on shore and the lighthouse flashing near Dieppe a firefly-beacon. They were nearly out over the water.

And then a sudden flare going out, mid-air, blue and hissing—in its burst, Iskierka was lit vividly against the flattened black of the sky, her reds and greens made shades of black and grey, and to the south, not three miles distant, were three Fleur-de-Nuit dragons all hunting together. Temeraire stretched out long and flew, as the beacon-fires went up beneath them.

Part III

"BY GOD, TO HAVE spent two days mid-air for this," Wellington said. "No, you may *not* have Roland. If you want another admiral in Spain, you may find another general while you are at it, and I will go home and sleep for a month."

"Your Grace, I beg you will understand the Admiralty's position," the Prime Minister said wearily. He threw a glance of distaste in Laurence's direction, which would not have had the power to wound him, save that Perceval had known his father, and been welcome in their home: he had only the prior year at last shepherded through the formal abolition of the slave trade, and had even begun to open tentative relations with the Tswana, in the teeth of much opposition from those whose estates, in the West Indies, relied heavily upon slaves. Laurence could not be glad to meet with disapproval in such a quarter, even if he were not surprised.

Wellington only snorted. "I understand well enough: you dislike requiring the services of a man you would rather see hanged. Since you do require them, more's the pity, you must take your bread as you find it and stop asking for pudding."

"Your Grace," Mr. Yorke said—the present First Lord of the Admiralty—"surely the urgency of the situation in Prussia—"

"The situation in Prussia!" Wellington said. "I have not fifty British dragons, with three hundred ragged Spanish and Portuguese beasts, most of them half-feral, to match against five hundred trained French dragons, and you want to bleat at me about Prussia. Bad enough you called Roland and myself away for a week: I dare say we will find half a dozen villages reduced to rubble by the time we get back, and the Flechas threatening to burn down Madrid. Now you tell me," with a sharp wave in Laurence's direction, "that Bonaparte will have four thousand beasts to throw at us in a year, half-trained and half-grown or not. And you want to snatch my aerial commander and waste her as a false front? Nonsense."

"Nonsense, indeed," Jane said, later that evening, in her house near the London covert. "Worse than nonsense. I am just as glad they did leave me out of the conference, after all. I do not trust what I would have said to them if I had been there. I have got spoilt, Laurence; I have not had to deal with any foolishness of this sort for a year and more. The Spanish officers would try and fuss me a little, at first, but I have got them flying straight by now."

She sighed, and reached for the decanter of port. She was incongruous in her heavy boots and aviator's coat amidst the velvets of her sitting-room, which better matched the coronet than its owner. Laurence knew she had applied to his own mother for advice on setting up her establishment, and her house-keeper was familiar to him—she had once been a young scullery-maid at Wollaton Hall and willing to permit a small boy to snatch an occasional pastry when a banquet was in the offing.

An informed taste had left its stamp upon the house, and its comforts were many: the fire laid to the precisely right degree, excellent wine at dinner, and all the furnishings of the best. Jane alone was out of place, and Excidium drowsing in the wide courtyard behind the house: his head was just visible through the windows, with the bone spurs gleaming white in the lamp-light.

"I have gilded the tool-chest, and kept the rusty old hammer inside," Jane said, reading his face, and laughed at him when he tried to demur. "No, I meant to do just that. The place is my sacrifice to propriety. I have even given a dinner here, if you can conceive it," she added. "It was your mother's notion, and I felt I owed it to her, after all her efforts on my behalf. I oughtn't have doubted her, either, as it worked marvels: a dozen girls applied to the Corps the week after. They were all ladies of small fortune, who preferred it to going for governesses, except one heiress who preferred it to being sold off like a heifer calf. Their families made a noise over it, but I told their Lordships I wouldn't turn any girl away who could keep her stomach and her feet mid-air, when we have six Longwing eggs in the offing to consider.

"And speaking of which: how does Emily, when you last saw her? I thank you for her step, by the way."

"Very well," Laurence said, struggling to decide what to say of Emily's connection to Demane, which had formed under his watch. He had not quite the pain of having failed in his self-appointed duty of chaperonage—although he certainly would have done, if Emily had wished to discard her virtue—but an uneasiness remained; he did not think she was heart-whole. "Has she spoken to you of Demane?"

"She has written volumes of nothing," Jane said, "but that is all right: *he* has made up for it. He presented himself to me the instant the *Potentate* arrived in Spain, declared that he should make himself worthy, and raved up and down my tent about Emily's graces for a quarter of an hour before I gave up waiting for him to be done and shoved him along—not too urgently, Laurence, you needn't look so worried. I haven't any complaints of the boy. A milder, sweeter-tempered creature than that monster of his, I have never met: it is just as well for Kulingile's captain to have some fire in his belly, when his beast has none. Do you mean to tell me Emily is going to break her heart over him?"

"Not break it, I hope," Laurence said, but slowly, and Jane read most of what he wished to say in his face. She shook her head a little.

"I never had much sensibility, myself—as you have cause to

know, dear fellow. I have found it a luxury beyond my means. But she might as well marry him as not. I put my foot down and insisted they legitimize her, when they put the titles on me: if Wellesley can hand his coronet on to his brats when he spent all of ten minutes begetting them, damned if Emily was not getting mine. But there was quite the squabble over it, and I doubt they'll let it go a second generation. So if she cares to hand it onwards, she will need to marry someone, and Captain Dlamini is respectable enough for anybody, I imagine."

Jane imagined incorrectly, at least so far as the polite world would see it: an orphan boy from Africa with only a dragon to his name made no match for Lady Emily Roland, the daughter of one of England's great heroes and the heiress to a coronet and a fortune. Of course, that Lady Emily was herself an aviator diminished her own luster a little, but when that service was the source of her titles, much would have been forgiven. Still, Laurence knew those considerations weighed not at all with Jane, who said only, "But she will scarcely see him one year to the next, chances are. Excidium is for Dover, and Kulingile will certainly be for Gibraltar, if ever we muddle our way back to peacetime. Well, it is a hard service." She rubbed her mouth. "I suppose I may as well keep him with me, and give them more of a chance to forget one another. I had considered sending him along to Prussia, and taking Granby back—but we have the Flechas for fire-breathers, even if they are not so handy as Iskierka, and you may be in want of Granby's advice, in any case. So they are giving you your flag?"

"Yes," Laurence said, staring into the wine glass. It seemed still to him almost a subtle mockery; he had not understood, until nearly the end of the meeting, that the ministers were arguing with Wellington over naming him to the aerial command, forming now, which would join the allied effort in Prussia. "Or at least, that seemed their intention, by the close; I can scarcely conceive they will do it."

"Oh, they will," Jane said. "A little bird has sung in my ear that the Tsar wants you: how did you manage that? I have never known you to ingratiate yourself with anyone whose influence would be really useful to your career, when you could make yourself as inconvenient to them as possible instead."

"I cannot claim any personal success in the matter," Laurence said dryly. "I appeared on his borders with an army of dragons when he was in imminent danger of defeat; I suppose it must have produced a degree of warm feeling."

"Well, we won't hold it against your record," Jane said. "And he is the man of the hour, make no mistake. I am never quite easy with these God-is-in-my-pocket sorts—begging your pardon—but if it keeps him zealous to be the savior of Europe, I shan't complain. We will certainly never get another chance at Boney, from what news you bring. Four thousand eggs! Our breeders would dearly like to know how he has managed it, and our supply-officers how he means to feed them. For my part, though, I will settle for having good old fat Louis back on his throne before they are grown."

She reached over to fill his glass: the port had been drunk, somehow. Laurence sat back into his chair, restless. The Tsar's request made the Admiralty's difficulty more clear: if Alexander had asked for Laurence, they must send him; and sending him, they could supersede him only with an officer of greater seniority, who must furthermore by necessity possess a dragon whose stature would outweigh or at least equal Temeraire's in the eyes of their fellow dragons. There were few British officers who could claim either distinction: thanks to Hammond's machinations, Laurence had been fully reinstated, so his seniority dated not from Temeraire's harnessing, but from his being made post as a naval officer, some five years prior to the date.

And yet that was not sufficient argument for his fitness for the task: nearly all his own education at sea, not eight years on the wing, and that spent in an irregular fashion. He could not sensibly recognize himself as anyone's first choice for command, even independent of animus.

"Should you *not* come to Prussia, Jane?" he said, low. The

Admiralty might think to send Jane as a comforting fiction drawn over his presence, but Laurence knew her abilities; and Excidium, with his long and storied career, and a Longwing's deadly vitriol, would easily command the respect of any fighting-dragons. Temeraire had been willing to defer to him before now. "If he is to be defeated, he must be beaten in Germany."

"No, Laurence," Jane said firmly. "He must be beaten in France."

He fell silent. To fight Napoleon back across the Rhine and the Pyrenees both, step by hard-won step, taking back all the victories fifteen years of war had won him: it loomed an impossible project.

Jane set her glass down, after a final swallow to toss down the rest, and drew open one of the rolled maps littering the table between them. "Don't look quite so gloomy. I dare say you have no notion how many men he is losing in Spain. The numbers from the battlefields don't tell the tale, but my scouts see it from aloft. The guerrillas nibble nibble nibble, like little mice, and his armies melt away on the road."

She drew her finger along the map, the jagged mountain-lines marking the borders between France and Spain, and then let it go to roll up again. "We *will* have Soult by next Christmas, or call me a liar. But it has taken Wellington three hard-fought years to stitch up this army, and it is held by frayed thread and dull tacks. There ain't someone to take my place in the air. I left Crenslow in charge this week, and you would have thought I was sending the poor man to the gallows, from the looks he gave. At that, there were seven Spanish and Portuguese officers at my heels clamoring for his head by the time we took flight.

"I don't say that you won't have troubles of your own in Germany, but the Prussian dragons have good cause to love you, and the Tsar can make the rest of them dance to his tune. So you must get across the Rhine without me, and we'll meet again in Paris, by and by," she finished.

"Granby would do better," Laurence said.

Jane snorted. "Iskierka won't," an inarguable return. "Besides,

you can give him ten years on the list and more. No, their Lordships haven't any other choice. Aside from everything else, we are
all hoping for some Chinese beasts to appear. Unless, could they
put this Hammond fellow in charge?"

Laurence almost smiled at the thought of Hammond made an
aerial commander, and that gentleman's certain dismay. "His
dragon might do. She has forty years' experience as an officer with
the Incan armies."

"If you wanted a prospect less likely than their Lordships'
making *you* admiral, giving the command to an Incan dragon will
do nicely," Jane said. "Not that the creatures don't know their
business, *I* can tell you: we have had a dozen of them to worry
about since last August, and they are worth three times their
fighting-weight in other beasts. The only saving grace is they hate
to lose even a single crewman, and if we manage to heave over a
boarding party of four or five, well-secured, we can bargain them
out of the day's fighting just to save a single bellman's life, even if
they outnumber us three to one. *Well-secured* being the real difficulty: they are quick as lightning at throwing us off, otherwise.
You will have a wretched time with those thieves in the Commissariat, by the bye," she added. "It has been nothing but bales of
rotting leather and rusted buckles, and what they call oilskins I call
barley-sacks," as though he were already in command.

She paused, seeing his look, and added, "You won't refuse it?"

"No," he said after a moment. "No, I will not refuse." Whatever his quarrels with the men of the Admiralty, there was in his
own understanding of duty a wide gulf between the necessary de-
fiance of an immoral order, and refusing to undertake a task only
because it was difficult, or demanded any private discomfort. If he
could have proposed a man better fitted for the urgent task, he
would feel the matter differently, but from that escape he was
barred by the continuing resentment of all the ministers and officers he had offended: they would argue far more vigorously than
he for the virtues of any conceivable substitute. If he were offered
the command, he might be sure he was the only choice.

"But Jane," he said abruptly, "I will not—I cannot accept un-less they reinstate Ferris, and promise him his chance. I cannot. That I should be reinstated, promoted, appointed to command, and *he* still bear the stain of the crime which I committed, entirely without his knowledge—it is intolerable to every feeling."

"Oh, I dare say that can be managed," Jane said. "His is an old family in the Corps, and they have a great deal of influence. The wolves were howling for blood too loudly at the time for them to make any difference, but this will change matters. I will write old Admiral Gloucester, who served with Ferris's great-uncle, and we will set the wheels turning."

They discussed the command a long time onwards; she gave him names of men to search out and others to avoid, both in the Commissariat and in his officers—as best he could; Laurence knew better than to suppose he would have much power of choice save among Temeraire's own crew, and perhaps not even there. The Admiralty was certain to name all the beasts of his company. But he made note of the men she recommended and spoke against; on the battlefield, the Admiralty would be far away, and the decisions his.

He had written a sheet both sides and crossed it, full of her good advice, and the clock had struck ten; then Jane said, "You may as well stay the night, if you like," and he was staring at a meaningless scratch of ink, his mouth gone abruptly dry with want. He had not permitted himself the license of hoping—of coming near enough hope even to think of—

"Jane," he said, all at once vividly aware of her bare hand on the table between them, strong and square, thinned a little by the years but deeply known, familiar, save for the yellow-jeweled sig-net and the white scar running between the two last fingers down the back, which had not been there before—before the shattering of his life. It had been late summer, an August night hot enough that they had left off the coverlet and lain naked together with the windows open, a devil's bargain between the London stench and the stifling heat. The next night he had betrayed her, and his coun-try, and flown with Temeraire to take the cure to France.

He had not touched her since. Nor any other woman. Not from loyalty—*loyalty* a word he had no right to use with her—but a deadening of some inward vital part, necessary to desire. They had spoken together; he had even been alone with her. But the door had been closed. He had not conceived that it might ever again open. "Jane," he said again.

She looked at him, with a little surprise, and then said, "Why, Laurence," and reached to take his hand.

He had been raised on decorum, that it should come as easily as breathing even in the face of death and tragedy. But his hand was twisted into her hair, the neat snug braid coming apart around his fingers, and the other shaking as he pulled open her neckcloth, on the Turkish rug before the sitting-room hearth with the table shoved over, the maps scattered and stirring in the draught.

Her mouth was wide and glad beneath his, laughing a little when he let her get her breath, and her hand bracing up his back. He dragged his cheek across the soft skin of her breast where the shirt hung loose, kissed her throat, luxuriated. He could not remember to be careful. They tangled themselves up, almost wrestling, until she said amused, "You will have us in the cinders: back your wings a moment," and sat up to push his coat off his shoulders.

His hands slid under the fine linen of her shirt, over the warm generous curving of her back, as she threw a leg over his hip. "Ah, there," she murmured, pleased. They moved together. The fire was crackling low, dying; she gasped.

He worried distantly that he might bruise her, his grip tight on her as he raised them both, her muscles shifting sweetly beneath his hands. She caught both her hands into his hair and bent forward to lean her forehead against his, smiling in the small, secret dark place between them, and he shuddered suddenly and completely, despite all the will in the world to hold off. He groaned in apology. "Graceless as a boy," he said, rueful, when he had his breath back again, and he tumbled her over onto her back to better use his hands to bring her. "I hope you will pardon me," he said, when she had sighed at last.

She laughed and kissed him. "I don't leave for Spain until to-morrow afternoon," she said. "You can make me a better show-ing in the morning," and then, practical, rolled up and went to wash.

They went upstairs carrying their boots, hand-in-hand, and left them in a heap in the corner of her bedroom. She pillowed herself comfortably against the headboard and lit a cigar, and blew a long, satisfied plume of smoke. He refused the one she offered him, lying flat on his back beside her and contemplating the can-opy without seeing it, his mind already catching on the hooks and burrs of planning, the immensity of the problem suddenly laid across his shoulders. "How many beasts will they give me, do you think?"

"Not more than twenty, I should think," Jane said. "If we can even supply that many. Two formations from Dover, and another from Edinburgh, I would expect."

Laurence was silent. He had learned enough of dragon-supply, he hoped, to make material improvements over the traditional standards of the Corps. He could not be fully confident of success, and he was wary of letting his force outstrip their means, but— twenty dragons would do very little, against the force assembling against them in France, and any legions from China would not arrive before late in the spring. "Would the Admiralty let me have more?" he asked. "If I should take unassigned middle-weights, and light-weights?"

"Light-weights are in short supply," Jane said. "Unless you can make Temeraire talk some ferals out of the stones for you, which I don't put past him. Of middle-weights, the Yellow Reapers have recovered nicely since the plague, most of them, and we have a good crowd of them *ex formatio*. There's a likely Reaper-Parnassian cross, too, a yearling now at Kinloch Laggan, under Captain Adair—a decent fellow. I expect they'd let you have her, if you ask after they've given you the rest of the beasts. How do you mean to feed them?"

"On corn and salt pork, and not beef," Laurence said. "Jane,

I will undertake to bring them to the battlefield, but I cannot set myself up as a tactician against officers with ten years' more experience in the air."

"The finest formations ha'nt done anyone in Europe a particle of good against Bonaparte these last six years," Jane said, "so as far as that goes, you know as much about facing him as anyone in the Corps: more, if you have learnt anything from the Chinese, which you ought have done. Besides, once you are in the air, the beasts will be following Temeraire, you know, and not really you, if that is a comfort." She snorted. "No-one can say he isn't a fair hand at talking other beasts into line. Although I hear he has met his match at last: tell me about this new terror you have visited upon us. I understand she is the despair of Whitehall, and has been issuing demands to be introduced to *our* prince, poor fellow, in case he should be more useful to her than Napoleon's heir, or the future Emperor of China?"

"And I wish to assure you, Temeraire, that I did mean to give this Prince of Wales of yours a fair trial," Ning said. "I would not like you to feel that I have acted with disrespect to your companion's nation and your home. But I am afraid it will not do: this business of Parliament must be an excessive inconvenience."

"That," Perscitia said, much ruffled beneath her sash and medal of office, which marked her as a member of that body, "is only because you do not properly appreciate the importance of the legislature, and its necessity to the promotion of our interests."

"I am afraid I cannot allow its advantages over a more direct exercise of power," Ning said.

"You are describing *Tyranny*," Perscitia said grandly—Temeraire heard the capital letter quite distinctly—"and a moment's reflection will show you its numerous flaws: only *one* can be a tyrant, and therefore such a political system will rarely be just, or serve the needs of all."

"That is lamentable, to be sure," Ning said practically,

"—unless one should happen to be the tyrant, whereupon it makes everything very easy."

"Temeraire," Perscitia said, when Ning had finished her cow and gone to sleep again, already ten feet longer than she had been that morning; now roughly three times the size of an elephant. "Temeraire, I hope you will forgive me, but that hatchling of yours has some peculiar notions."

"I am not certain she is *wrong,* however," Temeraire said doubtfully. Laurence had a very low opinion of tyranny, he knew, and therefore he felt himself obliged to despise it by commutation, but there was no denying that it had its uses. He looked around the London covert with some disfavor, remembering too well the beautiful grounds at Fontainebleau. There was a pavilion for them to sleep in now, which would once have seemed to him the height of luxury; but there was only one, extremely crowded, and not even as nice as the one where he and Iskierka had been housed at the training camps near the Alps.

There was nothing to beautify the arrangements, no fountains or even a pleasant courtyard; the pavilion had only been erected in the midst of the old clearings where they once had slept on bare dirt, and the paths among the trees were too narrow for anyone but a human to walk. The stones were not properly heated, either: there were several braziers going for warmth, but in all, the establishment did not stand up well to comparison with their recent prison.

"But it is entirely unreliable," Perscitia said. "*Now* Napoleon has decided to be fond of dragons, because he has learned to make us particularly useful in fighting his wars, and for that matter, quelling any of his enemies in France itself—but what of the tyrant who will come after him? What if the next emperor should decide that he does not like dragons? I would rather have the protection of law, and tradition, and know that whatever we have gained cannot be as easily taken away again. Temeraire, we must give real thought to the future. One day they will cast a cannon that can take a Regal out of the sky with one shot fired, and then where will we be?"

"Nonsense," Temeraire said uneasily. "I have been shot two dozen times myself, and there has been nothing so terrible about it. Of course a cannonball would be very unpleasant, but unless one goes too close to the ground, or flies into their path, they are not so difficult to avoid."

"There were no guns at all, five hundred years ago," Perscitia said. "I have been assured of it, by my secretaries."

"*That* is quite false," Temeraire said, glad to be able to contradict her. "They were invented during the Song dynasty, a thousand years ago: I have read of them in China."

"But even so they *were* invented—they did not always exist," Perscitia said, turning his information around to serve her own argument, which seemed to Temeraire unfair. "And Chinese guns are not as good as ours are now, and therefore guns have *improved,* and they will go on improving. What do you suppose will happen when they do not need us to make war anymore, and we are only very inconvenient and eat a great deal, and frighten most of them? They were quite willing to let a great many of us starve, when we were too sick to fly and hunt for ourselves, and they couldn't get eggs out of us anymore.

"No, it is no good our relying on any one king or emperor, and it is no good letting them only use us for battle. Oh! I am very glad you are come back, Temeraire. Even though I have been elected, there are still any number of dragons who will not listen to me at all, only because I am not large and do not like to fight all the time," she added peevishly. "But they will certainly mind *you,* and I am sure *you* can understand, if you only make a little push to do so."

Temeraire was not at all sure he wanted to understand. Perscitia did like to take alarm at things unnecessarily. It was surely nonsense to talk of shooting down heavy-weights as though they were geese—but Perscitia was clever, and he felt uncomfortably she might not be entirely mistaken about the march of progress.

In one thing at least, however, they were in perfect agreement: he did not at all trust the Government. They certainly would let dragons starve, if they could, and perhaps worse. He had seen *worse* in Russia, now, and could describe it; he shuddered again at the memory of the cruel hobbles.

"I see no reason why we shouldn't have more of us in Parliament anyway," Temeraire said. "And for that matter, why we oughtn't go into some sort of business, too. I must tell you more of this John Wampanoag fellow, that I met in Japan."

"You needn't," Perscitia said, "I am corresponding with him." Temeraire blinked in surprise. "I thought from what you said he must be well-known there, so I had one of my secretaries send a letter to Boston, marked very clearly to his name, and it did find him, for he was kind enough to write back. We have discussed arranging an overland trade route from Portsmouth to China, or perhaps just to India to begin with."

"For my part, I cannot see that we need this Parliament, or to trouble ourselves about business, either," put in a small beast, who Temeraire realized with a start had been listening all this while to their conversation.

He had been easily overlooked: he was sitting in the corner of the clearing beneath a windbreak of pine-trees, and was himself mottled dark green with a belly in purplish brown, just barely topping the line between light-weight and courier-weight. He was of no breed Temeraire recognized, although his accent was quite distinctly Scottish, and wore no harness. Smaller ferals had always slipped into the coverts to sneak some leavings when they could, and now the practice was grown more widespread: the porridge-pots made it easy to make them welcome, and once they were there, the aviators could even trade them meat for their labor.

"But it's a deal of work, carrying heavy things from one end of the earth to another," the green feral continued, "with not even a sheep to be sure of at the end of the day; and you may keep your Parliament. A vote never filled anyone's belly that I heard of, nor this pay we are meant to be getting, which I have never seen. I like that map of Napoleon's, if you ask me."

"What map is this?" Perscitia demanded, as Temeraire flattened his ruff in irritation: they certainly had *not* asked him.

"Napoleon has had the splendid notion of offering dragons territory which he has no right to offer, nor any power to give," Temeraire said, "and trying to trick them into fighting for it, all to distract his enemies: I had not supposed," he added coolly, "that any *British* dragon would be taken in by his chicanery: as though we had not learned before now that all he wants is to take all our territory for his own, and bring his own dragons over here."

"He hasn't any quarrel with me and mine that I know of," the feral said. "All right, he invaded, but that was to beat that mad old king the men have over here, and I didn't see any of his beasts setting eggs while they were here, did I? Meanwhile the men in this country go about taking *our* eggs when it suits them, and hunting up all the game, and coming after us with guns if we want a sheep to eat now and then. I'd just as soon take a chance on a fellow who has done right and proper by his own dragons. Two of my wing were in France lately for his big hullabaloo, and said their leavings at breakfast are better than what we get for dinner, and their pavilions make this," he flicked his tail dismissively at the small pavilion, "look like a wet hole as you'd put a pig in, to keep for later."

By the end of this speech, more than one of the other dragons sleeping inside the pavilion or around the fringes of the clearing had lifted their heads to listen. The Scottish feral—his name was Ricarlee—was informed well enough to sketch out Napoleon's map in the dirt for them all to examine, and Temeraire was sorry to see the interest it produced, particularly among the feral beasts. The Yellow Reapers crowded round the side of northern England which had been allotted to them and murmured thoughtfully in a way that made Temeraire uneasy, and not only the unharnessed ones, either.

"Outrageous," Perscitia said loudly, and, "Mercenary," and "A return to the Dark Ages, even if it worked, which it shan't," but she was the only one to raise a protest.

Even little Minnow, who had stopped by the covert to say hello to Temeraire, only gave a shrug, even though she had done rather well for herself since the invasion. She and Moncey, and the rest of the Winchesters from their old company, had established a private courier-route. They carried packages and urgent messages and the occasional passenger, for anyone who could afford their rates, and the leather satchel which she wore over her neck and forelegs was beautifully trimmed in gold and pearls.

"You can't blame anyone, can you?" she said, nevertheless. "It is our territory, too, or else why did we all fight, in the invasion? Why oughtn't we have the right to take a sheep or cow—along sensible lines, that don't spoil the herds, or anything else stupid."

"But the sheep and the cows are not simply *there,* by accident," Temeraire said, glad to have worked through this very subject with Laurence on several occasions; he had found it quite baffling, himself. "The humans have arranged their being there, by raising them and looking after them, and growing grain to feed them. Naturally they are angry if a dragon swoops down and snatches one, without making any return for all their trouble."

"Ah! Easy enough to say, it is all their work!" Ricarlee said. "And if those herds weren't there, and those great fields of grass the humans like to plant? Why, then there would be some wild goats or pigs, or a tasty venison, free for the taking. I have seen it myself a dozen times in the North: here comes a farmer, cutting down the trees and plowing under the earth, and soon enough the game have all gone away and there is nothing to eat *but* the sheep. Just because a man is small don't mean a hundred of 'em can't steal our territory if they work at it together, and I don't see why we ought to put up with it."

And Temeraire was sorry to see the dragons all around the clearing nodding enthusiastic agreement.

"Laurence," Temeraire said reluctantly, when Laurence returned to the covert in the morning, "I think, I am afraid, we may be going to have some small difficulty—some awkwardness—"

"Certainly we shall," Laurence said. "Have you heard already, then? I was coming to tell you, but I cannot be surprised that the couriers have passed you the word. I am glad you recognize the magnitude of the challenge before us. The Admiralty have already named me a dozen of our captains, and half of them the most hidebound formation-flyers of the service; how we shall use them without Napoleon bowling us over as thoroughly as he did the Prussians in the year six, I have very little notion at present."

"*Our* captains?" Temeraire said, puzzled, wondering what on earth this had to do with the ferals of Britain threatening to go over to Napoleon en masse.

"*De jure,* at least," Laurence said. "But judging by their choices, the Admiralty mean to assign those men they think more likely to disobey me than otherwise."

Temeraire hesitated, still at sea, and then Granby came into the clearing with his hat, beaming, and said, "Well, Admiral Laurence, may I congratulate you?" and shook Laurence's hand.

In half-appalled wonder Temeraire said, "Laurence, they have never made *you* admiral? Not that there is anyone better deserving the rank—!" he added hastily, only that the Admiralty should have done it was almost incredible. And yet it seemed they had—a very meager, very late sort of apology after all their misdeeds and unjust punishments, and nevertheless astonishing they should have made it at all.

"It has been done very unwilling," Laurence said. "Likely at the Tsar's behest, and in hopes of more aid coming from China. But yes, it has been done, and I have my orders. We leave England in a week. John, I have a favor to solicit: I must give a dinner for the captains, and I hope you will ask Iskierka to permit me to make use of her pavilion for the occasion."

"A dinner?" Granby said dubiously. "Laurence, have you heard who they have—I won't say saddled you with, but I do say it; I don't know what they can be thinking."

"They are thinking to have men at my back who will counter my heretical spirits, and who will not hesitate to disobey my orders if they suppose me to be doing anything contrary to Britain's interests," Laurence said. "They have chosen as well as they could, for that purpose. But I have no choice; I must take them, for all that. So we must begin with the fiction of ordinary relations, and hope to make it truth in time.

"But, Temeraire, I fear I must ask you to find some excuse to exert yourself, on the occasion, and if possible give their beasts cause to respect your abilities. I am sorry to make the request: offensive to those who must witness it, as implying they require any such display to maintain discipline, and painful to you to make, as implying the respect which ought to be due you cannot be taken for granted. But I think the urgency of the situation demands it."

"Oh, I do not mind that at all," Temeraire said, "but Laurence," and he opened his mouth to explain that there was an entirely different source of difficulty and trouble—to tell Laurence that Napoleon's Concord had somehow reached Britain, and the ferals thought much of it, and several of them were even trying to forward the arrangement.

But Laurence looked up at him, and Temeraire halted. There was color in Laurence's face, and though he had spoken so seriously, he was despite that smiling a little, as though some inward happiness buoyed him against all the difficulties of his new position. Laurence had said before that he did not grieve the loss of rank and fortune, of his reputation. But of course, he had been trying to save Temeraire's feelings. Temeraire could not bear to spoil this moment of vindication and triumph. And if he spoke, Laurence would at once report to the Admiralty, of course, as he would say was his duty; and undoubtedly they would find some way to blame him for it, and perhaps even take back the command, after all.

"Yes?" Laurence said.

"—ought you not have another set of golden bars for your coat?" Temeraire said faintly.

Laurence laughed—laughed, quite aloud!—and said, "I thank you for the reminder; indeed I must make shift to acquire them at once."

"He must not learn of the Concord going around," Temeraire said to Perscitia anxiously, when Laurence had gone with Granby to begin arrangements, for the golden bars and for the dinner. "At least, not until we have contrived some solution; only what am I to do?"

Chapter 13

"LAURENCE, I HAVE BEEN thinking," Temeraire said. It seemed an opportune moment: Laurence was busily engaged in figuring in a very large ledger the various expenditures required to fit out Iskierka's pavilion for the dinner. "I have been thinking, it might be suitable for *me* to host a dinner as well—for some of my old friends from the breeding grounds—veterans, and unharnessed fellows— and perhaps some ferals might stop in—"

Lacking a better idea, he had seized on Laurence's strategy as his own: a dinner, as he already knew, worked splendidly to solve any number of difficulties, and perhaps it should serve in this case, too. He did not quite know how to explain to Laurence *why* he wished to host a dinner, but as it proved, he did not need to: Laurence lifted his head instantly from his work.

"You answer the wish I had not yet made," Laurence said. "We must try to bring on some more light-weights and middleweights, and I would be glad to take as many of the ferals and unharnessed beasts with us to Europe as you can convince to take the King's shilling. You may offer them the usual rate of pay for harnessed beasts; their Lordships have grudgingly allowed as much—do you think some of them will come?"

"I will certainly make every effort to persuade them," Temeraire said, feeling relieved and also uncomfortably as though he were practicing deceit—although it did not really deserve the name; after all, he was not trying to hide anything from Laurence for his *own* benefit, but only for Laurence's; that ought to have some mitigating quality, even if the English language did not seem to offer a more satisfying and accurate alternative to the word. In any case, he would do his best to persuade as many dragons to come along as ever he could: that would certainly be a splendid solution, if everyone should come along to the Continent and help fight *against* Napoleon instead.

"Will you need my assistance with the arrangements?" Laurence asked. "You would not expect over twenty dragons, I suppose?"

"Well, I do not precisely know," Temeraire said, even more uncomfortably; just that morning, Perscitia had spoken very darkly of *hundreds of silly beasts ready to take Bonaparte aboard,* "but I thought perhaps the feeding station outside Dover would not object to our making use of their provisions for the day, and let us have the liberty of preparing them—I will be very happy to welcome any dragon who likes to come and eat, even if they do not think they will choose to come along with us."

This station had been established by degrees over the last few years, by a reluctant Government grudgingly recognizing that feral dragons meant to frequent the place, and had better be fed on the nation's terms than allowed to feed themselves. It was not yet *officially* a breeding ground—the Ministry finding it hateful to contemplate declaring a breeding ground in any insufficiently benighted location, and the many wealthy landholders in the area maintaining a loud rear-guard protest against the encroachment—but as many dragons were choosing to make it their home, and some of them as nesting grounds for their eggs, which the Corps gladly collected, there was as a practical matter very little difference.

There was no definite border to the territory, but if there had been, Temeraire's own pavilion would have stood near the center— the pavilion Laurence had built him, ages ago it seemed, before treason and invasion and transportation, and the loss of Laurence's first fortune. "We can hold it there," Temeraire said, thinking of the distance from Dover, and the isolation of the place; there would be few people about to report on the meeting, and perhaps Laurence would never need to know.

"Splendid," Laurence said, and made the necessary arrangements, which was to say, he wrote Temeraire a draft on his bank.

"And perhaps you would be glad to stay here in Dover, and leave the rest to me," Temeraire said, "as you must worry about your *own* dinner; I should not like to add to your work."

"If you think you can manage the feeding-station master," Laurence said.

"Oh! There will be no difficulty there; it is good old Lloyd, who used to run the breeding ground at Pen Y Fan, and who managed our supply for us during the invasion—and Perscitia has a handy group of fellows now, who will do anything for her if they are only paid for it," Temeraire said quickly. "No, we can manage perfectly, I am sure," and Laurence yielded. But that was surely doing him a service, and could not really be called concealment, Temeraire felt almost sure, as he hastily flew away to meet with Perscitia.

Unfortunately, his poor pavilion had never been very grand, and was lately much neglected. It had been used as a shelter for the sick dragons during the plague, and since then as a resting-place by any dragon who happened to like being an easy hour's flight from the coverts of London and Dover, at least for a night—which was a great many dragons: couriers, ferals sneaking around to get scraps off the Corps, unharnessed beasts who liked to get work in the quarries, or in the ports, or doing portage. None of them had taken the trouble to keep it at all nice. The corners of the chamber really could not bear too-close examination, and when Temeraire put his head in and sniffed too deeply, he jerked his head back out again with distaste.

"Well," Perscitia said doubtfully. "Perhaps we might find another . . . ?"

There were some others near-by, although none as large. After the invasion, some of the unharnessed dragons had used their share of the proceeds from the golden eagles they had captured to build themselves pavilions—more or less; three buildings and half a dozen unfinished structures clustered in a loose line. But of these, only Perscitia's own was not equally a mess—but that was not saying much, as hers was very small, and made of plain red brick and grey shingles, lacking entirely in elegance or charm.

"It is easier to keep neat, if it is not so big that men cannot clean it out without an enormous amount of trouble or expense," she said with a defensive note, as Temeraire eyed it from outside, "and also, I do not find the size at all a disadvantage: if it were any larger, and some heavy-weight took it into his head to say she was claiming it from me, I should have no recourse—unless I liked to try and take her to court, and just you watch how much remedy the law would give a dragon."

That was all very practical, Temeraire supposed, but he did not see why the pavilion needed to be a shut-up box, with only the most meager openings for air and light, and not a hint of decoration. "It is very nice," he said tactfully, "and so long as it suits you, I am sure no one else could find anything wanting," although she might at least have dug a garden, and put some interesting rocks along the side.

But she was quite right about the expense of keeping a larger pavilion clean: Perscitia's secretary said she could not arrange to have his cleaned properly for under fifty pounds—fifty pounds, when Perscitia's men had already to be paid fifteen pounds for their cooking services! A perfectly outrageous sum, and Temeraire could not bring himself to spend it only on *cleaning;* only he did not see how else it was to be done. He tried bringing water in a large barrel, and simply sloshing it over the floor, but he knew very well what Laurence would have said of this sort of house-keeping, and it did not have much effect. His attempt at using a small tree to brush out the corners met with little better success, except he did manage to knock away a piece of the wall.

"We could ask Iskierka to burn it out," Perscitia suggested, but this was impossible: Granby and Iskierka had already gone to Edinburgh to take charge of the second half of Laurence's force, which should leave from there instead of Dover due to some byzantine mystery of supply.

"I will ask Ning," he decided.

That, at least, could be managed, as she was still in London. The Admiralty had sent a courier to escort her to the training grounds at Kinloch Laggan, while they awaited an answer from China, but she had very politely said, "How excellent military training must be! I will certainly consider your kind invitation, when my time is not so occupied as at present. In the meantime, you may wish to consider sending some workmen to enlarge this pavilion, and perhaps arrange a higher quality of food."

Temeraire waited until cover of night to fly back to the London covert—only out of consideration, to avoid distressing the populace and the horses, and not of course to conceal his presence—and roused Ning out of the pavilion. She listened to his request with a tilted head. "It seems peculiar to me that you should be so urgent to clean this pavilion when you are imminently departing for the Continent," she said interrogatively.

"I mean to hold a dinner there," Temeraire said, a little warily. "Laurence wishes me to persuade some of the unharnessed dragons to come and join us," which was perfectly true.

"Will this dinner entail a great deal of difficulty and expense?"

"Yes," Temeraire said, with a sigh.

"Do you expect many of these dragons to join you?" she inquired.

"It is just as well to make an attempt," Temeraire said, and surely at least a few of his old friends would come, although he did not have the *highest* hopes—it was not like the invasion, when everyone had been worried about the French dragons taking their territory, and there was no denying that the Government had be-

haved in a scurrilous fashion since then; few dragons would believe in pay tomorrow when their accounts were a year in arrears
as it was.

"Hm," Ning said thoughtfully, but she acquiesced without further argument. Temeraire carried her on his back to the pavilion,
and once there, she spat out a single small ball of her white flame
directly into a corner—very neatly, Temeraire had to admit—and
the refuse scorched up instantly.

"That is a very interesting phenomenon," Perscitia said, lowering her head to examine Ning closely, even trying to peer down
Ning's throat. Ning drew her head back and gave her a flat stare,
which Perscitia quite ignored. "How is it accomplished?"

"Pray let us step outside until the air has cleared," Ning said in
a stiff and dignified fashion, turning away.

Temeraire flung water onto the overheated stones and fanned
away the hissing cloud of steam that resulted. Fortunately, the
stink went away with the smoke. The corner was a little blackened
perhaps, but he was sure that no-one would notice that much,
particularly at night.

Ning was quite willing to repeat the operation, too. "That is
very handy of you," Temeraire said approvingly, when all the pavilions were clean, if somewhat smoky. "Now I had better fly you
back," but Ning demurred.

"I will stay for the dinner," she announced, to his dismay.

"What have you to do at dinner?" he demanded.

"I am hungry," she said, which was no explanation at all; the
dinner was not until tomorrow, and meanwhile they would certainly feed her in London today, if she went back, but when Temeraire tried to point this out, she only yawned delicately, and said,
"I beg your pardon, I am so very fatigued! I will rest now," and
then closed her eyes and pretended to go to sleep.

"There is nothing wrong with that," Perscitia said. "She may
as well stay: anyone who has heard of her will be impressed to
have her on our side," except Temeraire was not certain Ning *was*
on their side, or of anything she would do for that matter: it was

an uncomfortable feeling, being round her, when she might at any moment burst out into some new and alarming start.

Perscitia's men—who it turned out were mostly women; Temeraire had mistaken them, because they all wore pantaloons beneath their skirts, and hiked these up to their waists while they worked—had already been engaged all that day in putting beef and mutton on roasting spits. There would be nothing really elegant about the meal, Temeraire mournfully recognized, but Perscitia had firmly rejected his every suggestion for more elaborate presentations. "We may have near a hundred dragons to feed," she said, "and many of them have never even had anything cooked: that must be enough novelty. Otherwise we will have half of them turn their noses up at it, and not enough for the other half, who will complain we are slighting them. No, a simple roasting must do, and we will make mash with the drippings, for anyone who is still hungry after they get their share of the meat."

She had been sending couriers everywhere, and dragons began to arrive early the next morning. They came hungry: Temeraire had a deal of work to do trying to keep them off the meat until dinner-time, particularly the Scottish ferals. A great number of those had come, including Ricarlee, who was rude enough to begin talking up Napoleon's Concord to them all. "I ought to run him off," Temeraire said, fuming. "He should hold his *own* dinner, if he likes to promote Napoleon's plans."

"I would not advise it," Ning remarked, from behind half-slitted drowsy eyes. "You ought to have quietly disposed of him before he came—" this sounded rather ominous, and Temeraire eyed her sidelong, "—but now it is too late: you will only give more credence and force to his arguments, if you establish him as worthy of being chased away. Allow him to speak, with a tolerant air, and do not permit anyone to see you think there is anything of sense in what he says."

"So you *do* want us to beat the French now?" Temeraire said, skeptical. "Or why are you offering advice?"

"You are very suspicious," Ning said. "You are my progenitor;

I am not ungrateful." Temeraire did not swallow this, and stared at her until she flipped a dismissive point of her wing. "Are you proposing to destroy the French entirely? To annihilate every one of them?"

"Of course not," Temeraire said, aghast. "We must only beat Napoleon properly, so he will stop having wars everywhere."

"Very well," Ning said. "So far we are agreed."

Temeraire remained doubtful, but he could not stay to pry a better answer out of her: a Winchester and a couple of the Scots dragons were creeping up on the beautifully roasted mutton that Perscitia's men had just finished turning.

He was more than a little exasperated by the time the dinner-hour at last arrived, and grew even more so when Ricarlee—who had the advantage of being smaller, and less nice in his manners—finished his own portion quickly and seized the floor to say, "Well, this is a handsome dinner indeed! I wouldn't mind eating so more often than once in ten years, I will say," and began again to rhapsodize about the Concord, and how it would ensure them an endless supply of delights.

More than one dragon made supportive noises, including, Temeraire was sorry to see, some of his old comrades from the invasion. Annoyed, Temeraire swallowed down his own side of beef more quickly than he liked—he privately could admit there was a great deal to say for the flavor of a nice piece of beef, properly spit-roasted, with only a little salt, and he would have preferred to savor it.

"That," he said loudly, "is nonsense. I do not deny that the Concord talks a great deal of sense, where it proposes rules for governing among ourselves, but there is no use imagining that Napoleon can give us rights to cows and sheep that have been raised by men who do not owe him allegiance. You must all see that Napoleon cannot really give you any land in Britain, as it is not his. He only means to set us quarreling with the Government here because they are his enemies; he wants us to fight them for *his* benefit, and bear all the cost, while he gives us nothing."

"There's something to what you say," Ricarlee said thoughtfully now, but before Temeraire could congratulate himself on swaying the Concord's most fervent supporter, he went on, "I don't see why we ought to do all the work, and Napoleon get the good of it all alone. We should make him pay us, in gold, if he wants us to fight."

This dreadful suggestion attracted many murmurs of enthusiasm, to Temeraire's horror, until he sat up as tall as he could and said loudly, "That is treasonous!" to interrupt them. "And it will only end in the most dreadful way you can imagine. When *I* committed treason—and not for any selfish reason, but only to share the cure—they took Laurence's entire fortune away—ten thousand pounds, lost!" This silenced the audience, except for several faint hisses of dismay. Temeraire, relieved to have headed off the worst, added, "If you did get any gold from Napoleon, the men here will only confiscate it, when he has been beat, and he is sure to be beaten; Laurence and I are going to the Continent this coming week, to finish him off. And even if he *did* win, it would only be after the British had killed any number of you, and then you may be sure he would sail in and snatch it all for himself, and give all your territories to French dragons, instead."

"Well, what else are *you* proposing, then?" Ricarlee said. "You are brim-full of doom, indeed, and reasons why we oughtn't listen to Napoleon, but I ha'nt heard any better notions from you, other than we shouldn't say boo to a lieutenant of horse. It's all very well for those who have wagons full of gold and admirals in their pockets to tell the rest of us we may put up with nine shillings threepence a day, which don't add up to a sheep in a sennight if it is ever paid, which it isn't."

Temeraire flattened back his ruff. "It is true my situation at present is an enviable one," he said coolly. "But my gold was won fairly on the field of battle, by doing my duty, and I do not think anyone can disagree I have acted in a most disinterested fashion where the welfare of my fellow dragons was at stake."

He might have added that there was no wagon full of gold

anymore. Ferris, back in Vilna, had arranged the sale of all the treasure they had been obliged to leave behind when going to the Alps. Through mysterious but—Laurence had assured him—reliable means, the value thereof had appeared in a bank account of his very own in Britain, and was now invested in the Funds and producing that very delightful thing, interest. But this was not a point on which he felt he ought to enlarge when talking with those who did not have so much as five pounds to their credit, and could not have gotten it out of a bank again, if they wished.

"Wagons of gold are not commonly found *save* upon the field of battle, I find," Ning put in unexpectedly, in a thoughtful voice, loud enough to carry.

Temeraire eyed her warily, but she made no further remark. "In any case," he went on, "there is a considerable difference between my saying you oughtn't simply swallow this plan Napoleon has held out to you, when anyone can see he has only made it up for his own ends, and my saying you must put up with our Government behaving in a scaly manner, which I do not say at all. Indeed," sudden inspiration striking, "we should make our *own* concord—and it needn't be one that is so unreasonable as to force a quarrel."

"Yes, indeed!" Perscitia said, sitting up sharp. "We must propose a bill, to Parliament, with our requirements."

"Now *that*," Minnow said, to Temeraire's satisfaction, "is the most sensible thing I have heard. It stands to reason we are better off not fighting with the people here: they have plenty of guns in this country, after all, and anyway we most of us have friends among the harnessed dragons, and don't care to put them in an awkward position. Now then, what do we want to ask their Lordships for?"

Fortunately, Perscitia's secretary Mrs. Elsinore was on hand to take notes. Her hand was excellent, although she had some difficulty in keeping up with the lengthening list of demands and requests: higher pay, more frequently and more honestly paid, and even for those dragons who did not choose to fight—"But then you ought to do *some* work for it," Temeraire said, to which Ricarlee a little disgruntledly said, "Oh, aye, *some* work; if they give us aught we can do without breaking our backs," but at least he and the ferals agreed to that much—and a host of improvements which Perscitia suggested, to make casting one's vote easier.

"And we must have more seats in Parliament for dragons," she added firmly. "We must ask for thirty, and allow ourselves to be bargained down to twenty; we must not accept less than twenty," which provoked some protests on the part of other dragons, who said they were happy to sit on stone, and would rather have more money.

"I do not mean chairs!" Perscitia said. "I mean *members*: there must be more dragons who have a share in making the law. Oh! And we ought to insist that they make some dragons officers, too. It is nonsense, only having humans as officers in the Aerial Corps."

"Yes, be sure and put that on the list," Temeraire told Mrs. Elsinore, and so forth and so on, until they all finished and looked at the list with some satisfaction—everyone pleased, and agreeing that they would all pledge themselves to enforce it, and then Perscitia announced, "I will take it to Parliament on Monday, then, and read it to the other members—perhaps I can arrange for them to hear Bonaparte's Concord, too," she added thoughtfully, "so that they have the contrast before them—I think it will be highly instructive—"

Temeraire suddenly woke to the realization that he had averted one disaster only to produce another. For the Concord to come to the Admiralty's attention would have been bad enough, but no-one would ever be persuaded that he had not had a hand in this new document—as indeed he had, but the point was that Laurence was sure to be blamed for it with even more violence. "You cannot read it!" he said hurriedly.

Perscitia scowled. "It is not *my* fault I was not taught early enough," she said, injured. "Besides, Mrs. Elsinore will read it to me until I have it by heart. You may be sure I will not make any mistakes."

"No, I meant," Temeraire said, but fell silent; he could not say, *Do not read it, for Laurence's sake.* That would be unfair, and worse than unfair; it was just what the Admiralty wanted of him and of every harnessed dragon, that they should betray their own interests and those of their fellow-dragons just to please their captains—and Laurence would not even be pleased; Laurence would never wish it of him.

"I only meant," he said, struggling, "that we must proceed with more delicacy. After all, if you should spring it upon the Parliament without warning, I dare say they will all refuse to listen. Laurence has told me how often the question of the slave trade has been argued, and how much difficulty there has been in getting the ban through."

"One cannot *spring* anything upon Parliament without warning," Perscitia said, with a lecturing air. "I shall announce tomorrow that I will make a motion to read in a bill, so everyone will know that it is coming. Of course I must first marshal support for the measure, but I have already thought of that. There are several gentlemen of the Opposition who will be glad of a chance to embarrass the Government by putting a question to the Speaker about Napoleon's Concord, which shall furnish me with an excellent opportunity of warning of all the dire consequences should it be adopted by England's dragons, and be the best introduction for *our* bill—which, by the bye," she added, "must be properly named— and I shall argue that the Government ought to adopt it, and thereby present an example of enlightened leadership to the nations of the Continent, and their dragons—"

"Laurence," Temeraire said, feeling rather desperate, "I must have a word with you."

"I am at your service," Laurence said immediately, turning away from the pair of wide-eyed young runners who had been delivered by courier that morning from Kinloch Laggan, along with four ensigns, seven riflemen, three lieutenants, and a ground crew of twenty men, all of whom had already been pressed into varying forms of service to prepare for the party.

"Oh—to-night will do," Temeraire said cravenly. "Or tomorrow; tomorrow will certainly be good enough, I am sure." The pavilion looked so splendid—lanterns hung everywhere, and silk hangings, and even if braziers and hot bricks were the source of warmth, there were so many of them as to make a really comfortable glow. The smell of the roasting cows rose marvelously over the fresh sea-air crashing on the cliffs below, and the pavilion's prospect could not be improved upon: the wide expanse of the Channel was already dark, as the sun sank westward, the boats with their lanterns bobbing jewel-like. The tables were laid with great magnificence: porcelain and crystal and silver all ablaze upon the inner, large platters of brass for the dragons set behind every captain's place, and liveried footmen already arranging themselves at intervals around the table. "How grand everything looks!"

"Yes, I mean to dine in proper state," Laurence said. "If only captains might be impressed so certainly by such things as their dragons, I would be content. But at least they will have no cause to feel I slight them, and I admit that I hope the formality of the table may encourage a like formality in the behavior of the guests; I can rely on no amiable feeling among them."

Laurence knew this was a polite understatement, but he had no intention of letting Temeraire know that Captain Poole had five years ago loudly expressed to Laurence's face the opinion that he ought to have been drawn, quartered, and thrown to dogs, in the good old fashion; nor that Captain Windle had on the same occasion struck him—in the midst of a general melee broken out in camp, where Laurence had been able to return the blow in kind rather than take insult—and still less that Windle's first lieutenant had tried, drunken and ineffectual though the attempt had been, to stab him with a table knife.

Temeraire, if he knew, would certainly have objections of his own to express to all of these gentlemen; violent objections. But Laurence himself could not blame them for their feelings, nor the honesty of their open avowal. The Admiralty had been brutal indeed in spreading the blame of his treason across all aviators, then compounding that injustice by postponing their own sentence and keeping him alive. Since then they had transported him, restored him, and now, to crown all, promoted him. Their actions implied too plainly that better was not to be expected, from aviators; that they were to be regarded much as were their beasts, as unreliable, half-controlled, and lacking in all discipline—a bitter swallow for officers who loved the Corps, and aspired only to perform their loyal duty to the Crown. Laurence would have gladly counted himself among their number, once; only extremity had driven him out of their ranks. The men who objected to his pardon were guilty only of loving their service, and resenting the insult to its honor.

He was nevertheless relieved that the first to arrive was Jane's recommendation, Captain Adair, whom the Admiralty had grudgingly allowed him. Adair was of an older Corps family and a gentleman; he and Laurence were even connected distantly, fourth cousins somewhere on the maternal side, and while he could not be called warm, his manners were punctilious. His dragon Levantia was young and not a little nervous; she had the claws of a Parnassian and the cheerful yellow coloration of a Reaper, and an anxious habit of mind distinct from either breed. But she was squarely middle-weight, well-trained and well-crewed, and Laurence had every hope of her making a solid anchor for their defense against the screen of light-weight dragons which Napoleon liked so well to put up at the head of his offensive maneuvers.

The rest of the party arrived in slightly tardy stages, and made Laurence greetings stilted when not verging on outright rudeness. Captain Poole did not verge: did not offer a hand, nor even make the smallest bow, and said only, "Laurence," in a cold and remote voice.

Laurence paused and said quietly, "*Admiral* Laurence; or you may report yourself to Whitehall for insubordination."

Poole stood a moment. Thin and thin-lipped, with almost a pared quality, as though someone had whittled him down like a stick; there was a hardness in his face, and his hair was shingled close to his head. But he was a young man still; he had been a lieutenant when Laurence had last seen him, on the eve of the ill-fated Battle of London. He had won his step sometime in the intervening years; his young Anglewing, Fidelitas, was larger than most of that breed, solidly in the heavy-weight class, and was likely one of the eggs bred up while the plague had been ravaging the British ranks with no prospect of a cure.

"Admiral," he said finally—adequate; Laurence nodded and stood aside. Poole immediately continued into the pavilion and crossed the length of the table to join Windle and three other captains, who were holding themselves well apart from the rest of the company, and speaking in low voices; the glances they threw at Laurence from across the table left little doubt of the likely subject of their conversation, nor their sentiments thereupon.

The dinner was not a success by any measure Laurence would ordinarily have used: the conversation stilted and labored, and the atmosphere heavy. His preparations achieved the quelling effect he had desired, but not by mere elevation of tone. He was sorry to realize that several of the captains had never before been confronted with the full array of a formal dinner service, and found themselves at a disadvantage. A quarter of the gentlemen refused soup until nudged by their neighbors, and nearly all of them plainly had to remind themselves at regular intervals not to eat from their knives. Captain Whitby called out across the table to say, "Hi, Alfred, light along those mushrooms you have there by you," only to make poor Alfred—Captain Gorden—startle violently and knock over his glass when one of the footmen made a desperate leap from behind him to fetch the desired dish before he could reach it.

So Laurence had without intending it established a distinction of social standing, and if he had made his captains polite, he had also made them uncomfortable. But the dinner succeeded in avoiding the worst dangers he had foreseen: there was no open rudeness, and the conversation though not lively was unobjectionable. The most resentful of the captains had been scattered around the table by the correct order of seating—although a little whispering had been required to arrange that, aviators as a rule not much given to working out their exact precedence—and as a result, had less opportunity for speaking among themselves in a small group. Laurence was willing to have their dislike a little transmitted, in exchange for having it dispersed and thereby restrained.

He proposed the loyal toast to the King, and afterwards necessarily saluted Windle, as the most senior captain present; all raised their glasses, even if Windle looked sour at the honor, and from there the round of toasts proceeded without incident. The excellent wines had a mellowing effect upon the company, and Temeraire meanwhile was having some success among the dragons seated in the outer ring to enjoy their own meal—an arrangement which if it surprised them and their officers plainly recommended itself to the former. On landing, one captain had said, loud enough to be overheard, "Bellamar, if they should try to feed you any foreign mess, or some nonsense of gruel, be sure I will see you properly fed back in Dover," but when they were ushered inside the pavilion to their places, the glittering array of the tables had an appeal which not the strongest captainly opprobrium could entirely overcome.

"Is this a dinner-party, then? Why, they are very splendid after all; I did not know how it should be," said Windle's own Obituria, a large Chequered Nettle, to the visible and scowling annoyance of her captain. It was a sentiment much repeated, particularly once the beef was served—one entire side to a dragon, roasted beautifully and showing to advantage upon the brightly polished platters, with whole oranges stuck upon the points of the ribs. Many harnessed dragons had developed an expensive taste for strong spice, much used during the plague to overcome the deadening of their appetites, which they of late had little opportunity to indulge. The curried sauce, delivered in large tureens, went around to especially loud enthusiasm, and, it had to be admitted, equally loud consumption.

The wheat porridge served after, which might have occasioned protests, was presented to them decorated with large lumps of rock sugar that had a look almost of jewels, so that several of the dragons leaned forward to ask their captains in undertone if they were really meant to *eat* such marvels, rather than take them away to keep. Temeraire had to give the company their lead and say, "Are the sugar jewels not remarkable? Pray tell me your opinion," to Obituria, on his right, as he took his own first large swallow.

The porridge-bowls were cleaned bare all around the table, and then the dragons' second course brought out: fish, overlapped and arranged on the plate into the shape of a sea-serpent, each appropriate to the size of the guest, with an enormous stuffed pumpkin for a glaring orange eye and masses of stewed greens for the ocean waves, oysters and clams and mussels in quantity rounding out the sea-bed, and for each plate a handsome lobster bright red as a flourish. Delight reigned; even Poole's dragon might be overheard whispering—as dragons whispered—"Roger, but he cannot be so very bad, only look at my plate—and the lanterns!" Poole looked irritable.

Laurence was glad to establish Temeraire, at least, in the esteem of the dragons. Meanwhile, at the officers' table every man had been toasted, as well as Nelson's memory. The second course was carried away in satisfactory ruins, particularly the same turbot which had furnished the dragons' dish, and the cloth being removed Laurence took his chance and rising said, "Gentlemen, we leave for the Continent in three days' time. We confront a tyrant whose genius for war has made him the dismay of every army he has faced, and the architect of misery in nearly every part of the world. He has seemed at times unassailable and invincible. But we have proven him otherwise here on England's soil and in Spain; the Russians have lately proved it in their own country. The hour advances when we shall prove it in Germany and in France, God willing. May we all of us, man and beast, do our part in ensuring his defeat."

It was not a long speech, nor very elegant, but it served the purpose: "hear, hear," went around the table, every man drank, and Laurence sat again conscious of relief and having bound his officers in at least so much unity of purpose. The dessert was spread out over the table and the company might now circulate more freely, but those early knots of opposition had been broken up, and the captains did not move far from their dragons, who were murmuring raptures over their own pudding, flickering blue with a monstrous expenditure of brandy. Laurence counted it well-spent to the last shilling for the ecstasies it produced among them. A small group of musicians—intrepid and overpaid—had been set to play for the company, and now began their work. Laurence had been used to this form of entertainment after shipboard dinners, if more informally produced by the hands, and if the music served to dissuade low conversations, that, too, was just as well.

He had never before given a dinner with so much calculation, but there was a familiarity to the undertaking: just so his mother had on many an occasion organized her political dinners, more akin to a military campaign than a convivial gathering. He thought of her with brief pain, and looked down at the black riband on his arm tight against the green coat. He would have no opportunity to see her: there was no time to fly to Nottinghamshire, and she had no heart to come to town; she had written to tell him so, and to congratulate him on his flag. She had not said, *Your father would be proud.* Laurence could not have persuaded himself to believe her, if she had. But that pain stood for a moment at a remove from the practical necessities of the moment, and he found the bitterness lessened, also. He could never have his father's pardon; but he had Jane's, and was content as he had not expected ever again to be.

"Oh, and look," Temeraire said, as the dragons finally emerged from the pavilion onto the crest of the hillside for some air, "there is the *Spartiate,* beating up the Channel. Let us salute her: I am sure if we roar all together, it will be as loud as a broadside, and it is only due her," that ship being the one survivor of the wreck of Nelson's fleet, after the battle of Shoeburyness.

The dragons were nothing loath, and even the most sour captain could hardly have made objection. The roar they made was a prodigious noise, once, twice, and then the third something else entirely. Laurence was braced, as was Granby; but all the other guests man and beast fell silent as Temeraire unleashed the full unthrottled roaring of the divine wind over all their united voices, and drowned them beneath that endless wave of noise. All was silent when he finished: the stones beneath their feet still trembling with resonance, and faint splashes coming from the surf below as gulls fell out of the sky dead into the sea.

The *Spartiate*—Laurence had sent a courier to her captain to warn him of the honor to be paid her—took a moment to recover, but then answered with all her guns, a distant rumbling at the distance but full of glowing fire and smoke. She was a fine and martial sight against the growing dark, enough to lift any heart with zeal.

After the ship had passed, Temeraire with sudden inspiration leaned over and whispered, "Laurence, ought we give everyone one of the lanterns, to take back to their coverts?" and the dragons, at least, were won. They carried away their paper baubles as jealously as gold, with many abjurations to their captains to be careful of the sides, and the hanging-cords, and not to let them fly off during the passage.

"Well, my dear," Laurence said to Temeraire with some satisfaction, when the company had gone, "I think we may have won the field, so far as it could be won. What did you wish to speak to me about, earlier?"

Chapter 14

THE FRESHLY MINTED DRAGON Rights Act 1813 received its first
reading in Parliament unopposed, to the great dismay of the Government: evidently no-one had felt equal to raising objections to
Perscitia's face, or rather teeth. Laurence was well aware that the
reception he met at the Admiralty, the next day, was restrained
only by the almost unwelcome intelligence, arrived that very morning, of the Chinese having promised six hundred dragons to the
allied forces.

He faced Yorke and his subordinate ministers with something
almost like amusement, knowing those men wishing to violently
castigate him for the one event and stifled by the other. Gong Su
had been sent with the news by Crown Prince Mianning, and he
had insisted on attending the conference, smilingly. He sat with a
placid and benevolent expression that implied—very falsely—that
he had only a vague understanding of the proceedings, and his
presence forced the admirals to maintain the appearances of respect towards Laurence.

"It seems you have once more encountered difficulties with
your King's ministers," Gong Su observed afterwards, as they

walked together from Whitehall—that gentleman's elaborate and impressive robes, and mandarin's cap and button, as well as his long queue, drawing much fascinated attention from the Marines on duty and every other passerby in the courtyard.

"I am grateful, sir, that your lord seems to have overcome the objections of his own," Laurence said.

Gong Su did not answer immediately. Only when they were ensconced in the privacy of a hackney carriage did he resume the conversation. "Matters in China have altered since your departure. It is my very great sorrow to inform you, Captain, that your dread imperial father is in failing health."

"I am sorry to hear it," Laurence said, although he understood at once how Mianning had carried his point against the conservative faction. Men who might stand against a crown prince many years from his throne would not risk the same opposition when he would very shortly be their emperor. "And sorry as well that he should have been robbed, since we last met: I believe their Lordships have already told you of the hatching of the egg."

Gong Su inclined his head. "It is part of my instructions from His Imperial Highness to visit the hatchling and make observations on her character, whenever it should be convenient."

Laurence still did not hold himself very knowledgeable in the court etiquette of China, but he had learned enough to know that this meant "without the loss of a moment." He opened the window and spoke to the driver, who very unwilling had to be reminded thrice of his obligation under the hackney regulation, and promised a half-guinea before he would carry them even to the intersection of Portland and Weymouth, still a quarter-mile's walk from the gates of the covert. To do the man justice, only so far would his horses go, either; they were already restive and stamping as Laurence and Gong Su disembarked, and shied at the shadow of a Winchester courier falling upon the cobblestones in passing. Fortunately Gong Su was accustomed to the isolation of British coverts, and the alarm the general populace took from dragons; Laurence did not have to make excuses, and a gaggle of braver

chair-men were waiting by the corner, hoping for similarly abandoned passengers, who could be prevailed upon to pay twice the
going rate to be carried the rest of the way.

When they had reached the covert, Laurence took Gong Su to
meet Ning, not without the liveliest concern; he could not help but
fear the consequences of an unfavorable report of her behavior.
The alliance between their nations was too tentative and gossamer
a thing to easily support the weight of disappointment: not much
interest united them, except the desire to see Napoleon over-
thrown, and a great deal divided. The Chinese port in Australia
and its sea-serpent hordes were still thriving, to the ongoing cha-
grin of Whitehall, and the opium trade continued to evade Imperial restrictions, to the wrath of Peking; resentments which would
easily stir up into a quarrel, on only slight additional grounds.

But Ning comported herself with perfect decorum, rousing
from another nap for the introduction and inclining her head to
Gong Su politely. "I am deeply honored by the concern shown me
by His Imperial Highness, and it is my great hope soon to have
reached that maturity of body and spirit which should fit a dragon
to assume the august responsibility of making herself a comfort to
one who supports the will of Heaven," she said, in fluent Chinese.
"Lung Tien Xiang has with great generosity furnished me with his
copy of the Analects, as well as many other works of significance
and real value, that my education need not suffer excessively on
account of the unfortunate events which caused the removal of my
egg from its harbor in the precincts of the Imperial City and pre-
vented the ordinary course of my hatching therein. I would be very
glad of any further guidance for my reading."

Laurence could not but notice that this speech in no way committed her, but Gong Su was satisfied. "I rejoice to have the pleasure of informing my lord that you are in excellent health, and that
no evil effects have attended on the theft which took you with such
harsh abruptness from your home," he said. "He will take much
comfort in hearing that you have endured the upheaval with a
spirit of resolution and equanimity. I will make every small and

humble effort in my power, such as it is, to acquire at least a few manuscripts for your further pleasure. As well, Captain," he added, to Laurence, "I would be honored deeply if you would permit me to offer on behalf of your elder brother," this another courtly fiction, as Laurence could give Mianning seven years without a stretch, "the proper festivities of welcome and celebration due the hatching of a new Celestial."

"I would like nothing better than to oblige you, sir," Laurence said, wary of how he might be expected to figure in such a ceremony, "but I must inform you that my present orders do not allow of any delay. We must leave for the Continent at first light tomorrow morning, and I go back to Dover to-night. That need not halt your plans; I trust my absence would not be felt with such a motive."

"If I may be forgiven for expressing an opinion in such a matter," Ning interjected unexpectedly, "I should feel it more appropriate to wait for a more auspicious moment. As I understand it, we stand upon the eve of war, where the armies of China shall strike against the very one who has so grievously offended the Celestial Throne by thieving away my egg. A celebration of my hatching might better be deferred until we may unite it with a celebration of victory, and thereby magnify the joys of the occasion."

Gong Su paused, and then said thoughtfully, "I receive your wise proposal humbly and with gratitude, Lung Tien Ning, and without substituting my own judgment for that of the Son of Heaven, believe there can be no objection to a temporary postponement under these circumstances."

"I am gratified by your kindness to our guest," Laurence said to Ning, afterwards, when Gong Su had left to return to his hotel, "and your patience in the matter." He was surprised to find her willing to postpone a ceremony which should certainly have gone far to establish her reputation in the eyes of the world.

"This island is too isolated," Ning said matter-of-factly, "and your own position too irregular: it does not seem to me very likely that any particularly notable persons are likely to attend, should

Gong Su offer a feast at present on my behalf—certainly no heads of state, or other personages of importance; I understand from Temeraire that he has never met your own king at all.

"When Napoleon has been defeated, it is certain a gathering will recommend itself to all the allies to decide how best to divide the spoils of victory: every ruler shall send a representative, and any formal celebration held at that time will naturally attract guests of the best quality, who will not wish to miss any chance of furthering negotiations to their advantage. And the presence of the expected force from China can only add to the consequence of that nation, and therefore myself. It will do much better. Do you find any flaw in my reasoning?" she asked; perhaps Laurence's expression showed something of his feelings.

"No," Laurence said. "No; your reasoning seems to me eminently sound. And if we should lose?"

"Such an unhappy outcome cannot really be taken into consideration," Ning said cheerfully: but certainly having avoided any public display of loyalty to China, or its future emperor, would make it less notable a treachery if she allowed herself to be won over by a victorious Napoleon, to claim the post of companion to his heir.

Laurence felt a qualm at visiting this scheming creature on an unsuspecting Mianning, who if he did not really have a familial claim upon him had certainly earned his gratitude. But an emperor of China required a Celestial, and Ning had at least proven she could be circumspect when her situation demanded. She might not indeed be so poor a companion for a ruler much beset by conspirators, once she had finally committed herself to his service.

"Meanwhile," Ning went on, "after consideration I have decided it would be best should I accompany you to the Continent. Although I cannot take part in the fighting directly, as the Chinese will think it inappropriate, I feel there will be much for me to learn by observation, and I expect there will be more opportunity of acquainting myself with other officers of high rank while in your company, now that you have been made an admiral—so long as you were not demoted to-day?" Her head came swiveling down to inspect him, tilting an eye towards the bars upon his shoulders. "There were some remarks I overheard made among the couriers that supposed this might be the case."

"No," Laurence said dryly. "I am happy to say I remain an admiral, and of more use."

"That is excellent," Ning said, quite unruffled. "It would have been inconvenient otherwise."

"I must however demur: you are not yet up to the flight," Laurence said. "We have near six hundred miles to cover in three days' flying, and every dragon of our company will be under full weight of harness and men; none of them can carry you. You must remain here."

"*That* will not do," Ning said. "No-one comes to this covert except low officers and couriers, and too few of those besides. But pray do not worry," she added. "You are beset with many cares, and must be desiring to return to Temeraire at once. You may dress for flying; I will make all the necessary arrangements."

Laurence did have to dress, so he deferred further argument even while wondering what arrangements she thought she might make. There was no dragon in the covert who could manage her bulk and the necessary speed of their flight both: she was growing with the same explosive speed Laurence recalled from Temeraire's early weeks, and more nearly approximated the size of a light-weight than a courier beast, by now. In an emergency, she might have been carried, but he would not slow the entire company for her and her unknown purposes.

But when he emerged from his cabin, she looked only satisfied and said, "Good, you are ready; our transport is nearly here."

Nearly in this case proved to mean the better part of an hour, and only when Laurence was on the point of refusing to wait any longer, and taking a courier, did a heavy ponderous flapping of large wings aloft clear the landing-ring of the covert. The massive Regal Copper of Temeraire's acquaintance from the breeding grounds, Requiescat, came thumping down.

"I regret that it was not possible for you to be more timely," Ning said, rather coldly.

"It ain't *my* fault," Requiescat said. "I don't fly a mile straight up for my own pleasure. But you can't guess the fuss the ground-lings make, only if I choose to coast in at a decent height—'stampeded everyone on Rotten Row,'" he mimicked a whine. "They don't take much stampeding, let me tell you. Climb on, since you're in such a hurry, and let's be off."

"A moment, if you please," Laurence said.

The Regal startled and peered very carefully down. "Why, I didn't see you there," he said, addressing a shrub somewhat to Laurence's left. "Who are you, then?"

"I am Temeraire's captain," Laurence said in some asperity. "Do I understand that you are volunteering to come to the Continent with us? And fight?"

"I might as well, I guess," Requiescat said. "I am tired of carrying rocks around. It may be good money, but it gets stale, there's no denying."

Laurence contemplated without enthusiasm the project of feeding a Regal Copper, with six other heavy-weights to manage already among their force—but there was no denying the breed exerted a kind of moral force upon their fellows disproportionate to even their immense scale. He was sensible of the advantage Requiescat's presence should offer not merely in battle, but in securing the uncertain discipline of his company. His worst fear at present was not defeat, but a mutiny among his captains, which might rob them of a victory otherwise in reach—and he would hold himself responsible regardless of the ill-management of the Admiralty which had served him with such officers as made that mutiny a prospect more probable than unthinkable.

Laurence looked at Ning, who regarded him with placid mien. How she had prevailed upon an unharnessed and indolent beast to volunteer for war, Laurence did not know, and suspected some inducement had been privately offered, which might well be held to his own account in future. But so far as the practical side of the matter, she had indeed found a solution: Requiescat could certainly manage her weight, even if he were armored to boot.

"Very well," Laurence said, yielding. "If you are set on this course, you are welcome; and you may accompany us as well, if you choose," he added to Ning, "but I think I will require your promise that so long as you remain with us you will undertake no action inimical to Britain's interests, nor hold any conversation with the enemy."

Ning considered this demand long enough to make Laurence glad he had made it, and at last judiciously said, "I believe I can commit myself so far: you have my word," and he could only hope that would be sufficient bond to keep her from either imprudence, or a dishonorable excess of the reverse.

"Requiescat is welcome: he is very handy in a fight when he likes to be, even if he does want the biggest share of everything, always," Temeraire said. "But I do not understand why Ning wishes to come along, and—Laurence, of course I do not mean to imply there is anything wanting in a dragon of *my* lineage, only I am afraid Ning—that she is—" He stopped, wondering how best to put it into words, without inviting any reflections on her breeding.

"Just so," Laurence said with a sigh, "but we are most likely better off bringing her than leaving her behind; she would certainly make some form of mischief in our absence."

"I am quite content to come," Ning herself said, when Temeraire tried to suggest that perhaps she would be better off remaining out of the noise and tumult of war, where she might easily be injured, particularly at her small size. "I will be careful to evade any danger."

"I am sure she *will*," Temeraire muttered, disgruntled, but there was no more time for persuasion to act upon her; the last furious bustle of preparation was under way, and Challoner, the new second lieutenant, was begging his pardon, but they needed his help with the armor.

Temeraire had scarcely remembered the enormous effort involved in getting a British heavy-weight under full arms and under way, and the size of the crew required to make the operation possible at all. He had once taken it for granted. Now he had learned to look with a critical eye upon the service which had then been all his world, and yet the cheerful ordinary shouting and cursing still had the power to raise a pang of pleasurable nostalgia—officers and ground crew all scrambling in every direction, checking over every buckle; the supplies all laid out and going aboard in their orderly fashion, as unchanged as sunrise. There was even something satisfying in the imposing weight of harness and chainmail, and more still in knowing his belly-netting held nearly fifty incendiaries, and a full complement of seven riflemen were already gone aboard his back.

He had been luxuriously scrubbed yesterday, under Challoner's supervision—Lieutenant Challoner herself entirely satisfactory, with a silver-buttoned coat in bright green, hair neatly braided and tied at the end with a matching ribbon, everything about her deeply comforting to Temeraire's sense of what was due their new rank and stature. She had also the charming quality of being the sister of one of Temeraire's former officers who had died at the Battle of Dover, and therefore seemed rather like a lost valuable recovered: although it was puzzling Rebecca should have described herself to him as the *younger* sister, when she was older than Dilly had been; but Temeraire put this aside; he did not like to think too much about the way time passed for people.

She had gracefully accepted Temeraire's hints on the subject of the appearance he should like the crew to present, and acted upon them: there was not an officer who did not have a tidy black neckcloth and a freshly pressed coat; their boots were all blacked to an equal shine, and the ground crew, too, were all tidy and had clean shirts and clean leather vests. The whole clearing offered a handsome portrait of industry and order to Temeraire's survey, and he could not help but regret that Forthing should very soon mar it again with his own disgraceful appearance, quite likely leading a good number of the crew astray with him.

He had tried to broach the subject with Laurence—"Surely we

ought have a first lieutenant more—more suitable"—but Laurence had firmly put a period to the discussion.

"My dear, I must ask your pardon. I know you are not fond of Forthing, but you must see the injustice of having accepted his toil and service all this long and thankless way, only to push him aside at the first opportunity where that service might receive its just reward. He has served honorably and to the best of his abilities, and I cannot entertain the suggestion of replacement."

Temeraire sighed again, but consoled himself: at least he had no reason to blush for his crew *now,* and battlefield conditions might excuse the lack of that formality and neatness of uniform which were under better circumstances considered appropriate.

Half their company was leaving under Granby's command from Edinburgh, but even the two formations which would back them made an enthusiastic noise full of consequence. Temeraire only wished he could think better than he did of the dragons behind him. Obituria, the senior heavy-weight among them, was impressive in the physical sense: she was a large Chequered Nettle, with a fourteen-barbed club of a tail which she could lay about as skillfully as if it were another leg, but she was a stolid, dull creature who flew her formation-patterns without the least spirit of inquiry. She would never say, *Why are we turning left and upwards here? Would that not expose our flanks to those little French harriers?* No, she did as her captain told her, and Captain Windle was as dull as his beast: seemed to only speak in words of one syllable, or two if he were much pressed.

Then there was Fidelitas, their Anglewing, who had the very peculiar habit of being *almost* interesting. If they were ever near each other, breakfasting at the pen perhaps, and Temeraire struck up a conversation with him, very soon he would be talking animatedly and getting quite excited—and then abruptly he would stop as though someone had clapped his mouth shut for him, and go wooden. There was no accounting for it, and anyway Temeraire nursed a private irritation against his captain, Poole, who often forgot entirely to call Laurence "sir" and never touched his hat.

But they certainly made a good enough outward show, with their formations assembled behind them, to make Temeraire pleased to lead them. It was not as glorious of course as flying at the head of the massed legions of China, but one could not have everything, all the time. And their complete equipage was perhaps even more impressive—if not *attractive;* Temeraire did not see why the Corps could not spare a thought, when laying out their gear, to provide them with banners, perhaps, or streamers—narrow streamers of thin cotton, attached to the front wing-edges, would have produced quite a remarkable effect, *he* thought.

At least Requiescat added admirably to their color. The formation-dragons were more than a little startled when he landed as they were forming up; he had been outfitted with mail, and Perscitia had further sent him along a new leather-and-steel head covering of her own devising, which only made him look more impressive. "I would have ordered one made for you," she had told Temeraire apologetically, "but it requires a great many measurements, to ensure it does not obstruct vision, and in any case I am not confident it would do for you, what with the divine wind—like being inside a bell when it has been rung, very likely."

"So, we are off to give the French another good drubbing, are we?" Requiescat said genially, as Ning leapt aboard his back and settled herself, with a rather preening stretch of her neck, between his wings. "Where is everybody?" he asked, looking around.

"The other formation is leaving from Edinburgh," Temeraire said, feeling this an unjustified aspersion on the size of their force: they had two formations, and besides that another dozen unharnessed beasts had been persuaded to join up.

"I don't mean formations," Requiescat said, "but there they are coming, I guess," and Temeraire looked round to see a cloud—no, a flock of birds—no, it was dragons; at least fifty smallish light-weights, all coming towards them—

It turned out to be Ricarlee, with a crowd of the Scots ferals. They produced a near-riot on their arrival—they had no notion of order, and directly they had landed they were scrambling into ev-

eryone's clearings, rousing up the Channel dragons from their
sleep, poking their noses into the feeding pen, until finally Temeraire roared loud enough to secure their attention, and also to
knock over one old oak, which crashed down into a barracks cabin
and brought out a dozen ground crewmen shouting and cursing.

This noise quelled the better part of the horde. "Requiescat, go
and round up those fellows away from the officers' mess there,"
Temeraire said, more than a little exasperated, "and Fidelitas, pray
chase those others out of the pen. It is quite intolerable your fellows should be making such a mess of all our arrangements," he
added severely to Ricarlee, who had landed with a handful of
lieutenants—small dragons in dark shades with bright blue streaks
painted upon their hides. "If you are here to steal, we will serve
you out as that deserves straightaway; if not, you had better come
to order and explain yourselves and this behavior at once."

"No call to be unfriendly," Ricarlee said. "You can't blame
anyone for wanting a bite to sup. We are for France, isn't it? A
long way to go on an empty belly. Now then," he sidled in peculiarly close, and put his head near Temeraire's. "It'll be share and
share alike, I trust?"

"Share and share alike of what?" Temeraire said suspiciously.

"Ha ha," Ricarlee said, winking one eye in a strange fashion,
"very good, I understand you. So long as we're agreed."

"I do not understand *you*," Temeraire said. "You cannot expect to eat as much as we heavy-weights."

"Hmmrph," Ricarlee said. "Oh, aye, fair enough," in a tone of
one yielding on an important point at a bargaining-table.

"Laurence, whatever do you suppose he is talking about?" Temeraire asked, in an undertone, while the covert's harried quartermaster began a scurrying effort to put out some hot mash with
leftover beef bones for the blue-streaked ferals, mostly to keep
them from hanging about the pen peering wistfully through the
stakes and terrifying all the cattle within.

"I suppose that word has got about that there are heaps of
treasure to be had, in fighting Napoleon," Laurence said, "un-

doubtedly aided by legends of your recently acquired gold." He was conferring with Challoner and his own supply-officer, a Lieutenant Doone. "We will have them, if they will come: I had not expected so many to answer your lure, but I think we can manage it, even if our commons must be a little short."

"Do I understand correctly, sir," Captain Windle said—he had walked over from Obituria—"that you propose to saddle us with this unruly gaggle for baggage, and feed them out of our supply? The winter is a hard time for feral beasts, I am sure, and as a form of charity this must recommend itself; I would be glad to know what *military* purpose you intend they should serve."

More than you, Temeraire would have liked to say, his ruff going back at Windle's tone, which he felt thoroughly disrespectful, but Laurence answered as though he had asked the question without rudeness.

"I propose, Captain, that they should be a screen for our formations, and a constant threat to the enemy's supply and cavalry— what he has left of it, after Moscow. If we cannot contrive to feed them, they must supply their wants somewhere, and better in French territory than in Scotland. We will not, however, delay our departure any further for their sake. Temeraire, they must be ready to go now, or not at all. Pray pass the word to check harness."

Temeraire called out with a pleasant sensation of significance, "Let everyone see to their harness, if you please," and himself spread his wings and rose onto his haunches to give himself a thorough shaking, politely ignoring the young rifleman Dubrough who lost his footing and mortified had to haul himself back up along his carabiner straps.

"Ha ha, like geese," Ricarlee said, too audibly, but from every side the dragons were calling back, "All lies well," and Captain Windle scowling retreated to Obituria as Laurence stepped into Temeraire's ready claw to be put up.

"Temeraire, your heading is east by north," Laurence said, clasping his own carabiners onto the harness.

"East by north," Temeraire called. Fidelitas and Obituria returned, "East by north," correctly, and then—a leap, a beating of wings, and they were all aloft, the formations taking their arrowhead shapes behind him to either point of wing as they climbed. Temeraire would have liked to pause hovering to look over the display, or at least to crane his head around for a good look, but it would have spoilt the picture they made and reduced his dignity; he restrained the impulse. Distantly he heard Ricarlee and his fellows coming along after them in a clamoring mass.

When his ear could catch no more of the beating sounds of dragons in their first climb, he wheeled away from the coastline and over the open water. A rush of bracing air met him coming in from the Channel, and he let the warmer air beneath his wings carry him up above it. It was a fine clear day, and the harbor speckled with white sails and rowboats, faint cries of people seeing them streaming past—only for a moment; then they were already whipping past and out to sea.

Temeraire settled into a comfortable pace, flicking out his wing-tips on the upper crest to make sure everyone behind him saw the beat. A quick glance to starboard made sure he had not exceeded Obituria's pace—she would be their limit. She was certainly making an effort, but not unduly so, Temeraire judged. He would have to slow a little in an hour, perhaps, to give her a rest, but it was so lovely to fly swift at the start of a journey, after so long in covert; he was sure everyone must be glad of the chance to stretch themselves.

The cliffs had fallen away behind them; the Continent was a faint smudge on the horizon. One of the large ships of the blockade—a first-rate, or a second-rate? He should have to ask Laurence—was beating up the Channel on patrol, working against the wind that was diving beneath them. Only mizzen and mainsails spread, but she was still impressive, and to Temeraire's surprised delight she fired a salute as their shadows came streaming over the waves and ran up her sails.

"Laurence, what is that ship?" he asked.

Laurence trained his glass upon her and after a moment said, "My dear, that is the *Temeraire*, herself."

Part IV

Chapter 15

$\mathcal{I}$SKIERKA'S FLAME SCORCHED THE air just short of Temeraire's leading wing—"I beg your pardon," Temeraire said indignantly. He wheeled round, and then discovered half the ferals had abandoned their positions, wreaking merry havoc among a handful of French supply-carts on the road to the south, quite away from any fighting.

"Temeraire, we must try and establish control over the left flank," Laurence called, his glass trained upon the field below, where all the infantry of both sides were tangled in what Temeraire found an indistinguishable mass, clouded by stinking wafts of black powder smoke. "I think we are near to breaking them. A run of incendiaries, united with Wittgenstein's advance, would have a material effect, if it can be done—a quarter of an hour from now, I think, or a little more."

"But Laurence, look what the ferals are doing," Temeraire protested. "If I do not go and chivvy them back into line—"

"We knew not to expect better from them, my dear," Laurence said. "This is not the moment to concern ourselves with their correction."

Temeraire without pleasure resigned himself to ignoring the ferals' pillaging; he recalled with pain the behavior of the Russian beasts, over the Berezina—and those dragons had not been under his command; it had not reflected on him. Now here they were with nearly the entire city of Berlin observing, and all their allies— General Wittgenstein himself was at that very moment taking a courier on an arc to the east, watching the battle through his glass—and everyone could see that nearly half his troops were behaving in this scaly and disorderly fashion. He writhed inwardly with mortification and threw a glance towards their right flank, where Dyhern and Eroica were maneuvering with their fellows. Perhaps they would not notice?

He turned his attention back to the battle and called to Iskierka, "Can you take that blue-green fellow over there, or will you need some help?"

"Oh!" Iskierka gave her present victims, a pair of French lightweights, a last pursuing gout of fire. "As though I should need any help to manage anyone at all," and she was tearing off after the big French cross-breed, who was serving as the anchor of their artillery-cover.

Quite naturally, a handful of the middle-weights from the left flank came to help screen him. "There," Temeraire said. "Requiescat, pray knock us a hole on the left."

"Do you mean their left, or my left?" Requiescat said, circling him lazily, as though they had all the time imaginable. "And which *is* the left; I am no hand at remembering."

"Over that large building with the green steeple!" Temeraire said irritably.

"Have him take the rest of the ferals with him," Laurence said, and Temeraire passed along the order—for what it was worth, as nearly all the Scottish dragons were busy rummaging through the sacks of the shattered wagons below; but some half a dozen of the smaller ones went after Requiescat when he called them to order, even if they were not likely to be much use.

Meanwhile, however, Temeraire's new signal-ensign Quigley

was putting out the flags—*ready incendiaries* and *fall in behind leader*. Temeraire fended off an attempt by a couple of over-daring young French beasts, who did not know better than to come at him from his lower flank—a quick hovering twist and he was doubled on himself. He roared at them as they closed. Both wheeled away with cries of anguish, a lighter lesson than they had asked for, Temeraire felt; but he did not have time to pursue them at present. Requiescat had gone barreling through the lines, his head down and the rifle-fire pinging harmlessly off his helm, and the ferals had gone in after him clawing about the dragons who had been first bowled out of the way and were struggling to beat back up into place.

"Excellent," Laurence said. "Make your pass when ready, Temeraire," and Temeraire plunged into the disorder of the French line with his legs tucked in carefully, the long-unaccustomed feeling of his bellmen scrambling about in the rigging below, which was growing noticeably lighter as they cast off the incendiaries in their careful way—he could feel each one being handed along a line of men until it reached the end of the rigging, just below his tail, and there down a line of three men suspended by lines, to the last one who ignited the fuse and let the bomb drop.

Obituria and Cavernus were with him—Cavernus another of their formation-leaders, a Malachite Reaper, who had come over with Granby from Edinburgh; she was a bit standoffish, and not above middle-weight, but a really clever flyer. All their formations came behind them, their crews dropping their own bombs. Not one in five landed anywhere useful, of course, and each one was necessarily small; that was the trouble with incendiaries—and worse, there was no sign of Fidelitas, who ought to have come along, too. Temeraire, startled, did a quick survey over the battlefield as he finished his pass; the dragons of Fidelitas's formation were circling uncertainly, many of them having small unhelpful skirmishes with French beasts—and Fidelitas himself was down among the baggage-carts, with the ferals.

"Oh!" Temeraire said, indignant.

"Can you manage another pass?" Laurence called, at the same

moment; they had created some noise and confusion on the ground beneath, but not as much as one might have hoped—not as much as *four* formations should have done. But the French dragons were recovering from their buffeting now, coming for them in their dangerous swarming numbers, and if he tried to lead the others back through that cloud instead of going round back to their own lines, Obituria was sure to take some injury; she was not quick enough. Fidelitas *would* have been, Temeraire thought resentfully.

He cast an eye quickly over the ground below—the incendiaries had at least thoroughly disordered the twenty gun-crews covering the French center; those would take several minutes to begin firing again. "Laurence, I might take those guns, myself, if the others could keep the French dragons off my back a little longer," Temeraire called back, proposing an alternative, and Laurence gave the word. The signal-flags flashed out, telling the rest of the dragons to cover his pass. But Obituria seemed perplexed; she was already climbing up out of combat-height to circle back to the allied line, without any orders at all, and even though the signal-ensign on her back ought to have been watching the flag-dragon, she did not turn round. Fortunately, Cavernus rallied her own formation to make a shield—but the smaller dragons, unsupported, would not be able to hold for long. Temeraire calculated quickly—he would have to go straight at the gun-crews, flying over the French infantry before them; he could not afford the time to circle round and come from their rear.

There was no more time to consider; either he must go at once, or they must give up, accept that their pass had failed in such a clumsy manner in front of everyone, when it *ought* to have gone well. Temeraire whirled and dived low even as he caught a glimpse of Laurence raising the speaking-trumpet to call him off, and steeled himself against the frantic spattering of musket-balls that struck his chest and legs from the French infantry below—like being bitten all over by rats or something equally unpleasant, and he could not even give vent to a hiss of displeasure; he required every last ounce of breath.

Halfway from the guns, he began roaring at measured intervals, just as though he meant to raise up a wave. Men and horses collapsed and scattered even before the shorter roars, and most of the already-disordered artillery-crews broke and began to flee in every direction; faintly he heard voices crying, *"Le vent du diable!"* as they ran. But one brave crew had stayed by the third gun in the line—blood streaming over their faces and hands, and the ground near them still smoking where an incendiary had landed not far away, but they were holding fast, exhorted by a tall young officer in a shako with its once-proud plume replaced by a makeshift bunch of chicken feathers. They were trying to bring the gun to bear—on him.

The wide mouth of the iron cannon gaped hideously round as they struggling turned it inch by inch. Staring down its dark maw, Temeraire tried not to think of all the dreadful things Perscitia had said about being struck by cannon-shot, and especially not of poor Chalcedony, who had gone down so horribly in the Battle of Shoeburyness with a ball to the chest. He could only try to outrun them: if he shifted his course now, the divine wind would collapse, and it would not do against all those guns; it was not enough just to destroy *one*.

He kept his roars coming, kept flying, even as the gunners frantically tamped down the wadding, and loaded in the shot. And then he was close enough: even as they were putting the slow-match to the tube, he gathered one last breath and roared enormously, collapsing the other waves into a single monstrous force, and the divine wind rolled out over them.

The gun rang so violently it might have been church-bells, pealing. The crew fell away like rag dolls, collapsing; Temeraire glimpsed with sorrow the officer with his feathers sinking, his eyes gone red with blood. And then the barrel exploded. Flames and bits of iron and splinters, red-hot and smoldering, flew in every direction. All along the ridge of the low hill, the oaken carriages of the guns were shattering as though they had been struck by cannon-fire. Those men who had not fled fast enough or far enough littered the ground unmoving, in a wide fan-shape marking the path of the divine wind.

And as Temeraire lifted away, wincing, the entire hill upon which the guns had stood abruptly collapsed, as though some essential foundation had shattered. Dirt and sand and pebbles cascaded away in a tremendous wash, burying the nearest ranks of French infantry to their ankles where they had not already been decimated by the hail of metal.

The French ranks near-by were dismayed by the attack, and the dragons above reeled back; Cavernus and her formation wheeled into a diamond-shape round Temeraire, sheltering him as he got back aloft, and together they climbed out of fighting-height and dashed back to the safety of the allied lines. Temeraire had the satisfaction of seeing Eroica's signal-ensign dip flags in a quick salute, as they swept past. His breath was short, and now that the moment of crisis had passed, the bullet-wounds stung fiercely; there seemed a great many of them.

"Report, Mr. Roland," Laurence called.

"Flinders lost, Warrick wounded, sir," Emily Roland called, hanging off halfway up his side. "A dozen hits to the chest, and the bellmen cannot stanch two."

"Mr. Quigley, signal Iskierka that we are going to the field-hospital, and to hold the line until we return," Laurence called.

"Surely that can wait until the battle is over," Temeraire said, flinching; oh, how he hated the surgeons. "Truly, Laurence, I do not feel them in the slightest."

But Laurence was inflexible; with a sigh Temeraire put down at the clearing, and tried to console himself that at least Keynes was with them again—the finest dragon-surgeon of Britain's forces, and the quickest hand at getting the wretched musket-balls out. It was not a very *good* consolation, however.

"What the devil were you about, giving them your whole belly for washing?" Keynes demanded in great irritation, having ordered Temeraire to sprawl on his side—a highly uncomfortable position, nearly squashing one wing—while he clambered about with his savage long-bladed knives, and his assistants scuttling behind him with the dish.

"Well, I did not *want* to!" Temeraire said, protesting. "But there was nothing else to be done, after Obituria had flown off. It would scarcely have gone better if I had circled around while Cavernus and the others were bowled over, and then the French could have come at me from aloft. Ow!" Another ball had dropped into the dish, with its inappropriately pleasant chiming sound, and the hot searing iron had been pressed to the wound to close it. "Surely that is all of them."

"I know a bullet-hole when I see one, damn your scaly hide," Keynes said, jabbing him again.

Laurence had with difficulty restrained his first instinctual reaction on the battlefield, which had been a murderous one; but hearing Temeraire say straight-out what ought to have been plain—which surely *had been* plain, to Obituria's captain—renewed his rage afresh. For a moment sight dimmed, one of those too-vivid memories seizing him, and he was in the night sky over the ocean, the *Valérie* below them: her lanterns and the muzzles of her cannon glowing red-hot, the only lights upon her decks. The wind in his face and the shock of impact: the barbed ball tearing into Temeraire's chest from her skyward guns.

He shook the darkness away and stood again in daylight, torn grass and mud churned up with thick rivulets of dragon blood spattered across his boots, the low groans of injured dragons and men. Temeraire still bore that scar, a knot the size of Laurence's fist, drawn flesh and dulled scales; he liked to paint it over sometimes for vanity. If there had been a skyward gun in the French emplacement; if they had fired off that last round in time, a difference of half a minute—

"That is all of them," Keynes said, straightening up, "and more than there ought to have been."

Laurence did not let anger go, but dismissed it to return later; the battle was not over. "Can he fly, Mr. Keynes?"

"I cannot keep out of the fighting," Temeraire protested immediately, pricking up his ruff.

"I should prefer a week's rest with no flying," Keynes said, "but I do not insist upon it—yet. Keep him out of musket-fire range, and see he has a side of raw beef to-night."

"Very well," Laurence said. "Has Mr. Warrick been taken off, Mr. Challoner?"

"Aye, sir," Challoner answered, from the belly-rigging; she herself had a bandage wrapped snugly about her left arm, and few of the bellmen had not been marked likewise.

Temeraire craning around to peer at them said anxiously, "You are not badly hurt, Challoner? I am glad to hear it. Where are they taking poor Warrick? And are you quite certain Flinders is dead? Perhaps he will wake?"

Flinders had lost nearly half his skull to a flying scrap of iron, likely a fragment of a cannon-barrel, and would certainly never wake again before the Judgment; Temeraire unhappily accepted the news, and said, "We will be sure to look in on his wife and children, Laurence, will we not?—I am very sorry he should be lost to them, and us."

"We will," Laurence said, going back aboard. He was not surprised at the inquiry, for Temeraire had before now shown all the signs of taking to heart the many strictures Churki had lain down for the duty of care the Incan dragons felt due to those men and women in their charge. Temeraire had begun to apply these even while crewed by the sorriest gang of untrained sea-dogs, conscripted under their duress and his own after the wreck of the *Allegiance*—the dregs of the Navy and half of them drunkards and former convicts pressed out of the bowels of Sydney Harbor. It was not wonderful that those sentiments should have enlarged themselves rapidly on so much better matter as his new crew offered: men of the Corps, trained up in the service and among dragons from childhood, and all of them respectable even if not nice in their manners.

But it was a novel expression to those men themselves, used to the European mode where dragons were encouraged to bind all their affections up in their captains, in hopes of giving that one hand a strong rein to pull upon. Laurence knew many crewmen thought it unremarkable to have gone ten years in service on a dragon, without ever once exchanging any conversation with the beast, direct; even most lieutenants spoke with them only rarely. He mounted back up hearing approving murmurs, mingled with the same anger he felt himself: the misconduct of Obituria's captain had left them, too, exposed to the danger their dragon had faced, and there was not a man who did not feel that Flinders need not have died.

"I will certainly have words with Obituria," Temeraire said, as he pushed aloft again with a few stifled hisses of discomfort to belie his earlier bravado. "I do not see what business she had going off in that fashion. Oh! And as for Fidelitas—!"

They reached fighting-altitude above a battlefield much altered by their handiwork, and the passage of three-quarters of an hour. Dyhern and the Prussian dragons holding the right still struggled against the more numerous and nimbler French—but they were making a far better showing than at the disastrous battle of Jena, where so many of the Prussian dragons had been brought low.

The Prussians had indeed turned the French strategy back upon them: the big dragons had exposed themselves early on, pretending to cleave to their old formation-flying habits, but their captains had been hiding below, safe in the belly-netting. As soon as the French boarding parties had dropped onto their backs, the heavy-weights had raced at top speed to the back of the lines, where the French boarders were seized at once by the many eager hands of their ground crews and imprisoned. It was a blow even larger than the mere loss of numbers: the French could ill afford to spare trained veterans at present from any part of their army, and with so many young and half-trained beasts among them, skilled aviators were an especial loss.

By now the French had belatedly grown wary of this maneuver. The boarders had ceased to go, and in their absence, the sheer muscle of the Prussian heavy-weights made a solid wall which even the numbers of the French dragons could not penetrate. Many of the young French beasts felt all the natural hesitation of a twelve-ton beast confronted by one of eighteen tons, spiked and plated in the bony armor common among Prussian heavy-weights. They had thus reached a stalemate, and below them the Russian and French guns were arguing the question back and forth, with an equal lack of resolution.

But on the left, the hole Temeraire's assault had opened was proving worth the cost: the French flank was weakening, and from their lofty distance Laurence could see the wreckage of two French infantry squares, broken by the explosion of the guns and trampled by the Russian light cavalry; another gun emplacement was being overrun, and Russian guns had been dragged forward and now unopposed were rapidly clearing away the French dragons from the air.

"We will let them work," Laurence said, watching the guns boom and thunder. "Temeraire, we can turn against the center, I believe. Mr. Forthing, signal a charge; Iskierka to take point, if you please. We will keep to the rear—"

"Oh, Laurence!" Temeraire protested.

Laurence continued firmly, "—and make a feint at threatening their guns on that hill near the green barn. We have put some fear in their bellies, I hope, and we may do more good there, by drawing away a significant portion of their force for an unnecessary defense."

But Temeraire's entire frame quivered with restive unhappiness all the while he hovered and darted around the hill, even though he was keeping a full six French dragons thoroughly occupied— two of them heavy-weights, and the French aerial center weakened materially thereby. Laurence was thoroughly satisfied with the arrangement, but Temeraire plainly not—and least so when he had to watch Iskierka lead a dazzling and ferocious charge straight at the French center, only to plunge with startling speed beneath the braced and waiting lines, and come up from beneath them.

The French were so entirely taken by surprise by that dive— contrary to all received wisdom, as putting the British dragons vulnerable below their claws—that they did not act to seize the advantage it offered them swiftly enough. Iskierka as quickly looped back up between their two ranks, followed by the full company, who then broke into two groups: middle-weights twisting to pounce upon the French light-weights in the forward rank, while the light-weights and heavy-weights together fell upon the larger beasts to the rear.

It was a daring maneuver—one which Temeraire himself had proposed, but it was perhaps not wonderful that its success should not be enough to content him when he was forced to see his design enacted by another. His ruff lay so flat against his neck that he looked nearly an Imperial dragon again. "I do not see why Iskierka needs to be flaming off in that showy way," he said, "and she quite nearly fouled Latinius's wing, on that last turn," this referring to the small Grey Copper from Fidelitas's formation, who was hanging on Iskierka's coattails and making clawing passes at the eyes of her recoiling targets, with every evidence of high delight.

Laurence laid a comforting hand on his neck, and told Forthing, "Pass the word to Requiescat." The massive Regal Copper smashed through the wavering French light-weights. Dragons scattered in every direction as he rolled onwards over them, and the British middle-weights turned eagerly to join the others in their assault in the remaining French forces.

Their own boarding parties now began going over. So many of the French dragons were unharnessed as to make the usual practice, aimed at capturing a beast's captain, ineffective. Instead men on long tethers leapt over, in moments planted spikes deep into the unharnessed dragon's bare back, and flung heavy cables over the side before they swung off themselves and were pulled back to safety. The crew of the light-weights seized the dangling ends and their dragons swiftly looped over and over around the enemy beast. Thus entangled, the French dragons had to flee or have their wings pinned, and more than one beast lost its wind and plummeted to the ground in a dreadful crash.

Laurence watched the operation without pleasure. The same technique had been used in the medieval age by the dragon-slayers

of the Norman court, who mounted on their own beasts had un-
dertaken a ruthless culling of the wild beasts of the British Isles.
The method had for a thousand years made harnessed dragons
with their large crews inevitably the masters of the unharnessed, at
least in the West; and these French dragons were too young and
unpracticed to have mastered the Chinese dragons' skill at defend-
ing one another from similar attacks.

Poole had suggested the tactic at the conference Laurence had
held with his officers, three nights ago, with an air of challenging
him to object—as though he thought Laurence some sort of idle
romantic, instead of a serving-officer who had been at sea since the
age of twelve, and at war nearly all his life. He wondered in grim
amusement how Poole himself would have liked to be on the deck
of a sixty-four taking a broadside, trying to keep his feet on blood-
washed oak. Laurence did not have the kind of squeamishness
which consisted in a refusal to harm the enemy upon the battlefield, in open and honest combat.

But there was still nothing like pleasure in seeing half-trained
young dragons flung down, and they were going at a shockingly
rapid pace. Ten French light-weights were felled in less than a
quarter of an hour, and then Cavernus made a daring effort on one
unharnessed Petit Chevalier. She dropped a dozen boarders on the
heavy-weight dragon's back, then she rounded up the ferals to
help: every small dragon seized on the dangling ropes and whipped
around the Chevalier, who grew clumsy with alarm and fouled
wings as they drew more than twenty loops around him: he might
have bulled his way loose at first, but the ferals were beating about
his head, and abruptly his wings were pulled too tight against his
body.

He dragged a breath, struggled—one of the ferals took a sharp
tumble, another was raked by outflung talons—and fell, fell, roaring in terror, to smash upon the ground below, crushing an entire
company of cavalry beneath his massive bulk.

The French aerial line broke: dozens of unharnessed dragons
fleeing away towards the Elbe, their panic infecting the harnessed

beasts and carrying many of these along with them; the remainder milling in uncertain confusion only to be harried away by Iskierka, pouring out flame as she descended on them. The center was theirs.

"Signal bombardment," Laurence said, and all the harnessed British dragons circled back, finding their formations, and began to sweep back and forth over the French infantry, freely dropping their incendiaries among them. The French were trying to turn their guns skyward; Fidelitas—now returned to the field—led his formation in a raking pass across two emplacements, and Cavernus went after another. But there were other guns beginning to threaten their position, and in any case Laurence judged the beasts would by now have spent the better part of their incendiaries. "Withdraw to heights," he said, and as the first gun-crew began their firing sequence, the British dragons were already circling up and higher, out of range.

They were also beyond the range of doing much damage direct, but Laurence was satisfied: they had established a secure command of the air. "Temeraire, if you please, send one of those ferals round to ask Dyhern if he could use a formation or two: we will spare him Cavernus and Fidelitas, if he requires their aid," he said.

"Very well," Temeraire said unenthusiastically, and collared one of the circling Scots, who had got herself a table-cloth out of the wagon-carts and thrust her head through it, so it now hung on her like a sort of capelet. "Oh, all right," she said, rather grumbling, but she went off in a hurry.

Meanwhile, the guns kept firing a steady barrage to keep them far aloft, but these were no longer trained upon the allied forces, steadily pressing their advantage, and then Laurence distantly heard as the Prussian cuirassiers shouted as one. Their horses were hooded and blinkered and nose-muffled from any glimpse of the dragons above; they made a thundering roll of a charge across the field, into the lessened hail of iron, and fell upon the guns. Laurence lowered his glass. He had seen enough: the day was theirs.

Laurence saw Temeraire settled in the field-covert with a side of beef and a bowlful of hot beef blood, sent over by way of thanks from the Prussian corps. "Mr. Keynes said he will look in on us in an hour, Admiral," O'Dea said, "and we will trust in the saints to keep himself," meaning Temeraire, "from taking blood-poisoning before then, or going mad from lead in the humors; like as not the knife has missed a ball here or there."

This provoked Temeraire to say uneasily, "I am sure there cannot be much lead left in me, after all of that wretched rooting about. Laurence, is going mad very uncomfortable?"

Laurence sighed privately. He would have been glad for a different ground-crew master, if he had dared ask for a replacement: O'Dea was clever enough, but untrained, and given to excess of both drink and poetic lamentations. In *his* case, Laurence would have had no compunction in removing him from the rôle and keeping him on as a personal secretary instead. But the Admiralty would surely have assigned them another scowling half-spy, or a man who would resist every advancement in practice. If O'Dea did not know his work as well as he ought, at least he had less to unlearn, and seven months' observation of the habits of the Chinese legions made him nearly as much an expert as any man in Britain.

"If you can feel any other metal remaining, pray inform Keynes; I am certain you will have no ill-effects before he comes. I will return directly I have seen my staff, and attended to the wounded," Laurence said, and went to collect Granby.

Iskierka had established a handsome bonfire in her clearing, for her crew, and was also eating; she was pleased with herself, as indeed she had a right to be. By her count, which was only a little exaggerated, she had told for some eight beasts, most heavy-weights, besides keeping their forward line clear and leading their telling strike. She had paid little for her daring: a few glancing musket-balls, fired from enemy dragons more interested in evading than fighting her, and one raking scratch already closed by the time she had come to earth—now poulticed and bandaged for the night by her surgeon, in an excess of caution which had provoked Keynes to mutter about mollycoddling. "And you may tell Temeraire for me that he did not do so badly, himself," Iskierka said. "I liked what he did with those cannon: it was quite handy, although I do think he might have been more clever about getting shot."

"A rotten mess," Granby said, when they were far enough from the clearing to be out of earshot from his crew, along the paths: their field-covert sprawled nearly two miles over a long stretch of foothills, with most dragons crammed in three and four to a clearing, but Temeraire and Iskierka were established on the upper heights, in prime clearings, and a considerable distance from the central farmhouse where Laurence had established his command. "Damn Poole, anyway; he ought to be broken the service."

"I cannot say so, John," Laurence said.

"Nor I, anyone would tell you," Granby said, "but I say it anyway. He wasn't overborne by some wild start of his beast; he *took* Fidelitas down, after those mad Scots beggars, and you will never convince me otherwise."

"You will oblige me by pretending, however," Laurence said wearily, and Granby raised an eyebrow.

"You have something deep in mind, I suppose," he said. "Do you mean to turn out a politician, after all?"

"God save me such a fate," Laurence said, with more force than hope behind it. He felt an inward revulsion at his own present thoughts: a species of scheming against his own officers, those in whom he had been used to repose the fullest trust. He had been assigned officers before against his will, men of limited abilities or whose characters he could not wholeheartedly admire. He had nevertheless always felt himself their captain and not their enemy; his work had always been the straightforward task of helping them to do their duty, and there was a bitter taste to finding himself instead obliged to contrive against them.

Before the battle, he had hoped—had felt nearly certain—that the engagement, well-carried, would see his command brought in tune. The joy of seeing Berlin liberated, its citizens cheering, and knowing their joint efforts responsible for pushing the French over the Elbe, ought to have swept all small and petty quarrels away, and established that urgently necessary *esprit de corps* which would sustain them through the long campaign ahead.

But instead all the satisfactions which their victory ought to have brought, all the sense of good-fellowship and shared struggle, had been wasted. Or worse than wasted. There was not an officer, not a dragon, in their command, who did not know that Poole had deliberately flouted discipline, that Windle had avoided his duty, and that Temeraire and Cavernus and her formation had been forced to run a dangerous risk to cover for their failures. They and their subordinates could not feel themselves part of the victory.

And no confrontation was possible, which might have cleared the air. Unquestionably they knew they had acted wrongly, and by now must have been feeling the shame of having done so, but Laurence had no expectation of that emotion procuring anything like an apology. They could not acknowledge fault to him, whose guilt was so much the greater in their eyes. Instead Poole would say that Fidelitas had seen the ferals pillaging, and had thought himself entitled to claim his own share of whatever treasure there was to be had; Poole had not thought it his duty to check him, as Laurence had done nothing to check the other beasts. Windle's reply would be equally pat—the ordered run had been accomplished, and he had known they lacked the dragons for a second pass. His slower beast was vulnerable to the highly maneuverable French light-weights converging upon them. He had acted to preserve her, as was his own paramount duty.

Laurence did not wish to hear their excuses—did not trust himself to hear their excuses without making such an answer as would only serve the Admiralty, who longed for any justification to remove him, which a quarrel with his senior captains could be made to provide. And he could not dismiss them, either: the Admiralty would delightedly send them back, confirmed and approved in their behavior, and a certain wreck to the discipline of the entire force: there would be nothing left to him then but to resign, and quit the field entirely, with all the evil consequences not merely to himself but to the entire war effort.

"What will you say to them, then?" Granby asked.

"Nothing," Laurence said grimly.

He stopped at his quarters and armored himself in dress uniform, then summoned the captains to conference, where he maintained the most formal reserve his manners could support: he inquired only after particulars—casualties, injuries taken, armaments consumed—and silenced two attempts at officers trying to say anything more of their dragons' conduct. No refreshment was offered; he concluded the meeting in remarkably short order, and dismissed them to their dragons. It was a cold reception for men who had won a notable victory against a larger force, and he was sorry not to be able to give a warmer word to Captain Ainley, whose dragon Cavernus had done such work for them today. But he could not say anything, without saying too much. As he preferred not to hear Poole and Windle make excuses, he could not chastise them openly at all, and if he could say nothing to them, he must say nothing to any man.

"You must make *some* answer, though," Granby said afterwards, as they walked back to the clearings together. "They must be thinking you are keeping silent for fear of the Admiralty. If you don't check them, they will only get worse."

"I know," Laurence said. They had reached the crest of the hill now, and a bright spring wind came rustling the trees; he took off his hat to let the cold air stir against his forehead, looking out over the battlefield: bobbing lanterns traveling over the ground as the corpse-robbers picked over the dead.

$\mathcal{T}$EMERAIRE LOOKED AROUND FOR Laurence in vain the next morning, all through breakfast and having his wounds dressed fresh—including the two additional bullet-wounds which he had reluctantly confessed to Keynes on the second visit. He had regretted doing so directly afterwards, but he had to admit that to-day they were much better; he did not feel any twinge at all, except if he extended his wings all the way back as far as they could go, and even that was not so very bad.

He had been ordered to rest, but there was no need to fly: the French had all pulled across the Elbe. Everyone was jubilant that Berlin had been liberated, and all the church-bells had been rung in rejoicing that morning; there was no fighting going, so there was no need for Laurence to be gone, and where?

"You do not suppose Laurence would ever fight *another* duel," he asked Emily finally, growing anxious when the noon hour had come, and Laurence was still away.

"No, not when he has given you his word," she said, "and anyway he is admiral now: I don't suppose you can go about challenging your officers, even in the Navy."

"Why would he challenge one of his officers?" Temeraire said frowningly.

"Nothing," Emily said hastily. "Nothing—those are the only fellows around, after all. He can't challenge someone he don't talk to."

She darted away before Temeraire could press past this bit of transparency. He tried to question several other of his officers, but Forthing only looked blank, and Challoner said forthrightly, "Roland oughtn't have said anything. Pray don't keep asking around, Temeraire: *that* will get around, and gossip will only make it worse," which only increased his worry, and removed any power he had of addressing it, at least until Laurence should come back.

"I beg your pardon," Ning said, breaking into his brooding thoughts, "but do you think you will eat that lamb you have there?"

"Certainly I will eat it," Temeraire said, rather indignantly: Ning had refused any part of the battle, even though she might certainly have been of material use, if only she had consented to set a few French guns afire. *She* had not earned any delicacies. Then he sighed: worry was interfering with the enjoyment of what ought to have been a treat, as the lamb had been sent him in the line of medicine, for his wounds, and Baggy had seen it roasted beautifully on a spit.

"Do your wounds distress you a great deal?" Ning asked. "You seem out of sorts, despite our victory."

"It is not my wounds, only no-one will tell me why Laurence should be angry with his officers," Temeraire said. "And I do *not* have confidence he will not fight a duel, if any of them should have insulted his honor."

"I am afraid I do not understand," Ning said.

"Well, Roland let it slip, that Laurence should *like* to challenge one of them," Temeraire began, but Ning flicked her wings negatively.

"No, no," she said. "I do not understand why you are perplexed: surely there was ample cause for anger on his part, in the failures of your wing dragons during the battle yesterday? You yourself remarked, last evening, that you intended to speak with them."

Temeraire paused: this construction had not occurred to him. "But whyever should that make Laurence angry with his officers?" he said. "Iskierka has behaved ten times as badly, on other occasions, and that was certainly not Granby's fault; besides, those ferals were worse than anyone else, and they have no officers to blame."

"Ah! Well, one does not like to speculate," Ning said, but she tilted her head as though she had something else on the tip of her tongue to offer. Temeraire nudged over the platter of lamb towards her. "Why, that is very kind of you," she said, and swallowed down an entire haunch in one neat gulp, crunching the bones with satisfaction. "Well, your admiral is not an unreasonable man, I think—" Temeraire enjoyed again, privately, *your admiral,* "—so perhaps you must consider if there might be some cause to have provoked his anger against them in these circumstances. I will regretfully mention," she added, "that I have heard Fidelitas's captain make certain unfavorable remarks, about Admiral Laurence, on a few occasions when I breakfasted in the southern clearing."

"Do you mean to say that Poole gave Fidelitas *orders* to go and pillage, while we were all still fighting?" Temeraire said, in dawning outrage. He could scarcely believe it, but when Laurence had at last returned, he did not refute the supposition.

"I must beg you not to repeat it, however," Laurence said wearily. "No good can come of such gossip: there is no proof, and I hope to God I shall be given none; I must not act upon it, if action can be helped."

"*This* is what you were afraid of, Laurence, all along, I see now," Temeraire said, seething. "Oh! It is beyond all that is shocking, and when I think that Fidelitas knows, perfectly well, how like a selfish coward he was behaving: I will certainly have words with him."

"You cannot," Laurence said. "He cannot be blamed for following his captain's orders."

"I do not see why not," Temeraire said, "when he knew perfectly well that those orders were outrageous. Told to behave like a greedy guts who doesn't care to know any better, when everyone else was keeping in line, and fighting—I wonder he is not ashamed to show his face at the porridge-pits. Laurence, you cannot mean to let him behave in such a scaly manner, without reproof."

"We cannot chide the dragon, and not chide the man," Laurence said. "And *he* is protected by the Admiralty, who would be glad of the excuse to force my resignation. No, my dear, I am afraid we must cut our coats according to our cloth. He cannot be punished directly: we can only withhold reward."

"Reward?" Temeraire said, pricking up his ruff.

"The Cossacks seized a French wagon-train fleeing the battle-field, last night," Laurence said. "Laden with charqui, and enough of it to feed us for two months. Wittgenstein has sent it over to our supply-officers."

"Why, that is excellent news," Temeraire said. "But I am afraid, Laurence, that one cannot really call charqui a *reward*: indeed, you would not credit how stubborn some of our company are, when it comes to eating anything but raw meat. Fidelitas would not even *taste* my dinner, the day before the battle, though that new cook we have hired did the mutton so very nicely, all rolled around the barley and chestnuts, with that charming sauce with all the peppers—he *looked* as though he would have liked to try it, so I felt obliged to offer him a bite, but he pulled back straightaway and said no, no, he would not."

Temeraire paused even as he finished speaking, and flattened his ruff. "Is *that* part of this same nonsense? Do you mean, Laurence, that he has been acting so very strangely at his captain's prompting?"

"That, I am afraid, must be the least of it," Laurence said. "But we cannot correct, so we must attempt to lure. Tell me: would you consider four thousand pounds a sufficient incentive, in the way of prize-money, to stimulate their interest, if divided among our force?"

"Four thousand pounds!" Temeraire cried, quite unable to stifle his delight. "Laurence, how splendid: of course it would. But wherever has four thousand pounds come from?" he asked, a little worried—he hoped Laurence did not mean to propose that *he* should furnish such a sum.

"The greatest unhanged scoundrels of the service," Laurence said dryly.

It was with the greatest satisfaction that Temeraire set himself up at the head of his clearing, later that afternoon, when the other dragons began to assemble: Iskierka and Requiescat, and all the formation-leaders, as well as Ricarlee and a handful of the other senior unharnessed dragons as well. Minnow had been sent round, to summon them all, and Temeraire received them with a stately calm he felt befit the solemn occasion, and frowned down Ricarlee into order, when he would have gone poking into the simmering leavings of breakfast. "What's it all about, then?" the unrepentant feral demanded.

"You must wait and hear with everyone else," Temeraire said coolly, "although I do not scruple to say, it shall be something of the *greatest interest,* and to the advantage of any *honorable dragon,* who is a member of our forces."

"Temeraire," Laurence said, walking into the midst of the gathered circle, "I hope you will oblige me by writing down these accounts as I read them off, large enough for all the beasts to read."

"Of course, Laurence," Temeraire said. "Baggy, light along my writing-table, if you please."

He settled himself above it, as Laurence opened the large leather-bound book he had brought—not printed, but full of numbers written by hand, organized in small neat columns. "I trust every one here will share in my satisfaction," Laurence said, "that the senior commander has ordered that our forces should receive the equivalent of four thousand pounds in prize-money, in recognition of our labors yesterday."

Temeraire, forewarned, preserved his countenance and the appearance of calm satisfaction; the other dragons did not manage as much, but made a great swelling noise of delight among them: they all knew *pounds,* of course, since they were paid now, and just what so dazzling a sum meant, in gold and in cattle.

"As there may be future prizes of this sort taken, I think it desirable that every beast should understand clearly the division of awards, both in this case and henceforth," Laurence went on, "and find it easy to call to mind at any moment during our campaign the reward due their efforts. As there are presently one hundred dragons in our company, our base unit will be a one-thousandth share, equal in this instance to four pounds." He nodded to Temeraire, who quickly wrote 1/1000—£4 upon his paper, and displayed it large.

"Middle-weights and heavy-weights are entitled to a double share," Laurence continued, "and formation-leaders to a triple share. Iskierka, Requiescat, Levantia, and Ricarlee, as flying captains, shall be counted as formation-leaders."

Laurence paused a moment, amidst a perfect hush: everyone had stopped murmuring and pricked their ears forward to hear all the details. "Naturally," he said, "any prize distribution will omit dragons who prefer to take private pillage in the course of a given battle."

This produced a half-cry of protest from Fidelitas, stifled, and an outright one from Ricarlee, who sat up sharp. "Why, there's naught fair in that," he said. "There wasn't anything in those carts we took but some sacks of grain, and a few scraps of this and that."

"*I* see nothing to dislike in it," Cavernus said, very loudly, and the other formation-leaders murmured in agreement.

"You may have a fair share, earned with the company, or you may scrape along as chance serves you," Temeraire said crisply, when the murmuring had died away. "We are certainly not going to encourage selfish pillaging, or even make an attempt, which anyone might see could only lead to endless argument, to carry out an accounting of pillage after every engagement."

"On the contrary," Laurence said, "any remaining shares will be allotted after each engagement in accord with the usual principles of prize-money, to encourage valor, attention to orders, and reward the wise exercise of initiative. Temeraire, if you will be so good as to make note of the particular awards. I am delighted to recognize Cavernus, first, for steadfastness under fire, and for bringing down the Petit Chevalier: ten additional shares."

This fascinating and highly agreeable proceeding occupied the entire golden afternoon to the satisfaction of all, except, it seemed, the captains, who began to fidget even before the first hour had concluded. Poole was even so rude as to break in and say, "How much longer are we meant to stand for this litany of—"

"Roger!" Fidelitas hissed, with a glance of mortification, while every other head turned censorious looks in their direction, especially Cavernus, whose wing dragon Maxilla was presently being allotted two additional shares for having held position in the face of a heavier beast opposite.

None of this silenced Poole. "You have already been shut out," he said to Fidelitas, just as though he were insensible to the importance of understanding the rules of division which should apply to *future* instances, "and you must be hungry by now; you have not eaten to-day at all, yet."

"Any dragon wishing to be excused may of course consider themselves dismissed," Temeraire said in austere tones.

"No, no!" Fidelitas said, curling his tail around Poole to block him from general view, and bending his head down to whisper urgently, "I will eat *later*."

"Pray, Admiral Laurence," Cavernus said loudly, her eye still fixed on Fidelitas, "will you be so kind as to repeat that last award? I should be sorry not to be able to convey the exact particulars to Maxilla."

Laurence obliged her, of course, and the other captains at least made no further attempts to interrupt, although they were all of them—even dear Granby, Temeraire was sorry to see—unreasonably inattentive, and insisted on walking up and down in the clearing and talking to one another instead of paying close attention to all the highly interesting details of the awards. Several of the captains even had to be nudged to the edges of the clearing by their beasts to keep them from becoming a distraction.

Sadly, one could not indulge in such pleasures forever; at last, Laurence had to finish. The lovely ledger was closed, and Temeraire with deep satisfaction reviewed his scroll, and the charming way in which the full tally of shares added precisely to one thousand, and how each number of shares should individually be multiplied by four, and many of them thereby increased to two digits.

"I should add," Laurence said, to crown the glorious occasion, "the goods taken having consisted in charqui, that any dragon wishing to take some portion of their share in this meat may have it at the value of two pounds three shillings the bale, equal in ration to a cow of twelve pounds six shillings four pence, for which they shall be credited."

The meeting broke up on this delightful conclusion, as everyone collected their captains and went away engaged in calculations. "Why, Windle, only think: that is ten pounds and three shillings difference," Obituria said, "and I have four shares, that is sixteen pounds, so I can buy six bales, and when I have exchanged those for the cows, that will make seventy-three pounds and eighteen shillings." Windle only gawked up at her in the most mutton-headed way, as though he had not followed.

"I will have it brought round to every formation-leader's clearing," Temeraire promised, of the scroll, as the others left, several of them inquiring about a chance of looking it over. "And to yours as well," he added to Ricarlee, magnanimously; he felt a good deal less irritated now by the ferals' pillaging. "Gerry, pray roll it and tie it carefully, and I suppose you had better have a couple of the ground crewmen to help you carry it—steady men, if you please, Mr. O'Dea, who will not let it get wet, or spattered, or dirty."

When everyone had gone, Laurence sat heavily down in a camp chair with rather an explosive sigh and said to one of the new runners, "Brandy-and-water, if you please, Winters." He drank this off without a pause and said aloud, "Like a very damned merchant," incomprehensibly, "but we will see if it answers; I think it may."

Laurence was half sorry to find the extent to which his and Temeraire's stratagem, which he could not help but find a little contemptible, did answer. He was surprised to discover in the circuit he made through their encampment the next day that the dragons had set their signal-ensigns to drilling them in the flags—this, even though older dragons by and large had a great deal of difficulty in learning anything resembling a new language. Laurence could not understand it immediately, until he reviewed the list of awards and discovered that he had mentioned *close attention to signals* seven times. And when Laurence visited the Scottish ferals' clearing, he found them all present and accounted for: the first time since their departure from Dover that such a remarkable event had occurred. Not a one had stolen out of camp overnight to try for private pillaging. The handful of Ricarlee's beasts who had stayed aloft and fought with Requiescat—and who had been rewarded with an extra share apiece—were cock-of-the-walk, and the subject of envious sighs.

He grimly accepted his own victory, and having finished his rounds asked Minnow to take him into the city, where the new headquarters had been established: Major-General von Wittgenstein beaming and delighted with everybody, and despite the surfeit of hangers-on surrounding him and the general chaos produced by too many men without any real work to do, a spirit of energy and confidence suffused the entire establishment, which Laurence could not but witness with a pang of envy.

"Admiral Laurence!" Wittgenstein cried, on seeing him, and came around to shake his hand again. During the terrible struggle of the previous year, he had been forced to abandon St. Petersburg to Oudinot and Saint-Cyr, and his satisfaction at liberating Berlin had been doubled into joy by having now avenged that painful loss. "The Cossacks tell me they have all certainly crossed the river: there is not a French soldier east of the Elbe, God be thanked! They have fallen back on the Saale. I have just sent couriers to the Tsar and to His Majesty King Frederick with a full accounting of the battle, and you may be sure they have both been acquainted with the noble performance of your beasts."

Laurence could not be encouraged by this generous remark, to him a painful reminder that their commanders had very little expectation of the discipline of dragons; he could only be glad in a sour way, that the report would go far to strengthen his own position. "Is there any word about Napoleon himself?" he asked.

Wittgenstein waved a hand. "Still in Paris, they say!" but added, "Come, step inside," and took him to a smaller back chamber; here were only a couple of staff-officers, laboring intently over a sheaf of intelligence-reports. "The latest word is he has raised an army of nearly two hundred thousand men and four hundred dragons, at Mainz," Wittgenstein said quietly, when the door was closed; a piece of intelligence that could not be called heartening, and it was no wonder he preferred to share it in private. "Blücher will cross into Saxony next week, to liberate Dresden and Leipzig, and we hope persuade the King of Saxony to join the alliance. I do not need to tell you, Admiral, how necessary to that end it will be to avoid pillage in his countryside. I understand from Admiral Dyhern that you are supplying your entire force on twenty kine, daily?"

"And twenty tons of wheat, sir," Laurence said slowly, already anticipating the coming question.

"Admiral Dyhern has been ordered by His Majesty to join General Blücher," Wittgenstein said—Dyhern having himself also been promoted; most of the senior Prussian officers had been quietly retired in the years since Jena, and every chance taken of pushing forward younger and more competent men. "In my judgment, and that of Field Marshal Kutuzov, you and your dragons are urgently wanted there, and our victory here to-day only makes that more desirable. But we do not demand it, Admiral, if you do not think it possible to supply your force there."

The question was a difficult one indeed. Laurence could manage it, he thought, but not without putting all the dragons on porridge, even the ones whose captains demanded the official ration of meat, and not without the risk of going hungry for a day now and again. Ordinarily he would have scorned such small concerns under these circumstances: if Napoleon truly had raised four hundred dragons already at Mainz, he could not be held unless the British dragons came. But Laurence could not rely on his captains to reconcile their beasts to short commons, and dragons themselves had little tolerance for going hungry when there was a handsome sheepfold to be seen over the next hill, whether or not the sheep were theirs for the taking.

This last concern at least, Laurence could air to Wittgenstein without feeling that he exposed the Corps to any particular shame; then he had only to swallow his personal pride, at asking for what seemed to him almost the power to bribe his own beasts. "If you will pardon me, sir," he said unhappily, "I will say what I know must have an unfortunate appearance of self-interest: it would be of inexpressible value to me to have further captures of supply, of the sort you made over to us yesterday, which I might award as prizes among the beasts to encourage them to maintain discipline."

"Among the beasts?" Wittgenstein said, frowning. "I do not understand. You mean your officers—you think they will keep them in line, if—"

"Sir," Laurence broke in, preferring to be rude than hear so mortifying a character given to his officers. "Sir, I beg your pardon; no, I mean among the beasts themselves."

Wittgenstein stared, then gave a small explosive snort of laughter. "What do dragons care for prize-money? We do not have heaps of gold to give them." But when Laurence assured him that the beasts did indeed care, passionately, he was ready to believe. "But money is in short supply everywhere, Admiral," he said.

"I am aware of it, sir," Laurence said. "I do not require funds: if you can only grant us further quantities of charqui, or cattle, or grain, acquired from the enemy, that will do."

He did not describe how he intended to convert these supplies into funds. Wittgenstein surely knew enough of the wretched graft of commissaries to suspect something of the method. Laurence had indeed made an evil use of Jane's intelligence about corruption in the Supply-Office: before leaving England, he had called upon those men she labeled as the most rapacious, and had quietly discussed with them the high price of meat on the Continent, and the difficulty in transporting even salt pork, much less cattle, to a force which traveled as the dragon flew.

"And may I say, Admiral, that it is a great pleasure to speak with a man of so much sense and understanding in these matters," the worst of these villains had said to him earnestly, shaking his hand, when they had tacitly agreed that the cattle meant for them would be sold in port, instead, and the funds made over to Laurence personally in gold. Certainly a handsome quantity of the sums would end in the pockets of his suppliers; just as certainly, they assumed an equal quantity would end in his own, while he fed his dragons on rotten meat, or off the farms of starving peasants.

Laurence had forced himself to care only that this arrangement would permit him to replace much of the exported cattle with local grain, and feed three times the number of dragons, more healthfully, at half the cost. He knew very well what Whitehall would have said, if he had proposed the substitution to them directly. Jane was feeding her dragons in Spain on corn and horse-meat, but officially the Commissariat was shipping her five hundred barrels of salt pork per day, not a quarter of which reached her. But the rules of supply were a wheel that did not easily move from the deep-worn rut in which they traveled. The thieves in Dover might take half the money they could get for the meat, and still leave Laurence with more than enough for their needs.

Only after the battle, when Wittgenstein had sent him the vast quantity of bales of captured charqui—"I understand you have a use for this peculiar stuff, Admiral," the accompanying supply-officer had said doubtfully, delivering him wagons loaded with enough of the dried and salted meat to feed two hundred dragons for a month—had it occurred to Laurence that he might instead use those funds to furnish prize-money, and thereby both persuade the dragons to eat the charqui, and make them more enthusiastic for their duty.

The entire business left an evil taste in his mouth, the sense of having pushed his hands deep into rotting effluvia. But Wittgenstein was only looking thoughtful, saying, "Admiral, I believe it can be arranged."

"You shall have whatever supply I can scrape together, if it will serve you for prizes," Blücher promised him, without hesitation. The old Prussian was loyal to a fault, when his loyalty was given, and he had before now decided for Laurence on the strength of Dyhern's testimonials, and the rescue of the Prussian beasts. "I cannot promise the quantity will be great."

The rewards were indeed not large, but it did not seem to matter to the dragons whether their share was worth four pounds, or one shilling threepence as was more commonly the case; nor was this due to any misunderstanding or mathematical confusion on their part. Every British dragon seemed able to maintain a full and perfect accounting, down to pence, of their funds. Even when there had been a further four allocations, after small seizures of individual wagons taken in skirmishing, there was still not a beast among them who could not stand before all the separate scrolls—Temeraire now kept these posted up outside his own clearing, under guard—and in an instant calculate the exact value of the shares of any dragon on the list, and compare this against their own.

This facility in no way diminished their desire of having the numbers written out for them, however, much to the dismay of their captains. "I had no idea of Iskierka's being so handy at sums," Granby muttered, as she announced with great satisfaction, "I believe I have one hundred twenty-four pounds sixteen shillings threepence, and Requiescat has one hundred twenty-one pounds eleven shillings tuppence; now pray check it for me, Granby, and show me all your work," which entailed a quarter of an hour's hard-fought calculations for him, with one mistake along the way, which Iskierka pointed out severely before he had quite finished writing it down.

Aviators did not get a great deal in the way of formal schooling. Mrs. Pemberton finally took pity upon the officers and offered her services to make individual copies of the lists, and as her head for mathematics was good enough to satisfy them, the dragons were eager to accept the substitute, although after a week she was obliged to begin charging them a shilling apiece for the copies, or she would have been applied to for a fresh set by every beast, every day.

One difficulty briefly reared its head: Windle, plainly resentful of the mechanism which had made his dragon an earnest advocate of pleasing Laurence's judgment, loudly said, "It is nonsense, Obituria. Where do you suppose this money is, really? It is jots on paper, not cash in hand, and so it will remain. And meanwhile you are eating this smoky charqui stuff instead of good fresh beef; you have dropped two stone of flesh, I dare say, in this last week."

Obituria had, and looked far the better for it; Laurence knew what General Chu would have said of the regular diet of British dragons. But she looked uncertain, and Ricarlee, never backwards in suspicion, presented himself that same afternoon demanding his funds in some less ephemeral form.

"Very good," Laurence said however, having prepared himself for this eventuality, and presented Ricarlee with a neatly bound sheaf of paper money, and a scattering of shilling coins and pence, which the dragon could not have held conveniently in any manner. "Perhaps you would prefer me to deposit it with your bank?" When Ricarlee professed himself innocent of any accounts, Laurence added, "Temeraire banks with Rothschild, and has had no cause for complaint, I believe."

He was glad, now, to have been forced to grapple with the difficulty of managing Temeraire's funds. Drummonds' and Hoare's had balked entirely; they refused to do anything but put the money into an account in his own name. Tharkay had come to his rescue: Avram Maden had a considerable acquaintance among the notable Jewish families of Europe, and the Rothschild bank in London had as a favor to him offered Laurence an appointment.

The young man he had first spoken to, in their offices, had been polite but skeptical; their business was ordinarily more in the line of coin-dealing, Laurence vaguely understood. But unexpectedly the head of the bank had come into the room: Mr. Nathan Rothschild, who had been distantly acquainted with his father through Mr. Wilberforce. The gentleman had paid Laurence his condolences, listened to the difficulty before him, asked briefly about the rate of pay dragons were entitled from the Admiralty and the length of their life spans; shortly thereafter Temeraire had become the proud possessor of an account, and if the bank-book were inconveniently small for his talons, at least he showed no signs of needing to consult it.

"Well, if Temeraire banks with them, I suppose I will allow them to hold my money, too," Ricarlee said loftily, willing to be satisfied by whatever Temeraire possessed.

The bank was equally willing; indeed, after all the hundred dragons of their force had followed suit, a representative was even sent to pay a visit to their camp. That young gentleman plainly entered the field-covert in a spirit of calm desperation, and as he hailed from the Frankfurt branch, his command of English was imperfect, which increased his miseries: the dragons—who had awaited his advent with a fervor rather like idolatry—kept putting their heads down to hear him more closely. But when no one had devoured him after an hour, he began by degrees to be less anxious, and to speak more fluidly of markets and shares to the enraptured attention of his audience, who by the time he left had all begun a lively debate on the merits of putting their money into the Funds as compared with speculating in currency or investing in shipping ventures.

Still, Laurence could not rejoice at his success. There was something low in this method of bringing dragons to heel, something nearly ignoble. He could not fault Poole's silent but visible indignation; even Granby looked a little distressed during the regular conferences which the dragons demanded, where Laurence announced each division. The entire enterprise had a quality of interference in it, thrusting himself between captain and dragon, which Laurence knew very well was anathema in the Corps. But even Poole could scarcely make a complaint that his commander was keeping his dragon in good order, against his will.

Nevertheless, he seethed visibly, and many of the other captains were more discreetly resentful, when they ought to have been in alt. Blücher had marched into Dresden and Leipzig nearly unopposed, and still Napoleon's growing army had not stirred out of Mainz: the campaign would begin well into the territory France had formerly conquered, and in every other part of the army, confidence brimmed over, with an eagerness for battle; meanwhile in the field-covert, his officers were sullen and silent, and performed their duties grudgingly.

"It seems to me I ought to get another share, for carrying her about," Requiescat said, squinting at the rolls. He and Iskierka had come by Temeraire's clearing to look them over and argue their divisions, yet again. "No-one *else* is lugging about another dragon on their back, and she ain't much like a feather anymore, either."

"I don't see why *that* should mean you get anything more. She hasn't done anything of use, herself, so it is not as though you are doing anyone a service by bringing her." Iskierka snorted a bit of flame disapprovingly.

"Certainly I am being of use," Ning said, popping her head up from the other end of the clearing. "Simply because you cannot yet *see* the Chinese legions does not mean they are not *coming*, and they are coming because I am here. And you must all hope they arrive," she added, "because otherwise, you will lose."

Temeraire flattened his ruff in some annoyance at this dismal interjection. "We will *not* lose," he said, "although naturally the legions *will* come, and be of great use, but that is not the same as saying we will *lose,* if they do not."

"Well, you will," Ning said. "I have been stretching my wings, while you all lie in camp all day—"

"And why are some of *us* tired, and you not, I'd like to know," Requiescat interjected.

"—and I have met any number of ferals, in these parts. Their conversation has been most illuminating. However, I do not mean to quarrel," she added, "and I am sure I wish you all every success."

"Then you might as well do your part, when we next fight," Temeraire said. "That fire you can make would have been very handy indeed in Berlin, if only you had bothered to exert yourself a little. I am sure if you did, Laurence would be perfectly pleased to award you a suitable share of the prize-money," he added.

"And what about me, hey?" Requiescat said.

"Perhaps Ning ought to then make over some of her share to you," Temeraire said, "for your services in ferrying her: that would be perfectly suitable."

"I must beg your pardon," Ning said, with some asperity, sitting up on her haunches, "but before you have quite concluded making these arrangements on my behalf, I must demur. I *am* doing my part, to preserve the alliance with China, and with that you must content yourselves."

"Doing her part not to take any side, until she knows who is going to win," Iskierka said, with a sniff, and Temeraire could not disagree.

"I know you are not *cowardly,*" Temeraire said to Ning, after Iskierka and Requiescat had both gone away still arguing, "as you have been perfectly willing to defend yourself, when necessary." There had been more than one occasion when dragons new to their camp had tried to deny Ning precedence—she was still small, although nearing the size of a light-weight by now—and she had firmly though politely made plain she would not stand for it; three or four dragons still sported a badly scorched toe, or tail-tip. "So

I cannot see why you would not like to do your share, and *earn* your share thereby. Surely you must see it gives a very strange appearance for you to be nowhere on the rolls, at all: you have not a single shilling to your name!"

Ning did cast a quick, wistful glance over at the rolls, but she only answered, "It is very well to count shillings and pounds. What is a shilling? It is the money that here, to-day, will buy you a rabbit. But in London, before we left, it would buy you *two*."

"Rabbits are harder to come by here than in London," Temeraire said.

"Just so," Ning said. "Because there is a war, and an army tramping through the fields, so there are fewer rabbits, and more mouths to eat them. Therefore, if the war were not occurring, there would be more rabbits, and perhaps you might even buy *three* rabbits, with your same shilling. Why therefore should I content myself to gather pounds and shillings, when I might instead command their value?"

"But so long as I have more pounds and shillings than another dragon, I may buy more rabbits, no matter what they are worth," Temeraire said. "And so long as you have *no* shillings, you can buy none, no matter how many there are."

"A consideration which would occupy my attention a great deal, if I did not have the prospect of becoming companion to a wealthy and powerful sovereign," Ning said firmly.

"Yes, but *which* sovereign," Temeraire muttered to himself, when she had curled herself back up to sleep. He did not mean to say so, but it made him feel a little uneasy that Ning did *not* care to join their side properly, just yet. Ning might talk of rabbits all she liked, but no dragon could really wish to be left out of anything so nice as prize-money, so she was only refraining because she really did think they might lose. She was wrong, naturally, but he would have liked to inquire a little further as to why, if he could have done so without suggesting he meant to believe her.

———

"And still the Austrians are flying back and forth between Vienna and Dresden every day," Dyhern said, grumbling even as he offered Laurence a cup of remarkably good coffee. "If he gives us one good knock, they will scurry back into his pockets, you may be sure."

They were encamped outside Leipzig, near the small town of Lützen, waiting for the order to move onwards. The headquarters of the allied forces had been moved forward from the east and established in Dresden: the Tsar himself was there with Field Marshal Kutuzov—whom report had very ill, which was certainly doing nothing to improve the coordination and communications of their army. And then the word had come last night: Napoleon had left Paris. Napoleon was coming to the front. The whisper had traveled around every campfire at a rapid pace, throwing an evil shadow over every man. Laurence had heard the murmurs as he walked through camp that morning, past the stirring fires and the dim wash of dawn, lightening a heavy grey sky.

He was meeting with Dyhern and the Russian Admiral Ilchenko, to review the supply manifests for the week ahead. Laurence had not managed to acquire more than a smattering of Russian in the last campaign, and Ilchenko was entirely innocent of English, while Dyhern's French left much to be desired; they communicated therefore in a patchwork of languages, often translating the same remark more than once, to be sure they had understood. But this awkwardness was the least of their difficulties.

Further reserves had joined them from the east as the Prussian Army mobilized fully, and more Russian dragons had come from the heartland, now that spring was reducing the need for them to keep the ferals from raiding. In numbers, they now even approached Napoleon's reported tally of four hundred beasts, although numbers alone were not a sufficient measure.

The Prussians now could field some 130 beasts, many of them having been liberated on the way to Berlin—but half of these were slow-flying heavy-weights. Even their middle-weights stood on the heavier side, and they had very few light-weights at all. Laurence would privately have preferred to keep the large beasts ferrying men and guns—especially guns. He knew it was a general tenet of the Chinese legions that dragons above middle-weight were a waste of muscle, but a middle-weight could not carry a twenty-four-pounder for any distance, and a heavy-weight could. Napoleon had previously made just such a use of his own heavy-weight dragons to bring a far greater weight of metal to bear upon the battlefield than horses over bad roads could arrange. But Laurence could not direct Dyhern, who with his comrades not unnaturally hungered for more avenging victories in the field. And in any case, the Prussian artillery-men were in no hurry to mount dragons.

On the Russian side, they claimed eighty beasts, but in practice only the thirty heavy-weights were under military discipline, and these could be used for nothing but battle. They cared too little for men—indeed barely acknowledged their existence save as the occasional providers of food and treasure, or the brutality of bit and hobble. A week gone, Vosyem had sent three hundred soldiers plummeting to a grisly death, because a knot of the carrying-harness had irritated her under the wing. She had not complained to her officers; she had simply turned her head round mid-air and torn away the silk with a few quick slashes of her serrated teeth, ignoring the cries and pleas of her passengers and the frantic spurring of her officers. The infantry had since refused to go aboard any of the Russian beasts, and Laurence could scarcely blame them.

As for cargo, one could give a Russian dragon almost anything to carry, but one could not rely on getting it back again. Only the day before, Admiral Ilchenko had very grudgingly come to Laurence to ask for Temeraire's assistance: Jevionty, one of his newly arrived dragons, would not surrender a cannon he had been ordered to carry from Vilna to the waiting artillery company whose charge it was, and he had begun to snarl and hiss at any officer who even attempted to approach him.

"Do not hiss at *me*," Temeraire said with great dignity, when he had descended into the clearing. "If I wanted a gun of my own,

I should *buy* one, with my money," and Jevionty a little abashed had muttered apology: the reputation of Temeraire's treasure had spread widely among the Russian dragons. "And I cannot see what you want with this cannon. They are not pretty to look at, and they are no use unless you have men to fire them for you."

"It is *mine*," Jevionty said obstinately, "and it *is* valuable, or else why do they want to steal it from me?" He had lost his own hoard in the devastation of Moscow, and was keen to rebuild it in any manner possible: the Russian beasts counted standing among themselves almost entirely based on their possessions.

"Well, they are an artillery company and they can fire it, so it is worth a great deal to *them*," Temeraire said. He scratched a claw thoughtfully along his eye ridge. "It is true that the value of things may depend upon how much someone *else* wants them. But I cannot call it anything but mean to keep it for yourself when you can get no good from it, and anyway, where are you going to keep it? You had much better let the men fight it for you. Have them paint your name upon the top of the barrel, so you can always see which gun is yours while you are flying above it, and then let them manage it for you."

After a little more nudging, and the promise of gold paint, Jevionty was persuaded to accept this solution, but the episode did not inspire any confidence in the Russian dragons as porters.

Meanwhile, the large body of Russian light-weights, who would have been by far the more valuable as part of their unified force, were nearly impossible to make use of or even to count: their numbers in camp varied widely from day to day. Barring a handful of beasts like Grig, who had established a stronger relationship with one or another of the officers, they would only perform errands given to them in the moment and with the promise of an immediate reward of food.

"The heavy-weights must eat first," Ilchenko answered flatly, when Laurence suggested he might establish a regularity of feeding time, to create the beginnings of discipline among the light-weight greys. But the ferocious heavy-weights were the pride of the Russian forces, and Ilchenko refused to care that they often left their feeding pits scraped clean, or spoiled what they did not eat with hot squabbles. So the greys were left to scrounge for scraps, and likely to go stealing from the local farmers. At least the irregular Cossack troops fed themselves: their fly-weight beasts were well practiced in living off the land without excessively offending their neighbors, and ate a cheerfully indiscriminate variety. But they were no use in a pitched battle, or against the French dragons, unless they came across one of them alone and unwary.

All the dragons were by now reconciled to the porridge-pit, but while this made feeding their enlarged force *possible*, it did not make it *easy*. With so many bellies of such enormous capacity to fill, their supply was in regular danger of running out and required the most careful and constant attention.

Laurence straightened up from the ledgers when they had finished their tallies, and nodded to the young aide whose duty it was to send their numbers on to Blücher's staff. He stretched backwards, hands pressed into the small of his back, thoroughly stiffened after the hours bent low: he ruefully thought he felt his years more sharply after an afternoon in a tent than after two days aloft. He and Dyhern stepped outside together, while Ilchenko stayed in to finish the letter which he would send to the Tsar with his report: a rather more formal affair.

"I cannot delight in this book-keeper's work, Laurence," Dyhern said, "but I have no right to complain. When I think how we gnashed our teeth at you for twenty dragons, before Jena! And look upon our coverts now. My heart must be appeased."

They were encamped in the bowl of a nameless valley perhaps a hundred miles from Leipzig, dragons strung along the heights and hillocks all around like decorations, nearly covering all the open ground. The steam rose in pearlescent gusts from the cooking-pits, in the center of the camp, and on every side the voices of dragons—the hissing of their breaths, their deep rumbling speech, the dry rustle of scales rubbing over one another. The sheer number of them echoed the tales of the uncountable hordes of the

Huns, of fairy-stories; Laurence could well share Dyhern's dissatisfaction and pleasure both, in the scale of their force and the difficulties of its management.

A tiny figure came gliding down over the tree-tops to the northeast, a bird Laurence thought at first, but moving very fast; the sentry-dragons did not even lift their heads until she was already far beyond them, and before they could raise a warning, she had darted twice across the bowl of the valley, her head seeking, and then dropped with startling speed to the ground directly before Laurence, folding her disproportionate green wings in. "Yu Li," Laurence exclaimed, very surprised, as the Jade dragon bowed very low as well as she could, with the dragging ends of her wings.

"Forgive this clumsy one's rude and hasty approach," she said. "I have been sent to establish lines of communication with Your Imperial Highness and Lung Tien Xiang—"

"Why, you are very welcome to startle us all ten times over, on that account," Laurence said, and turning to Dyhern explained, "She is the leading edge of the Chinese legions."

But Yu Li was not finished. "Honored Brother of the Dread Lord," she said, and Laurence turning caught the change in her address, and realized with a start that the Emperor must have died, and Mianning by now crowned, "I beg your forgiveness for my hasty and improper address, but I have grave news to impart. Having mistaken your location, I first sought to find you in the small town not three hundred *li* from here, where a great many noble officials were encamped."

By *small town* she must have meant Dresden; any Western city would bear a peculiarly shrunken character to a Chinese dragon, who expected to find in these places thoroughfares and pavilions suitable for draconic inhabitants and not merely humans—which meant, in turn, that she had flown some one hundred miles in an hour, a remarkable achievement even for one of the Jade Dragons. Her chest was indeed heaving rapidly, and her wings trembling. She extended one limb towards him, the golden mesh upon it carrying a letter.

"I was honored to meet there with your advisor Mr. Hammond," she said, "who has entrusted me with this letter and begs you consider it as soon as you think wise."

Laurence took the letter—a note, not even enclosed, and scrawled in an irregular and hasty version of Hammond's usually tidy hand, at least large enough to be easily legible. A moment was enough to read it; he handed it on to Dyhern and turned to Yu Li. "Did you see the French advance, yourself?"

"Yes, august one, and in hopes of offering you further intelligence, I crossed their body from aloft," she said: Jade Dragons flew at a far higher altitude than most dragons, and with her small size, she would certainly have been taken for a bird, even if anyone had glimpsed her. "Their beasts are not very orderly, so it is difficult to properly tally their numbers, but there were in excess of five hundred assembled. Their carrying-harnesses held perhaps a hundred men, for each dragon, and the larger carried guns, as well."

"My God!" Dyhern said. "He will smash them to pieces. There are not twenty beasts at Dresden, and those convalescent." He turned to explain the situation to Admiral Ilchenko, who had come out of the tent at the commotion; Laurence had seized pen and paper from his runner and was hastily scrawling a reply. "Yu Li," he said, "will you take this back to Mr. Hammond at once, if you please?" She accepted the note with another bow, and as soon as it was stowed away she gathered herself, leapt, and was gone.

"What is to be done?" Dyhern said.

"Gentlemen," Laurence said, "I am taking every beast that can travel at speed—every one that can sustain sixteen knots or better. *Les Cossacks, il faut que je les emmener avec moi*," he added to Ilchenko, who was nodding intently. "Dyhern, you must take my heavy-weights, and your own, to our depot at Leipzig. Stupefy every pig and sheep in the place with opium and bring them, with all the grain you can carry. The Russian heavy-weights must remain with Field Marshal Blücher here. We must take it as a certainty that the rest of the French infantry is coming up on our rear. Napoleon plainly intends to cut our lines of communication and supply—perhaps even capture the Tsar—and then smash us between the two wings of his force. We must try and hold him at Dresden long enough for you to come up behind him, instead. Do you agree?"

There was so little room to dispute the plan that Laurence had not hesitated to send to tell Hammond that he was coming: his force was the only one substantially composed of dragons who could manage the speed necessary to catch the French; certainly neither Eroica nor Ilchenko's dragon Sorokshest could do so. They shook hands in agreement, and Dyhern took Hammond's letter. "I will go and speak with Marshal Blücher," he said. "Begin your preparations! I will send as soon as he has confirmed the order of battle."

Chapter 17

$\mathscr{I}$SKIERKA DID NOT HIDE her delight that Requiescat had to be left behind, to go with the Prussians; although her pleasure was a little dimmed by Laurence's saying to him, "You may be sure that the rôle of providing supply to our forces is no less urgent, and will merit no less recognition, than direct engagement with the enemy—if we cannot eat, after the battle, then hunger will rout us as thoroughly in victory as any defeat Napoleon might inflict."

"But surely I will have better chances to earn additional shares," she muttered, with a narrow glare at the rolls. Temeraire sighed a little. He understood Laurence's position that it would scarcely be fair for him to award shares to his own dragon; and as the flag-dragon he was entitled to a handsome five shares of every division as a matter of course, but it was sadly disappointing to see Cavernus and Iskierka and Requiescat reaping the benefits of their labors, while he could not.

However, Temeraire was determined to hold himself above petty competition. He was for his own part not very sorry to leave Obituria, who was also too slow to come. Fidelitas could make sixteen knots, however—respectable, even if not up to *his* own pace, and Laurence meant to divide them into two companies anyway.

"The ordinary order of flight must be suspended," Laurence was saying to his captains, and several of the Prussian officers who had dashed over to hear his orders—one of them Ferris, who had been made acting-captain for one of the Prussian middle-weight dragons. Temeraire had meant to object to this in strong terms, until he had met her: she had a wild, hollow-eyed look. Her captain had died, during her long captivity. "I *will* have vengeance," she said, low and harsh. "I will, I will," and Temeraire had not had the heart after all to demand that she give Ferris up.

"Captain Poole, you and Fidelitas will take in charge all our Yellow Reapers, and the Prussian middle-weights, as well as the middle-weight ferals. All those dragons who can sustain a pace of twenty knots will come forward with us. When you arrive, if possible we will resume our formations, with the Prussian middle-weights forming a loose phalanx in the center under the command of Captain Ferris, for the ease of his transmitting British signals to the rest of the force. *Captain von Tauben, Captain Wesselton, j'entends que vous parlez bien Français: voilà ce deux ensign-signaleurs qui allons monter avec vous, de relayer les commandes.*" He nodded to the two ensigns, who went a little timidly to the Prussian captains he had named.

"Captain Poole, should you come and find that we are already overwhelmed," Laurence said, "you must consult your judgment. It is of the first importance that the French should not capture the Tsar. Lung Yu Li will report to you, when you arrive, if he should be in danger. Midwingman Roland will go aboard Fidelitas to translate for you." Temeraire flattened back his ruff; he did not see why Roland should go anywhere, much less to Fidelitas; he had certainly done nothing to deserve her, and after all, Gerry could speak a little Chinese by now, too. But with an effort, he restrained himself; he could not quarrel with Laurence on such an occasion, even if Emily's expression was perfectly flat, and she certainly did not *wish* to go. At least, Temeraire comforted himself, she would not ever stay with Fidelitas—she would return as soon as she could.

"Temeraire, if you will be so good, take all the dragons to eat, as much as they can hold," Laurence said. "Porridge first, and eat your meat on the wing, as much of it as you can carry: anything we leave will only go to feed the French. The Russian greys have leave to eat now as well: they are coming with us."

"We will go at once," Temeraire said, and leaping aloft he roared for attention, and then called, "Pray will all the heavy-weights go to your porridge, three to a pit; then middle-weights and light-weights fill in around them, and no jostling if you please: we must all eat together."

He went down himself, and after a little chivvying to keep everyone in order, he nudged a couple of the Scots out of the way to eat himself. But he had scarcely taken a bite when the Russian greys descended and began a really frenzied attack on the food. He had to interrupt his meal and go and pin several of them down—which made them squall and begin to plead for mercy, as though he were going to hurt them, and it took a small roar before each of them would quiet down enough to listen to him say, "You are *welcome* to eat, only stop clawing anyone else out of the way, or gobbling so quick that you spill half the porridge out of your mouth onto the ground: there is enough for everyone."

When he had repeated himself some nine or twelve times, to different dragons—and once to the *same* dragon, which annoyed him very much; "If I catch you at it again, you will have to sit out until everyone else has eaten," he told her sternly, the second time—at last the greys calmed down. By then they had all got something into their bellies, and also the rest of the light-weight dragons, especially Ricarlee and his fellows, had taken up the work of prodding them into better behavior using thwacks and nips, as they could not speak to one another. One could not help but feel sorry for the greys, they did look so thin and hungry; and when at last they saw most of the British dragons finishing and going away, with plenty of porridge still left, they did look a little abashed, and began to eat more sedately.

Temeraire heaved a sigh and went back to his own delayed meal. He had time only for a few bites more when Grig landed beside him—having finished eating already, Temeraire noted, disgruntled. "We have been allowed to eat *first*," Grig said full of gleeful malice, with a belch entirely disproportionate to his size, "before all of the heavy-weights: you should have seen Vosyem scowl! And that Laurence of yours says we will be fed again tomorrow, too, if we can only keep up with this Fidelitas, and do something on the battlefield: now, which one is Fidelitas, pray?" He asked the question very intently: even he looked rather hungry, although he was his captain's pet, and usually ate better than most of the greys.

Temeraire had to swallow down a gulp of porridge to answer. "He is that Anglewing, over there. The golden-yellow one."

"Almost all of you British dragons are yellow," Grig said, peering over in that direction. "That one?"

"No, *that* one, the large one with the extra ribs to his wings, and the darker shade," Temeraire said. Fidelitas was indeed talking to several of their Yellow Reapers, but the shape of the head was distinctly different, in Temeraire's opinion, and anyway Fidelitas did not have white stripes.

"We will be sure to keep up with him," Grig said, nodding firmly. "What ought we do on the battlefield?"

Temeraire considered this as he ate, doubtfully: he was well aware the Russians never troubled themselves with trying to train the light-weights, and only bullied them into coming along with the heavy-weights to distract the enemy and get in the way. "Well—if you see any of the French dragons trying to gather for a run at us, you should dash at them and bat them around the heads; or if you see anyone beset by too many of the enemy, you should go and help them. And whenever there is a chance, you should form into a long pack and go flying all around us, and especially in front of the enemy, to keep them from working out just what we are trying to do . . ."

He trailed off; he could tell, from the doubtful flick of Grig's ears, and that dragon's glance over at his fellows, that the greys would very likely do none of this. "Wait a moment," Temeraire said, struck by a sudden thought, and called, "Ricarlee, will you come here, if you please," and presented the two small dragons to each other, which was made possible by Grig's English—although this had been acquired to spy upon them in the last campaign, which Temeraire had not quite forgiven. Still, it was handy that the greys were better than most dragons about languages.

"Ricarlee and his fellows have grown very smart about harrying the French," he said, which made the feral thrust out his chest proudly, "and there are a great many of them, and they are nearly your size. Ricarlee, I should like you to pair off each of your fellows with one of the greys, before you come to the field. Then," he said to Grig, "you may tell your friends they need only do whatever they see their partner doing, and stick with them through the battle."

Grig nodded thoughtfully. "And naturally the Scots will report if anyone runs away and just hides through the battle, and they will have to eat last."

"Yes, I suppose," Temeraire said, a little taken aback; he had not thought of it that way, and it seemed very peculiar to him that any dragon would *hide* during a battle—although he recalled that Perscitia did not quite like fighting, either; but then, she *was* a very peculiar dragon.

"I will tell everyone, you may be sure," Grig promised. "We will do our share, and," he sidled up a little, with his head slanted, "perhaps those who distinguish themselves *particularly*, who assist you in some notable fashion, such as keeping others in order, will be entitled to a little more consideration, after the fighting?"

"Oh," Temeraire said, a little anxiously. He did not know if Laurence meant to include the greys, in the distribution of prizes—they were pretty sure to get a prize in this battle, Temeraire felt. "I certainly cannot make any promises," Temeraire said, as he dismally contemplated dividing the same thousand shares among more dragons, but privately he had the sinking feeling that Laurence would do just that.

Laurence for his part would have been glad for any hope of his having prizes to award after the coming engagement. While the dragons took their meal, he himself swallowed some bread and cold meat and drank a little wine, writing all the while: messages for the Admiralty, and for Jane; if Napoleon smashed them here, she must be warned before another five hundred dragons appeared on her doorstep. "I'll reach her, never fear," Minnow promised, as she ducked her head into the letter-harness. Laurence did not care to lose even a single beast at present, but Winchesters were so small they could do very little good in combat even against other light-weights, and Minnow was clever enough to slip her way along the coast past Napoleon's forces. Captain Wesley and his Winchester Veloxia had already gone for Whitehall; they would make for Berlin, and see the message relayed from there.

Then the dragons were finished eating, and everywhere the harness went on. The ground crews would have to be left behind, to march with the infantry; likely a good deal of equipment and matériel would be lost. But there was no help for it. Winters came hurrying with Laurence's flying-coat, struggling under the weight; Laurence took it from the small girl and shrugged into the heavy leather, checked his pistols and his sword—he would never forget having gone aloft with only a dress-sword in his belt, but his beloved Chinese blade was a satisfying weight there now—and stepped into Temeraire's ready talons to be put up.

The weather was extraordinarily beautiful, and the sky studded over with small puffs of charming white cloud which sadly shortened their field of vision. Laurence rarely took his glass from his eye, and the lookouts kept their own out, straining for a first glimpse. Beneath him, Temeraire's wing-muscles beat in steady lapping strokes, working nearly to his limits—his speed was extraordinary for a heavy-weight, but he was in armor, although with a quarter the usual weight of incendiaries. Only the fastest of the dragons had come with him: Iskierka, their light-weights, and the Cossack ranks behind them in their clannish groups, some forty dragons each carrying ten men crammed aboard. There would be no real hope of defeating Napoleon: they could only try to hold him long enough for more of their forces to concentrate upon the field.

It was three hours to Dresden at their break-neck pace; it would be another hour before the rest of the force could join them. Laurence put firmly from his mind the unwanted awareness that those desperately needed dragons would arrive under the command of an officer who hated and despised him, and who would be glad of almost any excuse to see him brought low. There was no use in entertaining the thought; Fidelitas was by far the senior of the dragons in the second wave. For a moment he had entertained leaving Granby and Iskierka back to command it—but only for a moment. If there was anything to be gained in the space of that first hour, it would only be gained by the most ferocious defense they could put forward.

"Smoke off forward wing, one point to starboard," Belleisle called urgently—one of his lookouts. Laurence immediately turned his glass in that direction. At first he was uncertain: smoke, or only a wisp of cloud in shadow? But the thin grey wisps were rising from the ground: smoke.

"I think we will go to battle-stations, Mr. Forthing," Laurence said.

"Aye, sir," Forthing said, turning to pass the word to Challoner, but this was scarcely required: every man was already in motion, their speed a mark of how tightly wound their spirits: like arrows held at the limits of their bow reach, ready to be loosed.

The smoke gathered rapidly ahead of them, not only from their drawing nearer: the city was burning. "Laurence, that is Accendare there on the other side of the city," Temeraire said, "I am sure of it," and Laurence scanning the sky managed to pick her out briefly. The Flamme-de-Gloire was nearly the largest dragon to be seen, and stark in her yellow and black as for a moment her wings hung open against the sky in their direction.

"She has never done all that herself," his midwingman Ashgrove blurted out, aghast. He was a young officer, and had come from a dragon run on rather looser lines of propriety than Laurence liked to see; but the remark was not unprovoked, as their passage brought the city further into view: a city bathed in flames. Easier to have counted those houses which were *not* burning, many of them emitting soldiers forced to flee stumbling through the lanes and alleys of the city. Napoleon had evidently declined to fight through the streets; he was smoking out his enemy—a brutality that bid fair to be as effective as it was callous. But Laurence, too, could not imagine how Accendare, for all her fearsome reputation, had single-handedly fired the entire city, its houses largely built of stone and well-supplied with water.

"Wing to larboard!" cried the fore larboard lookout. Not one wing but a hundred, two hundred, more: a cloud of dragons was rising en masse from a previously hidden valley, where they had evidently been resupplying. In pairs they carried large iron cauldrons suspended from yokes, steam rising from the innards, and as they turned and swept over the city, they tipped them over to pour out long billowing streamers of smoking tar and pitch. Behind them came a second wave, throwing out incendiaries to ignite the hot tar—these sometimes bursting in mid-air.

His glass trained upon the still-distant mass of dragons, Laurence could not escape the feeling there was more variation among them than he would have expected to see—variation not merely in color and size and pattern. There were too many dragons of sharper distinctions—the shape of the skull, or the mounting of the wings. "Roland," Laurence said, before he remembered she was gone. "Mr. Forthing," he said instead, "do you mark anything peculiar about those dragons?" He would have liked to consult Granby, but failing that any man who had been an aviator all his life, and more familiar with the variety of dragons.

Forthing peered over, holding determinedly to the straps of his flying-cap, which had lost its buckle in their tearing speed and now threatened to quit the field at any moment; he was trying to tie up the loose straps instead. "A lot of queer sorts, sir, if that is what you mean. Ferals—he has scraped the barrel, I suppose."

Laurence shook his head, dissatisfied. "Would you call them *French* ferals?"

"One feral's much like another," Forthing said uncertainly.

"Sir," Lieutenant Challoner put in, "I have been in the colonies, lately, and while I would not swear to it, those green ones on the left flank there have a look of Naskapi beasts—those are the natives up north of Halifax."

"What, Indians, here?" Forthing said. "How should they ever get here, and why would they?" But Laurence had already put his glass on the green dragons, who were carrying sacks of incendiaries, and although it was too far to make anything of facial features, the men aboard were certainly not French officers—one only to each dragon, wearing long leather coats embroidered all over in patterns, fur-collared. Their beasts had the same angular, narrow-muzzled heads common among the Incan beasts, although their scales were not of the long feather-like sort.

He shook his head, dissatisfied and puzzled, but he could not spare the matter more thought: in five minutes more they would be upon the battlefield, if they continued on their straight-line course. They could strike directly at the bombing run: the slow pace and coordination required for the operation meant that even a little opposition would be sufficient to disrupt it. But the city was plainly lost already, and the only hope of defeating Napoleon was to save the army, if it could be done.

The breadth of that monstrous force would make any rear-guard defense hopeless without the support of guns. But there ought to have been guns: at least three hundred of them. All lost, in the fires? On that chance all hung: if they could establish artillery positions, a successful retreat might yet be accomplished. "Temeraire," he said after a moment, "we will come around by the south, and get a better look at what Accendare is doing on the road over there."

The signals went out, and they swung wide around the burning city: people below streaming into the countryside, carrying the wreckage of their lives—small carts laden, wheelbarrows, mothers with babes in their arms, a parade of misery. Accendare herself was flying over a rise of land near the eastern gates, circling with a crowd of light-weight hangers-on, mostly Pêcheur-Rayés. She had nothing to do with the fires in the city at all: she was instead striking at the efforts of the allied forces to establish a line of defense across the eastern highway, along which a straggling line of Prussian infantry were attempting to retire.

Infantry squares stood in tight formation, locked in defense around the artillery-crews struggling to bring their guns to bear. Their bristling bayonets held off a direct assault, but Accendare's flames scorched and seared them, and the Pêcheurs, having spent their incendiaries, were dropping anything to hand upon them. One dropped a torn-up sapling, and crushed six men in a row—but the soldiers beside them heaved out the sapling and closed ranks, keeping their bayonets up; one of the fallen struggled up again, and another took the fallen rifles, and planted them in the dirt with the bayonets jutting up. Nearly every square was bristling with these unattended spikes, testament to the grinding toll the assault had been taking upon them.

Laurence could not help but admire the courage and steadfastness which had preserved the order of the Russian and the Prussian infantry under an aerial pounding so unopposed; he did not see a single beast in the air working to defend them. But no small force of dragons could have hoped to hold long against such a disparity of numbers.

Nor could his own. Still, he closed up his glass and nodded, not with relief but with certainty; the decision was made, and now there was nothing to do but to fight it out. "Tell Iskierka to take Accendare," Laurence called to Temeraire, "and we will put a stop to that bombardment, across the eastern side of the city at least: we must give the infantry some chance to get onto the road."

He gave the word to Quigley to signal the Cossacks to follow Iskierka: the smaller dragons clustering about Accendare were plainly French regulars, and the Cossacks were all veterans who had refined their boarding techniques against those troops over two years now of hard fighting. Granby's signal-officer waved an acknowledging flag, and then Iskierka tilted and peeled away with her following, leaving Temeraire with a sadly diminished band—only thirty dragons, many of them only out of courier-class by a generous assessment—half a dozen of the Scots, two Prussian Mauerfuchs, and then seven Grey Coppers and five Xenicas robbed from the British formations; none of them with real muscle to speak of.

But Laurence signaled them into a diamond-shape, behind Temeraire, and their sheer furious pace made its own impact upon the enormous cloud of French dragons. Temeraire roared out, the divine wind opening a path before them like the sweep of some enormous scythe, and even when the echoes had faded the fear of it kept the dragons spilling away to either side. There was no slackening. All the small dragons packed tightly in a mass behind Temeraire, the *chop chop chop* of their wings beating close and frantic, and they carved a channel directly through and burst out over the eastern gates, leaving the bombing-pass disrupted: cauldrons spilled too soon, incendiaries fallen too late.

They nearly passed Accendare, fleeing back to the safety of the French lines as Iskierka gleefully scorched her escort, and the faint sound of huzzahs reached them from the ground, a few shots fired off by way of greeting or celebration. But for the most part the Russians and the Prussians were making urgent use of every moment that had been won them. The guns sheltered inside the bayonet-bristling squares of infantry were now dragged swiftly into a line on the low hills overlooking the road, and began almost at once to fire steadily, establishing a slender cordon of safety the French dragons could not fly across with impunity. And almost at once, the main body of the corps began to make an orderly retreat—men marching out from the back walls of the city, despite conflagration behind them, and streaming away along the road to the east.

Iskierka and the Cossacks swung back to join Temeraire. They still made only a very small band, against the French numbers. And this retreat they should now have to defend with only that thin support of guns, for an hour. The French were already halting the bombardment, Laurence saw: the dragons were going to ground, in companies, and setting down their burdens. In a moment the full force of that attack would be upon them.

"We can make very little plan of battle, ignorant as we are of all knowledge of the enemy's dispositions, and so outnumbered as we must expect to find ourselves," Laurence had said before their departure, to his small knot of captains. "If a defensive line can be established, Temeraire and Iskierka will give the lead: let your beasts do their best to support them. We will at all times attempt to remain above boarding-speed, and accept the sacrifice of accuracy. I have full confidence that every man—every officer—and dragon will do his duty," he finished, a little awkwardly altering his remarks, as among the company stood all five women under his command—whom he should now have to expose to so extraordinary a risk. But the Xenicas were the heaviest of the fast dragons, and could not be spared.

The sacrifice of accuracy was complete indeed at the pace which Temeraire now set, freed from the constraint of slower beasts in his company. He led one furious corkscrewing pass after another, knocking or simply terrifying the French dragons out of his path, which the lighter dragons behind him mauled enthusiastically. Wind and a riot of colors tore at Laurence's eyes: he could not distinguish one dragon from another in the speed of their passage, but even when Temeraire slowed to turn back for another pass, he found it nearly impossible to make any sense of the battlefield, or the enemy's forces.

Laurence and his officers fired their guns blindly as Temeraire swept along, hoping more than certain that they occasionally hit a target: one pistol and another, and then the struggle of reloading mid-air, grains of powder blown scattering from the packet, pistolballs slipping away from numbed fingers. On his left, Baggy uttered a wordless exclamation and clapped his hand to his forehead: a bright red line drawn across the entire front as though someone had meant to take off the top of his head, blood running freely down his face; he had been grazed by a ball. Half a wingbeat slower, and he would have been killed: a shot impersonal as a bolt of lightning, in a sky full of storms.

It was very like doing battle with locusts—every blow landed, but there seemed no hope of headway. Temeraire savaged this dragon, roared another into recoiling flight—and still more came to take their place, erupting from the smoke-clouds like spirits boiling up from some infernal region. The French came at them endlessly, trying to win past to overturn the roaring guns and destroy the retreating army.

Laurence was conscious of every moment of that hour as he had never felt time in a battle before. There was nothing he could do to aid Temeraire but keep a lookout in every direction and warn him if the enemy approached—but the enemy was always approaching, and there was no respite to be had. If Temeraire slowed for anything but the briefest turn, the French converged on him at once. If he retired for a breath behind the safety of the guns, the French instantly resumed their attacks upon the artillery. It was not an effort that could be sustained for long, not after three hours' brutal flight.

His speed began to falter. Their destruction came on, steady and inevitable; Laurence searched the horizon after every turn. He had lost all sense of time, and the sand-glass had become useless thanks to Temeraire twisting in his evasions, frequently turning himself entirely over. The sun was shrouded in smoke.

Laurence measured minutes in increments of despair, and was nearly at its limits when one of the lookouts set up a cry. The glass nearly slipped from his fingers as he wrenched it from his belt just as Temeraire dived again, but then he climbed, and Laurence did not need the glass: the line of dragons approaching was visible in the distance, Fidelitas in the center of the force.

Their speed was slowing as they made their approach. The

French rear-guard were swinging guns around to set up an unwel-
coming barrage, and abruptly the air lightened around them as
several dozen of the French beasts pulled away to try to bar the
reunion of their forces. Poole would have to choose whether to
force a way through, at great risk, or sweep wide of the city with
the French skirmishing to delay him every step of the way, a safer
course which would mean the loss of another half an hour before
he could come to their aid.

Half an hour they did not have. There were more than enough
dragons remaining to face them, and even as Temeraire's flagging
energies were renewed by the sight of their fellows, so was the
enemy's determination to bring him down before his relief came.
Seven dragons surged at his head from all sides, a sudden
penning-up. Captain Gaudey flying alongside sent up a shout, and
her Xenica Glorianus made swift merciless work of the exposed
side of one red-and-blue Garde-de-Lyon attempting to foul Temeraire's left side, letting him escape—but Temeraire had been
checked for a moment; long enough for a dozen boarders to spring
over from the gathered enemy dragons, firing pistols and swinging
curved swords—Napoleon's famed Mamluk troops, their red trousers brilliant against Temeraire's hide.

Laurence knew nothing of the larger battle, for the next five
minutes. The world narrowed to the span of Temeraire's neck.
Carabiners clacked against the harness-rings as they were all flung
off their feet—Temeraire fighting furiously, earth and sky whirling
around them and blurred together with smoke. Laurence half-
blinded by wind and speed tried to reload, to block sword-swings
he could not see. Forthing went down before him, stopping one
blade; Laurence shot the man behind him—

The world righted itself, and stopped—or did so at least by
comparison; Temeraire had slackened to a resting pace. He was
falling back, behind the guns, and behind a wall of allied dragons:
Fidelitas had taken the risk and come straight through, after all.
Calloway clubbed the last boarder across the back of the head
with a rifle, knocking the man down, and shouted, "Mr. Ashgrove,

pass the word for bandages, and four hands to spare. Sir, you aren't hurt?"

"No, nothing to signify," Laurence said, though breath was a struggle; he had taken a blow to the ribs. He managed to haul himself around on his straps. Forthing sagged in his carabiner straps, bleeding and dazed. Fidelitas and Cavernus and Levantia had rounded up the light-weights of their formations and were raking the French, Ricarlee and his fellows making a gleeful rampage among their leavings with the Russian greys interspersed among them. Below, the allied troops were streaming away, bayonets bristling at their backs and cavalry guarding their flanks, guns rolling over the road.

Chapter 18

TEMERAIRE WAS CONSCIOUS MOSTLY of weariness, leavened
occasionally by the deep ache in his wing-joints, which throbbed
unpleasantly whenever he stirred them. The half-healed musket-
wounds in his chest made small knots of pain as though someone
were steadily pressing a blunted knife, not sharp enough to pierce
scales, against the flesh. Beside him, Iskierka, too, ate through her
porridge with dull silent effort, her own head hanging. He paused
and sighed heavily after a swallow: he had never quite noticed,
before, how tiring it was to gnaw away at a large piece of meat in
one's jaws, even if it had been stewed some time.

But he persevered, the food went down little by little, and he
gradually became aware of a strangely general silence around the
feeding pits. All of them from the first flight were very tired, of
course, but no-one from the second flight was speaking, either—
none of the usual chatter or squabbling. Even the Russian greys
were eating quietly, with many sidelong glances over at Fidelitas,
who had a hunched, strange expression as he ate—half-ashamed,
and he avoided Temeraire's look, even though he had done so well
during the battle and come to their rescue.

With a sudden sharp anxiety, Temeraire said, "Where is Roland?" No-one answered him. "Challoner!" he called urgently—but she had gone to eat something; Forthing was still with the surgeons—"What has happened to her?" he demanded of Fidelitas directly.

"What?" Fidelitas said, with a startled—a guilty, Temeraire thought—flinching. "I do not know. Who is Roland?"

"She is *my* officer," Temeraire said, infuriated by this cavalier response, "who was lent you only for this one engagement—*lent.*"

He was about to add several remarks about the care he might have expected, in exchange for such a gesture, when Baggy put down his own bowl of porridge—he had been gulping it with no benefit of a spoon—and belched and said, "Here, now, what's the fuss? Roland is with the admiral."

"Oh," Temeraire said. "She is not hurt?"

"No?" Baggy said. "Why would she be?"

"Well, I am very glad to hear it, although someone might have said so, sooner," Temeraire said, but he was not entirely placated; he still did not know what made Fidelitas look so strange—nor Cavernus, who also wore a stiff, disapproving expression.

Perhaps they were distressed over having retreated. But no-one could truly have complained of the day's outcome—no-one, at least, who had seen Dresden in flames—the scale of the opposition—the situation which had confronted them; no-one could fail to be impressed. They had escaped, and nearly all the Prussian and Russian soldiers, too, *with* their guns; or at least half of them. No-one would have called it likely that morning, knowing what they had faced. Of course it was not *exactly* like a victory—but only look how the Russians had beaten Napoleon last winter, all by running away in a particularly clever manner, and anyway Temeraire called it churlish to be dissatisfied, all things considered.

"Well, well," Churki said, coming down next to him, with a flurry of her feathers. "So here you are, after all, and here is the army still in one piece! I would not have looked for it this morning," she added, as though to affirm Temeraire's own thinking, and with strong approval. "That was some fine soldiering. Would there be anything to spare?" And then she even waited very politely until Temeraire made room for her to join him and eat. He did so with a dignified bow, although it made his wing-joints ache again: he felt it only due her own courtesy, and also the very good sense of her kind remarks; he hoped everyone else should have overheard, and that it might make them cease behaving so wooden.

Churki at least felt no constraint herself. "Naturally when I understood the circumstances, I knew Hammond had to be removed from the city at once," she said, as she ate: she had been with him in Dresden early that morning when the first desperate scouts had reported the oncoming force. "There were not more than ten other dragons in the whole place, except the couriers: there was no use trying to fight. So I brought him away, along with that young Tsar fellow—I do not think much of those Russians, let me assure you! Not one of them properly looking after their own emperor; and would you believe that *he* is not married, either? There is something very wrong in the management of men in this part of the world, I must say. I did not feel I owed them any assistance, but Hammond was distressed, so I agreed to take him along and that poor old Marshal as well. *He* did not sound very well. I told them he had better be wrapped up better, but they would be off, without blankets or hot bricks." She shook her head censoriously over the whole enterprise.

She had flown further east, to a town named Bautzen which was their destination, and there had waited until Yu Li had reached them with the news of the army's escape. "Which I did not expect in the least," she said. "Of course, then Hammond would have nothing but coming back to rejoin you. But if you ask *me*, he has no business being here, and neither does the Tsar. No-one could call this Emperor Napoleon a sensible man, after that war he ran in Russia, but there is no denying he is worth ten times over any general we have.—And he has fathered *four* children."

"Only one," Temeraire protested, "although Empress Anahuarque means to have another, Laurence says."

"*Four*," Churki said firmly. "He has two more by two other

women, in France, and one in Vienna, all of them old enough to walk; I inquired of Hammond on the subject. So the Sapa Inca is already expecting another child?" She emitted a sigh thoroughly laced with envy. "Maila cannot complain of *her* choices—if only Hammond would find a woman who had proven her fertility half so well as this French Emperor of hers! And that Lithuanian girl means to have a baby for Dyhern, I understand," she finished, in disgruntled tones.

Temeraire had almost forgotten completely about Miss Merkelyte—Mrs. Dyhern. It did not seem entirely fair to him, either, that Eroica should have simply appeared and snatched her out from under them—but there, he did not mean to be annoyed with Eroica, who had not done it on purpose, and who had been so remarkably helpful with the treasure: a true friend.

"But I see your Laurence, too, has done nothing in that line," Churki said. "Even though he is an admiral now? Surely that must make it easier for him to command the interest of a worthy woman. Not," she added, "that I see why you insist on being so choosy. But if you do *not* mean for him to marry Mrs. Pemberton, you had better settle her with someone else, so at least *she* may begin having children."

By then nearly everyone was finished with their meals, and moving away to make room for the cooks to scorch the pit clean and begin stewing tomorrow's porridge. Fidelitas had taken himself off as quickly as he could, so Temeraire took the opportunity of nudging over to Cavernus to ask quietly, "Why is everyone so awkward? What has Fidelitas done?"

"*He* has done nothing," she said, but refused to say anything more. "You had better talk to the admiral about it."

"I trust, Midwingman, that nothing more will be said on the subject," Laurence said.

"I am not a goose, to go about honking everywhere," Roland said. "But there shan't be any keeping it quiet, sir. Every man top-

side heard him, and every man aboard heard Fidelitas, and I dare
say a dozen beasts heard Cavernus putting in her mite on the subject; it shan't stay a secret."

"No," Laurence said, "but it may be known, without being
formally brought to my notice."

"It might be better if it *were,* now," she said pointedly.

Laurence knew what she meant. He had certainly just saved
the allied army, through extraordinary efforts, and Whitehall
could not dismiss him at this particular moment; if he meant to
call Poole to any official account, now was the time. "That will be
all," he said. She frowned, then touched her hat and left the room.
Laurence sat back heavily in his chair—a more comfortable one
than many he had used on campaign; he had been assigned a house
for his quarters, large enough to boast a sitting-room inhabited by
a writing-table. He understood Roland's resentment—shared it.
But any court-martial convened against Poole would face the remarkable difficulty of convicting him of dereliction of duty when
his duty had in fact been performed to the utmost: when his dragon
had led a dangerous charge and had won through to relieve Temeraire and Iskierka, just in time, and secure the retreat.

The case could only be won by a public argument that Poole
had tried to persuade Fidelitas to do otherwise—and that his efforts had failed; that his dragon had willfully disobeyed him. That
knowledge was even now traveling through the Corps at the speed
of rumor, surely to the anger and anxiety of every officer who had
taken it as truth that dragons were devoted blindly to their captains. Laurence was not even sure that a court of aviators would
be willing to admit that it had happened. Poole would be invited
to say that he had changed his mind and had told Fidelitas so, too
quietly to be overheard. Many would refuse to believe that a
dragon had committed the act from any sense of duty; he would
either have done it at the behest of another dragon, or, by a still
more uncharitable interpretation, for the sake of prize-money.

"And I cannot say Poole was unquestionably guilty, in any
case," Laurence said tiredly. "He might well have argued that the

risk of a charge outweighed the value of saving us—that he desired to take a safer course."

"But if he had gone round, he should never have come in time to save the guns, which were in much more danger than I was," Temeraire said, with an optimistic gloss upon his own peril. "And without the guns, everything should have been lost, anyone could see that. Poor Fidelitas! I am very sorry I was so abrupt with him to-day: he was behaving so oddly that I was sure he had done something to be ashamed of, but I see it is only that he was ashamed of Poole, and everyone else was pitying him. We must do something for him, Laurence. I do not suppose there is any hope of a prize?"

"No," Laurence said. They would be on short commons, if anything, by the end of the week. A great deal of supply had been abandoned behind the enemy lines.

"Then a medal," Temeraire said decisively. "He certainly ought to have a medal."

"We will consider the matter tomorrow," Laurence said. "For now, you should be asleep: I made sure you would be so when I came, and I am sorry to have found otherwise. You have eaten enough?"

"Yes," Temeraire said. "All the third flight handsomely said they would go without, because they had eaten in the afternoon before they fetched the supply here, so we ate well. And really I am not *very* tired," but here he yawned, enormously, and moments after putting his head down murmuring, "but now that Emily is back, and you have assured me all is well . . ." he was snoring in a remarkably stentorious way, which made the shrubs near his nostrils tremble violently with every exhalation.

Laurence rested a hand on the soft muzzle and left it there a few moments, feeling the steady thrumming of breath moving beneath, before he continued on to the courier-clearing, where Yu Li awaited him, herself drooping with fatigue. Laurence hesitated; he had heard enough of her report that he knew he must urgently hear the rest, and take the news on to the headquarters, but she had been going back and forth all day in their service and now was shivering badly; the night had turned cool, and Jade Dragons did not have the flesh to keep them warm when they were not flying. He looked towards the large manor, overlooking the encampment, where the senior staff were assembling, and slowly asked, "Do you think you might be able to come inside the house?"

She followed his courier to the manor, and came up the stairs behind him, to the great consternation of the guards. She was only some eight feet long from head to tip of tail, but her talons and teeth were remarkable enough for all that. But Hammond flung open the door from within and rushing out onto the top of the stairs seized Laurence by the hand, nearly wringing it in greeting. "Admiral!" he cried. "He has halted on the road outside Dresden. He has certainly halted. We have it confirmed beyond a doubt."

He required no antecedent, and the guards overhearing the news brightened as much as did Laurence. "I cannot think why," Laurence said, though he returned Hammond's handshake with all the enthusiasm this news invited, and came into the house with him, forgetting his own company. "He could have had us in striking-distance in two hours' flight—you are sure he has not merely stopped to bring up stragglers?"

"His stragglers are three-quarters of his army," Hammond said. "Now that Blücher has rejoined us, he does not have enough men to meet us. He has sent half his dragons back to Erfurt, to bring the rest of his infantry along by portage. We will have three days, at least. Come in, you must come in at once," Hammond continued, and drew Laurence along into the large dining room where the senior staff was assembled, without even noticing the dragon trailing behind them.

Even there, Yu Li at first escaped observation—Marshal Blücher coming forward to greet Laurence with a fervent embrace, and the other officers acclaiming him with all the energy of men who knew very well how closely they had skirted disaster and defeat. "His Majesty will wish to see you," Blücher said. "You have eaten?"

A stifled yelp interrupted their greetings: Yu Li had inquisitively come up to the table, which was littered with maps tacked together to form a sweeping whole. She put her head out on its long neck to examine their positions, very much startling the young staff-officer next to her, who nearly knocked over his neighbors as he went stumbling back. "I beg your pardon," Laurence said hastily. "Gentlemen, this is Lung Yu Li, who has been sent from the Chinese legions."

There was an enormous silence. Yu Li broke it herself, saying in Chinese, "This is a very handsome map, but those men are not over there," while leaning forward to make several alterations to the disposition of figures with the talons of her foreleg, nudging some here and there in small increments until she was satisfied with their arrangement. She straightened up from the table and blinked around at the company, who wore a general expression of disquiet: a dragon did not generally appear in a dining room, and even Laurence had to admit of a vague sense of something decidedly out of place, as though a caricature from the *Gazette* had abruptly come to life.

"Sir," Laurence said to Blücher, "her news does not permit of any delay, further than has already been occasioned. Marshal Kutuzov ought to hear it at once, if he can be disturbed."

"Ah! He cannot," Blücher said heavily. "Marshal Kutuzov has died."

The men gathered around the table with the Tsar were divided neatly by dress: the statesmen neat and in good order, the serving-officers unshaven and in clothing stained with sweat and retreat; their faces were equally bleak, however, and Yu Li's news was not calculated to make them less so.

"By the Dread Lord's order, the legions departed from Xian directly on receiving the Dread Lord's order," Yu Li said, "and proceeded without delay through Yutien and made the crossing of the Taklamakan Desert. Since then we have encountered a steady resistance which has hindered the secure establishment of our supply. As a consequence, we must establish a sufficient presence at each depot to defend it, and our supply-flights must travel in larger groups, which in turn necessitates an increase in supply, and thereby greatly delays our advance."

"Feral raiding?" a Russian officer asked, when Laurence had translated this far. "I dare say they do not know how to manage wild beasts, when they have none in their own country, but any respectable guards ought to be able to fend them off."

Laurence was sure Yu Li did not refer to ordinary feral attacks as might be made on any army's supply, and when he asked her of the arrangements made to avoid these, she said, with a severe eye upon the officer who had spoken, "Naturally, as is necessary to any civilized army, we have a sufficient supply allocated to be able to give appropriate presents to those dragons whose territory we must cross. But our gifts have been refused. These attacks are bent upon destruction, not theft."

There was a pause, as this sank in. Every man there knew that Kutuzov's intention had been, as nearly as could be managed, to arrange a trap almost exactly like the one which had nearly closed upon Napoleon's army in Russia, in the last campaign. He had meant to penetrate as far westward as he could during the winter, and on meeting Napoleon's advance retire by small piecemeal stages, grudgingly surrendering territory and stretching the French lines of communication, until the arrival of the legions from the East should abruptly shift the balance of aerial power, and allow him to strike a crushing blow—with, they had all confidently expected, the assistance of the Austrians, who would under those circumstances have finally come off the fence. Napoleon had already overset much of this design by leaping forward to seize Dresden and force them so far westward in a single blow. Even a small delay in the legions' arrival would now have been a cause for concern.

"How long?" Wittgenstein asked finally, breaking the silence.

"General Zhao Lien regrets that it will not be possible to assemble along the Vistula before two months have passed," Yu Li said.

"We do not have two months," Blücher said. "We do not have two weeks."

"If the Austrians came in?" one man said.

"The Austrians will not come in while Napoleon is on their border with five hundred dragons and two hundred thousand men, when we have half those numbers," Hammond said. "Count Metternich is entirely with us in spirit, gentlemen, but he is not a fool."

"If I may be so bold," Laurence said, "we ought first consider *how* Napoleon has obtained the services of five hundred dragons. Eugene had a strong aerial force at the Elbe, and Davout reportedly has two hundred dragons at Hamburg. The beasts here cannot all have been French. Not after Bonaparte's losses in Russia, which to our knowledge were immense. There were too many dragons of unusual conformation with them, and Yu Li's reports must further give rise to the suspicion that he has also established relations with the dragons in the east—that he has anticipated the legions, and arranged these efforts to delay their arrival."

A conclusion less to the taste of any man present could hardly be imagined: all Kutuzov's aims shattered. But the rational force of the argument was difficult to avoid, and no-one objected; Laurence paused a moment, saw that no-one would speak, and said forcefully, "This is the work of his Concord, gentlemen. Do any of you doubt it? He has for the cost of pen and ink bought a thousand dragons, who otherwise would have spent this war sleeping idle in remote caverns. Have there been reports of increased raiding, on our own supply?"

A steady rumble of muttering around the table. There had been, everywhere—

"The consequence of so much strife and unrest, we thought," a Prussian general said slowly, but at last a full understanding was taking hold among them, which Laurence had despaired of in the past months, when his every attempt at raising the specter of the Concord had been met with dismissal—ferals were of small numbers, of no account; Napoleon's offer could not even reach them, for the lack of language and letters; they would not believe in it, if it did.

"If he has truly gained the allegiance of the feral beasts, the unharnessed beasts, we must root them all out. How can it be done? Poison—" one officer began.

"He has gained it," Laurence snapped, "because *this* is the answer you would make them. When you offer them slaughter or even the mere slow dwindling starvation which has been their lot, these last few centuries, and Napoleon holds out the promise of liberty, and the enjoyment of rights in the territory which they consider their own, there can be hardly any wonder that they should flock to his banner. Do you imagine the harnessed dragons now in our service will long remain loyal, when they know you mean to destroy their fellows?"

Wittgenstein held up a hand, and with an effort, Laurence silenced himself; he felt as though his heart beat with a palpable force against his ribs. He saw Hammond glancing at him sidelong, worried, and Yu Li, despite being unable to follow his words, had understood his passion; she had sidled over to take up a position flanking him to the left with her forelegs held high—apparently at rest, but the muscles of her legs were gathered as though to launch her with all their considerable force, if necessary. He felt entirely capable of violence himself.

"The Tsar has summoned me to Bautzen," Wittgenstein said to the silent room—the Tsar undoubtedly meant to name him commander, in Kutuzov's place. He was nearly the only choice, and could scarcely refuse, but the position he would inherit could not have been less enviable. "I must inform him of this intelligence, and learn his will. We will convene tomorrow morning. For now, gentlemen, go to your rest. Mr. Hammond, if I may ask you for a word—"

Hammond went away with him, not without an anxious backwards look, and Laurence turning walked from the house and returned to the field-covert still in that settled mood of wrath.

"Come, you will sleep warmer with Temeraire," Laurence told Yu Li, when they had landed. She tucked herself beneath Temeraire's wing, which he raised murmuring without even opening an eye, but Laurence could not rest. He paced his fury out the length of Temeraire's body—aware as he did that his officers and crew watched him out of their tents, and whispered. He could not care.

The reply would come by morning. He did not know what the Tsar would decide. In Russia, Alexander had ordered the release of his own feral dragons from the hobbles that kept them imprisoned in the breeding grounds. But he had done so only from expediency—he had hoped to persuade those dragons to take carrying-harnesses, and transport his infantry, in exchange for their liberty and their bread, and to keep Napoleon from recruiting them instead. That same expediency might now induce him to attempt the wholesale destruction of the feral dragons, if he thought it easier to achieve.

Laurence knew with perfect clarity that he would not obey such an order, nor even stand by and see it done—and he did not have to wonder what Temeraire would think of it. They had met a like choice, once before. His steps slowed at last, and he halted by Temeraire's sleeping head, the calm of resolution settling upon him. He had determined not to regret his choice; if he were now to be taken at his word, and that determination tried, he could not complain. Their course would be clear enough, if as wrenching as he could imagine. He had refused Napoleon his service, twice over, when he could have served his own interest. But for this, they would go to him.

At least the distance would not be long, Laurence thought, with a black humor, and almost might have laughed. He breathed deeply once instead, and mastered himself. Six bells had lately rung—there were a few hours yet until morning. He was still wearing his flying-coat; he climbed up to the crook of Temeraire's foreleg, wrapped the leather skirts close around himself, and shut his eyes; sleep came easily and all at once, as though he lay in his cot, twenty years ago, without a care but the direction of the wind.

Temeraire felt really exasperated, the next morning, when everyone was very quiet all over again—his crew, this time, and once
more for no reason which anyone would tell him. It was all shrugs,
and "I don't know anything, I'm sure," except for O'Dea, who
would only make dark hints of some mysterious terrible event
which was certain to occur, and *then* say, "Ah, but I don't know
anything, I'm sure," which was not to be preferred.

Laurence had gone to meet with the generals again—he had
looked so very fine this morning, Temeraire had noted approvingly. He had woken to find all the runners scrambling, for once
summoned away from their schoolwork, and Laurence shaving
while they sponged his best coat and ironed his best shirt, ordinarily kept in the chest with Temeraire's talon-sheaths. Temeraire
had seized the chance of offering a few suggestions—and Laurence
had very obligingly put on his medal of the Nile, and freshly polished the hilt of his sword, and taken his dress hat with its handsome cockade, much to Temeraire's satisfaction; but then the hour
had grown late and Laurence had gone in a rush, and only then
had Temeraire realized, from the behavior of the crew, that he
ought to have asked what cause merited the display.

"Very well," he said, in some irritation, "then I am going to
the porridge-pits to see if anyone else *does* know anything, as you
are all quite useless."

Most of the ferals liked to gather there, and have a smell of the
food even if it was not ready for eating yet; and at least one of the
big dragons had to sleep near-by to keep them off it: it had been
Iskierka's turn last night, so she was lying beside them, but she had
nothing to offer. "I don't see there is anything to know," Iskierka
said, yawning. "Granby, is there?"

"I don't know, I'm sure," Granby said—Temeraire looked at
him with a strong sense of betrayal, but at least Granby had the
grace to look troubled. "I did hear Laurence was in a taking, last
night, but you know what he is: if anyone tells you he gabbed

about what set him off, you can be sure it comes straight from Banbury. Perhaps it is only old Kutuzov dying like that; no-one can like the commander popping off in the night with Napoleon on our heels. They say it is going to be Wittgenstein next, I hear," which was interesting at least, but did not answer Temeraire's immediate concern.

Grig landed near the pits and said loudly, "Is there any chance of an early bite?" which brought Iskierka's head up for a warning snort of flame. "I don't mean anything by it, I'm sure," he said, with a small hop that brought him over by her head, to make an apologetic bob, and then he pitched his voice very quiet and said, "Temeraire, what do they mean to put the poison in, have *you* heard?"

"What?" Temeraire said.

"I will not blab," Grig said hurriedly. "Not to anyone you don't like—"

Temeraire put his head down and nudged Grig firmly back towards the outer ring of trees. "Now you will explain yourself at once," he said, and everything came spilling out: a few of the small Russian dragons of Grig's acquaintance had eavesdropped upon a conversation among their officers, and passed the word to him, in hopes he might be able to learn how to avoid the traps.

Temeraire heard out the hideous plan, first with bafflement—it could not be, it was too infamous—but when he recalled that it came from those same men who had kept their beasts chained, hobbled, all in order to make them starved prisoners in breeding grounds, he ceased to doubt, and a settled, wrathful calm descended.

He had all too much confidence in their power of achieving such a dreadful goal. Everyone was so very hungry now—there was not enough food anywhere, it seemed, and ferals did not even have the advantage of porridge, to stretch what there was. If men only put out some cooking-pits full of food, in the pretense of keeping the ferals from raiding, many would eat, and sicken, and die. And with their numbers broken by this first slaughter, still desperate with hunger, the remainder would be easier prey for all the forms of entrapment that men could devise. Temeraire remembered with a shudder the burning frame so close around him, the crowding pitchforks—and those had only been peasants; those men had not had guns.

"Yes, I understand," he said, when Grig trailed off at last. "I understand very well."

"Then you see why I would like to know—" Grig began, but Temeraire rumbled a warning, and silenced him.

"I would certainly give you no private hints, if I had them," Temeraire said, speaking clearly, to be heard and understood by all the other dragons, who had been already listening in with interest, stretching to overhear. "I will not be satisfied, nor should any right-thinking dragon, to escape destruction only for myself and my personal friends—*I* will not stand by, and see such a project carried out. And neither will Laurence, you may depend upon it."

He was angry, and his voice betrayed it—Grig cowered away from him and the rising thrum. Temeraire closed his jaws until the urge to roar had subsided. He would not blame Grig, who had been raised so badly, and had never learned to trust any other dragon, or had any person worthy of trust, either.

"We will certainly put a stop to the entire business," Temeraire continued, when he trusted himself to speak again. "And any dragon, who does not care to be poisoned or shot for the convenience of men, may help us, if they choose—that is all I have to say on the subject, and when Laurence comes back, he will certainly agree; *he* will never obey such a command."

"Oh," Grig said, a little doubtfully. "But did you not say that you lost ten thousand pounds by it, the last time?"

This gave Temeraire a sharp moment, a painful start—and after he had only just restored Laurence's fortunes!—"I will lose as much again," he said, with an effort, and immense resolution. "I will do it again, if need be; if I really must. Even *that* consideration will not stop me."

Having made this painful declaration, Temeraire went aloft

and returned to his own clearing, to pace its confining limits round and round and making distracted apologies if he should knock over a tree, to the inconvenience of his crew. Laurence had certainly gone to stop the whole business—Temeraire saw it now. Laurence meant to stop it, and to tell Temeraire after the whole monstrous plan had already been averted, exactly to spare him the distress of the prospect which now lay so horribly close before them. If Laurence did not succeed—Temeraire shied away from too much contemplation of the consequences.

He turned his attention, rather, to the nearly as daunting consideration of how they should proceed, if the worst were to come to pass. They could not chase all over the Continent, themselves, to warn everyone. "We shall have to pass the word through the ferals," Temeraire said aloud, but what if not everyone should believe them? He turned around again, sweeping over two tents without really noticing. "I had better speak to Ricarlee—and I must try and get word to Bistorta, and to the ferals of Lithuania."

He was so engaged in planning out this network of communication that he did not pay any attention to movements outside his own clearing, until with a start he raised his head at several shadows moving in perpetual circles over his clearing, rudely, and looking around found Obituria and Fidelitas and their formations gathered closely around him, with their wing dragons circling overhead.

"What is it?" Temeraire said to Fidelitas, who ducked his head away with a queer, jerking unhappy movement, but said nothing.

"Why, I don't know," Obituria said maddeningly. "I have only come along on orders: we are to take up stations around your clearing. Is there going to be a battle? *I* did not get to fight, last time," she said glumly.

"I should not think so, for Napoleon was three days off, yesterday," Temeraire said, puzzled, but Granby was coming down the path—Granby, in a rage, halting where Captain Poole and Captain Windle had gathered with their officers, across the entrance to Temeraire's clearing.

"What the devil do you mean by this?" he snapped. "You will explain yourselves, gentlemen; you will dismiss your dragons, and explain yourselves, at once."

"We will do no such thing," Poole answered, very coldly—he looked very pale, with red splotches come out upon his forehead, "and I hardly would have supposed that explanation would be required by an officer of His Majesty's Corps—a *loyal* officer; I do not think any such man could entertain the least confusion, after the performance to which so many of us were witness not an hour since, about our actions, or indeed their necessity."

"By God, I will see you broken the service for this," Granby said. "You have deserved it twice over before this, in one campaign, and this crowns all—"

"That you should dare to speak of the *service,* in these circumstances, beggars all belief," Poole spat back. "When we consider what your own behavior ought to have been even before now, and when you have heard an outright avowal of the intention to commit treason, by those whose willingness to do it can hardly be denied—by those who ought long since have been put past the power of repeating their crime—"

"What?" Temeraire said, in rousing wrath. "Am I to understand that you—that all of you—" he turned to Obituria and Fidelitas, "have come here, have taken up positions against *me*—in defense of this poisoning scheme? That you are here to help poison other dragons, and not even enemy dragons; to poison and murder the smallest, starving ferals, who have not a bowl of porridge to be sure of, who have no coverts, nor crew, nor any sort of treasure at all, who are not a quarter of your size—"

The dragons were all drawing back from him uneasily—the divine wind was a growing echo in his throat, and he felt not the least inclination to rein it back. "And you would let them all be made sick, and left to die—I suppose *you* think," he stormed at Gaudenius, Obituria's wing dragon and a Yellow Reaper, even as that beast shrank ashamedly back, "that they would not think of poisoning the Reapers in Yorkshire, the ones who do not care to be harnessed? And none of you should mind it if dragons like Ri-carlee and his fellows, who after all have been good wing-mates all this while, should be tricked into eating poisoned sheep, and pushed into pens to be burnt up? To *this*, you mean to lend your assistance—"

"Oh! I don't, at all!" Obituria burst out, aghast. "I don't! How can you say such dreadful things? We are only here because our captains have asked us."

"That is as much to say, that you have not troubled to find out what they are about," Temeraire said. "I do not suppose any of you wondered, when they told you to take up a fighting-post over my clearing, what they meant by it?" He looked at Fidelitas, who could not meet his eyes, but dropped his head miserably.

"Do not listen to that treasonous, seditious beast another mo-ment," Poole called angrily. "Fidelitas, you know you have never been disobedient a moment before you met him—you must see how he is bent on leading all of you astray."

"Astray, I suppose, from your wishes," Temeraire said, swivel-ing his head down to Poole, "which have never consulted *his*, or those of dragons, at all."

"And this is what your marvelous *actions* are to get us," Granby snapped to Poole. "—a pitched fight, between our own dragons, in our own camp."

"Better that, than seeing treason go by, unopposed!" Poole said. He stepped back from Granby and drew his sword. "I will gladly die—I will die by my own dragon's teeth—" Fidelitas cried out in horror at this dreadful suggestion, but Poole only flung on-wards, "before I will turn a blind unseeing eye to treason, before my face. When *I* am called to give testimony, *I* will not say, I knew nothing, bleating."

"Why, damn you," Granby said, reaching for his own sword, and all the officers were suddenly shouting at one another, and Challoner and the crew, staring, were running to Granby's side, and they were all so closely packed in that Temeraire could not see a way to get a claw in among them, if needed—

"What is the meaning of this display?"

Laurence's bellow had rarely been so welcome. Temeraire gasped in relief; Laurence was there, on the path—and then his gasp became horror, for with a swift springing turn, Poole was by Laurence's side, and he had laid the edge of his sword at Laurence's throat.

Temeraire froze, halted completely. One push of the blade, and Laurence—Laurence might die, might be killed, right before his eyes. Fidelitas made a low terrible noise, crouching—of course he knew that Poole would die, too, immediately afterwards. But that could count for nothing with Temeraire; what would anything matter, when Laurence was dead?

Laurence stood very calmly, and looked Poole in the face— Poole panting heavily, his jaw clenched. Temeraire felt he saw and tracked every droplet of sweat that trickled down into Poole's collar, every slight—too slight—tremor of his arm. "Put up that sword, Captain," Laurence said. "You are overset." He looked at the other officers, paying not the least attention to the blade still at his neck. "Captain Granby, I am obliged to appoint you acting-admiral, of our forces—"

"Laurence!" Granby cried, taking a step.

"I have been required to assume the united command of the allied aerial forces," Laurence continued, as though he had not been interrupted. "We have only a few days before Bonaparte will be on our heels, gentlemen. We are to use them to recruit or sway every feral we can find to our cause, and make whatever defense of them we can. I do not despair of our success. Winters," he called— and after a moment, Winters timidly ran out to him, through the crowd of uncertain, stilled men.

Laurence reaching up pushed the blade by the flat away from his neck, easily. Poole watched his arm move as though he had no power to halt it, and then let it fall to his side. Laurence did not look at him, but took out an envelope from his coat and handed it to Winters. "Take that to Mr. Challoner, and have her set every man with a clear hand to copying it," he said. "Gentlemen, if any of you have any man in your crew who has any Durzagh, from serving with Arkady and his Pamir ferals at the Channel, you will oblige me by sending them to me at once."

He came down the path, through the men who cleared a way for him, and to Temeraire's side. He put a hand on Temeraire's foreleg. With a shudder of relief, as though he had seen a slow-match put out before it reached the cannon, Temeraire put his head down and nosed Laurence over carefully. Fidelitas was snatching Poole up, and flying away, but for the moment Temeraire gave that no attention; he only made certain Laurence was well, and after he had assured himself that there was no scratch, no drawn blood, he gave a great sigh and then asked, "Laurence, what is that?" meaning the mysterious document which Laurence had brought, which seemed so important.

"It is your bill," Laurence said. "Yours and Perscitia's. The Tsar and King Frederick have agreed to its terms."

Chapter 19

"YOU MUST ALSO CONSIDER," Temeraire said earnestly, "the French breeding program, and what it should mean for all of you, on the Continent. You must recall they mean to hatch no less than four thousand eggs."

"It does give one pause," Bistorta acknowledged, while a murmur traveled the gathered ferals—a great many Alpine ferals had come in answer to his urgent messages, and others from Saxony had come along out of curiosity. Naturally none of them could fail to be concerned with so many dragons hatching in a territory neighboring their own. "It does, but it does not therefore mean we can rely on your friends. I don't think there are any of us who have not heard of this very terrible business in Russia, now."

"I have seen one of those beasts who was hobbled up myself," one feral piped up, "going around with the French. His scars! I did not like to believe it, before then, not truly. But nothing else could account for scars like that."

Bistorta nodded firm agreement. She wore the largest, most magnificent of the platters from the golden dinner service around her neck, upon a chain—it gave Temeraire a faint pang still, every time a flash of the firelight gleamed off the lovely engraving—and the others were all very respectful of her. "I do not know I would not rather see this Napoleon win, when by all accounts he has behaved handsomely by dragons."

"I am the last to say anything in defense of the Russians' behavior," Temeraire said, "except that they have learnt better, and are showing they mean to do better, for the very same reason that Napoleon has been behaving so nicely to dragons lately: because they want our help. Napoleon's concern, like theirs, is first for himself and his own empire. I do not believe he is to be relied on, further than any other government. It is only that they can all see the importance of having us on their side, now, which makes them eager to be our friends. Of course, Napoleon has been *quicker* to see his advantage—I believe no-one has ever denied he is very clever. But that is not as much as to say he is the keeper of our interest."

"Well, no," Bistorta said, "but it does not make him *less* so, than this come-lately Tsar, who did not think anything of *hobbles*."

"And if the outcomes of their respective victories were equal, I should agree with you," Temeraire said judiciously. "But you must see that they are not. Napoleon only need hold his enemies off until all his new dragons have hatched and grown, and then he will have his own way, all across the Continent. There will be no-one to match him for ten years, no matter what the rest of us should choose to do in future.

"But if the allies should win, there will be many powers in Europe—Russia, and Prussia, and Austria, and England, *and* France, besides Spain, and any number of smaller nations and principalities. If any one of them should fail to keep faith with us, or should begin to treat dragons poorly, we shall have the power to threaten them by alliance with one or more of the others. So you see, it is very much to our advantage to have a balance of power upon the Continent—however thoughtful Napoleon may have been of dragons, personally."

"I do not know I would call it *thoughtful,* myself, to hatch out four thousand dragons without so much as a word to assure us he has enough food for them all," muttered one rather lean-looking Alpine beast, with narrowed eyes.

They all went away murmuring among themselves, and Temeraire congratulated himself that even if they had not been swept away entirely by the force of his arguments, some at least had been persuaded—there had been several inquiries about the rules of prize-money, and ordinary pay, which would hardly have been made if no-one thought them worth joining. He stretched his wings, and went to have a long drink of tea to wet down his dry throat: there were another forty dragons due to arrive in—only an hour, he realized in dismay, as four bells was rung. It seemed he had done nothing but talk, and talk, and talk, for two days.

"I do not suppose Napoleon will attack to-day?" he asked Challoner wistfully.

"No, I shouldn't think there is any likelihood of it," she said. Temeraire sighed.

But his labors were bearing some fruit: Bistorta came back the next morning for more conversation, along with many of the other dragons, and a little later Molic arrived also with some two dozen Lithuanian and Prussian ferals in tow. Temeraire spoke with all of them again, and also with a handful of Persian ferals, who had flown all the way from the east; Yu Li had promised to leave word with them, if she could, on her way back to the legions.

The Persians expressed a loud and very useful sense of injury. "For we were told we might have our territory back, and eat all the cattle that grazes upon it, if only we pushed to keep others out of it," their chief Tushnamatay said, complaining, "but instead we have been having one fight after another with these red fellows from China, who are extremely nasty if there are any number of them—all sorts of tricks."

"When you engage to fight the Imperial Legions of China," Temeraire said, not a little loftily, "you must expect to run into difficulties. I am not surprised that Napoleon should have misrepresented the situation to you, but I do not see why you should feel obliged to him for putting you in so awkward a position, and why you should keep on fighting us instead of accepting the respectable gifts the legions would be happy to make you."

"Gifts are all well enough," Tushna said, "but they do not make up for men rousting us out everywhere."

"I do see that," Temeraire said, "and I am willing, if you choose, to add you to our own separate concord, and to make every effort to persuade the men in your territory to agree to join it and give you your rights. I will not make extravagant promises I cannot be sure to keep—unlike *some*," he added significantly, "but I can say, we will take your part, if you take ours; and besides that, if any of you should choose to provide us with active assistance, you shall be entitled to prize-money, in a fair share—and you may ask any dragon of my company, that it *is* fair."

He was interrupted here by a clanging alarum, and Moncey dropping into the large clearing. "Well, we are in for it," he said cheerfully. "He has dropped ten thousand men on the road ahead of us at Bautzen, with sixty guns."

"I am very sorry to interrupt our conference," Temeraire lied to the listening dragons, "but naturally I must go at once. We should be very glad to have any of you, who would like to help— you need only follow along with Ricarlee, that grey dragon there with the blue markings, and he will show you where to go to have a share of the fighting."

He returned to his own clearing, Laurence already coming down the path himself shrugging into his flying-coat. "The army will fall back on Reichenbach," he said. "We must open the road, and then hold them for five hours."

"I am sure we can do it, Laurence," Temeraire said.

"Best not to take it on credit, my dear," Laurence said.

But Temeraire's confidence was answered, in this instance; when they landed late that evening at the new field-covert established outside the small village of Reichenbach, Laurence might dismount with a sense of weary satisfaction, and know they had balked Napoleon of his prey one more time. And Minnow was waiting for them as they came down, a little stained with travel but bright-eyed and with a letter from Jane; and before Laurence's boots had touched the ground she announced without preamble, "We have rolled Marshal Jourdan up at Vitoria—Joseph Bonaparte has fled over the Pyrenees, to France."

Every man in ear-shot shouted with joy, as tired as they all were, and the news spread outward in ripples that eddied back and demanded still more huzzahs; it was some time before Laurence could open his letter, and read, with inexpressible satisfaction:

> *I think he is nearly done in Spain, and if I say so myself, we have done a neat enough job of the thing. We will be over the Pyrenees soon: Wellington would like to cross as soon as we have mopped up Pamplona and San Sebastian, and I have my eye on that breeding ground east of the Nive. I would not say no to a few dozen French eggs, still soft in the shell, and neither would the Spanish, I am sure. Would the Austrians like a few? If it would help to tempt them in, by all means make them any promises you like.*
>
> *You may tell Emily that Demane came through without incident. Kulingile got boarded halfway through, but Demane restrained himself properly, I am glad to say, and let his topmen do their work; they pushed the boarders off again after only a little squabbling, and his first lieutenant took a nicely heroic scratch, which should let me promote the fellow, and has made them something like a happy crew.*

"Where is Hammond?" Laurence said aloud. "He must know of this, at once," and took a hasty leave of Temeraire; but he met Hammond hurrying out of the courier-clearing, with so delighted an expression that at first Laurence thought he must have heard the news already, by some other avenue.

"He has agreed to a cease-fire," Hammond cried, beaming as he seized Laurence's hand, before Laurence could say a word. "The courier came not an hour ago: Metternich has persuaded Bonaparte to listen to mediation. A week, Admiral, he will give us a week!"

It was difficult to say which of them pleased the other better, by their exchange of intelligence; Laurence took Hammond back to the small cabin set aside for him, where Dyhern and Granby shortly joined them in equal transports of delight, and with several bottles of a handsome port that had been unearthed somewhere by one of Granby's runners. They toasted Victoria, Wellington, Roland, Emperor Francis, and Metternich all in turn, rejoicing. That Napoleon should allow them even a week's respite, on the cusp of the Austrian border, with all the slow-moving advantages of supply and fresh troops creeping towards their side out of Russia, was as nearly inconceivable as it was desirable.

"Bonaparte is hoping to keep the Austrians from throwing in with us, of course," Hammond said, expansive with his happiness. "Metternich has done it as prettily as can be imagined! The Austrians cannot be ready to march for another month in any case; we will not be worse off by a moment for the lack of their aid."

"But can we be sure they won't throw in with him, while they are talking?" Granby said, a little dubious. "I should not give much for our chances if they do."

Hammond only snorted. "If he offers them half of Italy, accepts the natural borders of France, and agrees to hand over three-quarters of those eggs he has been at so much trouble to breed up, Metternich may find it hard to call him unreasonable, but I dare say something might yet be contrived. I cannot think it very likely the count will be put to the trouble. No, Captain: I am quite certain—*quite* certain—that Austria is of a mind with us; we all know very well that Bonaparte is the one insurmountable obstacle to any lasting peace."

Laurence could not wholly admire a stratagem which bought military advantage with something so much like deceit, but he consoled himself that the power to make acceptable terms, to make a real peace, nevertheless remained in Napoleon's hands. If his enemies expected him to prefer improving them through the hazards of battle, that was scarcely unreasonable, as he had always before now done so.

So he raised his glass to Metternich again willingly, when Hammond proposed another toast to that gentleman's diplomatic skill; and afterwards to the King, and then in justice to the Tsar, and even to Bautzen—officially recorded according to the day's dispatches, which Hammond had brought them, as a victory, although this was stretching the fabric of truth to the point of transparency—until at last they saluted one another in turn as well, still rejoicing.

The night ended in a thick fog; but by the morning Laurence was on his feet, only a little cloudy, and ready to work with a will. He well understood that the commanders of their force wished mainly to make use of his reputation and Temeraire's, and by that expedient recruit sufficient numbers of ferals to their cause, or disaffect enough of Napoleon's allies, to shift the balance of aerial power in their favor. Well enough: but given this priceless week, he meant to exercise his new authority further than those who had given it to him had perhaps intended.

There were guns strung out along all the roads from Russia, making a dawdling progress westward, and in a week Laurence thought they might gather up as many as three hundred of them, if the Prussian beasts were sent to carry them. Dyhern did not resist the order, beyond sighs, now that Laurence had the authority to give it.

The Russian greys he decided, not without some trepidation, to put to the task of supply. They were so ideally fitted-out for the task in every respect but their own unmanageable hunger: they could pick up languages with almost as much facility as Temeraire himself, could outcarry beasts nearly twice their size; besides this, they were not of much use on the battlefield, being neither particularly swift, nor maneuverable, and inclined to timidity whenever they felt themselves unobserved. Laurence had every expectation of their being far more valuable as a kind of replacement for the supply-dragons of the Chinese legions—so long as they did not go flying off madly with the supply to gorge themselves and hoard the excess in some concealed place.

"Oh?" Temeraire said, when Laurence had made the proposal, with a look so doubtful it nearly dissuaded him.

"We will make a single trial, at least," Laurence said.

"Perhaps it may be a *small* trial?" Temeraire said, with an anxious look over at the porridge-pits.

Laurence gathered the greys together, and with Temeraire and Grig as interpreters laid his intentions out for them. "You shall be responsible not merely for carrying the army's supply, but for knowing its state," he added, "and in particular its state after you yourselves have eaten; you must deduct your own share and eat first, to save the cost of carrying your own day's food." He emphasized this point with some calculation: he knew very well it would recommend the duty to all of the greys, irregularly fed as they were.

"And you must all keep in mind," Temeraire added, with a far more narrow and stern look from his lowered head, swept in a suspicious circle across the assembled dragons, who shrank away a little, "that anyone who should steal food will of course never again be trusted with so important a task. We have made these special sashes to mark those dragons allowed to receive supply," here he nosed at a heap of rather ragged strips of fabric, each embroidered with something approximating the shape of a number, which had been hastily produced by the hands of many ground crewmen, "and anyone who steals will have their number revoked *at once.*"

The greys asked many skeptical and repetitive questions—"We may eat every day? Even if we do not fight? We may eat *first*? Truly, every day?"—which illustrated so well their miserable state, and how little expectation they had of anything better, that Laurence had an effort not to upbraid Ilchenko, when he muttered none too quietly that the food would be thrown away.

Ten beasts were chosen for the first run, and returned the next morning full-bellied and heavily laden with sacks full of wheat and pendulous nets of stupefied pigs, much to the envy of their fellows. A second trial sent twenty along with the first ten; the third day saw sixty more gone, and by the fourth day all of the greys had been spread out across the Continent, bringing in supply on so steady a pace that the aerial forces for the first time exceeded their own requirements, and Laurence's supply-officer Lieutenant Doone was jubilantly reporting himself able to offer grain to the infantry, instead of enduring the scowls and mutters of their quartermasters for begging it of them.

Laurence received the news in his cabin with grim satisfaction, as he studied his maps urgently: two days only remained of his precious week, and a battery of small red flags, presently scattered along the line of the Caucasus Mountains, marked the still-distant positions of the Chinese legions. "How many more dragons of middle-weight size might we support?"

"Forty comfortably, sir, I should say," Doone answered.

Laurence nodded. He had not dared to ask the legions to send him any troops, when he could not supply them; now the time was short, but he thought not insurmountably so. He had to write at once, but Temeraire was their drillmaster now, and Laurence did not mean to distract him for even a moment from that task. Every fighting dragon of their force, and all the ferals who now steadily came in to join them, had been delivered to his rather ungentle care, and no small effort was required to bring them into any kind of unified order.

"Send me Midwingman Roland, if you please," he said, and sent Winters to find him a narrow paintbrush, and paper large enough to support a letter to a dragon.

Roland knew more of writing Chinese than any of his other men, and together they made an attempt. The result, Laurence had to admit, was not very graceful. "We might ask Ning if she can make it out," Roland suggested doubtfully, when they had finished.

Requiescat had flatly refused to carry Ning any further, after the battle of Dresden; he had been responsible for carrying two long guns, the whole day, as well as a great number of infantry-men. But she had only said, "I can fly for myself now, I expect, and I will catch you up if I must fall behind."

"And why haven't you been doing it before now, I would like to know," Requiescat said indignantly.

Ning had indeed managed to mostly keep pace with the company throughout their retreats, appearing perhaps a few hours after they made camp. She had established herself on a smallish outcrop on the heights, adorned by a delicate waterfall trickling over mossy rocks and exceptionally difficult to reach on foot, which gave her an excellent view of the maneuvers of the beasts under Temeraire's tutelage.

After Laurence ordered some flags waved in her direction, she flew down. "How energetic they all seem!" she remarked, landing. "I must congratulate Temeraire on his efforts. I wonder if he has noticed that those large and quarrelsome dragons from Russia are flying in an awkward way?"

Laurence laid the letter before her, and Ning regarded it as sorrowfully as a master gardener presented with a scraggly and unwatered seedling. "It is decipherable," she said, in tones of enor-mous generosity, "but perhaps you might wish to fix that charac-ter, in the second row: I do not believe you mean to say that you will attack the legions' supply." She drew the corrected version in the dirt, which omitted one careless streak of ink.

"It is indeed to be hoped that some part of the legions will ar-rive in time," Ning added thoughtfully, as she watched Emily re-pair the letter. "I have noted the increase of your ranks, and the improvement in your supply, but from what I have seen of Napo-leon's forces, I still fear he must defeat you in battle, if you do not have any of the legions. Do you suppose they will come?"

"I cannot allow your conclusion," Laurence said, although he felt a disquieting pang at Ning's certainty: their position would indeed be markedly more vulnerable, without the legions, although he did not subscribe to such a degree of pessimism. "But I think there is every likelihood of their arriving in time."

He climbed the heights after to observe their forces at drill. They were certainly improved already; Laurence could give himself the pleasure of believing that much. But he saw, also, what had inspired Ning's certainty: their forces were heavily slanted towards the separate ends of draconic size, light-weights and heavy-weights; looking upon them he could almost see the hollow space which that trained core of middle-weight beasts would neatly fill.

Well, the message had gone, and there was nothing more that could be done to bring them. He went down from the heights, and refused to permit himself dismay. Two days remained.

And yet they disappeared all too quickly. "I would be glad of another two *weeks,*" Temeraire said, yawning extremely wide, exposing all his teeth and a considerable stretch of gullet traveling back into a darkness which had lately enveloped many gallons of porridge and a haunch of venison besides, "but I think we will really do quite well, most of us. There is no teaching the Russian heavy-weights anything; that is the only point on which I cannot call myself satisfied. They are all delighted with the notion of prize-money, but they will not pay attention to signals at all. They will only go straight in and start fighting. Do you suppose there is any chance of armoring them better? I would just as soon load them with spikes and mail, so they cannot be either boarded or brought down, and then we may send them in whenever we should need some very hard fighting. One must do them justice; they are very *good* at fighting, if not at listening."

"I will see what can be done," Laurence said. "We may be able to shift something from the Prussians. I am inclined, if you think we can spare them, to place their heavy-weights entirely at the service of the artillery, even on the field. Napoleon will still have us outgunned, but if we can swiftly bring more metal to bear where it is most needed, we may overcome his advantage."

Temeraire murmured his agreement, but he was already falling asleep. Laurence rested his hand on the breathing muzzle a little longer, and sighed; he would have given much for two more weeks as well. But the armistice was over. No treaty had emerged from Dresden, where Metternich had reportedly spent the entire week closeted with the Emperor. Napoleon would be on the move at first light, and peace would be won only on the battlefield.

Laurence walked back to his cabin by way of the courier-clearing—a route which took him nearly half a mile out of his way and wasted precious sleep; but he could not help making one final visit. By his best estimate, the answer from the legions *might* have come yesterday, *ought* to have come to-day, and could yet come tomorrow without disaster. After that, hope would have failed: they would face Napoleon again before even a small part of the Chinese legions might join their force.

Word would be sent to his quarters at once, if a Jade Dragon landed; Laurence knew it very well. Nevertheless, his feet took him past the courier-clearing, and as he drew near, he heard the leathery flap of wings aloft, a dragon coming down, and saw the two blue flares and one green, which were the safe-passage signal for their camp. His steps quickened to an undignified pace, and he nearly ran up onto Hammond's heels: that gentleman was standing at the edge of the clearing, his hands clasped anxiously, and staring up into the dark.

"I beg your pardon, Mr. Hammond," Laurence said, extremely surprised to find him there.

"Oh—! Admiral!" Hammond cried aloud: equally surprised, with less right to be so, and a look of anxiety Laurence could not understand.

The dragon came down. She was an unfamiliar beast, a heavy courier in Austrian colors, wearing a white flag of parley. She was carrying passengers: gentlemen passengers, swathed thickly in furred oilskins for the journey, who climbed down with the awkwardness of men not used to go aloft very often.

One of them had especial difficulty, and required the support

of a gold-handled cane when he reached the ground; Laurence appalled realized it was none other than Monsieur de Talleyrand
himself, whom report had restored to Napoleon's service—as
though Hammond had chosen to invite a pair of the Emperor's
eyes to come and wander about their covert, and look in on all the
latest arrangements of their aerial forces.

That Hammond *was* responsible was plain: he had already
gone forward to his guests, greeting the second passenger as Count
Metternich. He had surely united the ministers here for some secret final attempt at negotiation. Laurence was sorry to learn of
anything so plainly not meant for his own eyes, but any sense of
intrusion he might have felt was under the circumstances exploded
by Hammond's indiscretion, which he now evidently meant to
crown by leading Napoleon's minister along the main track which
led down into the field-covert and directly past their assembled
forces—including all the ferals which had lately been recruited to
their cause.

"Mr. Hammond, sir, forgive me, you have been turned around;
I think you must mean to take *this* path," Laurence said loudly,
and catching Hammond by the arm drew him to the slighter track
at the opposite end of the clearing, which swung out wide around
the covert to reach the headquarters, and was used by those nervous of coming too near the dragons. "Sir," he said, low but
sharply, "if you have not before considered the material value to
Napoleon of any intelligence about the disposition of our aerial
forces, I must ask you do so now. Keep Monsieur de Talleyrand
from sight of the clearings, and do not bring him back here. I will
send the beast on to headquarters to wait for you."

Hammond colored and stammered an apology at once. "Very
sorry—I assure you there was no—all my apologies, Admiral, you
are right, of course," and after a moment's hesitation added, "We
will be on the west slope, at the green farmhouse—I did not like to
trouble you for a passage—"

"Then I will have one of our couriers escort the Austrian courier there," Laurence said, not much appeased; Hammond ought

not have put such a peculiar value on asking for the small inconvenience of an escort for his courier at the cost of exposing them
all to the bright, curious looks of Talleyrand, who even now observed their whispered conversation placidly, and without any evident qualms at overhearing whatever he might. The only comfort
was the lateness of the hour, which should have bleached away the
colors of the dragons and sent most of them to sleep; Talleyrand
could have got no very exact count from aloft.

By the time Laurence had made the arrangements and seen the
ministers off to their negotiations without further harm to secrecy,
an hour had been consumed, and the full dark had descended. No
other couriers had come.

He knew he ought to seek his own rest. But he lingered a little
longer, to the ill-concealed disgust of the watch, who plainly would
have liked nothing better than to go to sleep themselves even
though they were on duty. He paced away another half an hour, by
the glass, before at last he took himself away.

He was at the very door of his cabin when one of the watch-
officers came running after him, even more disgusted now and
panting, to tell him a Jade Dragon had arrived, and to hand him a
scroll, written in Chinese. Laurence turned it right-way up and
read it swiftly. "Very good" was all he said, and the watch officer
went away even more disgruntled, without even gossip to carry;
but Laurence went into his cabin and shut the door, and when he
fell upon his cot he slept at once, dreamlessly, and well.

Chapter 20

"Laurence," Temeraire said, a little nervously, "I think we have done it, although perhaps I ought not say so; but surely we have won a battle at last? Really won it, I mean, not only in the dispatches." He did not quite dare to believe it: after so much tiresome running away, to see the French retreating for once was very unusual, and he worried perhaps it might be a trick of some sort. "Perhaps we ought to send some scouts to our rear," he added, "to be sure there is no-one coming up behind us. Where is that Davout fellow? I still remember how very unpleasant it was when he nearly surprised us, at the battle of London."

"Davout is in Hamburg," Laurence said, which was very comforting, as that city was several hundreds of miles distant, "and we are quite certain that Napoleon has no troops anywhere in our rear; no, I think we have carried the day."

The poor little village of Reichenbach had not survived its encounter with two quarrelsome armies: there was scarcely a building left standing, and the sad wreck of a big French Papillon Noir lay sprawled in the smashed heap of a barn, fragments of stone and shingles and the corpses of soldiers scattered all around his body. The legions were methodically pressing the French corps back all along the leading edge of battle, exposing ever more of their artillery and infantry, and now at last Temeraire could really see some use in the Russian heavy-weights: it was not that they had begun to listen better, or follow sensible tactics at all, for they had not; but it did not seem necessary. Laurence had set a sizable bounty upon each gun captured, and in their eagerness the Russian beasts flung themselves ferociously and heedless down into the French ranks and began laying about with teeth and claws, and the poor artillery-men were fleeing wildly in every direction at once.

"I think we must add a bonus, the next battle, for guns taken unspiked," Laurence said: he was observing the same, through his glass. "We will take at least a hundred to-day, I think. Temeraire, pray will you pass the word to the legions to concentrate their attentions upon the French right flank? If we can break that group of middle-weights there, we will open them nicely to the Austrian advance."

"Certainly," Temeraire said, and roared a low sequence of three notes, which brought one of the Jade Dragons to his side immediately to relay orders, but before he could issue his commands, Yu Shen backwinged a little distance away in a respectful attitude, and Ning suddenly came up on his right and hovered beside him. *Now* she appeared, when all the hard work had been done, Temeraire thought resentfully; he had barely landed all day, and had scarcely had time for more than a few gulps of porridge, and that cold.

"Well, what do you want?" Temeraire said.

"I wonder if you might consider sending the legions against the center," Ning said.

"No, not in the least," Temeraire said. "The Imperial Guard is anchoring the center, with a hundred Incan beasts, besides their Grand Chevaliers, and you can see the guns for yourself. We should be rolled up straightaway if we pressed the attack, and then our general advance would be broken. The suggestion is quite absurd—

whyever would you propose such a thing?" he added, belatedly
curious. He could not make out any reason for it, unless perhaps
Ning meant to lead them into a trap for some peculiar reason of
her own, but even then, she would have had to think them really
quite stupid to listen.

"All you have said is perfectly true," Ning said, "until one
considers that there are sixty heavy-weights approaching the
French rear. If you should draw the French center forward even by
quite a small margin, you should weaken their line, and thus expose their entire retreat."

"But why should there be sixty heavy-weights in the French
rear, and where have they come from?" Temeraire said. As a wish
to be granted by some particularly benevolent spirit, perhaps the
God that Laurence was so fond of, the notion appealed to him
greatly: it would only be justice that *they* should come up from
behind Napoleon for once, although he did not see how they could
have managed it. "It cannot be Excidium and Lily, from Spain;
they have only just crossed the Pyrenees by now, and they had a
great many dragons to manage over there, anyway."

He finished on an interrogative note, hoping despite himself,
but Ning said, "It is not them: it is the dragons from the convocation, the ones you called the Tswana."

"There is no reason it should be the Tswana," Temeraire said.
"Not that it would not be very handsome of them to help us," he
added, "but I do not think they care a fig whether we should win,
or Napoleon."

"However fruitless it may be to guess at their *motives*," Ning
said, "one may nevertheless conclude their *intentions,* from their
having taken up a position ideally calculated to fall upon Napoleon's rear, and having failed to offer him any assistance in his
present difficult circumstances. In any case, I can hardly call their
motives very obscure: if we should defeat Napoleon, they must
prefer to have us in their debt."

Temeraire noticed, not without a little irritation, that suddenly
Ning had decided to include herself in their ranks, with all this *we*

and *us.* "Yes, but we—Laurence and myself, that is, and our friends," he pointedly noted, "—will not defeat Napoleon with one battle," but then he looked at the field again, and imagined sixty heavy-weight dragons added upon it, and slowly said, "Laurence—Laurence, if we *should* break their center—if we should rout the guard, and the Tswana should block a retreat to the west—"

"Yes," Laurence said, his voice taut. "Yes: we might have a chance to capture him, if the guard should break."

"One might have expected," Ning remarked a little tartly, "that my advice would be well-founded: had you not better get about it?"

Laurence stood up in his carabiner straps and stepped to the side of Temeraire's neck, looking down at her. "Ning," he said, in Chinese, "I beg your pardon: I must ask you to give me your word before these witnesses," and he beckoned to Yu Shen and also Yu Guo, who had come a little closer to listen in, "that the situation is as you have described it."

Ning said thoughtfully, "Well, I am prepared to give my word that the Tswana are there, and that they number between forty and seventy beasts, the better part of whom are heavy-weight, and that they are ideally placed to strike at the French rear; however, more than this I will not avow. If you disagree with my conclusions, you may draw your own, and proceed as you like. I consider that I have discharged my duty to China, in offering you the fruits of my observation and my own advice, and if you now choose to discard so notable an opportunity, for want of assurances which I cannot provide with perfect certainty, I cannot hold myself responsible."

Laurence was silent; Temeraire curved his head back towards him. "We surely ought not miss the chance," he said anxiously: he perfectly understood the caution Laurence must have felt, and of course they would be in a very nasty position if the Tswana did *not* attack in the end. But he felt he could scarcely bear to let Napoleon slip away, *again;* and who knew but that he would find some clever new way of defeating them. "Perhaps we might send someone around to see, and have a word with them?"

But Laurence said, "There is no time. Whatever chance there is must be a thin one; even a narrow avenue of escape must suffice for Napoleon to evade capture, and he will certainly begin his own withdrawal in short order now; the course of the day is decided, if nothing should change." He shut up his glass with a snap and said, "Pass the word to concentrate our assault upon the center, at once," and then went on, to Temeraire's rising delight, "and we must go in ourselves, to offer both support and reason; Napoleon and Lien especially will wonder less at the incaution of a frontal assault if we give them the excuse of your exuberance."

Laurence sent Yu Guo to inform Granby of the plan, and then they were flying across the field: Temeraire felt himself loosed as though from a cannon-mouth, with a wild propulsive energy behind him. The armies below were engaged in a thinning struggle: everywhere French soldiers streamed westward into the trees and fields, in rout and retreat, and on the flanks, the Cossack cavalry was harrying them along. But in the center the Imperial Guard still held their positions, magnificently firm, their tall shakos like ranged checker pieces from above in even rows, and above them Temeraire counted half a dozen Grand Chevaliers in full equipage, with a surrounding cloud of Incan beasts too large to enumerate. He did spy two Copacati, the venom-spitters, and Maila Yupanqui himself was here, circling nervously above the rear.

"I am surprised he should not have insisted on staying behind with the Empress," Temeraire said, with a snort.

"Napoleon can ill afford to leave his staunchest supporters behind in Paris, in his present circumstances," Laurence said.

They were closing: Temeraire gathered his breath and roared out his challenge, envisioning the force of it thundering like a wave upon the ranks of their enemies and crashing upon them. He roared again, and once more as he drew into striking range, the legions falling into place at his rear and roaring with him, heartened. The screen of lighter dragons at the fore of Napoleon's force

tumbled away like pebbles in surf, and Temeraire had the gratifi-
cation of seeing Lien's head come up, her ruff spreading wide as
she heard his approach.

She bent down towards a man on the ground beside her: Temeraire was able to pick Napoleon out, when she spoke to him. The
Emperor wore a plain grey coat and blue hat with no decoration
at all; he looked plainer than his Guardsmen. It would be so very
easy to miss him in the crowd, Temeraire thought anxiously, but
he had to take his eyes away: half a dozen Incan middle-weights
were converging upon him, bent on checking their advance.

The Incans' feathery scales had the effect of making them seem
larger than their size, and were handy besides for turning lead balls
and canister-shot. Forthing shouted, "Fire at will!" and the sharp
retort of the rifles went off as the middle-weights closed, but the
Incan beasts did not flinch.

Temeraire turned to slash with his talons and met an Incan
middle-weight's peculiar eye, vivid green on the outer rim, yellow-
blue-streaked on the inside; she looked squarely at him, their paces
matched for a moment, and then darted her head down trying to
bite his wing-joint. He folded his wing in on that side and rolled
sideways into her, blowing out a little of his wind; his weight
landed squarely on her and drove a great gasp of air from her
body. He kept rolling until he came off her other side, and both of
them dropped a hundred feet or so below the cluster of dragons.

He snapped out his own wing again and caught an updraft as
she tumbled away struggling to right herself. A scattering of bombs
fell away from his belly-netting, Challoner calling the orders faintly
below, and the Incan lost another hundred feet in evasions and had
to turn back and hurry to the safety of her ranks.

"Temeraire, ware above!" Roland called: and he darted a
quick look up. He had lost some height himself, and one of the
Copacati meant to try to seize the advantage, a silver-green arrow
darting towards him.

"Pass the word to ready boarders," Laurence said, and Temeraire flattened his ruff. Of course it would be splendid to take a

Copacati prisoner, if they could—this one was rather larger than the one Iskierka had dueled, back in Talcahuano, he thought. But Challoner would naturally lead the boarding party, and it would be of all things wretched to lose a fine lieutenant just when he had finally got a satisfactory one, and Temeraire had a struggle to repress the instinct to twist away too quickly for anyone to go over.

The Copacati spat: a thin black stream of poison jetted narrowly into the air, but with a skillful twist of her body she pulled up and fanned her wings at the stream twice, dispersing it into a fine cloud of mist. "Temeraire, your eyes!" Laurence shouted, and Temeraire shut them tight at once and twisted aside, Laurence calling the mark as he whirled blind through the sky. One hapless middle-weight came into his way, trying to claw at him, and was bowled over for his trouble; Temeraire cracked open an eye when the poor fellow began crying out noisily as he himself was caught by the mist of venom.

But Temeraire had got out of range himself; with a quick double-thrust of his wings he closed in on the Copacati as she circled back for another pass, too quick for her to spit again, and seized her from below, belly to belly. The feathery scales now offered him an advantage, better purchase than he might have had otherwise; he gripped onto her shoulder-joints and snapped at the underside of her neck, forcing her to dart her head up and away from him.

She raked at him with her back legs, hissing, and he could not roar, either, while he had to keep her head off him; but his bellmen were throwing grappling-hooks up to catch on her harness, and swarming up the lines.

"Pray be careful, Challoner," Temeraire called as he twisted away, when they had gone over, "and I will certainly have words with you, if you lose her," he added to the Copacati, in the Incan tongue.

"Then you shouldn't be sending her jumping through the sky!" the Copacati returned smartly, not without some justice Temeraire had to admit, and made another darting stab at him with her long glistening fangs. "Perhaps I will *keep* her," she added tauntingly.

Temeraire flared his ruff angrily, and with an enormous heave twisted them bodily over and thumped the Copacati soundly at the base of her neck with the side of his head. The blow made his jaw ache, but it was worth it to check *that* sort of talk, and it shook all her own scanty crew loose and dangling from their carabiners, so at least they had no advantages over his own boarding party gone over.

"Temeraire, we must fall back," Laurence called: the French forces were taking the bait, pressing forward everywhere to meet them.

Temeraire reluctantly let go and threw himself away from the Copacati, beating furiously, and managed to roar briefly into her face. He could not build enough resonance to *properly* roar and knock her back, but she recoiled enough he could open up some room between them. He fell back on the legions, who had split into their three-beast squadrons, and were skillfully fending off the French beasts pressing upon them.

They could not hold their ground long against numbers and weight so much the greater than their own force. They did not really want to hold it, of course: as they fell back, the French dragons pressed forward to keep on them, and in so doing left exposed the infantry and guns of the Old Guard at their rear.

But Temeraire began to feel a little anxious, as their position was becoming undoubtedly awkward. The flanks of the French aerial corps had begun to close in upon their sides, and they were increasingly in danger of finding themselves enveloped. Many of the Chinese dragons were beginning to take real injury: it seemed that in every direction Temeraire looked, he saw one of the red-gold beasts falling out of the ranks to retreat to the surgeons, many of them trailing black blood as they flew. The remaining squadrons pulled together, and re-formed themselves in a disciplined manner: along the line in reverse order from left to right, any dragon who lost a fighting-partner shifted over to fill a gap in the next squadron with an opening. It was elegantly done, without disruption to their maneuvering, but their ranks were steadily compressing as a consequence, exposing the survivors to more of the enemy's force.

The Chinese commander Zhao Lien winged around from her position at the rear of the force to join Temeraire. "Honored one, may this humble soldier suggest that we make arrangements to withdraw over the shelter of the artillery, if it is not inconvenient," which was a polite way of saying he had got them thoroughly into the soup, and there was now no way out of it except to simply run away, which would certainly give the French every opportunity to wreak disaster on the allied troops beneath them, and perhaps even turn back the tide of the battle as a whole.

Napoleon, too, had seen their plight; perhaps even before they themselves had marked it. Down on the ground, the ranks of the Old Guard were moving forward, and with that anchor the French withdrawal everywhere was halting. Companies were re-forming and wheeling around, light-weight beasts dropping to pick up cannon and replace them in firing position, the enormous clockwork of Napoleon's war machinery turning under its master's hand.

But the movement was accompanied from some distant place over the hills by a steady deep drum-beat, growing louder and louder even above the cannon-roars, a great pounding noise that resonated peculiarly in Temeraire's skull as it climbed, and climbed still further. The other dragons around him all paused, turning as they looked back towards the French rear. Shadows were forming out of the deep bank of grey clouds to the west, and then the clouds were streaming away as a wide row of dragons was suddenly pouring down over the western slope directly at Napoleon's rear: dragons in every vivid color, and on every back a drummer sat, pounding furiously to keep the time of their wings.

Their bellies had been covered with pads of thick grey leather. They did not fly separately or even in formations, but in short lines of four and carrying a peculiar device that looked like the front edge of a plow more than anything else Temeraire knew. The teeth were made of curved elephant tusks, bound into a thin frame of wood and metal. The Tswana dragons plunged them down among the troops and swept forward, turning over men and guns and earth all together.

The French dragons wheeled around in alarm to meet their advance, but as they did, a second wave of Tswana dragons came arrowing down from far overhead: they must have climbed very high, to be able to come swooping out of the clouds so, and their plummeting speed was enormous; they struck the body of the French corps with shocking force, and drove dozens of beasts to the ground, smashing them into their own artillery and men before they climbed a little shakily off again, and shook themselves and jumped back into the air.

Temeraire stared, a little. He had never seen the Tswana fight properly, dragon to dragon: he had seen them tear apart the Cape Town settlement, and its fort, but that assault had been carried out in a fury of rage and revenge by dragons maddened at the loss of their tribes, and anyway it had nearly been over, by the time he had arrived. This was a great deal more systematic and impressive, not to say a little alarming; but after a moment he shook himself off, and roared a welcoming challenge before he led the legions forward to help. The French center was collapsing entirely; Iskierka and the Prussian dragons were turning their left flank, forcing the remaining dragons there onto the already-great disorder behind them, and as the dragons cleared the field and began a steady bombardment of the infantry squares below, the Russian and Prussian cavalry charged, sabers raised and shouting, into their disorganized ranks.

The French retreat, half turned around, now fell into complete rout. Men were fleeing the field in masses, companies disintegrating. Temeraire swept back and forth trying to see past the confusion and pick out Lien. On the left flank he could see Marshal Saint-Cyr lifting away on a Petit Chevalier with a clinging mass of staff-officers aboard, making their escape towards the western road still held by the French rear-guard, their guns firing steadily and hot.

The Old Guard had drawn together, above and below, to make themselves a sheltering box with the Emperor inside. Blowing horns were summoning the heavy-weights back into a knot, and Temeraire roared in fury as he saw Lien at last, well-hidden behind a screen of artillery and heavy-weight dragons: Napoleon was being thrust bodily aboard her back by his soldiers. "Laurence, Laurence, she is getting away!" he cried, hovering, half-hoping Laurence would order him to charge, to throw himself through that crowd of dragons.

"I am sorry, my dear," Laurence said heavily. "There are too many of them—"

But suddenly there were not. The Tswana had gathered their first fruits of surprise, and now re-formed into a large company on the French right flank, spear-shaped, preparing to sweep around and engage the French heavy-weights. There were sixty of them; Temeraire had thirty left of the Chinese legions at his back, and Eroica was leading some forty Prussian beasts, with Iskierka supporting them. The French had nearly a hundred beasts still gathered, and in tight formation could have held for an hour even against all of them pressing in.

But the Tswana roared, and Temeraire roared with them, and suddenly Maila Yupanqui, who had climbed aloft, gave a loud bugling cry—and broke.

Temeraire stared in astonishment. It was not just him, either. All the Incan dragons were turning to follow him as he fled, snarling up all the other French dragons in their passage. The proud ranks of the Imperial Guard's aerial forces scattered. There were only thirty dragons left together, in the center, and Temeraire heard Laurence shout; his wings were already beating, launching him forward even as Lien flung herself into the sky.

Chapter 21

Laurence endured with some impatience another two dozen congratulatory messages as he returned to Temeraire's clearing from the headquarters, the morning's dispatch still crumpled in his hand. It was a slow progress: officers he had never met stopped him to make him their bows, and as he passed he overheard himself pointed out by his aviator's coat, over and over again.

He would have been honored by the acclaim and grateful for the warm feeling, if bestowed for his own labors. Indeed, half his irritation was for the sense of being robbed of his and Temeraire's justly earned laurels, in exchange for a crown of fool's gold. But the dispatches said nothing of the daring assault upon the center by the Chinese legions, which had lured Napoleon into exposing his Guard to the Tswana attack; indeed the Tswana themselves had been given only a grudging part in the victory at all, a brief mention of their strike into the French rear. And nothing whatsoever was mentioned of the collapse of the Incan ranks. Instead, so far as Laurence could see, the world was to believe that he and Temeraire had, in a fit of valor and what should have been the

most extreme stupidity, flung themselves headlong through a hundred dragons, and defeated Lien in a single chivalric combat, pre-
sumably while those hundred dragons looked on and did nothing
to interfere.

He had read the dispatch that morning himself, appalled, but
no-one at the headquarters had listened to his protests long enough
to promise any correction; they had been too busy to shake his
hand, and even the Tsar himself, who had received him personally,
had only clapped him on the shoulder, and interrupted to praise
his modesty.

So he returned the bows shortly, and walked onwards without
making much conversation except to return the compliments to
his service. All through his slow progress a disquiet crept over him
by degrees, and even when he at last passed beyond the reach of
his well-wishers and reached the clearing where Temeraire stood
vigilant over Lien's silent and huddled form, Laurence could not
take his ease, or settle to the large obligation of letters and reports
which waited on his desk.

He came out of his tent again, restless, and put a hand on Temeraire's side. "I do not see why they need so many guards upon
him," Temeraire said, a little disapprovingly: he referred to the
cottage visible near-by which was now Napoleon's prison, ringed
by three companies of heavy infantry all standing to close attention. "It is not as though I would not see, if he tried to come out
and rejoin Lien; they might trust me for *that,* I think."

"Their presence must discourage any hope of a rescue, which
his Marshals might yet entertain," Laurence said. "Even you might
be distracted briefly, if they managed to descend with a large force
of dragons." He stood looking at the small house, and then said
abruptly, "I will return soon, if you will pardon me."

He walked to the cottage slowly. He felt little compunction
about the worry which his appearance caused the Prussian colonel
in charge of overseeing the guards, who plainly did not like to
deny entry to the hero of the hour; but Laurence did fear his presence might be felt as an insult. "Pray ask His Majesty if he will
receive me," Laurence said. "I would not wish to intrude."

The colonel, relieved, sent to inquire; he plainly thought and hoped that the Emperor would refuse any visitor whom he could avoid, and was crestfallen when Laurence was invited to go inside. "I would scarcely try to take him out of his prison," Laurence said to the man, taking pity, "when I put him in it, only yesterday."

"Yes, sir," the colonel said, dismally, and let him go in.

The cottage interior was dark, after the brilliance of the morning sun; Laurence stood blinking in the entryway, and then went down the hall to the one real chamber of the house. Napoleon was standing before the small window, looking down the hill towards Lien, with his hands clasped loosely behind his back. He turned round at Laurence's step, and inclined his head: calm and composed, even amidst the wreck of his hopes. "Captain—or Admiral, I should say: I hope you are well? You took no injury in the battle?"

Laurence bowed. "I am, Your Majesty." He hesitated, then; he did not know what to say. He did not fully know what had brought him, except a dislike of being given more credit than was his due, but that could hardly matter to Napoleon. Nor could Laurence make him any kind of apology: he could not be sorry to have captured the Emperor; still less to see peace finally within reach.

"You are a dull companion," Napoleon said, breaking the silence. "What stifles your tongue? Have you been sent to offer me terms?"

"No," Laurence said, with a private relief; he could imagine no task less to his taste. "No; I beg your pardon, Your Majesty, I only wished to—" Here he halted, struggling again, but the Emperor came to his rescue.

"Ah, come," Napoleon said, crossing the room to him, and holding out his hands, clasped Laurence by the shoulders; he drew him close and kissed him on both cheeks, in the Gallic fashion, and then more familiarly patted him upon the cheek gently with a hand. "Do you suppose I would ever reproach you, of all my foes? I am sorry only to have faced you across the field, when you ought to have been by my side. Loss is the hazard of battle. One who cannot bear to taste it cannot be a soldier. Now come and sit with me, and tell me how the fighting unfolded, from your side. There is nothing like being dragon-back for observing, but I could not always be aloft, yesterday, myself."

They sat together talking quietly of the battle and sketching maneuvers on the top of the one small table with the charred end of a stick from the fireplace. Laurence had never admired him so well in victory as in defeat: the Emperor's resolution in the face of disaster, and his generosity to the man most directly responsible for his captivity, had true grace in it. No-one disturbed them for nearly an hour, and then a noise from the hall drew Napoleon's head up suddenly alert, the attention of the hawk. Steps came along the hallway, softer than boot-heels, and Laurence rose as three men entered the room, attired formally: Hammond, who started to see him there, accompanied by Talleyrand and Count Metternich.

"Admiral Laurence," Hammond said, nearly stammering, "I wonder at—have you—"

"His Majesty was gracious enough to receive me," Laurence said, and would have excused himself, but the Emperor waved a hand.

"Perhaps you will give the Prince de Bénévent your chair, as there is none other," Napoleon said, meaning Talleyrand, "but there can be no objection to your remaining. What is done in this room must soon be known in all Europe, and you cannot leave it with a tale of dishonor, save if I fail in my oaths to France, which I trust these gentlemen know I will never do." He spoke with an almost jocular air, but there was steel in the grey eyes.

There was a pause, an awkward silence, as the three ministers exchanged looks. Hammond in particular plainly wished Laurence anywhere but in the room, and Metternich looked little better pleased. But Talleyrand said genially, "Surely His Majesty only speaks the truth," and limped over to the chair; seating himself he leaned in to the Emperor and said, "Sire, I have the pleasure of delivering to you this letter, from the Empress: by the courtesy of the Tsar, I was granted the liberty of sending her a courier to inform her of your good health, and to receive this reply for you."

"Ah!" Napoleon said, and seized the letter with real enthusiasm; he opened and read it with an intent, hungry look, nodding to himself a little. It was not long: he read it over quickly, twice, and then put it away in his breast. "I am grateful for your kindness to Her Majesty. Now, gentlemen, I beg you not to hesitate further. Speak plainly: there is nothing to be gained by delay."

Talleyrand bowed towards him from the waist, in his chair. "Sire," he said, "I will obey. It is the united demand of the allied forces that you must be removed from your throne as the price of peace. I regret that those who stand arrayed against France, on the cusp of invading her territory, refuse to consider any other outcome."

Napoleon made a gesture of impatience, a quick flicking up of his hand: this was of no importance. "My enemies know my life is in their power. They may kill me or banish me, as they please, but do not let them suppose that either to preserve my life or my freedom I should ever willingly yield my throne to the Bourbons, nor sacrifice the gains which the Revolution won for the French people."

Talleyrand remained placid in the face of this dramatic speech. "It has been agreed that Your Majesty shall abdicate in favor of your son," he said, "with the Empress as regent."

Napoleon paused, silenced. After a moment, he said, "What of France?"

"Upon your abdication, the enemy nations are prepared to sign an immediate armistice, recognizing her natural borders," Talleyrand said. "So long as France yields to each of the allied nations a share of the dragon eggs presently laid in her breeding grounds."

"Belgium?" Napoleon said quickly.

"Flanders shall be made part of the Netherlands," Talleyrand said. "Wallonia remains to France." There was another brief silence. "In exchange," Talleyrand continued, when Napoleon had made no answer, "you are to surrender your throne, and retire permanently to the island of St. Helena. The British," here he nodded to Hammond, who had a stiff, uncomfortable expression, "will undertake to guarantee your safety and comfort there, and that of your faithful dragon."

Laurence overheard all this, standing awkwardly by the rough fireplace and staring at the dully glowing logs, conscious of both the impropriety of listening and the impossibility of doing anything else. He was determined at first not to really hear, to listen only in the base shipboard sense of some audible noise reaching his ears by the accident of enforced proximity, which was not to be understood or repeated, or treated as knowledge in any way. But he could not help it; he heard, and knew, and he was surprised—there was no other way to describe his feelings. He was very surprised.

The exile would be a remarkably harsh one. St. Helena was an isolate half-tenanted rock under the control of the East India Company, valuable only as a way station on the sea-journey to Asia. Its population had been entirely imported, more than half of them as slaves, and there was but a single town which catered only to the shipping. Its distance from any other shore would make it a secure prison even for a dragon, and even the long-range couriers came but infrequently, which would bar any regular communication. To imprison Napoleon there, divided so thoroughly from his wife and child and all the world, was undeniably a cruelty, and of a sort which he had never visited upon his own conquered enemies despite many opportunities to do so.

But in every other respect these were terms offered to end a war, not ones dictated afterwards by its victors. Laurence knew it had long been the position of the British Government that Belgium must be wholly stripped from France, to safeguard Britain from another invasion; it had long been the position of all the monarchs of Europe that the legitimate kings of France should be restored. If Napoleon had been free, with all France eager and united at his back, Laurence would have been surprised to hear him offered such terms; when he was prisoner, after a sharp defeat, they seemed absurdly generous.

He was not alone in surprise. Napoleon, too, said nothing. He sat back in his narrow, hard-backed chair, gazing at Talleyrand for a period of silence with an almost baffled expression, as though he did not know what to make of what he heard. And then abruptly his face changed. The confusion went out of it, and for one moment his hand went to his breast-pocket, where the letter from the Empress had gone. He sprang up out of his chair and walked away to the window and stood there, his back to the room; his shoulders were very straight.

Laurence stared at him, his own confusion unabated, and then looked round at Hammond. Hammond did not meet his eye, giving every appearance of finding the bare wooden floor of their chamber an object of intense interest, and Metternich also had a constrained expression, very still and controlled, with his hands clasped before him. Talleyrand only made no appearance of discomfort or consciousness; his looks remained perfectly easy and open, milky mild. He was the one to break the silence, gently prompting, "Sire, will you make an answer?"

Napoleon moved his hand slightly to his side, a gesture not of refusal; only of denial. He was silent a little longer, then he said, "You have the papers?"

Metternich produced a document from his coat; after a moment Napoleon turned from the window to take it. His face was changed wholly, gone utterly remote; he might have been cut out of stone. He read over the papers quickly, without sitting down, then put them on the table and reached for his pen and bent over and signed with a single swift flourish: *Napoleon.* He turning handed them back to Metternich, who received them with a bow.

"If I may express to Your Majesty—" Talleyrand began.

"You may not," Napoleon said over his shoulder, cold and contemptuous; not what the work of a servant who had brought him such remarkable terms ought to have deserved. He went back to the window, his hands clasped behind his back; a dismissal without a word.

———————

Coming out of the cottage behind the three ministers, Laurence lengthened his stride and caught Hammond by the arm. "Mr. Hammond," he said, "I hope you will come and greet Temeraire: he will be glad to know you are well."

"Oh," Hammond said, stifled. He looked longingly at the sedan-chair waiting to carry him away, back to the headquarters, and then said, "Gentlemen, I hope you will excuse me," with a bow to his counterparts.

He walked away with Laurence across the field towards Temeraire, stumbling now and then, and picking his buckled shoes up out of the churned ground. Laurence waited until they were private enough, out of earshot, and said, "I find myself in a false position, Mr. Hammond, and I would be glad of your assistance to escape it: I am sorry that all the dispatches, this morning, should have spoken in such excessive and inaccurate terms of my and Temeraire's part in the Emperor's capture yesterday."

It was a shot at a venture, but it bore fruit: Hammond darted a look at him, hunted—enough, if Laurence had needed anything more than Napoleon's own reaction, to tell him there was something underhanded at work.

"I will certainly correct the misapprehension, as widely and as soon as I may," he continued grimly. "If the Tswana had not disrupted his retreat, we could have done nothing, and our final capture depended entirely on the panic and flight of Napoleon's Incan escort. The dispatches have all proposed that we captured him in the face of an enormous force of dragons, making us figure in a truly heroic light, when we have only done our duty, in I hope an honorable but not an astonishing manner."

"Admiral," Hammond said, "I beg you not to repine upon— not to make an effort to—There are certain considerations—"

Laurence stopped and turned to face him. "And what would these considerations be, Mr. Hammond, which have induced you and the ministers of four nations to jointly publish a fabricated report of the battle?—And moreover, to have made the French an offer of terms which I should have been astonished to hear London approve under these circumstances: the Emperor our prisoner, the war certainly ended, and yet you hand the throne on to his son—"

He broke off even as Hammond raised an anxious hand to try to halt him. Too late: Laurence had understood at last. He saw before him suddenly the inexplicable flight of Napoleon's escort—the vivid colors of the Incan dragons fleeing in a pack, the handful of Grand Chevaliers and the other French dragons swept up in their midst.

"Or I should say, to his wife," he finished, after a moment, with a sour taste of disgust in the back of his throat. "Tell me, Hammond, how long have Talleyrand and the Empress conspired with you, to deliver the Emperor into our hands?"

"Admiral—" Then Hammond flung up his hands in frustration, letting them fall limp, and said bluntly, "Laurence, what would you have had us do?"

He turned and walked away, his shoulders bowed, back to the sedan-chair. Laurence stood alone in the field, the cottage in the distance small and dark against the brilliancy of the blue summer sky, and the shadow of a man standing solitary by the window.

Chapter 22

THE EMPRESS, STANDING AT the head of the stairs of the palace, kept one hand lightly resting in the crook of the Tsar's elbow as though she were fatigued by the effort of maintaining her position, and required his support to welcome the guests ascending to the Tuileries. For his part, he gave that support with a regal, cool expression, and if he felt any concern regarding the slate of highly anxious Incan dragons, all ruffled up into enormous size and peering over at the proceedings from the square, he did not show it, though more than one guest threw alarmed looks in their direction. She let go his arm for a moment, however, to welcome the King of Prussia with an embrace, and beckoning to reunite him with his son, standing beside her.

"I regret that I never met his mother," she said, "but I have tried to offer him a little of that comfort which I might wish my own son to find if he were ever a guest in your own court, and I hope he one day shall be, now that our nations stand once more as dear friends."

Her voice was clear, and projected well; Laurence overheard it where he stood waiting his own turn on the stairs, and the low approving murmurs which followed. "They say she protected the prince, even after we came into the war," he overheard one Prussian officer saying to another. "Who knows what would have become of him, otherwise, in Napoleon's power!"

The celebration was very little to Laurence's taste. He had not yet learned to reconcile himself to the betrayal of which he had been made an instrument, and he had no pleasure in being presented to the Empress and being obliged to receive her hand. He said as little as possible, but he suspected his looks spoke for him, and said more than they should; the Empress looked at him with a certain thoughtfulness when he straightened.

He knew it for certain, later that evening, when little Winters came tapping on his door all yawns and a rumpled nightshirt, roused from her bed to find Laurence: an escort of French Guardsmen had come to take him to the Empress. His former gaoler Aurigny was at their head, bowing, and Laurence did not feel he could refuse the summons, as little as he wished to speak with Anahuarque again.

Laurence silently followed his escort through the hallways to the Empress's sitting room, a small snug chamber with a balcony overlooking the garden where Maila Yupanqui slept with a slitted eye trained upon her lit window. Music still drifted over the trees from the distant ballroom, but the Empress had taken off her elaborate gown, and sat now in a brightly woven dress in the Incan style, loose and comfortable, which nearly disguised her growing belly. "Come and sit with me, Admiral," she said, and nodded a dismissal to the guards, who glanced to one another in some concern for a moment before they reluctantly withdrew.

"I hope Your Majesty is well," Laurence said, remote, and only bowed rather than taking the seat she had offered him; he preferred to preserve all the distance which the intimacy she offered would have closed, and he was resolved to behave only with formal courtesy.

But she said, "I am as well as can be hoped," as though lamenting the loss of the husband she had so neatly disposed of, and Laurence could not suppress a tightening of his jaw. She smiled a little, as though she had seen what she expected. "But I think few of the Emperor's friends regret him as much as do you, his enemy."

In the face of this provocation, Laurence could not restrain himself. "That *some,* on whose love he ought to have been able to depend, do not regret him, is certain."

"And you think me among that number," she said bluntly. "You are wrong." She paused a moment, regarding him with her steady, dark eyes. "I would like you to understand me, Admiral; I should be sorry that you thought such evil of me."

And would be sorrier, Laurence thought, if he spread a story that did her so little credit. Few others had the power to do so, and he the only one who did not have good cause to conceal it. "Your Majesty scarcely owes me any explanations, nor can I invite your confidence."

"I do not seek your silence, beyond what your judgment should consider best," she said. "It grieves me that you should imagine me happy in the present circumstances. If I could have my husband here at my side, triumphant, once more the conqueror of Europe, only then could I call myself a happy woman."

"You might have had him here as the Emperor of France," Laurence said. "Would that not have been enough?"

"But I could not," she said. "*You* know that I could not. You know my husband, Admiral."

This silenced him. Anahuarque added, after a pause, "You may more justly say, I should have been content to go into exile along with him; to take him away to Pusantinsuyo. But it was my husband's duty to hazard everything for victory—mine, to rescue our empire from defeat."

Unwillingly, Laurence did begin to understand her a little more, and that peculiar retreat of her dragons in the final instants: she had offered only to let Napoleon fall into their hands, if he had already been defeated in battle—and thus to end a war swiftly that had almost certainly been lost, but which his gifts and determination could have long prolonged.

"Tell me, if the choice had been put to him, do you think he would have preferred to flee with me to my country, or to keep his son upon the throne he won?" Anahuarque asked, watching his face. "Do you still accuse me of disloyalty?"

There was much to be admired, in the strategic sense, in a plan which had permitted the Empress to enjoy the chance of complete victory, while hazarding very few of the risks of defeat. Laurence could only despise it a little less, for being a more limited conspiracy. But he remembered too clearly the father running through flames at Fontainebleau to save his son, heedless of his own risk; the swiftness with which Napoleon had signed the documents to accept his own exile, in exchange for handing on his throne.

"You have chosen, Your Majesty, as he would have chosen," Laurence said briefly. That, he could not deny.

He did not think she would ask him to say more, and indeed she nodded his dismissal, satisfied. He left angry, because she was right to be satisfied; she had indeed silenced him as thoroughly as she might have wished. He would have liked to spread the infamy of the conspiracy widely, and to heave away the credit he had not earned; he would have liked to expose her and those who had abetted the betrayal of which he had been made an instrument. But he could not, without serving a worse blow to the man who had been their victim. That she would keep Napoleon's son upon his throne, Laurence could not doubt, nor that Napoleon would have preferred that outcome to any other form of defeat.

"But Laurence, surely we have been trying to see Napoleon defeated, all these years," Temeraire said, a little perplexed. "Do you mean that you are sorry, now, that he has lost?"

"No," Laurence said. "No, I would not see him restored if it were in my power, only—" He halted and shook his head, as though he could not put his feelings easily into words.

"Well, Napoleon has never seemed to me such a very bad fellow, but I am not in the least sorry that *Lien* has lost," Temeraire said. "And this exile is by no means less than she deserves after the very underhanded way in which she behaved about the egg. I only wish they planned to put more guns on the shore, at that island, and they ought to station four heavy-weight dragons there at least. I do not think they properly respect what she is capable of doing." He sighed a little.

Laurence shook his head in silence. He had given his opinions briefly, and advised how best to safeguard against Lien's sinking the ships, but he thought she could not be held captive long by guns or guards, however numerous. A single accomplice ship equipped with pontoons, somewhere off the shore, would make escape possible. Napoleon's true gaoler would be his own son. The ministers had bribed him so, to keep to his island, and so long as they left the boy on the throne, Napoleon would keep the bargain.

"I should like to express my gratitude," Temeraire said a little uncertainly: he had come to the clearing where the Tswana dragons had made their camp with only the best intentions, and they had received him, but none of them had returned his introductions, and they *would* all stare so unblinkingly, as though they expected him to do something alarming; it gave him the uneasy feeling they might be right. "—mine, and of course Admiral Laurence's as well; and I dare say everybody else is grateful also, even if they have not shown it as they ought, yet. But I believe Mr. Hammond means to speak to your prince, when the opportunity arises, and discuss perhaps reopening some of your ports, at the Cape or—"

"He may save the trouble," one of the Tswana dragons, a large fellow in orange and green, interrupted rudely. "You do not suppose we are ever going to let any of you slavers back in our territory?"

"Oh!" Temeraire said, a little indignantly; *he* was not a slaver. "I am sure I have no idea why you wanted to be helpful, then, if you choose to lump us all together."

Another dragon snorted. "Why should we have *helped* any of you? We didn't want this Napoleon running things, and he would have, with a few thousand dragons under his hand. Now the rest of you can squabble it out among yourselves, and leave us alone."

"And I had meant to be so gracious," Temeraire said to Lily afterwards, when he had flown back to their own covert: which was not at all like a British covert, but a handsome ring of pavilions, each large enough to comfortably house a dozen heavyweights, or more if they did not mind leaving a tail or a leg poking outside, and piling in. They were situated atop a high hill overlooking Rochefort harbor, presently a very picturesque scene with three dragon transports and a second-rate in harbor, and a flotilla of frigates and ships' boats scattered around them. In addition, the pavilion floors were raised from the ground with room to put coals beneath, in the best design; the weather was not so unpleasant that they were needed today, but thought had been given to the matter. It was rather an unhappy reminder of the conditions which did not await them in Britain, when at last they boarded those waiting transports and sailed back up the coast. "I had even meant to make them a present."

"What sort of present?" Lily asked interestedly. She and all the old formation had been gratifyingly pleased for his good fortune, and had come from the Peninsula with their own to report: King Joseph had attempted to flee Spain with tremendous heaps of treasure, and they had captured a caravan with no less than six wagons of silver plate, the prize-money for which had made them all respectably rich, even divided up.

"A golden chain," Temeraire said, "with some very handsome emeralds: that Incan dragon gave it to me, when she so wanted to keep Challoner." He sighed a little; but as the Copacati had professed herself perfectly willing to go into the Aerial Corps, it meant Challoner should make captain straightaway, and Laurence had persuaded Temeraire that they could not stand in her way. Temeraire could not really like it, but the necklace had been a handsome consolation. "I am sure it could not fail to please, but of course I am not going to give it to them now, when they have been so churlish."

"You might give it to me instead," Ning said; she had been apparently sleeping in a comfortable curled place upon the stones in the sun, but she lifted her head as though she had been listening, all the time.

"Whyever would I?" Temeraire said warily.

"As a gift for the Emperor," Ning said, "a gesture of respect and gratitude, and of congratulations on his ascension. I would be delighted to present it to him on behalf of yourself and Admiral Laurence."

Temeraire flattened his ruff. "So you are going to China, after all, and want to make a handsome appearance when you get there; I see."

"Yes, I think it the best course of action at present," Ning said calmly, ignoring his remarks. "I cannot find that the new Emperor of France will even be able to talk for two years, much less go flying, and in any case one should like his situation to be of somewhat longer standing. In a few years, it may be time for me to pay a visit, and see how matters are progressing, but for the moment certainly I ought to be in China."

"I do not know why you mean to come back to visit, then; you cannot have *both* of them," Temeraire said.

"I do not see any reason against it," Ning said. "They are both excellently placed, strategically, for the coming century, and one ought to plan ahead. It would not do to close any doors unnecessarily. Which is why you ought to give me the necklace," she added, "and preserve those ties which the present victory must render much less politically useful. After all, the need for an excuse to make alliance is past, and with the death of the Jiaqing Emperor, the adoption of your admiral must have considerably less personal force. You would be well-advised to strengthen bonds with the new Emperor now, while the satisfaction of a joint victory warms his feelings towards you. It cannot but serve you well in future to have the relationship recognized. After all, I cannot find that Admiral Laurence will even have a post, when you have gone back to Britain, and he does not seem a particular favorite with your rulers."

This last understated the case, and Temeraire had not really considered that of course, now that the allied armies were disbanding, Laurence was no longer in command of anyone. He realized uncomfortably he did not really know if Laurence was even still an admiral at all.

"Oh, on that you may be easy," Excidium said, when Temeraire had roused him for a consultation, "for my Jane was still an admiral even when those croakers in the Admiralty had stripped her of her post, back before Napoleon invaded us. But they may send you to the north of Scotland to fly patrols, or some other make-work. Anyway, Ning ain't wrong that it is always good to have more influence. Jane has said to me that she would collect a year's worth of letter-writing in influence by taking her coronet to some hostess's rout for a night, even if she would as lief be hanged as go to a ball. So it is well-worth preserving the connection, if you have it."

"And which I am sure Ning likes preserved for her *own* sake," Temeraire muttered afterwards, "perhaps so she has an excuse to come visiting." But that did not mean she was not right; however, perhaps Laurence would not like to send such a gift, after all.

"Certainly I should not like to be encroaching," Laurence said, however, "but I can hardly say *he* has not acknowledged the relationship, in a manner which permits *me* to ignore it. Aside from all the very real service Mianning has done our nation, his personal kindness to us more than merits the greatest warmth and respect, and it must be for him to first grow cold, before we can consider ourselves to be pursuing an unwanted connection. Perhaps you might consult with Gong Su, as to whether the gift would be suitable; some gesture at least, I think must be desirable."

And naturally Gong Su was of the opinion that an elegant golden chain sized for a dragon, of the finest Incan craftsmanship, adorned with a dozen beautiful and valuable jewels, would be an eminently pleasing gift: who would *not* be pleased, Temeraire would have liked to know. So there was no help for it, and Temeraire disconsolately saw it laid into a handsome wooden box, with much padding of soft wool, and delivered to Ning just before her departure: the legions had already nearly all flown back, leaving only an honor-guard of forty dragons to accompany her home.

"Well, old fellow, at least you didn't have to buy it," Maximus said, nudging his shoulder by way of consolation as the box flew away; which was some comfort, except if one considered the lovely alteration the chain would have made to his bank-book, if it had been sold instead, and viewed its departure as the loss of that amount.

"Fare thee well, and I hope we have seen the last of him," Jane said, joining Laurence on the dragondeck of the *Vindication*. The *Bellerophon* was visible out on the horizon, with Lien a little awkwardly disposed on the deck, a heavy band of chain marring the clean white line of her neck. They were making sail. Jane shook her head. "I shan't give ha'pence for the chance, though. I dare say that beast could make shore from St. Helena in a day and a night if she put herself to the trouble, and it is sure enough he will find *some* excuse to be off, after he gets tired of the place; and there ain't any cause *not* to grow tired of it, either. Perhaps his wife will have him poisoned, and save us the excitement, though."

"I dare say your hopes may be answered," Laurence said.

"Very good," Jane said approvingly. "That was almost uncharitable: we will make a cynic of you yet. You are for Dover in the morning, and London?"

"I am," Laurence said, and heaved a breath. "I will see you there, I think?"

"Yes, though the Lord knows they are running out of honors to heap on my shoulders, and Wellington is in even worse case: I think they will have to make him a new order of knighthood. You are getting off lightly by comparison, with your mere baronetcy. But I have come to drop a word in your ear: I have been invited four times in letters this last month to say something about the need for a strengthened presence in Halifax. Will you go if you are ordered there?"

"No," Laurence said. "I mean to retire, when we have returned. I have enough money to keep Temeraire, now, and enough of a countenance to ask my brother to put us up on one of the farms."

Or they might return to Australia, or to China: Temeraire had every right to ask that of him, now that the war was won. Laurence did not mean to refuse him; he only hoped to go back to Wollaton Hall first, and find a way to carry it with him, somehow. He longed in a deep inward part for Britain, for home: to see the house standing at twilight with all the windows lit, a child's memory of peace. He could even be grateful there for the counterfeit honors that had been heaped onto his head, if they gave his mother some peace, and if his brother need not be ashamed to give him a field for Temeraire to sleep in, for a little while.

"I am glad to know," Edith said, low, when Laurence had finished. She sighed once, deeply, and looked out into the south field, where her son was now climbing all over Temeraire's forelegs with Laurence's three nephews. They had spent the first week of Temeraire's residence plastered to the windows of their nursery, under the confining hand of their nurse; but a few of the village boys, less supervised, had made a game of daring one another to come and touch Temeraire's tail, and observing them from the window had been too much for high spirits to endure. The middle boy had dared his elder, the dare had been reciprocated, and by the time Temeraire had woken, the boys had managed to scale his back and were busily defeating Napoleon in a grand aerial battle bearing a strong resemblance to the highly fictional accounts which had lately filled the newspapers.

"Well, that is not how it happened at all," Temeraire had informed them, turning his head round, and all three children had gone very still and quiet, but the story recommended itself too highly not to overcome what, their exasperated mother lectured them that night, was a relatively slight concern for the preservation of life and limb.

Her lectures and the protests of their nurse had not had much effect. Old wooden swords had been unearthed from a chest the next day, and endless battles fought since then. Edith's son had lasted five minutes clinging to her skirts before he had run out through the garden gates to join the irresistible game, and she had not held him back, though her hands curled in her lap as though she half-wished to restrain him.

"I am glad he should not be afraid of dragons," she said, despite a little anxiety in her looks: the boy was her only child.

"I assure you Temeraire will have a care," Laurence said to her. Temeraire indeed was in danger of showing too *much* care, as he had begun to inquire of Laurence whether the boys might not really be considered as under his protection, by virtue of their connection.

"Churki writes," he had said a little wistfully, "that she has met Hammond's family at last, and there are *twenty-six* of them, if one counts the smallest children and his cousins, which she does." He sighed a bit enviously. "She has already set about building them a larger house," he added, "and helped their tenants plow their fields more quickly, which she says was of the greatest assistance, because so many of the young men have been away at the war, and are not returned yet. Laurence, oughtn't we plow this field?"

"No, it is resting this year," Laurence had answered. "But if you are in want of occupation, I am sure my brother's steward would be delighted to have your assistance." He had been surprised to find a thriving clan of Yellow Reapers established just outside Nottingham, who were now a regular sight throughout the city and the surrounding countryside, most commonly carrying large loads of coal from the pits but willing to take on other work as well; they had been of use on the estate more than once, his brother had said.

Temeraire had indeed found some satisfaction, since then, in bringing in prodigious loads of timber and stone required for repairs, and offering to bring more, if they should care to repair the

ruins of the abbey behind the house, which had burnt down sometime in the eleventh century. He had even offered his services to
their neighbors, one of whom was Edith's father.

Lady Galman had included Laurence in a subsequent invitation for the families to dine together, and he had with some hesitation accepted. No number of accolades would ever make him easy
going into society again, but he had wished to speak with Edith.
He had written long years ago, by his mother, to acquaint her with
the manner of her husband's death during the invasion of Britain,
which had borne a sufficiently heroic character for him to wish her
to know of it, in hopes of its relieving some of the pain of her loss.
But he felt the inadequacy of such an indirect account, and the
obligation to do better, if she wished to know more.

"I am glad to know," she said now: they had spoken briefly at
dinner, and she had called this morning, for a chance of more privacy. "And glad to have the power to tell my son, when he is older.
I only wish . . ." She stopped a moment, and Laurence was not
certain she meant to continue. "I only wish I might not feel Bertram had pursued a course for which no training or inclination
had fitted him," she said finally, low, "in an effort to secure my
good opinion. He ought to have been certain of it."

Laurence was silent. It had been long years since he and Edith
had spoken on such terms of intimacy, but there had been long
separations between them before, demanded by a naval career, and
he did not pretend that he did not understand her. If Bertram
Woolvey had never made himself notorious, neither had he made
himself notable, before his death. He had been a gentleman, and
he had offered his wife a comfortable home and a place in respectable society, when Laurence could no longer aspire to either. But a
man might well have wished to figure in his wife's eyes as something other than a safe harbor, if she had once looked for more.

"His aid was material," he said finally: the only comfort he
could give. "I do not know if we would have succeeded in freeing
Iskierka, without his help, and her loss would have been disas-
trous."

Edith nodded a little, her head still bowed. Then she lifted it and smiled at him, with an effort. "Will you be in Nottingham long? Or does duty call you away again soon?"

"Duty, no. I have retired from the Corps," he said. "Inclination may yet: Britain is not a hospitable country for dragons. But we have made no plans."

That night, after the light had begun to fail and Laurence had closed the book, Temeraire said, "Laurence, there does not seem to be anything more that needs doing, on the estate, where I can be of any material use: Mr. Jacobs," this being his brother's steward, "has assured me of it."

"It was kind in you to undertake the effort," Laurence said. "You need not feel that you must earn your keep, my dear: we are well in funds. We ought not outstay our welcome, but we have not done so yet. My brother has assured me he does not regard our presence as an inconvenience, nor does the neighborhood object." Laurence had rather met with expressions of satisfaction that Britain's heroic dragon was staying near-by. As the news of Temeraire's presence had spread, he had even lately seen plates with Temeraire painted upon them displayed for sale in the city, and coaches were given to pausing, on the road passing the estate, so passengers might climb out and have a look from afar. He did not expect the fad to last for long, but he was glad not to have forced his brother to endure the complaints of his neighbors.

"No, only, I am not quite certain what we ought to do with ourselves," Temeraire said. "I thought I had deferred so many things for the sake of the war, and now I cannot think of any of them; or perhaps I am thinking of all of them at once, so none of them are coming clear in my head." He sighed a little. "I am glad you have retired, and the Admiralty cannot send us anywhere unpleasant now, but there is no denying there was something useful in being *sent*, and given something to do."

Laurence drew a deep breath. "Do you wish to return to China?" He had expected as much, and prepared for it. He was only glad to have had the opportunity to come home for so long.

He had seen his mother, and seen her at peace; she had moved to the dower house, only a little distance from the main, and he had ridden across the fields to see her daily. He had knelt by his father's tomb. But spring had gone to summer, and summer would soon enough go to fall, and there was no building on the grounds where Temeraire might sleep; nor would Laurence trespass so far on his brother's good-will as to propose putting up a pavilion. In any case, if they meant to go to China, the overland route would be the easiest to take, and the sooner they set out, the better weather they would have.

Temeraire was silent. "I would like to *visit* China again," he said slowly, "but I do not know what there is for me to do there, if we were to remain, besides being as awkward a guest as here. And I would be sorry to leave all my friends, just when we finally have the power of seeing them anytime we like. It is only half a day's flight to Dover, and Lily and Maximus, or to Edinburgh, if I would like to see Iskierka—not that I would precisely *like* to see Iskierka," he added quickly—there had been a certain degree of unbecoming smugness on the subject of Granby's promotion to Admiral, which had provoked a quarrel that was not yet made up, "but Granby is with her, of course, and you should like to see him sometimes, I am sure.

"It is not as comfortable here as in China, of course, and even where there are pavilions they are not nearly as nice, but I must be fair: things have come along a considerable distance. I remember when I could not go anywhere, without people running and screaming—I thought it was only something people did, like cows. And now they wave handkerchiefs at me from the hill, if I look up at them, and the steward spoke to me in a perfectly sensible way. Perscitia tells me that it is because of our work—well, she says it is mostly due to *her* work, but I know she would rather have me stay, and help her. Only, I am not sure how we would go about doing so, if we did."

A carriage had been coming along the road as they sat together, the lanterns bobbing to show its progress through the twilight, and the well-hooded horses clopping along steadily, blissfully ignorant of Temeraire's near presence. The carriage had halted on the road, and a gentleman had come out of it; he had not been content merely to observe from afar, but had come across the field towards them, and now Temeraire raised his head, his ruff pricking up, and said, "Why, Tharkay, how elegant you look."

"I hope you will forgive the intrusion," Tharkay said; he was indeed dressed with unusual splendor, in magnificently polished Hessians, with a many-caped greatcoat, and a walking-stick topped in gold.

"You are very welcome, Tenzing," Laurence said, rising to shake his hand, "if unexpected: we looked for you in Paris."

"As enjoyable as the display of the Empress's powers must have been to observe, I was called away on my personal business," Tharkay said. "One might have supposed a law-suit which has consumed the better part of twenty years might support a few weeks' further delay, but under the circumstances, I did not wish to hazard it."

"You have won your case, then?" Laurence said.

"I have," Tharkay said. "Not without several interventions on my behalf: I must thank you again for your testimony."

"I suspect it has served you more ill than good, since I made it," Laurence said, "but if my present fame has made it of value again, I can only be glad."

"Oh, your star falls and rises with enough regularity that it was only a matter of time," Tharkay said. "And Her Grace's power is at present very great."

"So you have your estates at last!" Temeraire said jubilantly, and without delay inquired, "And pray, what is the rent-roll; do I have that right? Or the income per annum?"

"Shamefully low," Tharkay said. "My cousins and the trustee have neglected all improvements, and plundered as much as they could; it will be some time before I have restored things to order. However, in one particular, the estate is desirable: perhaps you know about the new seats which have been set aside, for dragons?"

"Oh, yes!" Temeraire said. "Twenty of them; Perscitia wrote to me."

"The Government has established nearly all the seats in isolate regions of the countryside, and managed to put all the population of serving-beasts and retired dragons, in the breeding grounds, into three: the boundary-lines have been quite creatively drawn. The others are peopled almost entirely by ferals, and the Government supposes them unlikely to appear for voting."

Temeraire snorted. "We must trust them to always carry out their promises in the most scaly manner, I suppose. Well, Perscitia and I must just manage it. I will ask Ricarlee to run: I am sure Parliament deserves him."

"I am informed," Tharkay said, "that my own lands fall in one such empty district. As the area is entirely devoid of dragons so far as I know, I am sorry there is not much company on offer, but I have a notable forest for deer-hunting, and I should be delighted to make you free of any place you like to put up a pavilion, and make yourselves at home."

"I am afraid we are inconvenient houseguests," Laurence said, bemused. "Are you certain you wish to make so extended an invitation?"

"I quite look forward to figuring as a tyrant in the imagination of my tenantry," Tharkay said, in his way. They spoke a little while longer, as the sun went down, and made arrangements to meet for breakfast the following morning, at Tharkay's hotel; then he took his leave again, with the tact that plainly meant to permit them private conversation.

"Why Laurence, I call that handsome," Temeraire said. "Do you suppose you should like it? But perhaps you would rather we went back to our pavilion, in Australia: I know you are not fond of politics."

For a moment, the sun rose out of the Blue Mountains and shone red-gold on the cut stone floor of the half-finished pavilion, spilled down light into the valley below and over the softly lowing herd of cattle: another memory of home, of peace and simplicity. But that could only be a flight, almost a surrender. The reward of true service, surely, was to be asked for more; and Laurence could not claim Temeraire's work was done, even if his own might have been called so.

"No, my dear," Laurence said. "I do not think a life of quiet retirement is our lot, nor yet should be; and our valley will wait until that has changed." He laid his hand on Temeraire's muzzle and looked north and west, towards the curve of the ocean, towards home. "Tharkay's estates are in the Peaks: I think you will like the countryside very much."

"I am sure I will, Laurence," Temeraire said. "And surely it will be famous, to be in Parliament."

ABOUT THE AUTHOR

NAOMI NOVIK is the acclaimed author of the Temeraire series: *His Majesty's Dragon, Throne of Jade, Black Powder War, Empire of Ivory, Victory of Eagles, Tongues of Serpents, Crucible of Gold, Blood of Tyrants,* and *League of Dragons.* She has been nominated for the Hugo Award and has won the John W. Campbell Award for Best New Writer, as well as the Locus Award for Best New Writer and the Compton Crook Award for Best First Novel. She is also the author of *Uprooted* and the graphic novel *Will Supervillains Be on the Final?*

Fascinated with both history and legends, Novik is a first-generation American raised on Polish fairy tales and stories of Baba Yaga. Her own adventures include pillaging degrees in English literature and computer science from various ivory towers, designing computer games, and helping to build the Archive of Our Own for fanfiction and other fanworks. Novik is a co-founder of the Organization for Transformative Works.

She lives in New York City with her husband, Charles Ardai, the founder of Hard Case Crime, and their daughter, Evidence, surrounded by an excessive number of purring computers.

naominovik.com
Facebook.com/naominovik
@naominovik

ABOUT THE TYPE

This book was set in Sabon, a typeface designed by the well-known German typographer Jan Tschichold (1902–74). Sabon's design is based upon the original letter forms of sixteenth-century French type designer Claude Garamond and was created specifically to be used for three sources: foundry type for hand composition, Linotype, and Monotype. Tschichold named his typeface for the famous Frankfurt typefounder Jacques Sabon (c. 1520–80).